The Anatomy School

THE
ANATOMY SCHOOL

Bernard MacLaverty

W. W. Norton & Company
New York   London

FOR JUDE

Part One

1. A Weekend Retreat

His mother came into the bedroom carrying an empty suitcase and whacked the curtains open.

'It's time, Martin,' she said. Martin moaned and got out of bed. There was white frost on the window. He scratched the pane to see if it was inside or out. His fingernail left a clear track.

'How many nights?'

'Three.' She counted them off on her fingers and mouthed the days as she did so. 'Why do they have Retreats at this time of the year? So many days off school, coming up to exams?' His mother was folding the right number of drawers and socks, fussing backwards and forwards from the dressing table to the bed where the suitcase now lay open.

'Exams aren't for a couple of months.' His voice was still thick with sleep. She was always doing that – exaggerating – trying to prove her own arguments. She could stretch time whichever way she wanted. If he lay in his bed until 10.30 it became 'sleeping in till midday' and if he came home at 11.30 after a night out it became 'streeling in here at one o'clock in the morning'.

'That's when you should be doing all the work,' she said. '*Before* the exams. There's not much point in studying afterwards.' She folded a shirt so that the arms disappeared. She threw him a pair of clean underpants. 'Don't be such a Slitherum Dick. Do something. Get dressed.' He hesitated. 'I'll not be looking at you.' He turned his back to her and changed out of his pyjama trousers. 'I always say there's no point in standing around with your mouth hanging open.' He sat on the bedside chair to put his shoes and socks on. 'And be careful with this case. It was more than good of Nurse Gilliland. I don't want to be returning something in tatters.'

When he was dressed he went downstairs to the kitchen. She shouted after him,

'That battery is on its last legs.' It was still fairly dark so he lifted

3

the torch from the kitchen cup-hook and went out into the yard. He walked carefully with his feet wide apart for fear of slipping. The ice underfoot made a sound like static when he pressed down. His breath clouded the cold air. He went into the toilet and bolted the door. It smelled of damp and cobwebs and bowels. The torch shone a pale milky circle on the whitewashed wall. He set it on the bench so that it lit the ceiling, and by reflection, faintly, the whole place. He took down his trousers and clean underpants and slid on to the bench over the hole. The wood was worn smooth. An icy draught came up from the darkness. The toilet paper was semi-transparent and written across the bottom of each sheet in green letters were the words MEDICATED WITH IZAL GERMICIDE.

When he went back into the kitchen she was making up a piece for him. He went to the kitchen sink and turned on the tap.

'Wash your hands,' she said. He sighed. 'When it comes to hygiene we have to be *more* careful than people who have the proper facilities.'

He nodded in an exaggerated fashion.

'What are they?'

'Salad.'

'With salad cream?'

'Of course.'

He dried his hands on the roller towel on the back of the door.

'There's tea in the pot,' she said.

'I don't think I have time.'

'Your case is in the hall.'

She cracked a hard boiled egg against the bread board. Lots of small taps, so that the shell cracked all over. She began peeling back the crazy paving of shell showing the slippery white underneath.

'How long is this going to take?'

'Not long.' She moved to the sink and held the peeled egg under running water. 'There's nothing worse than getting a bit of shell – when you bite into it. Like sand at the seaside.' From the cutlery drawer she produced a thing for cutting up eggs – like a little lyre. She laid the egg in an oval depression and hinged the

4

metal strings down on top of it. The egg fell into slices, each with a yellow circle of yolk at its centre.

'Come on, they're not for Father Farquharson.'

'Less of your cheek, Martin Brennan.'

'I'm gonna be late for school.'

'You should never mock the clergy.'

'It's the clergy who'll thump me if I'm late.'

'Especially somebody as good as Father Farquharson. He's a living saint.'

'Aye.'

'But not aloof,' said Mrs Brennan. 'He's ordinary at the same time.'

'You can say that again.'

'Martin, you're a big man but a wee coat fits you. I feel like throwing these sandwiches in the bin. You're about as grateful as . . . What notion have you taken against Father Farquharson?'

'It's a few sandwiches for lunch time – not one of your supper nights.'

'You should be eternally grateful to the same Father Farquharson. It's not every house in the parish he visits. And it's not the high and mighty up the Somerton Road. No, it's here – our house. Even though we don't have the proper facilities. You should go down on your knees to a man like that.' Martin rolled his eyes and willed her to finish making the sandwiches. 'It's a sign of respect for your father, God rest him. If there was anything to be done your father would always be the first to volunteer. Who'll we get to pass the collection plate on Sundays? Your father. Who'll do the digging and keep the graveyard tidy? Your father. He was in the St Vincent de Paul and the Knights of Columbanus and God knows what else. He never told me the half of it. And the Legion of Mary. All I can manage the time for is the Ladies of Charity – but that's me. I'm selfish. I'm like you – always on the lookout for number one.'

'Father Farquharson's a bit . . .' Martin searched for a word that wouldn't be rude, '. . . boring.'

'Very well.' His mother spoke in a clipped I've-nothing-more-to-say-to-you voice. She put the top on the sandwich and sliced it into four triangles. 'Crusts on or off?'

5

'The way they are.' She took the waxed paper from around the loaf and folded up the sandwiches.

'Just because your mother chooses to do things a little better than anybody else . . .' The queen of the unfinished sentence. 'But that doesn't suit the likes of our Martin. Oh no, he'd prefer to scorn things that are just that wee bit better . . . Mary Lawless doesn't stand up for you any more. She used to worship the ground you walked on. And Nurse Gilliland says you're a changed boy. Being seventeen doesn't suit you.'

'I thought you liked change,' he said.

'What do you mean?'

'The furniture.'

'I like *improvements*. Not quite the same thing.' Occasionally, when he was a child, Martin would come down the stairs in the morning to find that his mother had moved all the furniture. The table would be under the kitchen window, instead of at the wall; the sideboard would be moved to the other wall; the china cabinet would be brought in from the parlour; the armchairs switched to different sides of the fireplace. She would be standing there waiting, watching his face.

'Well?'

He knew if he said he liked it better the way it was, she would be hurt. He thought the reason she did this was because they hadn't enough money to buy *new* furniture so she just moved the old stuff around. After a lukewarm reaction she'd fold her arms and say, 'I think it's a complete transformation.'

She handed him the parcel of sandwiches and he picked up the suitcase from the hall and ran.

'Say one for me,' she called after him.

At lunch time Martin sat in the hired bus eating his sandwiches, hoping nobody would sit beside him. It was at the top of the school drive and guys who were *not* going on the Retreat milled around it, making faces, giving 'up ya' signs to the ones inside. Kavanagh was one of them and he gave Martin a look which said – more or less – you poor religious bastard I hope you enjoy yourself but I've better things to be doing. Kavanagh's mate, Brian Sweeny, was there too, just lounging up against the wall, his hands in his pockets. There was a lot of interest in the driver because he

6

was an outsider. He sat high in his cab, smoking, wisecracking with the boys in the driveway. The boy who eventually sat down beside him was called Eddie Downie – Martin didn't know him well, not well enough to joke anyway. If Kavanagh wasn't there it didn't matter who sat beside him.

The bus drove along the twisted, narrow roads of County Down towards Ardglass and the boys sang Republican songs. A boy called Sharkey knew all the words and shouted them out in advance. 'Up went Nelson in old Dublin.' In Ireland things had hardly happened before there was a song about it. Everybody swayed in unison at every corner. Near Downpatrick one guy broke ranks and stuck his chalk white face out the window. Everybody cheered. He puked what was discovered, when they arrived at the Retreat House, to be an almost horizontal line along the side of the bus. Martin took a couple of photographs of it to show Kavanagh. When he and Eddie Downie examined it they could see it was definitely breakfast in origin.

The Retreat House was on top of a hill. Gardens sloped down to a high stone wall. There were daffodils and things growing in its shelter. A hawthorn tree had white blossom and some of it was swirling off and mixing with the fine snow which was blowing from the north. Beyond the wall, the town of Ardglass fell away to the sea. The boys all stood about shivering, waiting for the driver to unload their bags from the hold. The horizon was grey, barely distinguishable from the sky as the snow shower passed. The sound of crows mixed with the sound of seagulls.

Inside, the place was huge – like a castle. The boys carried their cases up a polished wooden staircase to the dormitories. The stomping and banging and creaking was deafening. The whole place smelled of Mansion polish. A Redemptorist stood in the hallway, his hands thrust into the opposing sleeves of his soutane. He was tubby and wore a biretta on the top of his head. He had heavy horn-rimmed glasses.

'Make the noise now, boys,' he shouted at the top of his voice. Then chuckled to Martin as he passed: 'For there'll be precious little of it later.'

'Excuse me, Father. Is it OK if I take photos? I'm supposed to be doing an article for the school magazine.'

'Click away. Click away, boy. What's your name?'

'Martin Brennan.'

'Good man yourself.'

It was hardly worthy of praise – the fact that he had a name. Why did he always have to ask permission to do things? What kind of a crawler was he? Do I dare to eat a peach? Do I dare disturb the universe? Anybody else would just go ahead. Wee Jacky had done T.S. Eliot's poem with them. Said it was modern poetry – talked about Eliot's quest for the spiritual. But Kavanagh had whispered that the poet's name was an anagram of TOILETS and the whole thing ended in a terrible fit of the giggles. Martin climbed the stairs with his teeth clenched. Suddenly from below he heard the dark and unmistakable voice of Condor – Father O'Malley – the school's Dean of Discipline.

He had addressed them in the school chapel before they left.

'I cannot believe I am having to say this – but last Easter the behaviour of adult boys from this school on Retreat was *so* bad that this year I have been invited to attend. I will be there – like a fire alarm – just in case. That should make each and every one of you feel thoroughly ashamed. That young men *capable* of becoming priests should need such supervision.' Then he had driven himself to Ardglass in his black Volkswagen. Now, once his voice had been heard, all the chattering and laughing died away but the creaking of the wooden stairs went on as the boys moved up and down.

Upstairs in the dorm there was a runner of fibre matting between dark green cubicles. There were no doors, the cubicles just had three walls. Martin chose the first empty one and sat down on the bed. The blankets were grey. Beside each bed was a plain wooden cupboard. Over the end of the bed was a clean folded towel. It had been laundered so many times the nap on it had almost disappeared – it was like a cloth his mother used for drying dishes. Or the kind of towel they gave out at the public baths.

He stowed his things and slid Nurse Gilliland's case under the bed. Everyone was gathering downstairs in a large sitting room. Half of it was a conservatory covered with a glass roof. The place was littered with cane chairs and tables with glass tops. Martin thought it looked like a posh ice-cream parlour. Except for the shelves of books. A good deal of messing was going on as guys grabbed seats. Some people had to sit on the floor.

'Who's that naked girl in the garden? Very salubrious.' Several guys stood up to see and others slid behind them into their seats.

'I was here first.'

'Rat arse.'

'For fucksake knock it off.'

The fight was hissed quietly because they were in a new place. The door swung open and Condor walked in. Silence. He was followed by two Redemptorists. One of them was the fat priest who had ushered them up the stairs. The other one was tall and thin with an Adam's apple the size of a hen's egg. Condor looked at the upturned faces. He smiled at the Redemptorists then indicated the audience.

'My boys.' He turned and walked out of the room.

It was the one with the big Adam's apple who spoke first, blessing himself elaborately. He looked a bit like pictures of Pope Pius XII.

'In the name of the Father and of the Son and of the Holy Spirit.' He joined his hands correctly and said the Our Father, Hail Mary and Glory be to the Father.

'You're all welcome, boys. My name is Father Valerian. And this is Father Albert. Welcome to this beautiful place.' He put an arm into each sleeve and began to pace about. 'Now you'll all have heard of Lough Derg – where pilgrims do not sleep, where they eat only dry toast and drink black tea and they walk around on sharp stones in bare feet – come rain, hail or shine. Well, that's not the kind of place we are here. Thanks be to God, says you.' There was an amused murmur, little exchanges between the boys. 'You may laugh but we are gathered here on a serious mission this Eastertide. We are not testing our bodies – we are examining our minds, our souls.' Martin heard the last two words as 'arse holes'. So did others. The murmur became a snort of laughter. Father Valerian looked in the direction it had come from, close to Martin, and smiled vaguely in appreciation – thinking it left-over laughter from his previous joke. 'Gentlemen, you must all ask yourselves *Why am I here?* In the primary sense of in this world, on this earth, and in the immediate sense of in this place, this retreat house. *What has brought me to this place?*'

9

'A vomit-covered bus,' somebody whispered. There were snorts and giggles and a lot of silent shoulder shaking. Martin straightened his face and tried sincerely to find an answer to the question. He had handed the typed note to his mother and she had said, 'Of course you *must* go. I couldn't afford it last year but this year – of all years – I'll find the money from somewhere. There's a lot of studying to be done and a lot of praying if you're going to pass this time.'

'But I prayed hard last year.'

'Not hard enough by the looks of it. St Joseph of Cupertino's the examinations man. You should be storming the gates of heaven every hour that God sends. Easter's a good time. At Easter the Man Above is all ears. And a bit more application wouldn't go amiss.'

His mother had gone the next day and drawn from savings. She said it'd be money well spent. If he prayed and worked hard enough then he'd pass and get himself into a good job, a job that paid well. The Retreat was an investment.

Father Valerian removed his biretta, holding one of its three fins delicately between his finger and thumb and set it on the table in front of him. He was trying to disguise his baldness by over-combing his thin hair from left to right. The priest seemed to love using his voice – the way it soared and swooped – the way he stressed certain words. He had obviously been taught to preach. 'You've all reached that age – shaving between the pimples.' He waited for them to react to his joke. 'This, for all of you, is the last year at school – and in this last year decisions will have to be made about the future. Shall I be a doctor, or a lawyer, or a professional jockey?' The three options were accompanied and underlined by hand gestures. He knew the last option was a joke but his face did not show it. Again the murmured amusement from the boys, 'But we all have a duty – a solemn duty before God – to at least *think* about devoting our lives to His service. To give it consideration. To offer Him our lives, to prostrate ourselves before Him and say "Be it done according to Thy word." Boys, when Jesus threw back his head on that cross all those years ago and said "*Consummatum est*" – "It is finished" – it was only just beginning. By his suffering and death he opened the gates of heaven for the likes of you and me. And I think it is only right that we should think of giving something back. For us to make a sacrifice. Many years ago I thought these selfsame thoughts and came to the right decision – for me – and, believe me boys, I have not regretted it for one instant. That is our task this Easter. To examine ourselves, to see if we can find the generosity to put our lives in the hands of the Lord and say to Him "Do with me what Thou wilt." In what corner of the vineyard you end up labouring does not particularly matter at this stage – we are not partisan – the Cistercians, the Canons Regular, the Passionists, the Redemptorists – whether you work in the foreign missions or stay in the home diocese – it matters not two hoots. What matters is that you make the commitment. But I don't want to talk about the ins and outs of it at this stage. We, Father Albert and myself, will be talking to you at some length over the next few days. Vocations are falling off. We must do our damnedest – if you'll pardon my French – to reverse this situation . . .'

Father Valerian paused at this point and looked around at their faces. He locked his hands together and covered his mouth. Then he lowered his hands as if freeing his mouth to tell them something of extreme importance. 'One thing that can help the atmosphere of introspection over these few days is the voluntary silence. We are going to submit ourselves to being quiet. Until Saturday midday we'll be away from the hoot and holler of the world. Absence of talk. No silly jokes, no rock and roll, no horse racing. As I always say, "Boys shouldn't squander their meagre resources by hazarding them on the comparative velocities of canine or equine quadrupeds."' Again the face was deadpan. But the boys all laughed, including Martin. The priest waited for the laughter to cease, gave it plenty of time. 'You can read and walk and think as much as you like – but all in silence. Except, of course, for the words we will speak – either inwardly or aloud – to our Lord and Saviour. And that silence begins *right now.*'

He stood staring at them. For a very long time. Until everyone was conscious of their breathing and the very movement of their clothes. 'The reason for it is to stop the flow of nonsense that normally courses through the head of any schoolboy. If we have nothing to say, we do not distract others. And if we are silent inside ourselves, everything, all our thoughts, all our emotions are directed towards our Lord and Saviour, Jesus Christ.' He paused yet again. His pauses seemed to be very dramatic, as if he was thinking up the next important thing to say. 'I don't want to do any special pleading, but for anyone who thinks he has a vocation could I put in a word for our own order – the Congregation of the Most Holy Redeemer. Saint Alfonso Liguori would welcome any boy, provided he was the right kind of boy, with open arms. Missionary work among the poor and the sick – bringing the word of God to the dark places of the world – Africa, the tropical forests of Brazil, the glades of Borneo echoing to the cries of monkeys – to be able to get in there among the native people and bring them the light of our Lord Jesus Christ – that, boys, is a real satisfaction. And you don't have to go that far. On our own doorstep we have the pagan English. And not far beyond that we have the Scotch who have one priest per sixty thousand Catholics. Pity them, boys. Thank your lucky stars that you have been raised in Holy Ireland.'

He was tight-lipped and nodding. Martin thought the priest was on the verge of tears. Father Valerian swallowed hard and went on. 'But maybe I am racing ahead. Throughout the next couple of days, let us pray with all our hearts and let us think with all our minds. And I want to leave you with this thought about religion. If it matters at all, it must matter completely.' He took several paces about the floor. He joined his hands and placed both his index fingers against his lips and stared downwards some distance in front of him. He raised his eyes and said, 'If it matters at all. It must matter completely. I want you to remember that boys for the rest of your lives.'

Father Valerian lowered himself back down into his seat. There was no restlessness like there was in school. This was serious. Apart from the presence of Condor somewhere in the building it was a kind of entry into the adult world. They were about to make decisions which would affect them for the rest of their natural lives. The other priest, Father Albert stood.

'Just a couple of housekeeping points.' He looked over his shoulder at the door by which Condor had left the room and pretended he was afraid. 'I know I am addressing *senior* boys. We operate a no smoking policy in this house.' Then he dropped his voice and addressed them sideways on, his eyebrows raised. 'If however there are those among you who are slaves to the weed, then the bottom of the garden, behind the yew trees is the place we never look. Just in passing can I point out – yew trees are the favoured species for graveyards and, unlike smokers, they live to a ripe old age. Just one more thing. Are there any boys who know what they're doing on the altar?' Martin looked around but none of the other boys moved. 'Anyone know the drill?' The priest crouched a little as if to encourage them, his hands now propped on his knees. He looked from side to side. Martin put up one of his fingers. Father Albert spotted the movement. 'Good man – what's your name again?'

Martin thought it was a trick. Like playing Yes or No. He looked wary and remained silent. Father Albert suddenly realised and laughed. Martin felt a blush invade his face. There was nothing he could do to stop it. Being in front of all the others made it worse.

'In the business of the Lord everything is permitted. You can speak. What's your name?'

'Martin Brennan.'

'Good lad.'

'But Father – it's been a long time . . .'

'There's nothing to it since Vatican Two.' Father Albert smiled again. 'Five to nine in the sacristy – just here.' He pointed to the chapel along the corridor. 'Thank you, Mr Brennan, for this very nice example of the rule of silence.'

The refectory had long wooden tables attached to benches, like a banqueting hall, where the boys sat face to face. The Redemptorists, six of them and Condor, sat at a top table. Martin sat staring down at his place-setting of knife, fork and two spoons on the bare wood in front of him. The spoon they had given him for soup was a dessert spoon and one of the prongs of his fork was sufficiently bent to touch its neighbour. If he looked at the guy opposite he might start laughing. At intervals along the table were battered aluminium jugs for water. Father Valerian stood and everybody followed suit. It was difficult for Martin to stand upright because, being the height he was, the attached bench caught the back of his knees. He stood partly crouched. Like an old man.

After the prayer they all sat. Then a door burst open and a

procession of Brothers wearing black soutanes came in to serve them. A ladleful of soup was given to everyone. It was the colour of painting water and tasted vaguely of lentils and dust. In the silence, all that could be heard was the clinking of spoons on soup plates. One of the Brothers clumped along the floor to a rostrum and began to read in a very loud voice.

'There was a certain rich man who used to clothe himself in purple and fine linen and who feasted every day in splendid fashion. And there was a certain poor man, named Lazarus, who lay at his gate covered with sores and longing to be filled with the crumbs that fell from the rich man's table; even the dogs would come and lick his sores . . .'

When Martin finished his soup he set his spoon down on the plate. It made a strange sound against the remaining grit.

The place was in darkness. The only light was on the ceiling, coming from some street lamps down in the town. Shadows of tree branches moved. Occasionally car headlights would swing around, up one wall, across the ceiling and down the other. Kavanagh would really love this place. He'd fall about laughing at everything. Reading about licking a beggar's sores when you were trying to eat. But Martin was still a bit mad at him for refusing to come. The bastard said he knew, without having to go on Retreat, that he didn't want to be a priest. He was aiming for Medicine. Martin had tried to coax him. It'll be a laugh. Something out of the ordinary. But Kavanagh had shaken his head and said he would see him when he got back.

Kavanagh's best mate from last year was Gus Brannigan who had transferred to St Columb's in Derry – something to do with his father's job. Which left him with Brian Sweeny who wasn't up to much. He was an affable, shambly sort of a bloke who hadn't all that much to say for himself. Each movement Martin made in the bed registered in the springs. A bigger movement made the bed frame squeak. The purpose of the Retreat, Martin reminded himself, was serious. 'If it matters at all it must matter completely.' Some people snored, others were whispering – breaking the silence – even though Condor's room was on the same floor. He wished he hadn't agreed to serve mass in the morning. But that was the way of things. He could never hold back when authority wanted something. 'Anybody want to sell raffle tickets?', 'Who wants to give up their Saturday morning to shake a tin for the Famine in Africa?' Martin Brennan couldn't keep his hand down. In class if a question was asked and there was a long silence, it was him who always had a go at answering. Even if he hadn't a baldy notion. Anything to relieve the embarrassing silence. One of the teachers had praised him in front of the class. 'Brennan's not backward about coming forward.' And everyone had laughed. Bastard.

Martin went over again the things he had to do serving mass. It was five or six years since he'd done it. They were forcibly retired from being altar boys in their own parish when they went to the grammar school. He tried to remember the sequence of the hand washing. It was all symbolism. The priest had probably washed his hands forty times in carbolic soap before he came out to say mass. Forty was symbolic too. People went into the desert for forty days and forty nights, but it was just a way of saying a long time. John the Baptist didn't say to himself: this is my thirty-ninth night here, I'm for home tomorrow.

He took his hands out from underneath the blankets and joined them behind his head. The bed creaked loudly. It had been a disaster when he'd failed last summer. There was just him and his mother at home so there was precious little money coming into the house – the widow's pension and some odds and ends from part-time jobs.

They put up the exam results on a noticeboard in the main corridor of the school. Everybody had been hanging around the drinking tap in the back quad for what seemed like hours. Eventually the Reverend Head appeared from the direction of the office with an enormous rolled sheet of paper. Everybody rushed to the noticeboard. The job of putting up the results could have been done by anyone in the office but the Reverend Head enjoyed the power it gave him. The Revealer of Truths. The Bringer of Tidings.

'Gentlemen, gentlemen – please. Gangway – gangway.' He fumbled in his pocket for something. 'Some of you may *not* want to see these.' The boys were all silent with apprehension, jostling to try and see. Martin was at the back of the crowd. He felt sick in his stomach, felt he was about to faint. The Reverend Head produced a box of drawing pins and rattled them like matches to make sure the box wasn't empty. Some of these he put in his mouth as he began pinning up the sheet. Guys were trying to see over his shoulder even at this stage. At one point he turned as best he could to confront the boys pressing close. But he couldn't speak because of the pins in his mouth so he spat them out into his hand.

'Get back, Brian. You too, Finbar. If there is any more of this nonsense – this crushing – I am going straight back to the office and I am taking these results with me.' The boys leaned back and created an empty zone around the Reverend Head. Deep down Martin knew he hadn't done enough. But the possibility existed that he might be wrong. He might have underestimated himself and done brilliantly. And there would be backslapping and parties and his mother would look at him, her eyes shining with pride.

When the Reverend Head left the scene the boys all surged forward. Martin's eye hunted the columns for his name. People behind him were pushing. Alphabetically he was always near the top. He found himself and tried to trace the horizontal line to his subjects. But it was difficult without a ruler. His guts fell. He knew for certain. He'd gone down in all three subjects. He stared and stared. But the result would not change. Guys around him were yelling and jumping. Whooping like cowboys. If they'd had hats, they'd have thrown them in the air. The bastards. The summer ended right there and then. All Martin's plans and possibilities disappeared. It had been aiming too high to think about university, but he had quite fancied the idea of teaching: going to a training college or even the priesthood. Any kind of a job, the Civil Service, the Customs & Excise, the Post Office – earning money, a pay packet at the end of every week – everything disappeared the instant he looked at that fucking noticeboard. He would have to go back to school for another year.

When he told his mother she was subdued.

'I just knew by the way you came in,' she said. She remained low key about it until one Saturday morning she came stamping into his bedroom. She crashed open the door and stood at the end of the bed, a brown envelope in one hand and a letter in the other. Both were shaking.

'There's the confirmation of it.'

'What?' He sat up in bed wearing only his pyjama bottoms.

'You've lost the scholarship.' She threw the letter on to the quilt in front of him. He looked at it and saw the words *We regret to inform you . . . .* 'The school says you can re-sit the year – but only if you pay the fees.' Martin shrugged and bit the inside of his cheek. 'Sighing is no good at this stage. You should have thought of this when you were lazing around. You must learn to apply yourself. Where in under God am I going to find that kind of money?'

When she stomped out he stared at his image in the wardrobe mirror and thought how pale and thin his body was. If he was going to seriously consider becoming a priest then he would have to do better this year. A lot better.

During the Retreat the hour after devotions and before supper had been devoted to spiritual reading. That evening Martin had browsed the shelves of the conservatory room and had come across a book on saints. His mother was always on about praying to St Joseph of Cupertino, the Patron Saint of Examinations, so he looked him up. He was born in Italy in 1603 of very poor parents. He was a dunderhead, nicknamed the gaper – presumably because his mouth was always hanging open – who, when he finally really applied himself, got no further. He had reached the limits to which his brain would take him. All he could do was pray. And he did. And when he got the questions he knew from the examining bishop he was ecstatic. And he passed his examinations and became a priest. The other thing about him was that he levitated – so the book said – rose up in the air at unexpected times, causing considerable inconvenience to the other members of his order. As well as the Patron Saint of Examinations, the book said he was the Patron Saint of Nervous Flyers. He'd have to remember that to tell Kavanagh. On the way to school. Have him killing himself first thing in the morning.

Someone got up and began to move about. Martin heard the quiet scuffing of bare feet on boards, then a little later, the distant flushing of a lavatory. Immediately he felt he needed to go too.

One of the other things he'd looked at was a book of poems by

St John of the Cross. It was weird. In one poem a deeply holy man chased Christ as a bridegroom. He could only remember bits. Upon a pitch black night, this man went abroad when all his house was hushed. In darkness he crept up a secret stair and made love to Christ. He came away with a love bite – 'my neck he wounded'. He knew it was symbolic, like the forty days and forty nights, but he was a bit confused about St John of the Cross being a man and Christ being a man. But he had loved the sound of it – 'Entranced I stayed, my face against my lover having laid' – something something – 'all endeavour ceasing, and all our cares releasing, I threw them among the lilies there to fade.'

A poem they'd studied in class was by a priest, Gerard Manley Hopkins. They'd done a sonnet of his – 'I wake and feel the fell of dark, not day'. Fell was an animal skin, smothering the poet, the teacher said. Martin liked the one – 'As kingfishers catch fire, dragonflies draw flame'. It would be a beautiful thing to be a priest – give yourself to Christ for the rest of your life. Have a good comfortable house with big rooms and all the facilities. And a housekeeper. Maybe write poems. Say mass every day. He'd feel good coming back to the parochial house for his breakfast. 'Hello Missus So-and-so.' Maybe a big fry with bacon and eggs and potato bread. But there were terrible responsibilities as well. Anointing the dead after car crashes.

He was getting a boner. He tried to hold it down by clamping it between his thighs but this only made the situation worse. It wouldn't go away. In such a place. When he was here to make important decisions. He got out of bed. The elastic in the waistband of his pyjamas was slack. He bunched a handful of it so that his trousers wouldn't fall down and reveal his condition. He tried to remember where the bathroom was. When he strayed off the coconut matting the boards were dry under his feet and he was afraid of picking up a wood skelf in the sole of his foot.

It took ages to find the bathroom's pull-string light. It was an amazing place with plumbing from a different century. Oak doors, brass bolts, brass taps, thick white porcelain. The luxury of any kind of a bathroom made him feel good. By now his thing had gone down and he was able to go without difficulty. It was funny how he couldn't piss when it was up. He washed his hands with lemon soap. The corridor was even darker on his way back. He had to reach out his hands and touch walls gently to make sure where he was. Then his pyjama trousers would begin to slip and he had to grab them again. He remembered Mary Lawless telling them once about going into a cinema from bright sunlight: she couldn't see a thing, and she was feeling her way down the middle aisle by doing the breaststroke. She wondered why everybody was laughing – she thought they were laughing at the picture. Then later, when her eyes adjusted, she realised that she could be seen, clear as anything, doing her mock swimming down the middle of the aisle. Like an eejit. He'd had a worse one than that. The day he genuflected, coming out of a row at the pictures. Right the whole way down. Not even a jig of the knee which he could pretend was a football injury or something. It was unmistakable. A genuflection. In the cinema. In front of everybody. Fucking hell.

He found his bed and climbed into it. Getting settled made the bed creak and twang. If that went on for too long guys would accuse him of all sorts of things. One thing really. *Brennan's pulling his plonker.* He kept his hands well away from it. They smelled of lemon.

On supper nights his mother served everything with such a palaver. Napkins and paper doilies, tiny sandwiches, sausage rolls and vol-au-vents and mushroom patties, cup cakes and apple tarts.

The same people had been coming to the house ever since he could remember. Mary Lawless and Nurse Gilliland never missed. Nurse Gilliland had retired many years before but for some reason she still got her job title. Father Farquharson made it when he could. Martin saw him as a sultan surrounded by his harem of three women – the master with slaves at his feet. One of whom was Martin's mother. Mary Lawless called herself 'the fair and flawless Mary Lawless' but she was fat and breathless. Nurse Gilliland was the opposite: thin and bony with high cheekbones and her grey hair scraped back in a bun. She wore maroon spectacles with wings. She had a liking for 'shower-o-hail' patterns in navy or brown and had manly brogues to match.

'I was never able to master the high heels,' she said.

There was always a sense of occasion when the priest was there.

'And how's Mary?' he would say.

'Aw, poorly enough, Father . . . When you've a body like mine, you haven't far to go to seek your sorrows', and she'd lower herself into an armchair on the pivots of her elbows. At the last moment she'd fall and half wheeze, half shout 'Jesus, Mary, and Joseph'. When she'd settled in the armchair and arranged her huge bosoms she'd turn to the priest and say, 'Excuse me, Father. It was a prayer and it was well meant.'

'I know, I know. You don't have to tell me.'

'I'm bate to the ropes this evening.'

'And you, Nurse Gilliland?'

'Soldiering on, Father,' she'd say. 'For my sins.' Nurse Gilliland had been a midwife and she said that she'd looked up the wrong end of more women than enough. She'd said that one evening when Father Farquharson wasn't there. The priest spoke to Martin as to a fellow scholar. Man to man stuff. The parlour, he said, was derived from the French word *parler* to talk.

'It's an entirely appropriate room,' he would say, 'for our little coterie. Another French word.'

'And doesn't she have the place looking lovely,' Nurse Gilliland spoke up. 'It's a credit to you, Mrs Brennan.'

'I know some people don't like the saying, but I must say you have the place looking like a wee palace.'

'You have indeed.'

'Martin,' said his mother, 'I think it's that time.' Martin left the room and put the kettle on to boil. When she heard the whistle his mother came out and made the tea in their largest pot and both of them, mother and son, brought in all the food she had prepared in the afternoon.

'This is no criticism Mrs Brennan,' said Mary Lawless, 'but a wee sprinkle of salt would help the mushroom patties tonight.'

'Excuse me, constable!' said Mrs Brennan. 'But I hate being criticised for doing something I intended to do. When I was cooking them I was thinking about our blood pressures. And I put the salt cellar down.'

'You were just right,' said Father Farquharson. 'Too much salt is a danger to us all.'

'I read about it in *Woman and Home*,' said Mrs Brennan.

'I didn't know you got the *Woman and Home*.'

'I was in the launderette.'

'Oh.'

'I thought that those who liked their salt on the strong side could add a little more – a little shaking, if you like. Whereas those who have no option cannot *remove* the salt.'

'My granda used to smother every bite he ate with the stuff,' said Mary Lawless. 'He just held the salt cellar over his dinner like this.' She demonstrated. 'His dinner had to be almost white before he'd start into it. And he lived till he was eighty-seven.'

'Crumbs! He was fortunate,' said Father Farquharson.

'It's a complaint of the developed nations, is the blood pressure,' said Nurse Gilliland.

'The world is ill divid.'

'There's those that have.'

'And those that haven't.'

'Put the priest back in the middle of the parish,' said Mary Lawless. Nurse Gilliland put the salt cellar back in the centre of the tray. 'I'm just realising what I said.' Mary Lawless put her hand over her open mouth. 'Excuse me, Father. That was an expression we used in our house all the time. For putting the salt back in the middle of the table. No offence meant.'

'No offence taken,' said Father Farquharson. Nurse Gilliland picked up the salt cellar and scrutinised it.

'It's a one-holer. If you're so concerned for our blood pressures you should get a different kind of a salt cellar. One with lots of wee holes. Like for pepper. Then less will come out.'

'Not if you shake it for longer. Like Granda.'

'Could you not use a pepper shaker for salt then?' asked Mrs Brennan.

'I suppose you could. There's no law against it . . .' said Mary Lawless.

'I'll maybe try it some time. Experiment a bit.'

'Where would we be without science?' said Father Farquharson, laughing.

'Up a gum tree.'

'Father, have you ever been to the Dead Sea?'

'No, I have not. I have been to Lourdes and Knock but I have not been to the Holy Land. It's an ambition of mine to go – some day before I die.'

'They say you can't sink, what with the concentration of salt,' said Nurse Gilliland.

'Isn't that called buoyancy?'

'Or floating – to you and me. It's the same thing when all's said and done.'

'Yes – you can float and read your *Irish News*.'

'And find out who's dead. And which priests have been to what funerals.'

'When were you in Lourdes, Father?'

'Nineteen fifty-eight. The year Pope Pius the Twelfth died.'

'Here's a thing I've been meaning to ask you, Father. Pope Pius the Twelfth – does that mean he was . . . does that mean there were eleven other Popes called Pius?'

'It does.'

'Would you credit that?'

'Was there a run of them?'

'I suppose so. I haven't studied it. That could be an interesting research project for Martin here. The naming of popes.'

There was a long pause.

'I don't know about the rest of you,' said Mary Lawless, 'but some of the happiest moments of my life have been spent doing jigsaw puzzles.'

His inability to sleep was annoying him. And it was even more difficult to sleep in a state of annoyance. He tried to think of soothing things that were not sex. Of warm water. Of firelight. When he was very young, every Saturday night he'd be given a bath in the kitchen. The fire would be built up to heat the room and music on the wireless turned on. They had a green bath made of papier mâché, which hung in the coal hole. His mother filled the bath from the big kettle and cooled it with tap water poured from an enamel bucket. Sometimes after the music an English comedian would come on. That was a bad sign because he knew that before long his mother would switch off.

'I've no idea why people always have to let themselves down.

Every time.' Afterwards he put on clean underwear. But when he got older — he reckoned it was when he grew hair — his mother gave him the money to go to the public baths. There they gave him a crisp corporation towel and a slice of red carbolic soap. Most times he brought a fluffy towel from home and stood out on the other one. In first year at grammar school he learned to swim. A breadth. Then a length. He then always took the choice of going to the swimmers instead of the public baths, where all the old men went. If he didn't get to the swimmers he washed, stripped to the waist, at the kitchen sink.

One day a week after school he took a bag of washing to the launderette and he'd sit there listening to the drone and tumble of the machines until one would go into fast spin and vibrate the floor beneath his feet. He'd flick through women's magazines pretending not to linger over the underwear adverts. They never got magazines like that in his house. On the way home his bag of washing was much heavier.

And that night he would watch his mother smoothing. What a strange verb — smoothing. She would splash water from a bowl, sprinkling it by shaking her wet fingers. The iron would hiss over the damped material. There'd be tiny clicks against buttons and the creak of the ironing board when the pressure of the iron was put on it. The board had an asbestos pad at one end and the flex made a noise against this as it was pulled backwards and forwards. The radio low in the background. The bag of entangled washed stuff from the launderette on the one side and on the other the neat pile of warm and folded clothes smelling of soap. Smoothed. Like when she moved the furniture — a complete transformation.

A vocation would completely change his life, would give him a sense of direction, a goal. To devote his life to religion, to helping others. To take up a life of prayer. His mother would be *so* proud of him. At home there was a Black Magic chocolate box full of photos of him at the various stages of his childhood. With hands joined in prayer, wearing a white armband on his sleeve after First Holy Communion. A similar set for after Confirmation but now as a soldier of Christ. Join hands for the camera. Brave enough to take the slap on the cheek from the Bishop. It was stupid, really. Beforehand there had been such a fuss in his class. The kids exaggerated everything. He hated that. They went around acting the Bishop, taking a swing like John Wayne in a fist fight. Making slap noises with their mouths and collapsing sideways on to the ground. It was symbolic — like the forty days and forty nights. He hadn't felt a thing when the Bishop had tapped his cheek. Will you fight to keep the faith, was all it meant. And who wouldn't do that? He tried to imagine photographs of his ordination in the Black Magic box.

The thing about falling asleep was that you never knew when it happened. There was no other human activity like this. You knew you were doing things or else you couldn't do them. Falling asleep was an intentional act of giving yourself up — allowing yourself off the hook. Sometimes it was not intentional: sometimes people just dozed off. But you could never say from this point onwards I *am* asleep. Or in the next few moments I *will be* asleep. Moments of fudge were necessary. The instant of entry into sleep was obscure. Hidden, the way an eyelid covers the eye. His mother was there but there was not a tree in sight — it was a kind of heath. It became utterly dark and he kept reaching for the strap of her handbag but instead kept clasping her hand. She was annoyed and slapped his hand away. 'Stop that you!' A machine approached, its noise becoming louder and louder. They knew they must get out of its way but did not know which way to escape because the driver could not see them in the darkness. And before he knew it, he was in the machine, somehow scooped up, parted from his mother. He was in a cockpit of a sort and the pilot was talking to him, giving him instructions, telling him that everything was going to be all right and that on no account was he to panic. No matter what happened. The flying machine was a cross between a wire and balsa wood biplane and a helicopter. And the wind was rushing past him. Little bits of material were tied to the cross struts so their wind speed could be judged. There was a chattering rotor above his head and beneath him he could see hills and dark forests. Roads and rivers threaded between pocket handkerchief sized fields. And when he looked up again he was not in the cockpit but standing on the wing. He was holding on to an inflated yellow life jacket but that was for saving him at sea. Quite useless for this situation. There was nothing to save him from falling through the air. The plane banked to the right and he began to feel himself sliding. He saw the flash of a car windscreen travelling the road miles below. As well as banking the plane was putting its nose down and he was beginning to slide forward. His grip tightened on the life jacket until his knuckles and fingers were white. But to no avail. He fell. The plane flew on and he was falling from it. His stomach swooshed. He was so terrified he could not make a sound. It was as if his vocal cords did not work. Eventually after what seemed ages he did manage to howl. So much so that he wakened himself and became conscious so quickly that he heard the tail end of his own howl. His first thought was that he had broken the silence.

The next morning he thought of washing his face with one hand, while the other held up his pyjamas. So he dressed before washing. It was a weird experience to see so many boys half stripped at the basins washing their faces and scrubbing their teeth, without speaking a word. There was the sound of water escaping down plug-holes and of toilets being flushed, of wet feet slapping around on the marble floor.

He walked the corridor to the sacristy.

'Good morning Mr Brennan,' Father Albert was waiting for him, his fat face smiling and shining. He was going up and down on his toes. 'I know we shouldn't be talking – but it is the Lord's business. Let's get you kitted out.' They went into a dressing room off the sacristy. Some cupboards, a low bench and a row of coat hooks. 'What size of a lad are you?' Father Albert produced a black soutane and handed it to him. 'This is the biggest we've got.' Martin looked at – it was far too small. 'Go on – try it on.' He got into it, just about, but it cut up into his armpits and his bony wrists hung whitely out from the sleeves.

'Naw,' Martin said. 'I'm too tall.'

'A growing boy. Just a minute.' Father Albert opened one of the cupboards and produced a scarlet soutane. Oh Jesus – no. He'd be like a choir boy, like something off a fuckin Christmas card. 'This will definitely fit.' It did. And he gave him a white lace surplice to wear over the top of it. He had never seen lace of such a complicated sort: tumbling at the sleeves and saw toothed around the waist. It was like a tablecloth on a queen's dinner table. The Redemptorist touched both Martin's shoulders and held him at arm's length. Then took a further step back.

'That's you. Perfect.'

He was going to have to parade out in front of the school like this. A door slammed outside.

'There's Father O'Malley now. Come along Mr Brennan, come along.'

The Redemptorist hurried Martin out of the dressing room. Condor was standing in the robing room, his head bowed, before the elaborate dressing table. Father Albert asked him if he knew where everything was. Condor nodded. Father Albert gave him the key to the tabernacle, saluted Martin and left. It was only then that Martin fully realised he was going to serve mass for Condor.

When he had finished his prayer Condor slid a hand into his pocket and took out some change. It rattled as he set it to one side.

'The sound of Mammon,' he said. If anything, his voice was even deeper in the morning. 'The noise that prompted the Lord to throw the moneychangers out of the temple.' From his other pocket he took a bunch of keys and a hanky. A second dive produced a box of Swan matches and a thing pipe smokers had – a thin probe, a tamper and a spoon, all in one. From his breast pocket he took two pens and set them beside the other stuff. 'Why do we have to carry all this junk?'

The drawers of the dressing table were huge, like the ones in geography for storing maps – big enough to take the vestments laid flat. The handles were of brass and when Condor pulled the drawer and let go of them they swung making tiny clacking noises. He put on a white alb which covered him to the toes of his polished shoes. He uncoiled the white cincture from the drawer where it lay like a curled snake.

'Silence and sanctity are twins. What have you on your feet, Brennan?' Martin showed him his leather shoes. 'Have they no gutties about this place? I remember lads with nails in their boots, steel tips – thought they were hard men. Well, on the altar I made them wear gutties. When you're serving mass you should be like a wraith.'

Condor walked through to the other dressing room and rummaged beneath the bench and produced a pair of white gym shoes. 'What size do you take?' Martin told him. Condor remained squatting. He smelled of tobacco, even through the alb.

His teeth were yellowed from smoking the pipe, especially the lower ones, like thin brown stalks. Mahogany teeth. 'Here. Try those.'

They were too small but they didn't hurt enough for him to refuse to wear them. He could smell a feet smell off them as he tied the laces. They were very flat. When he went back into the sacristy Condor had all his vestments on. The priest reached for his handkerchief and thrust it up his sleeve. Martin had only seen women do that. Nurse Gilliland in particular. Condor indicated that he wished to go and Martin led the way onto the altar, his hands firmly joined. He kept staring at the marble floor as he walked. He didn't dare look at any of the boys. He could feel the heat rushing to his face, knew his blushing was like a reflection from the red soutane.

When it came to the hand washing, he folded the linen towel over his wrist, took the water cruet in his right hand, the silver bowl in his left and approached the altar. Condor came to him and extended his fingers over the bowl. His nails had a rim of black — pipe smoker nails. The finger and thumb of each hand were together, the rest of the fingers fanned out. It was as if he was making two shadow rabbits. Martin poured the water from his cruet. The fingers were awful, chubby, knuckled, each one with a tuft of black hair on the back. Martin stared as Condor dried his hands and recited the prayer. He folded the linen towel and draped it back over Martin's wrist. The fingers looked no cleaner and he still smelled of tobacco.

After mass Father Albert was waiting for them in the sacristy. He clapped his hands together and beamed.

'That was well served, Mr Brennan. No faults whatsoever. Not even foot faults. Rod Laver would have been proud of you.'

The day was taken up with sermons and talks and prayers. In between times there were opportunities for spiritual reading and self-examination. Occasionally Martin went down behind the yew trees for a smoke. The gravel there was littered with cork tips. Walking in the grounds was strange. Normally the boys would walk in twos or threes but because of the silence everyone was alone. They stood, their hands in their pockets, looking away from one another. Out to sea, mostly. It was good for pictures, everyone being on their own – with guys standing here and there all over the gardens. Like statues. Martin went back inside for his camera. There was still some snow where it had blown into corners. The whirr and clunk of the shutter mechanism was satisfying as he took picture after picture. Suddenly Father Albert was beside him, his hands joined behind his back.

'Mr Brennan at work, eh?' Martin nodded. He was unsure whether to speak or not. This had nothing to do with the business of the Lord.

'You realise it is somehow breaking the silence, to take pictures?'

'But you said I could.'

'I know, I know. But it distracts – the noise of the shutter. The activity. The purpose of what you're about.'

'Do you want me to stop?'

'What do *you* think?'

Martin nodded and put the camera away.

Before the evening sermon and devotions Condor came striding out on to the altar.

'It saddens me to have to say this but today I've had a complaint from the people directly below this place. It seems some boy or boys have been throwing stones.' A ripple of amusement went through the congregation. 'THIS IS NOT FUNNY,' he roared. Faces straightened – everybody went still. 'When are you *ever* going to grow up? I had the indignity of being summoned to inspect this gentleman's property – a gentleman, I might add, who is not of our faith. A number of panes of glass in his greenhouse have been smashed. He assures me they were intact yesterday. The stones could only have come from here. The school will be obliged to make good the damage. I'd like the boy or boys involved to own up. You are now supposed to be *mature* individuals, God help us. The whole school should not be tarnished for the evil-doing of a few.' Boys at the front looked around to see if anyone was going to own up. No one did. 'This gentleman was extremely upset and was threatening to involve the police. But I wouldn't want them here on Church property. Those particular gentlemen would be the last people I'd involve in a matter of law and order. Lorranawda, according to our friends in

England – so we will have to police this one ourselves. If anybody saw anything Father Albert and Father Valerian will be available at any time. A word in either of their ears . . . would be sufficient.'

After Condor left the altar, Father Albert came out.

'A word in either of our ears,' he began. 'But if you're coming to me my left ear is my best.' He cupped his hand behind his left ear and smiled. The boys laughed. To have Condor reprimanded for his grammar . . . Indeed, let off the leash like this, the boys made more of the joke than they should have. Father Albert spoke loudly across the laughter to stop it: 'If anyone saw anything, or anybody who was involved in this . . . then it would be the right place to become a man. For truth is a manly thing.' The boys went quiet. Father Albert stopped and cleared his throat, then looked up into the rafters. There was a pause, to prepare them for his sermon. 'And purity is a manly thing. Looking around me at your bright and handsome faces . . .' he coughed artificially. 'A-hem! I can tell that none of you are strangers to a good white tablecloth. The first day that tablecloth comes out of the drawer, it is crisp and white – a thing of beauty – it'll have the little ridged creases where it was ironed – if your mother was anything like mine.'

There was no pulpit. Father Albert seemed to prefer it that way – to be on a level with the boys. Once or twice he moved down off the altar to be among them. To clip a boy round the ear for fun, draw a halo in the air above someone's head to make a mockery of him. There was something about this Martin didn't like – like in a Western when the female singer came down off the stage and toyed with the cowboys. It embarrassed him for some reason he couldn't put into words. Martin felt his eyes begin to be heavy.

'That, boys, is like your soul the day you were born. God given. Pristine. And you keep it like that for some time – until the first food arrives. The *hors-d'oeuvre*. The starters, as they like to call them nowadays. The horses doovers. But as the meal of our lives proceeds things begin to go wrong – small things – maybe a slip here, a slip there – a sprinkling of salt, a scattering of breadcrumbs, the carafe of water slops over. The venial sins have begun. But we can cope with that. With the flick of a serviette, with a little brushing here and there, maybe a rub with a damp cloth. These are tools, boys – like the sacraments, daily mass and communion, prayer and devotions – ways to keep the soul spotless. We can say an Act of Contrition and, provided we have a firm purpose of amendment, our tablecloth will be . . . almost as good as the day we took it from the linen cupboard.' Martin closed his eyes. He could hear what was being said just as well. Better indeed because he could concentrate more, not having any visual distraction. 'But the meal goes on, boys, and we get more and more dangerous things coming to the table – gravy, blackcurrant jam, tomato sauce, maybe that soiler of everything, that spoiler of everything, red wine – with beaded bubbles winking at the brim. We get careless and eventually an elbow will hit something. And, before we know where we are, mortal sin has entered our lives. Our tablecloth is stained, ruined. What's to be done? A visit to the laundry. Why else do you think the Church has the Sacrament of Confession . . .'

Because he had slept so badly the night before and because of the early start that morning Martin began to drift . . . The chapel was hot and he was conscious of the boys' shoulders on either side of him keeping him upright . . . At the moment he was about to go, his head JERKED up. And he was awake again. Then the same heavy eyelids, the same falling asleep sensation and again he would JERK himself awake. He was ashamed. As Christ in the Garden said, 'Can you not watch one hour with me?' He concentrated, dug his fingernails into the back of his hand so that he hurt himself awake. 'Then comes the day when we have to die. And we have to display our tablecloth for inspection, for examination. You're at that stage in your lives when you are totally taken up with examinations. Well, believe me, boys, this is the only examination that matters – and if we fail it, we fail everything. And what's more – *there are no re-sits*. On the Last Day, Judgment Day, the conduct of each one of us will be held up to scrutiny by Our Lord. The secrets of our hearts will be brought into the light. What we are considering here are, as St Paul says, things that no eye has seen and no ear has heard, things beyond the mind of man, all that God has

prepared for those who love him.' The resurrection of the body. The Last Day. The Apocalypse

John

there

are . . . . . . might . . . . . . Jesus Christ . . . . . .   unconditionally   frangwine

melopites   caringe   St Paul   smee   gloofort

30

mong

JERK!

'. . . Matthew's memorable words "But when the Son of Man shall come in his majesty and all the angels with him, then he will sit upon the throne of his glory; and before him will be gathered all nations, and he will separate them one from another, as the shepherd separates the sheep from the goats." The examination to end all examinations. A levels will be chicken-feed compared to the Last Judgment. Every action, every thought, even the ones you tried to hide – ESPECIALLY the ones you tried to hide – will be pulled out and examined before the Court of Heaven – and sitting in that court will be the ones you love – your mother, your father, your brothers and sisters. Your friends. The ones you deceived. The ones you disobeyed, the ones you had your impure thoughts about.

fuckface   Fuckface?   Can't be   Can't possibly

sep   farnick   barglish   . . .

sin   day

32

On Good Friday after the Stations of the Cross they were all asked to write out questions. 'They can be anonymous,' said Father Valerian, 'and can be about anything.' A ripple of amusement went through the boys and, recognising the drift of their thinking, the priest rolled his eyes to heaven. 'Yes, even that.'

Cut squares of paper and halved pencils had been left around the large sitting room. A wooden box with a slit stood on a table at the centre. It was locked with a small brass padlock. The silence was still being kept but there was a lot of winking and grinning at one another as everyone wrote on their squares of paper.

After dinner it was dark and everyone moved into the sitting room. Some boys had to go to another part of the house for extra chairs. Both Father Albert and Father Valerian sat behind the table at the head of the room. Father Valerian produced a small key, opened the box and shook the papers on to the table.

'Democracy,' he said and smiled. The priests began to sort through them. Father Albert raised his head.

'Normally in a situation like this I would say "Just talk among yourselves." But given the circumstances of a silent retreat I will say no such thing.' The boys watched the faces of the priests as they read the questions. Two piles of papers were gradually developing. Father Valerian patted one pile.

'These are questions,' he said. He patted the other pile, 'and these are impertinences.'

They took it in turns – Father Valerian answering a question about Original Sin, Father Albert answering one about whether or not it would be sinful to use force to make the British withdraw from Ireland. Martin was sure that that one had come from Sharkey. The question 'Will Sunday mass be compulsory in heaven?' made everyone laugh. As did 'Is it true that Shakespeare founded the Legion of Mary?' These were tossed to one side but on each serious question they talked for ages. Then, as if on a signal, they both stopped and eyed the pile they had not yet touched. They both sighed together.

'I don't think I'm even going to read these out,' said Father Albert, 'because they are all asking about the same old story. There's a lot of talk nowadays about clean air and clean water – the environment. We all accept restrictions on our freedom to achieve these ends. But how many of us will go along with the censorship – how many of us will root out the hard core pornography. It's everywhere we look, in plays and films, in magazines, on hoardings twenty storeys high. Everything nowadays is beyond the bounds of decency. To object to that kind of thing is not *with it*. There is a conspiracy to corrupt our youth and it's all coming from across the water.'

'But we must do all in our power, boys, to stop it,' said Father Valerian. 'An effort must be made to re-establish purity in our young men.'

He picked up one of the written questions between his finger and thumb and held it well away from him.

'*Is it a mortal sin to be intimate with a girl you love?* What kind of a question is that? We don't serve God like employees – in expectation of our wages. We must be good for itself. Virtue is its own reward. Anyway is this the kind of thing boys of your age should be asking? You should be out playing football, enjoying yourselves, instead of getting into such occasions of sin.'

'Sighing over women,' said Father Albert. 'Swoonsville.'

'Pandering to your passions.' The session had taken on the character of a Laurel and Hardy act. 'None of you will be in a position to marry a girl for many's a year. And there's no point in getting all hot and bothered. A lot of it is showing off in front of your chums: aren't I the one – I've got a girlfriend.' Father Valerian inclined his head towards Father Albert and looked over his glasses at him. Albert responded by averting his face and patting his hair with his hand.

'There is, of course, a serious point we are trying to make here. Chastity is a beautiful thing in a young man. A strong character is one who doesn't give in to his passions. Failure to master oneself is to be in thrall to the most complete slavery imaginable. A boy *has* to be able to say no.'

'It's the same for a young woman.'

'And if we dedicate our efforts to remain pure to the greater glory of God it will all be something *worthwhile*.'

The first time Martin had kissed a girl was when he was twelve or thirteen. At a daylight party, on a summer's evening. There were girls in dresses, perfume smells, the feeling of being tongue-tied, nervous. Music with a pounding beat was playing. Someone suggested a game. Martin sat on the sofa until his number was called by Pauline Lunny. She was older than the rest. She was standing close to the door of the room – which was wide open. There was a draught-excluding velvet curtain on the door which could become a dark tent. Martin stood, grinning – as if it was going to be some kind of a test he had to pass. Pauline had her hair in a ponytail. She stretched out her arms and beckoned him in behind the door. She lifted the curtain and when he was in she let it fall around them. There was a confessional darkness. He knew from the movies to put one arm around her neck. She was wearing lipstick. He moved his face towards hers, not knowing what to do next. She closed her eyes, allowing him to kiss her. His mouth came against her mouth. At first her mouth felt dry, then it adhered to his and became moist, became huge inside his mind, like a universe. He closed his eyes. The sound of the party went on vaguely pounding in the background. He was totally surrounded by the moistness and size of her lips. It was as if he was mesmerised by this one sensation – an enveloping bed, an extravagance of comfort he had never experienced before. And the scent of her. The taste of her mouth and tongue. The smoothness of the skin of her cheek and the lobe of her ear which touched against the finger of his right hand. He became aware that his other hand was resting against the tight feel of her waist, a muscle feel, a flickering live feel, faintly hidden by the cloth that was between his hand and her. Beneath it she was like an eel, a rippling body, a single muscle. But before he could relax into the sensation he was utterly startled to feel her tongue probe and flicker in his mouth – it tasted of acid, like a sucked penny, felt of rough skin – and he wanted to tell her that that wasn't how it should be done. It was unhygienic. But he knew that she knew better than him. If Pauline was doing it then that was the way to do it. And because she was so good at it, he felt inadequate. He didn't know how to respond. *She* was kissing *him* – and she quickly became bored with it because she broke from the kiss and moved out from behind the door curtain to look for someone else. Martin was startled to find that something was happening in his trousers. At a time like this. It happened unexpectedly on the top deck of a bus or when he was going to communion or when

35

he fiddled with himself but why on earth it should happen when he was kissing a girl he hadn't the faintest idea.

And it was happening *now* – at a religious question and answer session. Father Valerian was talking about controlling bad thoughts – at the very moment Martin was enjoying them. He crossed his legs and hoped to crush the intruder out of existence. 'Think of something,' said Father Valerian, 'which the Mother of God would approve of. Joyful pursuits – walking the hills, diving into the sea, a particularly exciting handball match you may have seen.' Father Albert with a large gesture looked at his watch then brought the question time to a close, saying that if anyone wanted to discuss any problem further then they could bring it up in confession. The proceedings ended with a prayer.

The evening meal was rice with bits of smoked fish and hard boiled egg. It tasted like eating an ashtray. A Brother with a wavery voice did the reading.

> 'He struck Job down with malignant ulcers from the sole of his foot to the top of his head. Job took a piece of pot to scrape himself, and went and shat in the ash-pit.'

Martin wondered if he'd heard correctly. He didn't dare look at anybody in case he'd take a fit of laughing. The reader paused and said, 'I'm sorry – *sat in the ash-pit.*'

Martin kept staring down at his plate. The bits of fish were brown. Eventually the urge to laugh went away and he ate enough to show he was trying. The guy beside him, a school boarder, finished Martin's. The whole thing left a yellow stain on the plate. For afters the Brothers set before everyone a plate with a wedge of hard biscuit and a tinned plum on it. The biscuit did not yield to pressure from Martin's spoon. He moved his elbow high and got the weight of his shoulder behind it but, instead of breaking, the thing scooted off to the side and fell on the floor. Everyone saw what happened.

Martin sat by himself on a wooden bench in the corridor outside Father Valerian's room waiting his turn for confession. He checked the grandfather clock at the end of the corridor. A quarter past. His stomach rumbled emptily. He felt good about himself the way he planned this. He had done nothing much since his last confession, which was on Saturday in his own parish. He had deliberately avoided playing with himself all week because he knew he was coming on this Retreat. The boys who had been here last year told about the open confession you had to make – sitting opposite the priest in an armchair with the lights on. The idea of this man-to-man stuff put the fear of God into him. It was beyond him to tell a lie in confession. If he had wanked he would have to tell it because confession was talking directly to God. The priest was only an intermediary, like a telephone: you talked through him. You told *him* your sins and God heard them. How could you hide things from God? The window opposite him was stained glass but at night it was black. On the walls between the windows were some African works of art – masks, heads. Beside them pictures of Redemptorists in white soutanes standing having their photographs taken beside black men. Like the kind of thing he'd seen in the magazine *The Far East*. His mother had it delivered every month by the Legion of Mary. Support for the missionaries, she said, it's the least we can do. She also said it would be one hell of a job to keep a white soutane clean throughout the length of a working day. White was a totally impractical colour for Africa.

Martin looked at the clock again. Twenty past. What was going on in there?

At last the door opened with a squeak and McGarrity came out. He pulled a face – half grin, half warning – and kept his hands joined as he walked away down the corridor. Martin stood up and took a deep breath. Holy fuck.

The room was dimly lit. The door squeaked in reverse as he closed it.

'Come in, boy. Over here. I'm not going to eat you.' Martin looked around. The voice came from the armchair beside the fire. 'Sit, man, sit.'

Martin sat. It wasn't an armchair but a hard, straight-backed chair. Father Valerian was wearing a purple stole around his neck and his biretta was perched on the top of his head. Martin tried to remember the formula of words he said every week but the priest wrongfooted him by asking, 'How long is it since your last confession?'

'A week, Father. Bless-me-Father-for-I-have-sinned. It-is-a-week-since—'

'And . . . ?' There was a long silence. Martin tried to think of something to say. The priest encouraged him. 'Has it been a clean sheet this week?'

Martin hesitated, wondering if the question had something to do with wanking or wet dreams.

'Yes, Father.'

'Good man, good man. But, you know – you can always do better. A good man like yourself can benefit from a more rigorous examination of conscience. Know what I mean? On an occasion like this let's take an overview – do a kind of overall spring-clean. Do you indulge in any morbid habits?'

'What . . . are . . . ?'

'Self-pollution?'

'I'm not sure . . .'

'Impurity with yourself?'

'I . . . I . . . I'm not sure . . .'

'Well if you're not sure I'm certainly not going to put it into your head.' The priest leaned forward, his hands resting on his knees.

'Father, I have bad thoughts, if that's what you mean. Also I touch myself.' Father Valerian sighed.

Martin went to the chapel to say his penance and to be by himself. The place was small and dark except for the lit candles. The sanctuary lamp glowed red. He knelt at the back and concentrated, trying to pray. He clenched his eyes tightly and tried to think in words he would use himself – none of the *We beseech thee O Lord* stuff. If You want me to devote my life to the priesthood, to You, tell me in some way. He did not want to ask for a sign in case it happened. He did not voice the thought. Because as soon as he had voiced it the possibility existed that the place would be filled with a roaring light and he could find himself on the flat of his back with God talking to him. In Ireland it was more likely to be the Mother of God talking to him. She seemed to have priority. But on the other hand he did want some indication whether or not he had a vocation. The candle flames pulled themselves upright — long and yellow with barely a movement from side to side.

Lord, do you want me to become a priest? Martin said into himself.

Another boy, Brendan O'Connell, came into the chapel and knelt down. He took out his rosary beads from a purse. A purse — for God's sake — with a snap fastener. Martin heard it opening, and then the tiny rattle of the beads. The candle flames flickered and danced after the air had been disturbed. The guy scratched his head and cupped his face in his hands. He was sighing a lot and sniffing — generally being a pain in the arse — letting everybody see he was making a heavy-duty decision.

Martin stood up and went out into the night for a cigarette. It was bitterly cold. The flagstones in front of the building glittered with frost. He could see his breath on the air as well as the smoke. When he looked up there was no moon: the sky was black and cloudless, but full of stars. He walked behind the Retreat House where it was even darker, shielded from the lights of the town. He moved away from the lit windows down to the shelter of an ivy-covered wall. He didn't like the gravel crunching beneath his shoes so he walked on the grass which was stiff with frost. He looked up again, and from this point the stars were amazing. The swirl of the Milky Way was obvious from one side of the sky to the other. A town boy, he had never seen anything like it. There was no part of the sky which wasn't filled with stars — impossible to put a finger between them, impossible to put the nib of a pen between them. The constellations he knew from books seemed to have been swamped by lesser stars. Gradually he began to pick the star groups out — first the Plough, then the W of Cassiopeia, Orion with the sword at his belt. And he was aware of their absolute silence. To be so vast and yet to make no sound whatsoever. His neck was beginning to hurt. If he could lie down. Also his teeth were beginning to chatter, like when he came out from a swim. If he relaxed the muscles of his face, it would go away. When he tensed against the cold, his jaw would begin chattering. He put his hands in his blazer pockets and tried to make himself a smaller target for the cold air. He was out here to make a decision, not to think about how cold he was, not to look at the stars. He inhaled the last of the cigarette and spun the glowing butt away over the wall into the dark. Yes – if he passed his exams he would strive to become a priest, to devote his life as best he could to the service of others; above all, to the service of God. He felt the weight of his decision lying on him and was turning to go in out of the cold when the word 'no' came into his mind. He walked with his head down. It was as if someone had spoken it. En Oh. NO. It had definitely come into his head from somewhere outside himself. He turned his face up to the sky. No. And no again. A very definite no was inside his head. Could this be the sign he had asked for? NO. He wondered was the no an answer to the question he had asked himself – could this be a sign? – or the overall question of whether or not to become a priest. No. There it was again. From outer space – a message. It must apply to the big problem and not to the problem within a problem. He felt a surge of gratefulness to the word that was repeating inside his head. The weight of the decision he had just made was beginning to lift. In the beginning was the Word and the Word was with God and the Word was God and the Word was NO. He could do something else. God was letting him off the hook. Martin Brennan was surplus to requirements as far as the Almighty was concerned. As Father Albert had said, a boy has to be able to say no. And here he was doing it. No – he said it to himself again. And at the same time felt a surge of gratefulness to, of all people, God. The lights of the town came into sight again as he rounded the building. They shone distinctly in the harbour, it was so still. The water stood the town on its head. He came to an area of the wall which was waist-high and leaned on it looking down. The wall was two or three feet thick and he climbed on to it and lay on his back, looking up at the stars again. To save his neck. His breath hovered above him. He would not become a priest. He had moved from one element to another. As his mother would say – it was not for him. He would do something else with his life which would be equally good – he hadn't a clue what it was just yet. Now it was a Good Friday night and he was lying on a wall shivering, grinning at the stars. Suddenly a meteor blazed across the sky – quick as a nib scrape. And a joy shot through him. Everything was the right colour and in the right place and his feelings were in defiance of gravity.

2. A Morning Walk to School

Martin kept his collection of books on the mantelpiece in his bedroom. He couldn't decide which way to stack them. Vertically, like a real library or horizontally, like a pile of books. He only had four of his own, the rest were schoolbooks. He lifted his homework diary which was falling to bits. It had assumed the curve of his backside because he kept it in his hip pocket most of the time. He got the books he needed for the day's classes and slipped them into his bag, then plunged down the stairs two at a time.

'I'm away,' he yelled.

From the kitchen he faintly heard his mother shout, 'Go easy.' The front door slammed.

He slung one strap of the bag over his shoulder and walked quickly to the main road. The sky was blue and full of rushing white clouds. It was a good feeling the first day back after Easter. There was no homework to be handed in, just your mates to see. He eased up, coming to O'Grady's, the paper shop on the corner. It had a sandwich board outside on the pavement with scrawled capitals: VIETNAM CALL UP REFUSED. Kavanagh should appear at any minute coming down the hill. It was a quarter to nine by the Bank of Ireland clock. He didn't want to be seen hanging around actually waiting so he walked up and down. The other side of the sandwich board had some guff about Captain Terence O'Neill. He looked at FOR SALE ads in the window – handwritten filing cards. It felt good having enough money for a day's supply of smokes. But O'Grady's didn't sell singles – he'd have to wait until the wee sweet shop beside the school. He'd have preferred the money for ten but he was not a millionaire. Somebody was selling a gents racing bike. Was there such a thing as a ladies racing bike? Neat little headlamps? Reading the ads Martin could have his back to the hill and still keep an eye on it, reflected in the window.

He had only known Kavanagh for two terms and they had never agreed to meet, apart from 'I'll see you in the morning' as they parted each afternoon. It was always better when they just coincided on their way down the road. Kavanagh was the guy everybody wanted to know and Martin felt – just lucky – that they walked the same route to school. Martin knew very few in his present year. All his mates had moved on when he failed. There was an ad which said TUTORING FOR RE-SITS. He looked away from it. Too close to the bone. He had to convince his mother that he was applying himself – so that meant very few outings at night. He read a few more cards. He hated noticing spelling mistakes. Somebody was selling a 'perambulater'. He could see a reflection of the bank clock. He took his time, reversing the image – like working out one of those intelligence puzzles in the eleven-plus exam. He deciphered it as ten to nine.

'Come on, ya bastard.'

He turned from the window and looked directly at the hill. No sign of him. Maybe he was sick. Maybe he'd gone off somewhere with his family for Easter and not come back. Condor would be out thumping the latecomers at the top of the drive even though it was only the first day back.

When he turned to the window again he glimpsed Kavanagh's reflection come into view. Martin moved off immediately as if he had just paused to glance at the cards. He looked over his shoulder and Kavanagh saw him from a distance. Martin waited until he came alongside.

'What about ye?'

'Grand,' said Kavanagh. 'What about yourself?'

'OK. We're cutting it fine.'

'We'll make it for nine, no problem.'

'I've gotta get fags.' Martin quickened his pace and gradually matched Kavanagh's. Kavanagh was big, basketball big, and his stride was longer. And he had great hair. Martin only came to his shoulder. They both carried the same kind of bag in the same kind of way. A khaki canvas haversack, one strap slung over the right shoulder. It was utterly unthinkable for anyone to wear it properly – on the back with loops over both shoulders. Val-der-ree, val-der-aa, hill walking in the Alps whistling merry tunes. The khaki colour stood out against the black of the blazer, a dangerous black and tan combination. And there was brass too. Cheap buckles and canvas straps fastened the top flap to the bottom. There were never enough books to fill the bag and it was stylish that they should flop about loosely inside.

Kavanagh heaved his bag a little higher on his shoulder and said, 'Jesus, I hate this.'

'What?'

'Going back to school. The worst thing's the getting out of your bed in the morning.'

'Maybe you could go to night school,' said Martin.

'Be far better if you could get pushed to school in your bed. Very salubrious.'

'Yeah – big castors on it, the size of pram wheels. And your ma pushing it.'

'Up the drive – past Condor. In your pyjamas. With your cock still up like a tent pole.'

'I'm totally amazed at the things people get up early to do,' said Martin. 'Like duels. Imagine getting out of your bed at that time of the morning to be fucking killed? Even worse, imagine getting out of your bed early to kill someone. Behind the cathedral at eight.' Martin had to run a couple of steps to keep up. But he didn't mind because he knew they were late and Condor never gave anybody the benefit of the doubt.

They came to the wee sweetie shop and Martin went in.

'I'll not be a minute.'

'It'll only stunt your growth,' said Kavanagh as he followed him in. The place was very dark – one 60-watt bulb. The middle-aged woman behind the counter stared at Martin. She had her hair up in a beehive.

'Three Regal,' he said. Martin produced his money. The woman rolled her eyes and all but snorted. She opened a wooden drawer and selected a packet of Regal. She took out three and trundled them across the counter.

'Have you got a packet?' The expression on the woman's face did not change. She opened the wooden drawer again. Barely looking down, her hand raked the contents. She dropped a ten Park Drive packet in front of Martin. Kavanagh came up behind him.

43

'Did I not see the gleam of gold in there?' he said to the woman.

'What are you talking about?'

'All I ask is a touch of class for my friend.' He laid a hand on Martin's shoulder and pointed at the drawer. The woman produced a different packet.

'Would a Benson & Hedges suffice?' she said.

Both Kavanagh and Martin nodded. Martin handed over his money and she flicked the empty gold packet on to the counter. He slid the three Regal into it and closed over its neat hinged top.

'Thanks,' he said.

'Mutton dressed as lamb,' said Kavanagh to the woman. She smiled. Kavanagh knew how to talk to old people. He could use their lingo.

Outside Martin said, 'I never saw that before.'

'What?'

'Your woman, smiling.'

'Maybe you gave her no reason,' said Kavanagh. They continued to walk. 'Did you get much done?'

'What?'

'Studying.'

'Naw . . .'

'Did you get your hole?'

'Naw . . .what about you?' said Martin.

'What about me?'

'Did you get it?'

'That's for me to know and you to find out.'

'What did you do over Easter?'

'It was horrid.' Kavanagh put on an upper-class voice. 'I kid you not. Laid up with measles . . .'

'Poor old thing.' Martin took up the voice as well.

'I kid you not. I had to stay in the dorm until Matron gave me the all clear. Uncle Quentin took me for a drive in the country – lots of adventures.'

'Where were Lucy-Ann and Philip and Jack and . . .?'

'They'd fucked off on an adventure of their own – Five Go to Pudenda Island – with Kiki the parrot.'

'Philip is marvellous with animals.'

'Hey – look at this . . .' On the other side of the road from the

44

school alongside the graveyard wall there was a crowd of workmen laying cable. The surrounding pavement was taped off.

'Aw fuck,' said Martin.

'What?'

'I forgot the camera. I was doing an article on the Retreat in Ardglass. And I was supposed to bring it back to Cuntyballs today.'

'He won't make a fuss.'

'I'm not so sure.'

'If he does, just you send him to me.'

Condor was at the top of the drive. There were some first-years standing around waiting to see the executioner at work. It was the same every morning. Just before nine he – as Dean of Discipline – would saunter down to the main door to take up his position. He wore a black soutane with a small shoulder cape. As he stepped out he would slip his hand inside the breast of his soutane and withdraw a yellow bamboo cane and flick back his shoulder cape. He'd hold the cane upright behind his back, so that it just playfully touched between his shoulder blades and tap-tapped the hair at the back of his head. Then he'd listen for the six pips for the nine o'clock news to sound from the kitchen. He'd elaborately check that the BBC was right against his own watch. He'd gaze at it, his under-lip jutting. Boys still in the drive would break into a run. Condor would bring the cane into sight – then hold it up like a sword. Everyone was running now. Condor was smiling. When he felt like it he would bring the cane down and everybody after that would get walloped. He'd listen to excuses with his head to one side, as if he was hard of hearing, but he rarely accepted any story. When he waved your excuse aside you had to put your hand out. He'd whip the cane down and catch you across the fingers. One on each hand. And on the follow-through there would be a loud *whap* as the cane hit his soutane. After ten past nine it was two on each hand. Cold mornings were the worst. It was like an electric shock. Pain beyond belief in the fingertips. Then a moment or two of numbness. Then the second kind of pain as the blood tried to push back through the hurt tissue. It was so fucking humiliating that grown-up guys had to put up with this shite. From a priest, too. If anybody complained about their

45

punishment Condor would say, 'You boys are but gristle, not yet hardened into the bone of manhood.'

It was on a par with the idea that discipline was something to be developed and taught. Somewhere in your being you had a discipline muscle which, if exercised enough, would always be in perfect trim. Certain no-good riff-raff were too lazy to exercise this muscle but the good thing was that it could be done for them. Condor would beat them and this would exercise the discipline muscle and everything would be all right. They would *become* disciplined because they had *been* disciplined.

But this morning they were OK. In – by the skin of their teeth. Martin was still feeling good about what had happened in the wee sweetie shop. Kavanagh's hand on his shoulder. And calling him *my friend* even though it was in a cod sort of way. They heard the first whacks of the latecomers as they moved into the corridor.

There was a group who met regularly in the locker room. The lockers had been removed years ago, but the place was still known as the locker room. They all greeted Kavanagh and Martin. It was good to be seen coming in together like this too. Kavanagh and Brennan. Brian Sweeny came over and there was a lot of backslapping went on between him and Kavanagh. On the first day it was always the same.

'Any jokes?' Sweeny asked.

Everyone gathered round and Kavanagh grinned and they all leaned forward.

'There was this guy, right?' he said. 'I kid you not. From the country – a big fuckin ganch – and he took this woman out. She was lovely, a real cracker – beautiful hair, big mouth, tits out to here. Anyway, after the night out, she says to him would you like to come back to my place? And she takes him up the stairs and into the bedroom and she strips off and lies down on the bed with her legs wide open. And your man says to himself, *Jesus, if I play my cards right, I might be on to something here.*'

Somebody at the back of the crowd who hadn't quite heard kept saying, 'What? What did she say?'

'Sexual intercourse is all right,' said Brian Sweeny, 'but there's nothing like the real thing.'

46

'This priest,' said Kavanagh, 'asked a boy *Do you masturbate a lot?* And the boy says *About a teaspoonful.*'

The bell rang.

'Aww fuck.' Almost everybody said it. Kavanagh and Martin were in different classes for the first two periods. Before they went their separate ways Kavanagh said, 'See you at lunch time. Here?'

'Yeah, yeah sure.' Martin couldn't stop smiling the whole way to his first class. 'A touch of class for *my friend.*' The gold cigarette packet – the hand on the shoulder.

'Very salubrious. I kid you not,' Martin said aloud to himself.

Ned Kelly, the Latin teacher, was reading his morning paper with his bald head cocked slightly to one side. Everybody was working on a translation. The classroom was silent – in the distance the sound of a pneumatic drill. There was a knock at the door.

'Come in.' The door opened and the Reverend Head came in with a new boy dressed in civvies. Ned Kelly's head shone as he bent over and listened to the Reverend Head. He then nodded for the boy to sit down. Before going to a desk the guy smiled and, as a kind of parting gesture, offered his hand to the Reverend Head in front of everybody. For a moment the Reverend Head didn't seem to know what to do.

'Thank you for all your help, Father,' said the boy in a voice too loud for the classroom. The voice was refined, easily mocked. The Reverend Head shook hands with the new guy. When he did it, he looked like he wished he hadn't. He rubbed his hand on his haunch and pushed it into the folds of his soutane out of the way.

Martin was at the back of the class sitting on his own in an old-fashioned two seater desk. The new boy came down the aisle and slid on to the empty bench beside him. Martin nodded but the new boy looked through him. Other guys were turning, trying to get a look.

The Reverend Head said, 'This is a new man – Blaise Foley.'

'Blaise is with an ess – not a zed,' said the new guy. The Reverend Head looked over his half-glasses at the new boy and stared at him. 'It's spelled the same way as Pascal, the philosopher, spells it.'

'Thank you for the lesson,' said Ned Kelly. He and the

47

Reverend Head whispered some more, then the Reverend Head said before he left,

'Treat Mr Foley as you would wish to be treated if it was *you* who were joining a new school.'

'Brennan, can you clue the new man in to what we're doing this morning.'

Martin nodded. He pushed his book across the desk and pointed to the passage. The guy looked down at it as if he'd forgotten his glasses. He also sat like he was wearing a neck brace or else had a bad back. He seemed to have neither pen nor paper with him. Martin smiled and pretended to go back to his translation.

'How long is there to go?' said the new boy. He had dropped his voice to a whisper.

'Ten minutes.' The new guy reached into his inside pocket and produced a pencil, which he set in the groove at the top of the desk. He began to look around him, at the high ceiling, at the skirting boards, at Ned Kelly reading his newspaper.

'Do you want something to write on?' said Martin.

'No.'

The translation passage was from Cicero. Martin was having difficulty with the tense of the main verb.

'A couple of minutes,' said Ned Kelly without looking up from the paper.

The new boy leaned over and said, 'Who is that big cunt?'

'His name's Ned Kelly. He's not that bad – he's OK, compared to some.'

The new guy raised an eyebrow.

'All Latin teachers are dumbfucks. Hatchet-men.'

When the time came to correct the translation Ned Kelly went through it line by line, phrase by phrase, sometimes taking an answer from one of the boys, sometimes supplying the words himself.

'*Silent enim leges inter arma?* Anyone?' Nobody volunteered. 'What about the new man? Any idea?'

'I haven't a baldy.'

Ned Kelly stared at him. There was a silence. Nobody moved. Ned Kelly maintained the eye contact and the boy stared back.

'I don't know where you've been before this but that is not the

48

way we answer questions in this school. Next – Brennan what do you make of it?'

'In war laws are redundant.'

'Yes. Like manners in schools nowadays.'

The corridor was empty one moment then, the second after the lunch bell, it was full of boys pushing and shouting. Martin leaned against the wall. Everybody was surging towards the door. From a distance he could see Kavanagh's head above everybody else's. He was fighting towards him through the crowd.

'So. What d'ya think?' Martin shrugged. They allowed themselves to be borne out through the door by the mob. The sun was shining. Martin said, 'What about Brian?'

'He goes home.'

'You got anything to eat?'

'Naw. Get some chips. Maybe walk to my place,' said Martin. 'I could get the camera. Calm Cuntyballs down.'

'Is he mad?'

'I haven't seen him. There's a few left on the roll. I could take some artistic ones of you eating chips.'

They wandered down the driveway and Martin told Kavanagh about the weird new guy.

'His name is Blaise, for fucksake. Can you believe a name like that?'

'I suppose if it was your father's name it wouldn't seem so bad. Like if your da had a tattoo then your attitude to tattoos would be different.'

'But he used a great word,' said Martin. 'A real good curse word. Fuck, what was it?' They turned left at the huge iron gates of the school.

'And Ned Kelly asked him a question and your man says *I haven't a baldy.*'

'Fuck you're joking. To baldy Ned Kelly?'

'I kid you not.'

'Shit the bed. That's asking for it.'

At the other side of the road a squad of men was still digging up the pavement in front of the graveyard wall. Pneumatic drills roared and hammered away. Traffic was being waved around large wooden spools of cable. Martin had to shout to be heard. But

49

Kavanagh shook his head to show he couldn't hear. Martin leaned close to his ear and yelled at the top of his voice, 'It's hardly worth saying anyway.'

'If it's not worth saying, it's not worth shouting.'

They smiled and didn't speak for a while. Gradually as they put distance between them and the school the noise lessened, until it was just traffic. Kavanagh said, 'So how was the Retreat thing?'

'You should've come. It was OK. I got some photos – one of a guy's sick along the side of the bus.'

'I can hardly wait.'

'Seeing everybody silent was weird.'

'Did everybody keep it?'

'More or less. There was some messing about in the dorms but most of the guys took it seriously.'

'Jesus. I don't think I could've done it.'

Brennan's front door was always open. Martin went in and Kavanagh sat on a wall, kicking his heels. If Martin had brought him in, his mother would have wanted to know who he was and why wasn't she being introduced. 'Sometimes I think you're ashamed of me.' Then there would have been a whole palaver about exams and Medicine and how difficult it was to get into and how long it takes before you earn a penny piece. Six years wasn't it? And could he not help Martin *apply* himself. Because if Martin applied himself he too could get into anything he wanted. And how Martin had failed last year but it wasn't going to be like that this year because he was a boy with brains to burn, what he lacked was *application*.

So it seemed easier to leave Kavanagh outside while he ran upstairs for the camera. In the hallway there was a great smell of something cooking.

'It's only me,' he shouted.

When he came back down his mother, at the foot of the stairs, said, 'What has you back at this time?'

'Forgot this.' He showed her the camera.

'Have you had any lunch yet?' He made a face, unsure what was going to follow. 'I've just made a pot of soup.'

'I can't. Someone's waiting for me.'

'Who?'

He nodded outside. His mother opened the door and saw a young man in school uniform sitting on the wall opposite. She beckoned him.

'No – we don't have time, Mum.'

Kavanagh hopped down and crossed the road.

'There's a brave spring in your step anyway, whoever you are.'

Martin introduced Kavanagh to her. He shook hands and he even bowed a little in her direction.

'That's what I like – a good firm handshake. Sometimes I think our Martin is ashamed of me.' Martin sighed. 'Have you time for some soup?' Kavanagh looked at Martin.

'No, we're in a rush,' said Martin.

'It doesn't take long to sup a drop of soup.' She spoke directly to Kavanagh.

'Yes, that would be great, Mrs Brennan,' he said. She directed them into the parlour, said she wouldn't be a minute. Kavanagh sat down in the chair Mary Lawless usually sat in and in the confined space he looked all jutting knees and awkward elbows. He seemed to be trying to make himself fit the room. Or to make Martin less self-conscious about the size of it. Martin slung the camera over his shoulder and sat in Farther Farquharson's chair. He rolled his eyes and made a face.

'It's OK. Smells good,' said Kavanagh. 'What is the school using now?'

'A Leica.'

'I like it.' It seemed only moments until Mrs Brennan arrived with a tray. On it were paper napkins, two bowls of soup, salt and pepper, a plateful of buttered bread and two soup spoons.

'Here's all your orders.' She set the tray down and the boys reached for the bowls.

'Lovely,' said Kavanagh. Mrs Brennan stood just inside the parlour door. She was wearing a blue nylon housecoat and now that her hands were empty she slid them into her pockets. Kavanagh spooned the soup and blew on it. He tasted it and made a noise of pleasure. Mrs Brennan smiled.

'That's really great soup.'

'There's nothing like soup from a bone. It has everything. Carrots and leeks and soup mix . . .'

'Soup mix,' Kavanagh almost shouted with enthusiasm. 'I know all about soup mix . . .with the split peas and the lentils and barley and all.'

'Yes, indeed.'

'Everything but the kitchen sink,' said Kavanagh. Mrs Brennan laughed. She was fiddling nervously in her pocket.

'I'll just leave you boys to get on with it,' she said. But she didn't move. 'So what are you going to be doing next year?'

'Medicine. I hope.'

'A doctor?' Hearing this, Mrs Brennan sat down on the arm of the sofa. Her nervousness seemed to increase. She took a potato peeler and some coils of browning apple skins out of her pocket and laughed. 'Would you look at me with the potato peeler.' She looked slightly shy about it and put it back in again along with the peelings.

'It's a very difficult faculty to get into,' said Kavanagh.

'So I believe. It's a very long course. It's ages before you earn a penny piece.'

'Yes, it's going to be a long haul, Mrs Brennan. Six maybe seven years sometimes.'

'God save us. But it's worth it.'

'Not to worry – Martin here will keep me in pocket money when he publishes all his photos in magazines.'

'Aye he'd need to *apply* himself more. Because if our Martin *applied* himself he could get into anything he wanted. Last year was a bit of a hiccup but it isn't going to be like that this year, is it?' Martin raised the spoon to his mouth and nodded his head rhythmically from side to side to the chant of his mother's voice. 'Our Martin has brains to burn, what he lacks is *application*.'

'Oh, not to worry Mrs Brennan. We'll get him through this year – by hook or by crook.' Kavanagh threw back his head and laughed. Mrs Brennan smiled.

'Good for you. It's a real pleasure to meet you eh . . .I must be off back to my kitchen again. And don't leave it so long the next time.'

'If the soup's as good as this I'll be back.' Even as he cradled his soup bowl Kavanagh made an attempt to rise from his chair but Mrs Brennan stopped him with her outstretched hand. 'No need,' she said. Martin was pushing bread into his mouth. 'I'll leave you both to it. Martin! You *may* be in a hurry but there's no need to stuff like that.'

When she had gone Martin rolled his eyes. Kavanagh said, 'She's OK.'

'Let's get outa here,' said Martin. He lifted the remains of the buttered bread from the plate and they went down the road to buy a bag of chips and made chip sandwiches. In the chippy there was a new girl. She was fat and wore new white overalls. She blushed deeply when she looked up and saw Kavanagh. She made the other older woman serve him and ran laughing into the back.

'She fancies you,' said Martin when they were outside.

'I'm deeply flattered,' said Kavanagh, 'but I'll allow you to take her off my hands. Frying tonight, eh? What about it?'

'Piss off.' Martin wiped his fingers on his hanky before he took some pictures of Kavanagh biting into his bread; chewing with his mouth wide open; spitting out like a drunk.

'That's the bolus,' Kavanagh said. 'The chewed mass just before you swallow it is called a bolus.'

'A bolus soup.' Martin came to the end of his film. 'I'm really glad to know that.'

'If you'd no teeth in the old days they gave you bolus sandwiches. Nothing nicer.'

Martin lit one of his cigarettes.

'Do you know what those things can do to you?' said Kavanagh.

Martin wound back the film and put it in his pocket. They sat on a concrete block until Martin finished his smoke. Then they both walked towards the school.

'Oh-oh,' said Kavanagh, 'something's going on.' There were policemen gathered opposite the school gates.

'Maybe somebody's murdered Condor?'

'We should be so lucky.'

When they got to the school gates the interest seemed to be on the other side of the road by the wall. Martin and Kavanagh crossed over. There was a crowd, mostly from the school, being held back by the police. Kavanagh had the height to see over the other people.

'What is it?' asked Martin.

'I dunno.' Kavanagh turned his head. 'There's a guy in the hole.'

Martin burrowed his way to the front of the crowd. He asked a first-year, 'What's going on?'

'How the hell would I know?' There was some green canvas with sticks lying on it beside the trench which had been dug. A workman's head appeared above the level of the pavement. A policeman rested his hands on his thighs and stared down into the hole. Then the new guy, Blaise, elbowed his way to where Martin was.

'They're bones,' he said. 'They've dug up a pile of fucking bones.'

'Jesus.'

'It's not really surprising. A couple of feet under that wall is the graveyard.' Blaise did not seem to be talking directly to Martin but to anyone who would listen. 'At first they thought they were on to a murder. But anyone could have told them who they've got there.'

'Who?' said Martin.

'Henry Joy McCracken,' said Blaise. Everybody laughed.

'Away and feel your head.'

'I kid you not. Those are the bones of the most famous United Irishman of them all.'

'Your arse.'

'His grave is right there on the other side of that wall. I've been to it. There's been a bit of movement . . .'

'An underground movement,' said Kavanagh.

'A little slippage. There's no doubt that's who they've got. It's what the cops are saying anyway.'

'Christ and I've no film left,' said Martin. He looked at the sticks on the green canvas. They didn't look like bones.

'It's street theatre,' said Kavanagh. 'They're doing that scene from *Hamlet*.'

'Which one?'

'Which one d'ya think?'

'The closet scene,' said Martin and everybody laughed.

'How would they know if it was Henry Joy?' Kavanagh was grinning from ear to ear, not believing a word Blaise was saying.

'The police said they found the glass phial.'

'What glass phial?'

'The phial with the parchment in it.'

'He's been reading Enid Blyton too,' said Kavanagh. 'The Graveyard of Adventure.'

Blaise turned and stared at him. He said, 'At the beginning of the century McCracken's bones were dug up from the old graveyard in High Street and reburied here. They put a parchment in a bottle saying who it was.'

'The only reunited Irishman in the world,' said Kavanagh.

'You may well scoff,' Blaise said. 'But I'm telling you the truth.'

Brian Sweeny turned up with red stuff at the corners of his mouth.

'What's going on?'

'You got tomato ketchup here,' Kavanagh pointed to the side of his mouth and Brian wiped it away with the sleeve of his blazer.

'Jam,' said Brian. 'Bread and jam.'

Faintly above the traffic noise they heard in the distance the warning bell for the end of lunch. The four of them – Brian, Martin, Kavanagh and Blaise – walked up the driveway together.

'There's Bungalow,' said Martin.

'Who he?' said Blaise.

'A boarder. They call him Bungalow because he's got nothing upstairs.'

'None of the boarders have anything upstairs,' said Kavanagh.

'I'm going to board,' said Blaise.

'Oops.' Kavanagh pulled a face and said he was sorry.

'You poor bastard,' said Martin. 'Where are you from?'

'Here. Belfast.'

'Then why board?'

'My old man wants it that way.'

'There's the Sexual Athlete – he's another boarder,' said Martin nodding towards a daft looking boy with a crew cut.

'You know why he's called the Sexual Athlete?' said Kavanagh.

'No,' said Blaise. 'But you're going to tell me anyway.'

'Every night he goes up to the running track for a wank.' Martin and Kavanagh looked at Blaise to see how he'd react. The new boy just smiled.

'He'll have the hands of a sprinter, then,' he said.

★

55

First after lunch was double Physics on the top floor of the science wing. The boys sat around on the staircase trying not to get walked on. The air was full of for-fucksake and take-it-easy and mind-how-you-go.

A voice said, 'Cousteau.' Silence as the teacher came up the stairs jangling his keys. He opened the door and everyone crowded in.

'Easy. Easy does it,' he said. He was a mild mannered, oldish man who always wore a waistcoat.

The boys sat on stools around island benches. The benches were empty except for gas taps. Sinks with swan neck taps were on the benches nearest the windows. Martin and Kavanagh sat together. Brian Sweeny didn't do Physics. When Blaise introduced himself to Cousteau, Cousteau gave him a new experiments notebook and told him to sit down. Blaise moved down the room and slid on to a stool beside Martin and Kavanagh. There was a low murmur of conversation as the teacher cleaned a section of the blackboard. The blackboard had alternate graph and plain sections and moved round like a roller towel. Cousteau began to write up and draw an experiment on the board. Martin whispered to Blaise, 'He's only got one ball.'

'Which one?'

'It's his left, I think.'

'How would anybody know,' said Kavanagh. 'It's a schoolboy joke – a total fucking rumour. It started because of his real name.'

'What's that?'

'O'Loan.'

'Oh lone ball.' Martin was trying to be helpful.

'Cousteau's name is O'Loan?' said Blaise. The others nodded.

Cousteau turned and pulled down on the points of his waistcoat.

'There is too much talk going on.' His voice was quiet and slightly annoyed. The noise died away. He turned to the board and continued writing. The chalk clacked and dotted against the canvas in the silence.

'Also it fits the song.'

'What song?'

Martin leaned over to Blaise and whisper-sang,

'Cous-teau has only got one ball.'

'When we do experiments it is usual to be in pairs,' Cousteau turned and said to the new boy.

'Like testicles,' Kavanagh whispered.

'But unfortunately we have an odd number in this class. For experiments you can team up with another pair. Or work by yourself.'

'I'll work by myself,' said Blaise. Cousteau dusted the chalk from his fingers and turned to read what he had written on the board.

'Take this down,' he said. Blaise shrugged and asked the question out of the corner of his mouth as if it was an inevitable one.

'So why is he called Cousteau?' Kavanagh leaned forward to tell him.

'In second year he was setting up an experiment which involved a filled sink. And some of the water had pissed over the side. Anyway he was leaning forward and wearing the wrong kind of shoes and he slipped and went head-first into the sink. Jacques Cousteau – Underwater Explorer.'

'Absolute fucking crap,' said Blaise.

'There is far too much noise today,' Cousteau turned. 'If you want to be treated like senior boys you've got to *behave* like senior boys.' There was silence. Cousteau walked to the side of the board and picked up a pointer. 'Acceleration of gravity. When an object falls it does so with increasing speed.'

Martin put his elbows up on the bench top and covered his mouth and nose with his hands. He whispered to Blaise, 'Why does your old man want you to board?'

'He thinks I'll be forced to study if I'm in here. And there's an element of imprisonment in it.' Blaise seemed to be able to talk naturally out of the corner of his mouth.

'Why would he want to imprison you?'

'Because he thinks I've fucked things up. On the studying front. Last year, there was an unfortunate hiatus in my education.'

'A what?'

'An interruption.'

'Sounds familiar,' said Martin.

Cousteau said, 'Is my teaching interfering with your conversation? Would you prefer me to stop? What did you say your name was?' Everyone looked innocently around. 'The new man. I've forgotten your name.'

'Blaise Foley, sir.'

'Well, Mr Foley, I would be very grateful if you would stop talking out the side of your mouth like some sort of a jailbird. And apply yourself to what I have to say. You may be falling through the air some day and wish to know the speed at which you are going. Perhaps from this very window.'

Cousteau talked on and on about acceleration and gravity. Martin stared ahead. The sun came out, slanting window shadows across the cream wall. Blaise sat on a stool just in front of him. The back of his head looked strange. Or else it was the way his hair was cut. He had yellowish sandy hair cut in layers so that his skull seemed ridged. Like grass on an escarpment. What was this thirty-two feet per second per second? Had Cousteau developed a stammer? The sunlight caught a set of prisms on top of a cupboard, making an intense horizontal rainbow appear on the wall. Richard Of York Gave Battle In Vain. Martin had seen film of people free-falling out of planes. They seemed to be able to fall for ages. He wondered if you would ever get used to it. What would happen, for instance, if you went very high to start with and had to go on falling for a couple of days? Maybe, if it was physically possible, a couple of weeks. Would your eyes ever stop watering with the wind of falling? Would you feel hungry? Would you fall asleep? *Fall* asleep! Jesus – that'd be some awakening, wouldn't it? Opening your eyes and fucking hell your stomach is in your mouth. Then trying to adjust to it. Getting up and getting dressed and the tears blinding you – nothing new there – but all at thirty-two feet per second per second per second per second per second. Trying to chew your toast, and the hot tea going up your nose like Coca-Cola.

'I suppose you know all of this, Brennan?'

'What sir?'

'You're not taking any notes – so you must know it.'

'I wrote it up last year, sir.'

'For all the good it did you.'

And what would happen to that other morning event in free fall. If he had a crap would the crap fall at the same speed. Would his own crap accompany him for the rest of life's journey? At turdy two feet per second per second?

He liked Cousteau. Apart from hard work and committing stuff to memory he liked anything to do with science – the experiments, weighing stuff in Chemistry and Physics – the boxes of bronze weights – the way they sat snug in their holes. The box was held shut with a small hook and eye. Inside the lid the green velvet was bruised where it had come in contact with the weights. The knobs were to give something for the tweezers to lift. Never use fingers: the sweat would alter the weight and render them inaccurate. He liked all the weights, from the 50 grams – a real bruiser – right down to the lightest, no more than bits of metal foil so fragile they needed to be covered with a glass lid lest they be lost, lest they blow away. The balance itself was enclosed in a glass and wood box to protect it from draughts. Wind could skew the results, said the teacher. In really critical weighings they were told to close down the glass front so that their breath would not prejudice the result. The weight of your breath. The dark needle would swing against the white calibrated scale and it would come to be exactly vertical with the addition of the smallest silver wisp.

'Dead on,' Martin would say.

And in Chemistry classes titrations amazed him. How could something change so utterly and so completely? He would have a conical flask of navy or scarlet liquid in his left hand. He would have to swirl it to keep the liquid moving until it would suddenly – with the addition of a single drop from the burette – turn clear as tap water.

Every time it happened he got a jag of pleasure. Like when a sum worked out. Or when he suddenly understood something the teacher said. A clarity. Like the day he understood weight, that it was dependent on gravity, how hard a thing pressed downwards was its weight.

Cousteau finished talking and gave the go-ahead to set up the experiment.

Martin said to Kavanagh, 'Do you know what we're doing?'

'Yeah sure.'

There was a traffic jam as everybody tried to get the same pieces of apparatus at the same time. Kavanagh got a candle and lit it from the Bunsen.

'Get a glass plate from that drawer,' he said to Martin. Martin did as he was told. Kavanagh held the plate obliquely over the candle. The flame licked at it, smoking it black. Kavanagh moved the candle so that the whole face of the plate was covered except for the fingerprints by which he held it at the very corners.

'Ya beauty,' Kavanagh said and set it upright against a tripod. Martin looked round to see how Blaise was getting on. He was standing with his hands in his pockets, watching them. Martin nudged Kavanagh. Kavanagh looked at the new guy and said, 'Need any help?'

'I think I *will* work with you two,' Blaise said. Kavanagh blew out the candle and the smoke drifted around.

'Where do we get Madame La Guillotine?' he said.

Martin shrugged. The two guys working beside them had already got the apparatus.

'Where'd you get that?'

'Up my arse.'

'Nah – come on.' One of the guys pointed to a cupboard by the sink. Martin went over and brought back a thing shaped like a guillotine but with no blade.

'This place smells like a fucking church,' Blaise said.

There was a to-and-fro spring in front of the guillotine. A needle had to be fitted to the end of this. Then touched against the smoked plate. The spring had to be twanged and the plate dropped in a guillotine fashion. There would be a needle trace on the plate and by measuring its peaks and troughs a graph could be drawn from which the acceleration due to gravity could be calculated. Their first trace looked like a snake. They cleaned and re-smoked the plate and conducted the experiment again. This time it worked much better. Measuring the peaks and troughs of the trace Kavanagh's hands became black and the soot transferred to his workbook. Martin started laughing, falling about.

'What? What is it?' Kavanagh was smiling at Martin laughing.

'What did the sheep say falling over the cliff?'

'Don't know.'

'Fuckin graaa–aa–aa–vity.'

'That's terrible.' Kavanagh leaned over to the next pair of boys. They were Gaelic football players, two defenders from the McCrory Cup team.

'What did the sheep say when it fell off the cliff?'

'Haven't a clue.'

As Kavanagh told them, the door opened and Condor came in. The class moved from an easy working murmur to silence. Condor talked to Cousteau then turned and beckoned Blaise.

'Foley, could I have a word?' The new boy moved to the head of the class and Condor took him outside. But Martin figured it couldn't have been too serious because Condor kept the door slightly open. They could just see the bottom of his soutane and hear his deep voice. Martin went to the front to leave back the guillotine apparatus but he could not hear what was being said on the other side of the door.

When Foley came back in, all eyes were on him. He pretended nothing had happened and went down to join Brennan and Kavanagh.

'What did he want?' said Kavanagh.

'A little more information on Henry Joy McCracken.'

'You're taking the piss about all that, aren't you?' said Martin.

'But *he* doesn't know that. He's away to report the whole thing to the *Irish News*.'

'But how do you know all that stuff – about the glass phial and all?'

'One hears, one retains,' said Blaise. 'In company one keeps one's ears open.'

'The same way I know about soup mix,' said Kavanagh.

Martin toiled up the road by himself because Kavanagh had to stay on for basketball practice. He was looking forward to making a sandwich from yesterday's meat when he got home. With mustard on it – a thing he had just learned to like. An ambulance passed him, speeding down the road. It was preceded by a police car. When he came within sight of his street he could see there was something wrong. Small groups of people were standing about, talking and staring at the road. They weren't dressed for outside – people in shirtsleeves, the butcher in his apron. Martin tried to see what it was, but there was just a lot of sand scattered on the road. Then he realised what this was and felt his stomach sink. The sand was there to hide something. Martin hung around and listened.

'What happened?' he asked the woman from O'Grady's.

'Two people killed by the bus.' Martin was stunned. In our street? The woman went on. 'They were on a motorbike. It just slid under the back wheels. A boy and a girl. Neither of them was wearing a helmet.'

There was a motorbike pulled up on to the pavement and lying on its side. The front wheel was buckled badly. Nobody seemed to want to go away. They stood around in little groups, mostly women, whispering and talking and pointing across.

'Both dead, God love them.'

'We're not used to it.'

'Two of them?'

'Death on such a scale.'

'She was wearing a wee white frock.'

'It's frightening.'

'I'll never get over it.'

'The light nearly left my eyes.' Those who had witnessed it were still ashen faced. Numbed. One woman said, 'What a place.' She pointed. 'To think there was a poor woman murdered not half a mile from here only two years ago.'

'He gave her a terrible death.'

'He got off because he was a Protestant.'

Martin tried not to look again at the sand but, in spite of himself, he did. He thought he saw, or imagined he saw, dark red beneath it. He tried to envisage the pressure of a bus tyre on a head. And the blood and brain stuff in the sand. And felt his stomach heave.

He wandered down the street, hovering between thinking about it and trying not to think about it. He looked around him for distraction. The red brick gable ends had election posters pasted to them like stamps on envelopes – all at one corner. Vote Unionist. Vote Nationalist. Vote Fitt. Vote Kilfedder. When elections were over nobody took any responsibility – they just left the posters there to become tattered and fade away. They became wet and ragged. The sun and wind dried them. The red and blue, the green and yellow faded to shades of grey. The faces of the politicians wrinkled and cracked like icons. Men with moustaches and horn-rimmed glasses – men without looks. Men who had no other reason to be photographed. They were not used to it: they all had fixed smiles. Children clodded mud at them, at the faces from the opposite side. They ripped them where they could reach. And where they could not reach they got their pals to lift them up. Join hands. Make a stirrup.

Once he had heard a cat run over by a navy blue van. His mother had asked him to bring in the milk from the door. He had opened the door and stooped to lift one of the bottles. He must have disturbed a black cat because it dashed out into the road and a van ran over it. He could still hear the squeal and the rubbery thump it made. Not wanting to see, he ran inside with the milk bottle. The milk was to make tapioca. But when his mother put it in front of him, with its jellied globules, he could eat none of it. The feeling now was the same. By the time he arrived home his notion for a meat sandwich, with or without mustard, had gone.

His mother had invited the usual people that night. 'The fine and flawless Mary Lawless,' as she called herself, was there. Once Martin had substituted the word 'fat' for 'fine' and his mother had ate the head off him.

'What an awful thing to say. Anyway she's not fat. It's hormonal.'

Martin's job was to bring in the supper his mother had left ready on two trays. Then he would be allowed a cup of tea and something to eat.

'Wasn't that an appalling tragedy today,' said Nurse Gilliland.

'I went past about a half an hour afterwards,' said Mary Lawless. 'I'm not right yet. I can't get it out of my head.'

'A double tragedy.'

'Merciful hour!'

'Was it the seventy-seven or an Antrim Road bus?'

'The seventy-seven.'

'Be a terrible shock for the poor driver as well.'

'We just have to accept such things with a heavy heart,' said Father Farquharson.

'But He knows what He's doing,' said Mrs Brennan, 'the Good Lord.'

'He's crossing your path and asking you how you like it.'

'Some of His decisions may seem hard but . . .'

'He knows what He's about.'

'It's a terrible pity all the same. Two young lives.'

'Were they Catholics?'

'I believe not.'

'All the same . . .'

'We must all have the patience of Job,' said Father Farquharson. *'How much can you take before you turn your face away from Me?* That's what the Lord is asking.'

'It's always your face – isn't that *so* true, Father? Never anything else. Your face.'

'Where the soul is. In the eyes.'

'The face is the soul of the body.'

'Look in a person's eyes hard enough and you'll see the soul. I'm not far wrong, am I, Father?'

'Indeed you are not.'

'You'd have to look pretty hard into the eyes of the young ones today, before you'd find any enthusiasm for religion,' said Mrs Brennan. 'How many young ones would you see doing the Nine Fridays? What ever happened to sanctity?'

'There's more than that has disappeared, if you ask me. They take everything for granted nowadays. Clothes, food – money itself . . .'

'Stop any girl on the street and ask her if she can darn and she'll look at you as if you had two heads.'

'Time was . . .'

'Excuse me, constable. Ask her can she make soup from a bone.'

'It just goes to show.'

'That was a great boy came in here one day. A friend of Martin's. Going to be a doctor. Knew all about soup mix.'

'And if they lose a button off a wee jacket or something the whole thing goes in the bin.' They all nodded.

'When did you last see a young one wearing a "wee jacket"? I ask you.'

'If you ask them what a thimble is they think it's something you hunt for. They only know it as a parlour game.'

'Catch yourself on, dear. They wouldn't even know what a parlour game was.'

'I suppose you're right. It's disco, disco and more disco.'

'Houl yer wheesht.'

'Now that you mention it,' said Father Farquharson, 'even *parlour* sounds very old fashioned.'

'I really hate the way the world is changing. All the old values. The old ways.'

'They have no conception of what it is to leave a clean plate.'

'I've seen young ones leave what would've done me a week,' said Mary Lawless.

'Aye, with the knife and fork crossed over it.' Mrs Brennan shot meaningful glances at Martin when she said certain things. 'Not side by side to show they were finished – oh no, table manners are too good for this generation. How's a hostess supposed to know when anyone's finished, eh? A young one could starve waiting for the next course because he didn't know how to put his knife and fork down properly. If you talked about a place setting to young ones nowadays they'd just look at you.'

'It just goes to show.'

'And God preserve me from pen holders. They're on the increase.' Mrs Brennan's face went sullen with a kind of passion. 'Why can't people hold a knife the way God meant you to hold it and not like a pen. It's so cissy – especially when men do it.'

'A woman looking cissy is all right, because she's a woman.'

'Aye it's strange right enough,' said Nurse Gilliland. 'But it's not *how* you eat that does the damage it's how *much* you eat. You can have too much as well as too little.'

'I can't have big feeds at night,' said Mary Lawless. 'No offence meant, Mrs Brennan. But they put me off my sleep. You're lying there, with your eyes wide open and your guts digesting away for all they're worth. Everything's slooshing about and you feel like you'd swallowed a swimming pool.'

Nurse Gilliland took a small hanky from up her sleeve and wiped the tip of her nose.

'Oh don't tell me about it,' she said. 'The scalding water-brash coming up the back of your throat. You'd be far better off, getting up and being sick. Getting it over with.'

'Christmas Day is the worst,' said Martin's mother. 'Remember that Christmas, Martin? Instead of doing the dishes, me having to lie flat on my back on the floor for two solid hours – before I could even get a belch up. It was like a ball of hard air in me here —' she knocked just below her throat with her knuckles. 'I'll never forget it.'

'Good times, right enough,' said Father Farquharson. 'We should all be thankful for such full and plenty. Holy smoke, it wasn't always that way. So how is our growing boy getting on, our final-year scholar?'

'Fine,' said Martin.

'I hope you're working hard?'

'Yeah.'

'*Natura vacuum abhorret.*'

'Yes, it does.'

'Isn't that marvellous,' said Mrs Brennan. 'The two of you, sitting there, conversing away in Latin.'

'He's for the priesthood, Mrs Brennan,' said Mary Lawless. 'Nothing surer.'

3.   Lunch Time

It had rained all morning. At lunch time the sun came out and Martin and Kavanagh went down to the shops. In the chippy the older woman called over her shoulder.

'Isobel, somebody out here for you.' The fat girl in the white overalls came out from the back and, seeing Kavanagh, blushed. But she came, scowling a bit at the older woman, to serve at the counter.

When he got his order from her Kavanagh said, 'Thanks Isobel.' Outside he said, 'Her social skills must be improving.'

The boys ate a bag of chips each, sauntering along the road.

'I've been keeping an eye on the *Irish News*,' said Martin. 'But there's been nothing in it yet. About the bones of Henry Joy.'

'Blaise was taking the piss.'

'That's what I mean. If it had been real it would have been in the paper. Condor phones up the *Irish News* – they check it out. It's bollicks and they don't print. Condor has egg all over his face. He'll get even, one of these days.'

The streets were still wet but the sky was blue. When he had finished Kavanagh bundled up his papers and threw them in a waste bin.

'Very responsible,' said Martin. Kavanagh washed his hands in the wet of a privet hedge and tried to dry them on the back of Martin's blazer. But Martin saw it coming and managed to run away. He made a ball of his own papers and drop-kicked it on to the waste ground.

'Fuckin lovely,' said Kavanagh. 'That's really lovely behaviour.' He stood drying his hands on the back of his trousers.

'What do we do now?' said Martin.

'We gather up your fuckin rubbish.'

'It's a waste ground. A place for waste – you won't be able to find mine because there's so much other friggin stuff.'

'Come on, let's go back in – go up round the track?'

They walked up the driveway and through the main corridor to the back of the school. They passed the Wee Field, a muddy football pitch covered in fine black ash which, when you fell on it, tore the knees to bloodied shreds. The goalposts were H shaped for Gaelic games. They once were white but now were covered in brown moons and half-moons where the ball had hit the woodwork. The pitch was so frequently used that the goal mouths had become dished. When it rained these depressions filled with water. The midfield was black mud peppered with stud marks. The school had both a Gaelic football fifteen and a hurling fifteen. The idea of a soccer team was frowned upon by the school authorities as being too British.

At the top of the Wee Field were two handball alleys back to back, built of grey, rain-soaked concrete. Kavanagh called the game 'poor man's squash'. No racquets required. Very few people ever played it. The alleys were a leftover from another era. Anyone who did play it developed specially toughened hands – and a caning was less of a problem to them.

'Would Brian be back yet?'

'I dunno. It's unlikely.'

'Should we wait on him?' Kavanagh shrugged.

'Brian's OK, but he can be a bit of a pain at times,' he said.

'Like what?'

'Dull. He's just fucking dull. He'll become a librarian who plays golf.'

They walked beyond the handball alleys to the Big Field, a much better grass pitch surrounded by a cheapskate running track. On either side were two walkways screened by lines of trees. At the far end, on top of a grass slope, dominating everything, was the prison wall. Black stone, wet and soaring to some thirty or forty feet. There were watchtowers at each end of the wall with horizontal viewing slits. In the evening, lights came on in the jail and the prisoners could be heard shouting or rattling things against the bars. Somebody was sitting hunched on the grass slope beneath the wall. It was Blaise. He was easily recognisable in his tweed jacket and cream trousers. Where he was sitting was out of bounds. To get there you'd have to step over a low wire fence. Police with machine guns frequently patrolled this area beneath the wall. People said they could have a go at you and say afterwards that you were trying to help a prisoner escape.

When they came near, Blaise said, 'Hi.'

'Blaise, you are not allowed in there and if you're caught several things are liable to happen,' said Kavanagh. 'Firstly the cops will blow your fuckin head off. Then the Reverend Head will bite your balls off for giving them the excuse to blow your head off.'

'I take it I'm not supposed to be here, then.'

'I kid you not.' Blaise leaned back on his elbow and smiled. 'Well, well, well.'

'Sometimes you talk like an old lady,' said Kavanagh.

'Oh yeah,' said Martin. 'What was that word you used the other day?' Blaise shrugged. 'You called Ned Kelly it. You said all Latin teachers were . . .'

'Dumbfucks?'

'Yeah.' Martin turned to Kavanagh. 'It's a great word.'

'Dumbfuck,' said Kavanagh as if weighing it. He nodded his approval. 'Nice one. But right now an armed dumbfuck is going to come out of that door and shoot us all if you do not move your arse.' Blaise rose to his feet, smiling, and put out his hand. Kavanagh took the outstretched hand and steadied Blaise as he sidestepped back over the wire on to the cinder track. Blaise looked down at his feet and toed his shoe into the black ash.

'Where exactly does the Sexual Athlete come?'

'On the ground,' said Kavanagh. They all laughed.

'Allowed,' said Blaise. 'Now that is such a fucking awful word. You're not *allowed* on that grass. You're not *allowed* out of bounds. And it's even worse outside a place like this – at home. You're not *allowed* out to that time. Picking your nose in public is not *allowed*. It implies that some fucker is making up rules for us all, that we are all the undercow of somebody else. Inherent in "I don't *allow* you" is the master–slave thing. So NEVER allow it to go unchallenged.'

They began to walk strung out across the track. Blaise sounded like he was wound up.

'I cannot believe that in this day and age censorship still exists,' he said. 'In Ireland people are not *allowed* to read certain things. The Bishops of Ireland read a book and put it on the Index. It's OK for them – but for us? It's a way of one set of people saying to

69

another set of people, we're better than you. And in the North we get it from both fucking sides. Church *and* State. Did you know that every play that goes on stage here has to be given the OK by the British Lord Chamberlain? And he can ban it, if he likes? Or cut lumps out of it wherever he thinks fit?'

'I've never been to a play,' Martin said.

'I'm not surprised,' said Blaise. 'In this provincial hole.'

'Why wouldn't it be provincial? It's a province.'

'A godforsaken backwater where they lock up the swings on a Sunday,' said Blaise. 'And what about this dump of a school? Is it like every other fucking Catholic establishment in the North of Ireland? Do you have a debating society?'

'No.'

'An orchestra? A choir? Does the school have a library?'

'No.'

'Jesus — a school with no library. A chess club?'

'If you don't like Gaelic football, that's your lot.'

'What a benighted hole. Is there a place where a fellow could have a smoke?'

'That we *can* provide.'

'The Reverend Head keeps his eye on this place,' said Martin. 'From his room. Through binoculars. He gazes upon us from afar, the bastard.'

'Does that not put the Sexual Athlete off his stroke?' said Blaise.

'He's a nocturnal animal, mostly. A creature of the night.'

The Reverend Head was unusually pale. One of his nicknames was the Moon. When it began to get dark on winter evenings his face could be seen at his study window — almost luminous — looking down at what was going on. He knew every boy in the school by his first name.

'And what does he do if he sees me breaking rules?'

'He bloweth his whistle. Of the referee's variety.'

'Loudly — so that one is nearly deafened,' said Kavanagh. 'One then proceedeth to the Reverend Head's room.'

'To have one's balls bitten off,' said Martin.

'If he is in a good mood he'll let you off with a severe beating. I kid you not.'

'I wouldn't mind a smoke myself,' said Martin. 'The safest place is the daffs . . .'

'The toilets,' Kavanagh explained to Blaise.

'Or behind the handball alleys where binoculars reacheth not,' said Martin. They continued walking round the track heading in the opposite direction, but nobody made the decision to turn. 'You remember you said, never allow the thing to go unchallenged.' Blaise nodded. 'Well if we did that – we'd be being the slaves. *You're* telling *us*. And we're obeying you.'

'Have you been thinking of that all this time?' said Blaise. He shook his head in disbelief. 'Repartee.'

'What?' Their shoes were making scuffing noises on the black ash.

'Never mind.'

'Steady on, chaps.' Kavanagh put a hand on Martin's shoulder, then his other hand on Blaise's. 'The rain's gone off. The sky is blue.' He gave a little bounce on his toes and heaved himself into the air, straightening his arms and putting all his weight on the other boys' shoulders. Immediately Blaise and Martin knew what was required of them: to walk steadily and keep Kavanagh up there as long as possible. But they managed it only for a few tottering paces before he came down to earth again. 'Not the best lift I've ever had. You need to get more co-ordinated.' He patted them both on the back.

'Fuck – listen to the finely tuned athlete,' said Martin. 'What sort of a name is Blaise?'

'The same sort of a name as Martin.'

'What d'you mean?'

'After a saint. He's supposed to have saved a child from choking on a fishbone hence all the palaver about sore throats. And according to Jacobus de Voragine he is a defender of dumb animals and diseased creatures – a bit of a Saint Francis. And he's the patron saint of woolcombers.'

'That'll teach me to ask questions,' said Martin.

'How come, Brennan, the other day in Physics, you had the experiment already written up?'

'I'm repeating this year.'

'Why?'

'I failed last year.' There was an edge to Martin's voice. 'I have to do them all again.'

'Are you stupid?'

'Fuck off. I just didn't do any work.'

'Sounds familiar.'

'Why are you doing O grade Latin?'

'They recommended it,' said Blaise, 'to keep my career options open. Dentistry, Medicine, the Law. Roman soldier. Also I'm good at it.' He didn't laugh or anything when he praised himself. 'These fucking examinations – they're ridiculous. They make us jump through hoops in order to become expert hoop jumpers. How long have we to go now?'

'About seven weeks,' said Kavanagh.

'Jesus.' Martin shivered.

'Is there any way we can narrow the odds?' said Blaise.

'Yes.'

'How?'

'Work. Four or five hours every night. More at weekends.'

'It doesn't appeal.'

'Past papers are a good way,' said Kavanagh. 'You can go over all the past papers, see the patterns, have a stab at what's going to come up. Cousteau is supposed to be good at spotting questions.'

'I just *have* to pass,' said Martin. 'Jesus, my mother had to *pay* for me this year. She had to borrow it. I said I'd pay her back but if I fail . . .'

'Screw your courage to the sticking place and we'll not fail,' said Blaise.

Martin's fists were balled up and shoved into his pockets.

'By the skin of my teeth would do,' he said.

'Fuck you. I have to get the best grades in *all* my subjects,' said Kavanagh.

'Is this a personality defect?' asked Blaise.

'Naw. I want to get into Medicine.'

'Like Daddy? I suppose.'

'Who told you that?'

'Somebody said.'

'Why the sneer?'

'I wasn't sneering. This is just the way I talk.' Blaise edged the group away from the track on to the avenue of trees. The leaves were just coming out. The path at this point was not broad enough for the three of them to walk abreast and Martin fell behind.

'Fuck past papers,' said Blaise. 'What we want is this year's papers.'

All three boys laughed.

'That'd be smashin.' Martin jumped up and snatched a leaf from a branch. 'Going in knowing the questions.'

'If you knew the questions,' said Kavanagh, 'you could nick some answer booklets – no bother – and do the exam at home with all your books and quotes and all, then go in and pretend to do it and leave your good answer and take your drivel one out with you. That'd be some cheating.'

'To take the nearest way,' said Blaise. 'Did either of you ever cheat?'

'You wanna hear what he did at his O grades. Tell him, Kavanagh.'

'An ordinary matchbox – OK. You write out all your quotes with a mapping pen, as small a nib as you can get, on tiny bits of card. Then you wedge them into the matchbox. I kid you not. Top right is organic formulae, bottom right is inorganic, top left is definitions, bottom left is . . .whatever . . .I don't remember.'

'How do you know top from bottom?' said Blaise.

'The sandpaper is only on the right hand side. Of Swan Vestas. If you use Bluebell just peel off the sandpaper on the left hand side. Anyway, your bits of card are so small you can palm them.'

'Elegant enough.'

'We used to cog all the time. Just so long as you don't get caught. Everybody does it.'

'I remember last year when Ned the Ted was in charge,' said Kavanagh. 'Ned doesn't give a fuck about *anything* – just gets behind the paper and sits on his arse the whole time. They were only Christmas exams, nothing important. Anyway the door opens and in walks the Reverend Head. You could hear books thumping on to the floor all over the place.'

'In first year,' said Martin, 'I was doing the Bishop's exam. Did you do that at your last school?'

'Yeah – every Catholic in every diocese has to do it,' said Blaise. 'It's like the Spanish Inquisition all over again.'

'And I had this boil on the back of my neck. Jesus, it was so sore you could feel your heart beating in it. Like the biggest pimple you've ever had. Hard as a brick. Anyway I wrote as much as I could on the first question – but I hadn't a clue about any of the others so I burst the bastard. Squeezed it.'

'Ah fuck, you dirty pig,' shouted Kavanagh, pushing him away.

'I did – I did – then I went up to the guy and pointed to the gloop going down my collar. And he could hardly look. Get out, he says, get outa here. And I never came back. Retired injured.'

'One less bishop for Ireland,' said Blaise.

'Remember the first time we got a woman invigilator?'

'Aye. She was OK. Not a complete bag.'

'She was lovely. The grey suit, the high heels and all.'

'Anyway she announces at the beginning *if there is anything she can do to help. Just ask.*'

'And Brennan here wanted to put up his hand . . .'

'You dirty bastard . . .'

'No – no he wanted to put up his hand to make your woman come down, all concerned like, and bend over and listen to what he has to say. Which was . . .'

'And I'm supposed to say *Please, Miss, I have an erection.*'

'Confusion. Sharp intake of breath,' Kavanagh elbowed in again. 'Your woman thinks. Then she says *If you would just step outside we could try hitting it with a cold spoon and if that doesn't work perhaps a jag from a compass point would bring it down.*'

Martin was laughing, walking backwards now. He had a habit of framing stuff with his fingers – making a finger rectangle approximate to a movie screen or a photograph. The sunlight was slanting down through the lime trees and shadows of the new leaves were moving on the ground. The trees and path stretched ahead like an example of perspective. Martin ran round and framed it up.

'Don't be such a fucking pain,' said Kavanagh. Martin went on doing it for a while. He didn't want to stop just because Kavanagh had said. 'It's just showing off.'

'It certainly is not. It's practice. I'm developing my eye.' Martin felt he had to keep doing it for long enough to show that he wasn't Kavanagh's slave. 'Aren't photographs astonishing?' said Martin. 'In a scientific way? Paper soaked in silver nitrate – light darkens it. That's the whole of photography. That's the best of all the photographs that have ever been taken – the masterpieces *and* the box Brownie snaps from nearly every household in the

Western world – all the emotion, all the politics, all the news pictures of disasters . . . all the love, the posturing, people caught off guard . . .'

'All the pornography,' said Blaise.

'All of it is there because silver nitrate darkens with light. Fuck me.'

'What about LPs? That's better science,' said Kavanagh. 'Recorded vibrations in plastic. So you can record all the greatest music in the world.'

'This is all bollicks,' said Blaise. 'The science has nothing to do with it. That's like saying what about charcoal. A burnt bit of stick. Then you pick it up and make a mark on paper and before you know where you are it's a fucking drawing by Leonardo. That is, if your name is Leonardo. Why get amazed at that? It's like saying you add chromium or strontium to glass and it turns different colours. So fucking what? It took a bit more than science to make the rose window at Chartres.'

'How could a stained glass window be just one colour?' said Martin.

'Jesus, do you know nothing? A rose window is a shape – not a fucking colour. The window at Chartres is rose *shaped*.' There was an embarrassed silence. Blaise had raised his voice and Martin had been wrongfooted. Kavanagh spoke to save the situation.

'A good mate of mine, Gus – he was here last year – he told me that maths was as beautiful as music. Maths had the ability to make him cry. Isn't that amazing?'

'Yeah.'

'The simplest and the shortest way of solving is the most beautiful. Result. Tears.' They all laughed. 'Have you seen the windows in the chapel here?'

'This is my first week.' said Blaise. 'Chapel is hardly a priority.'

'I thought boarders *had* to go to mass every morning,' said Kavanagh. Blaise looked at him with a raised eyebrow.

'There are other places one can seek sanctuary.' By now they had reached the end of the avenue of trees. They moved towards the Wee Field.

'Hey, if we're going to have a smoke we'd better go now,' said Martin. 'I don't want to be going into class smelling of it.' They headed towards the toilets. Blaise asked Kavanagh,

'Do you smoke?'

'No,' said Kavanagh. 'I prefer my health risks to be venereal.'

'I like that,' Blaise said.

As they were going into the toilets some of the Gaelic football crowd were coming out. Logan stopped Kavanagh and said, 'What did the lemmings say when they charged off the cliff?'

'No idea,' said Kavanagh. 'What *did* the lemmings say when they charged off the cliff?'

'Fuckin graaa-aa-aa-vity.'

Inside, the three of them found space against the white tiled wall. Martin pulled out a ten packet of Regal with two in it.

'Put those away,' said Blaise. He produced a full twenty of Marlboro and opened it.

'Where'd you get them?' said Martin.

'Duty free.' Martin took one and lit it.

'Do you like them?'

'Yeah, they're OK.' Blaise took a cigarette out. He looked clumsy with it – lit it awkwardly.

'You're mad, all of you,' said Kavanagh. 'Destroying your lungs. More than your lungs. Did you know that smoking makes your feet drop off?' They laughed. 'It's not funny. The arteries in your legs degenerate, you get gangrene. Your feet go black then drop off.'

'Not after one cigarette,' said Blaise.

'Don't be such a fuckin doom merchant.'

'I only do it occasionally,' said Blaise. 'I'm only being sociable. Here.' He handed the rest of the packet to Martin. Blaise held the cigarette between his middle and ring fingers. His eyes squirmed when he brought the cigarette up to his face. Eventually he gave up and dropped the cigarette to the floor, only half smoked, and squidged it out with his shoe.

'Do you like Balkan Sobranie?'

'What are they?'

'Very posh tobacco. Have you never seen them? Pastel colours, gold tips? I can get them, if you want to try them.'

'How?'

Blaise grinned and thrust both hands into his pockets.

★

For some time Blaise was glad to wear his tweedy jacket and light trousers. He told Martin and Kavanagh that there was a wardrobe at home stuffed with various school uniforms. But the authorities were adamant that he had to get this particular school uniform quickly. An oldish woman, not his mother, it was said, came and took him to Fergal Quinn's. Quinn's had a monopoly on the contract for the school blazers. Fergal Quinn was a brother of the Bishop.

So Blaise appeared in the daffs at lunch time in his bright new uniform. Nobody whistled because they were still wary of him. He was carrying a small holdall. From it he produced a box of fifty Balkan Sobranie. He opened the box and passed the multi-coloured cigarettes around. Then he took from the bag a bottle of Bison vodka. It had a pale stem of grass from the Russian steppe standing upright in its centre. Then a column of triangular paper cups like tiny dunces' caps. He passed them around and poured a splash into each paper cup. He apologised, saying that in an ideal world vodka should be drunk ice cold. Also that there were not enough paper cups and when people were finished it would help if they could pass the cup to somebody else. There were so many takers for the vodka that nobody got drunk. One splash each. They all *pretended* to be drunk, staggering around, bouncing off the tiled walls, shouting and whooping, some smoking pastel-coloured cigarettes as they imagined sophisticated but drunk women would do, others holding the cups to the top of their heads as if they were dunces – drunken dunces, at that, as they clowned around. But when the bell went everyone composed themselves, straightened their blazers and ties and headed for class. Blaise stood at the daffs doorway – it had a brick protecting wall to prevent people seeing directly into the toilets – with his holdall open and the empty vodka bottle inside it, collecting the used paper cups. 'Cover your tracks – always cover your tracks,' he said to Martin as he went out. Kavanagh told Martin later that Blaise had gone around picking the paper cups out of the toilet bowls because the wax paper would not flush away.

One day a typed notice appeared on all the main doors inside the school which said that due to circumstances beyond the control of the authorities the school would close early at 2.20p.m. Every pupil chose to believe it and left. Investigation of the note traced the typeface and its slightly eccentric e below the line to the Spiritual Director's typewriter. The Spiritual Director had allowed boys to type articles for the school magazine. It was after this that the school put up a notice to say that 'official' school notices would be displayed only on the noticeboard with the lockable glass doors.

Two weeks later another notice appeared – this time inside the glass case – dismissing the school at 2.20p.m. and there was a stampede for the gates before any of the teachers could prevent it. The notice said that there would be a celebration of a special mass for ST MARY EUPHRASIA PELLETIER, *Virgin* at 6 o'clock in the school chapel for those who wished to return for it.

These things were blamed on Blaise but he stood with his hands up and said: not guilty. He didn't even know where the Spiritual Director's room was. What would be the point in him doing something like that? He was a boarder and couldn't get out anyway.

4.   An Evening Stroll

The photograph is of a split second. A man attempting to leap a large puddle. But you can see that he's not going to make it – he has *no* chance of making it. His heel is cocked like a gun and about to strike its own reflection in the water. The man is moving so fast that he is out of focus, fudged, but somehow his reflection seems sharper. He has launched himself from a half-submerged wooden ladder and the reactive force has set up ripples close to the ladder. They have not yet had time to spread and break the stillness of the water surface.

Martin pored over the Cartier-Bresson book. He was totally absorbed in it – had spent a lot of time over each incredible image. He heard someone laugh, too loud for the public library Reference section. It was Kavanagh. He was at the far side of the reading room leaning over, talking to this girl. Martin could see that she was embarrassed by the noise he'd made. She put her head down so that he could see the straight parting that ran from brow to crown, but her shoulders were shaking with laughter. She was Philippa Dobson, but people called her Pippa. She looked up at Kavanagh and said no to whatever he was proposing.

Martin yawned and got to his feet. He could do with going downstairs to the toilet. The doors of the reading room closed with a breath of air behind him. The staircase was of white marble and Martin liked the way the steps were shallow. You could glide down, rather than step. He stood there resting his left hand on the balustrade. On the landing was a glass case where a book exhibit was always on show. There was a girl standing looking into the glass case. Immediately he was taken with her. She was lovely. Not so much beautiful, but somebody he felt he could fall in love with. This was always happening to him, but somehow with this woman it was immediately more intense. He felt certain. She was half crouched, holding back her hair from her face in case it interfered with what she was looking at. Martin slowed the pace of his descent right down: he wanted to have her in his sights for as long as possible. He could adore her. She was in jeans and a white blouse, holding a folder and some books against her chest. Martin decided to have a look in the glass case even though he had passed it hundreds of times in the past month. The girl moved around to the opposite side, concentrating on the display, totally unaware of him. She was tanned and her hair was streaked with blonde. She had soft, deep brown eyes. There were spotlights focused inside the case and he saw her profile reflected on the glass at a mirror angle. She was lovely from both sides. Like an Italian film star whose name he couldn't remember. He could see through one of her images in the case, making her seem like a ghost. The image was paler than her reality. An apparition. She tilted her head sideways the better to see something and he imagined her as Snow White. In her glass coffin. Fuck, he had her dead before he'd even met her. She had a small silver cross on a chain at her throat. Her hand went from her hair to the cross and she slid it to and fro along its thin chain. Even her hands were lovely. Then she raised her eyes and looked up at Martin. Looking at her. He nearly died. The girl's eyes were so deep and dark. Her gaze held for a moment, then she switched it off and looked down into the case again. He swooned – saw himself cartwheel and tumble down the marble of the staircase. The more shallow the steps the more frequently he would bang his head. Like trailing his fingers down a glass washboard. Causing vibrations inside him. Martin looked away, afraid to be caught staring at her if she was to look up at him a second time. He felt the hairs on his neck prickle, either in anticipation or reaction, he didn't know which. Through the stuff of her white blouse he could discern curlicues of even whiter lace. Jesus. He was pretending to look intensely at the display as they circled the case. And yet if he had been examined on what was in the case he would have been unable to answer. There were books. Yes, of that he was sure. But whether they were in English or Latin or Irish . . . or were about cookery or bridge-building or word origins – he hadn't a clue. She continued to stare down at the exhibits, then she raised one eyebrow, a bit like the way Blaise did. She disapproves of something. Maybe think of something to say. *So – you don't agree?*

Or open a conversation with *I have found inconsistencies here myself.* She straightened up, flashed him a quick smile and climbed the stairs away from him. Shout now – *Hey, come back, I've something more to say to you* . . . . Or *Excuse me, you forgot your* . . . Or *why did you smile at me just now?* She climbed the staircase with just the soles of her shoes coming in contact with the marble. Her heels made no contact. She walked with a straight back, with elegance. And not once did she look over her shoulder at him. If she'd been Lot's wife she'd have lived. One pillar of salt less for the world.

He had to be careful when he went back up. Should he tell Kavanagh he had seen the most amazing woman, a woman he fancied way beyond the call of duty? If he pointed her out then Kavanagh would be over beside her like a shot, saying, what's your name and what school do you go to and my mate holds you in the highest esteem, fancies you something awful, I kid you not – he thinks you the most salubrious thing he's ever seen. Then he would grin and point Martin out. 'Him – there. The one with the scarlet throbbing face.' And that would be the end of it. The girl would be embarrassed, pack her books and leave. And never come back. 'Some skinny geek I saw prowling around the stairs in the library fancies me.'

When he went into the reading room Kavanagh was back in his place and the Pippa woman had her head bent over, studying. Martin sat down and scanned the room. Where was she? The ghost woman, the reflection? Then he saw her, halfway down the room, sitting with her back to him – her blonde streaked hair, her straight back.

Kavanagh said, 'What are you smiling about?'

'Nothing.' Martin snapped open the rings of his physics file and hooked them into the holes of the last sheet of notes he had written up.

'There's skulduggery afoot. Shenanigans of some sort in progress,' said Kavanagh.

'Honest. Naw,' said Martin. Then he couldn't stop himself. 'I just saw an extraordinary woman.'

'Who?' Martin shrugged. 'Which one?' Kavanagh scanned the room. Martin smiled and shook his head. 'Who would Brennan fancy?'

81

'Brennan is remaining silent on this point.'

But for the rest of the evening Martin contrived, several times, to walk to the filing cabinets opposite where she sat and riffle through the cards, his brow knitted at the elusiveness of the volume he was looking for.

At about eight o'clock she stood and packed her books and left. He watched the white of her blouse and the tilt of her head all the way to the door. He wanted to run after her, to say *Fancy a coffee?* Or *Even a tea?* but the fear of her reply stopped him. *With you?* Incredulous voice. *Are you serious?* Laughter.

Just as if to show him how it was done, Kavanagh got up and went over to talk to Pippa again. He looked so easy, so relaxed, leaning his hip on her desk, bending over to point out something on her page. A wink in Martin's direction, a smile, a tilt of the head.

Martin hoped that the ghost woman would come back again. *I forgot my purse. Thank you so much. Not many are so honest nowadays. Oh, you had considered the priesthood, had you? I don't think it would be for you, either. Yes, a coffee would be nice. Let me pay, now that I've got my money back.* He kept looking between Kavanagh and the door. Instead of the ghost woman, he was amazed to see Blaise come in. And the coincidence reminded him of the line which accompanies Macbeth's first entry into the court: 'He was a gentleman on whom I built an absolute trust.' Blaise was wearing a dark sweater and trousers. He stood looking around him, his hands in his pockets. He saw Kavanagh talking to the girl but continued to scan the silent room. Then he came walking over to Martin.

'Hi.'

'Hi,' Martin said. He could feel a blush rising into his face but there was nothing he could do about it. Blaise had chosen to come to him first. 'You shouldn't be here. You should – at this very moment – be locked up.'

'Yeah,' said Blaise. 'I went to the pictures.'

'What about evening study?'

'I don't enjoy it.' Martin smiled and said,

'What was the movie?'

'It was brilliant. A thing called *The Killing*. With Sterling Hayden in it – always chewing a match. It's a scam to rob money from the bank at a racing track. And they distract attention by shooting the bloody horse that's winning the race.'

'Sounds good.' Martin felt that Blaise was actually talking to him, as opposed to making statements in his presence.

'But it was the *way* it was done. Jumping about backwards and forwards in time. Building the story up in bits of scenes. Totally brilliant.'

'Had they bet on the horse?'

'No – why would you fuckin bet on a horse if you were going to shoot it?'

'Well then had they bet on the horse running second?'

'No! it was a fucking diversion – to get the cops out of the way. And it had this great actor in it, the wonderful Elisha Cook Junior. You'd know him if you saw him. The Patron Saint of Cowards. A man with sweat always on his upper lip.'

Martin was almost afraid to say anything else. 'I thought you guys might still have been around here.'

'And we are.'

'I'd better get back. Are you walking up the road?'

'Yeah, sure.'

'Get Kavanagh – I don't want to interrupt his dalliance.'

'His what?'

'Just get him,' said Blaise. He slid into the chair next to Martin and began to inspect his book. 'Cartier-Bresson – not much work being done tonight, eh?'

The three of them went for a coffee and afterwards walked up Clifton Street towards Carlisle Circus strung out across the pavement. Martin and Kavanagh had bags slung over their shoulders. They were talking and walking so slowly that they seemed to have no purpose or direction to their steps. Kavanagh would make some point and lean on a lamp-post, then swing around it. Martin would brush his shoulder along the black stones of the wall of the Old Poor House. Blaise was in the centre putting his feet firmly on the square sets, as if avoiding the cracks. The sun had gone down and the light was beginning to fade. A blackbird was singing its head off at the top of a tree in the Old Poor House gardens. At one point Martin found himself in the middle. He dropped his bag on to the pavement,

'Steady the buffs,' he said and put a hand on Kavanagh's shoulder, then on Blaise's shoulder. He jumped and tried to heave himself into the air by straightening his arms – but Kavanagh was too tall – and, instead of walking forward the two boys moved out sideways, so that Martin barely got off the ground.

'Thanks – thanks a million,' he said. The other two were laughing. They seemed pleased they had both come up with the same strategy at the same moment.

'What kind of music do you like?' Kavanagh asked Blaise.

'All sorts. Everything. I like all kinds of music.'

'Like what?'

'German baroque, eighteenth-century classicism, modern,' he shrugged. 'You name it. Even some Vaughan Williams, given the right circumstances.'

'What about the Stones?' said Martin.

'I'm sorry.'

'Do you like the Stones?'

'I thought you asked me about music.'

'Fuck off. What about Dylan?' Martin began to sing – *The times they are a-changing*. Blaise pulled a face. It was difficult to know whether he was taking the piss or not. Martin began to take slow giant steps away from the other two.

'Come back,' Kavanagh made a mock and mournful cry. Martin stopped giant stepping. Kavanagh bumped into his back and said, 'So you're not going to tell us who this wonderful woman is?' Martin shook his head.

'I can't. I don't know who she is. I just saw her tonight.'

'What about Pippa?' said Blaise.

'She seems distinctly saved,' said Martin.

'She's not as bad as all that.'

'No make-up. V-necked drawers.' Kavanagh made as if to kick Martin on the backside. But Martin evaded the swipe.

'Anyway what's wrong with that?' said Kavanagh. 'It makes her even more gorgeous. I kid you not. The ice maiden, the unattainable one. Ere long the lovely Pippa will succumb to my not inconsiderable charms.'

'Women only interfere with good friendships,' said Blaise.

'Overheard one night in a Belfast entry,' said Martin. '*Hold my bible and I'll take them off myself.*' This time Kavanagh grabbed Martin in a stranglehold from behind.

'Fucking bastard. Besmirching the woman I love. Retract.'

'Ahh – ahhhhh – you're choking me.'

'This is no behaviour for the sons of gentlefolk. Desist ere I smite you both.'

'Unhand me.'

Kavanagh let Martin go and he staggered across the pavement. Kavanagh said to Blaise, 'Are you one of the gentlefolk?'

'Yes – if you're referring to a working-class intellectual background.'

'So what does your old man do – for a living?' Kavanagh asked.

'He falls off logs.'

'What?' Martin screwed up his eyes.

'It's not a difficult job.'

'What are you on about?' said Martin. Kavanagh was laughing.

'As in *It's as easy as . . .*' said Kavanagh. '*He falls off logs.*'

'No – I can never make out,' said Blaise, 'whether he's a physicist or a mathematician. He's away most of the time – Australia, America. It's probably why I want to do Philosophy.'

'Because your da's away, you want to do Philosophy?'

'Learn to make connections, Martin,' said Blaise. 'Don't be such a dumbfuck.'

'I'm sorry, sir.' He bowed and kowtowed.

'Maths and Philosophy are governed by the same logic.' Kavanagh pushed Martin's crouching body onwards with a shove from his knee.

Martin said, 'What precisely *is* a dumbfuck?' Blaise looked at him in the heavy-lidded way he had.

'You are, Martin.' Blaise continued to stare at him. 'You are.'

'Cut the niggle,' said Kavanagh. 'How do you *do* philosophy?'

'By thinking. You take a problem or an idea or a statement and examine it.'

'For example?'

'We are doing it at this very moment.'

'What? It can't be as easy as that.'

'OK. If the Barber of Seville shaves all the men in the town, except the ones who shave themselves – what's the situation?' Blaise put his head to one side and raised his eyebrow.

'The Barber of Seville makes a fortune,' said Martin.

'Wait, there's a catch,' said Kavanagh. Blaise smiled and went on,

'If the Barber shaves himself, he is not to be shaved *by* himself. If he *doesn't* shave himself then the only one who can shave him *is* himself. It's a paradox.'

'That's not a para-dox – it's boll-ox,' said Martin.

'Say that again slowly,' said Kavanagh to Blaise.

Martin and Kavanagh were walking on towards the school driveway when Blaise stopped. The school had taken to closing the big gates in the evenings. Blaise nodded his head up the side street to a row of converted red brick houses. This row had been bought over by the diocese to house university students who were going on for the priesthood. The row was attached by an extension to the school.

'I'm going in through the Wing,' said Blaise.

'This I must see,' said Kavanagh. 'What about getting caught?'

'The Wing is for apprentice priests. It's designed to stop people getting in, not getting out.' All three of them walked up the street.

'So how do you get back in?' said Martin.

'Through my cat flap.'

'How d'you mean?'

Blaise stopped in front of a window and sat down on the stone sill. He began to fumble in his pockets. He said, 'This window is opposite the Spiritual Director's room – and it is open.'

'How do you know?'

'Because it's the one I came out of.'

'And you left it open?'

'Yeah. I believe Father Barry is away for the evening.'

'What if somebody has noticed it was open, and closed it.'

'Yeah – that's happened before now.' It was the first time Martin had heard a note of regret in Blaise's voice. 'In the last school but one I had to stand on a second floor windowsill until dawn. Five fucking hours. So never again, says I. In this case they couldn't,' said Blaise.

'Why not?'

He took a brass window lock and two screws from his pocket and showed them. Then a small screwdriver.

'How many schools have you been to?' asked Kavanagh. Blaise shrugged.

'This one's the worst.'

He reached round behind him and inched the window up. He did not even drop his voice.

'See you tomorrow.' Then he stepped over the sill into the darkness. Martin and Kavanagh waited. The window frame slid back down with a thud and they saw Blaise's shadowy figure screw the window catch back into place. They laughed a bit and made signs of goodbye to him with the flat of their hands pressed up against the frosted glass, including a V-sign.

One Saturday, about lunch time, there was a ring at Brennan's front door.

'Martin, get that. My hands are all wet.' Martin went to the door. He didn't recognise the shadow beyond the dimpled glass as the bread-man or the man who collected the rent. He opened the door and Kavanagh was standing there, stooped, trying to look a bit smaller.

'What about you, Martin?'

'Hi.'

'What are you up to?'

'Nothing.' Martin felt a blush rising in his face.

'Fancy going into town?'

'OK.' He felt the reddening of his cheeks so intensely that he had to duck back into the hall leaving Kavanagh propping up the wall outside. He could hardly believe it. Kavanagh had called for him. He plucked his jacket off the hall stand.

'Who is it?' his mother shouted.

'It's for me,' Martin rushed into the kitchen. 'Any money?'

She was standing at the sink in pink rubber gloves washing dishes.

'What's it for?'

'Spending.'

'Do you think I'm made of money? Who was at the door?'

'Kavanagh.'

'Ooooh – why didn't you bring him in?'

'He's in a hurry.'

'You look a bit flushed. Are you OK?' He nodded. 'Get me my

purse.' He brought it to the draining board. 'Open it.' He undid the catch and took what money she allowed him. And he was away pulling on his jacket, dashing out the door on to the street. With Kavanagh for the whole of Saturday afternoon.

Martin sat at the kitchen table trying to make a start on his essay. His mother was in the scullery baking, preparing for one of her supper evenings. Different kinds of bread: soda, wheaten, currant bread. When the flat sodas were cooked she leaned them up against each other on a wire cooling grid. They slithered together with a dry, floury sound. She kept dashing in and out, all energy. Sometimes talking to herself.

'Now buns,' she said. She put a hard block of margarine in a baking bowl and covered it with a hill of sugar. She set it on the hearth with the heel of the bowl up on the fender so that its open face was to the fire. 'Keep your eye on that, Martin. I'm way behind – chop that up a bit for me.' He put down his pen and cut the margarine into smaller pieces with the wooden spoon. It melted and he saw the sugar go clear. He called her when it was ready. She came in from the scullery and beat the mixture furiously with her right hand, holding the bowl on her left hip. When it was the consistency she wanted she dashed back into the scullery. Martin followed her. She lifted dollops of the mixture on the end of the spoon and plopped the right amount into fluted papers set in the recesses of a black oven tray. Martin ran his finger round the bowl and put it in his mouth.

'That'll kill you with indigestion,' she said. 'What on earth is the time?'

'Almost seven.'

'Oh Holy Frost! They're coming at eight. Help me, Martin. Bring some of that fire into the parlour. It's like bloody winter. I want it looking red and comfy when they come – not all yellow blazes. *And be careful.*'

Martin pulled all the chairs back to clear the shortest path. With tongs he picked up blazing coals and set them on the shovel. They had welded together and sounded dangerous – gritty, cindery, tinkling. The heat wafted upwards. Both the kitchen door and the parlour door were open as wide as possible. When the shovel was full but not too full he made a dash from one fireplace to the other, his face screwed up against the coal smoke and the flame. His mother shouted, 'Watch that mat.'

Once the burning coal was in place it had to be covered with fresh coal. The coal house was in the yard next to the lavatory. It had no door and there was no light in it. In the black hole Martin had to work by radar. He put the shovel flat to the uneven ground and pushed forward until it met resistance. He made shovelling motions until he heard the rumble of falling coal and the shovel felt sufficiently heavy. Then he reversed out. When it rained the water ran off the yard into the coal house. There was a kind of black soup on the floor which he had accidentally scooped up with the shovel.

The fresh coal caught and with the bellows he pumped the fire to a blazing pyramid. After the dash from one room to the other the air was full of motes, leaving pinpoint flecks in the air and on the mantelpiece. His mother came round after him with a damp cloth inspecting and wiping cream surfaces.

'Look what you've done,' she yelled. 'Dribbling that black stuff all over the hall lino. Martin, love, wipe that mess up and give it a wee polish before they come. Just a wee rub over.'

'I've a lot of homework.'

'When there's something to be done, you *always* have a lot of homework.' Martin moved towards the scullery where the basket of polishing things was kept. 'And you're too old to be putting on that lip, boy.'

He knelt on the hall rug and rooted among the dusters and canisters of Pledge for the Mansion floor polish. There was a tiny metal butterfly at the side of the tin, to lever open the lid. It was a new tin and the waxy, brick red surface was untouched – unbroken like fresh snow. He wiped the cloth on it and ruined the smoothness. The lino was a squared pattern and he did it in areas. Dulling it with polish, letting the polish dry before wiping off with another drier cloth. Seeing each area as a small accomplishment – accumulating a shine. He remembered doing this job when he was just a kid, being resentful. He thought about informing someone from the government – somebody from the Cruelty, as Nurse Gilliland always called them. He was far too young to have to work this hard. His mother was treating him like a slave. He was being abused. They'd take him away and he'd have an easy life in a home somewhere and they'd put his mother in jail.

'Don't polish *under* those rugs,' his mother said, stepping over him with the good plates from the china cabinet. 'For fear people would slip. Can you imagine what would happen to Mary Lawless's bones?'

The newness had gone off the fire when the doorbell rang and Martin's mother shouted for him to answer it. She was upstairs, in the middle of getting dressed. Mary Lawless looked quite pale and shaken. Martin took her coat and hung it on the hall stand. It was the size of a black circus tent.

'Thanks be to God for the growing boy. What I have just seen . . .' she kept saying over and over again and shaking her head. Martin's mother was coming down the stairs.

'What's wrong with you, Mary? You look like you've just seen a ghost.'

'I wish I had, Mrs Brennan. I wish I had. It would've been a thousand times better than what I *have* just seen.'

'Darling dear — what was it?'

'A boy, not that much older than Martin here, coming blundering out of a pub. And he proceeded to throw up in front of me. I'm sure my shoes are ruined.' She had to bend over quite a distance to be able to see her feet.

'They're splashed, right enough. I'll get you a wee cloth,' said Mrs Brennan, going to the kitchen.

'Get me a big one,' yelled Mary Lawless. As his mother said, Mary Lawless could always see the funny side. 'Thank God for that perfume you're wearing too much of,' she shouted after Mrs Brennan. Martin loved the smell of it. In fact he had bought it for his mother at Christmas.

'What is it?' asked Mary when Mrs Brennan came back with a wet cloth.

'*Le chien mort*,' said Martin.

'Nonsense.'

'Chanel,' said Mrs Brennan, getting down on her knees at Mary Lawless's feet.

'Gorgeous.'

'What a thing to happen and you trigged out in all your finery.'

'What are you talking about? Finery? Everyday duds, that's what I'm wearing.'

They got Mary's shoes cleaned. Father Farquharson arrived at the same time as Nurse Gilliland. When they were all settled in front of the fire, which they praised excessively when they heard Martin had lit it, Mary related the drunken story. Father Farquharson agreed that things were getting worse with regard to the drink. Being a teetotaller himself he could not see the charm of the stuff but he supposed a drink or two was a way of relaxing. But moderation in all things. Martin excused himself, saying that he had homework to do.

'You're fairly shooting up, Martin,' said Nurse Gilliland.

'I'm a growing boy,' said Martin. He said it to get it in before Mary Lawless could say it.

At about ten o clock he heard the parlour door open and his mother call, 'Martin, would you be so good?' He made the tea and carried in one of the laden trays.

'Just a wee bite to eat,' said his mother. 'Set it down here, Martin.'

On plates covered with paper doily mats Mrs Brennan carried in more sandwiches. They were cut into tiny triangles, the top slice of each was brown bread, the lower white. The crusts had been removed. Between the different colours of bread were lines of filling – yellow egg, pink salmon, green lettuce with red tomato, brown roast beef, purple ham. A few sprigs of parsley lay on top.

'Glory be to God. There's what would feed a regiment here, Mrs Brennan,' said Father Farquharson. Mary Lawless, as she always did, tapped the arm of her chair in appreciation.

'First class – the gentry wouldn't get any better.'

'What are you talking about, Mary? The gentry would never taste the likes of these,' said Nurse Gilliland. 'Not the way herself makes them.'

Mrs Brennan handed each person a paper napkin for their knee and a china plate.

'Och away on,' she said. 'It's just thrown together – nothing but a cup of tea in your hand. Some night I'll take the time and do things properly.'

Mary Lawless selected a sandwich and bit into it.

'What's this?' she said with feigned wonderment. Mrs Brennan looked.

'Roast beef.'

'That meat's so tender you could ate it with your nose.'

'Here, Father, take a napkin,' said Mrs Brennan. 'You wouldn't think black would stain but it's nearly worse than anything else.'

'You're right there,' said Father Farquharson. 'It practically highlights a stain.'

'I hope my shoes don't stain,' said Mary Lawless. 'The language of the young ones nowadays coming out of that pub – it would frighten you.'

'Merciful hour,' said Mrs Brennan. 'They're a holy terror.'

'You were coming out of a pub, Mary?' said Nurse Gilliland.

'Indeed I was not. It was a crowd of young ones.'

'Slang,' said Father Farquharson, 'there's a lot of slang about.'

'Who's talking about slang? It's the cursing I'm talking about. Giving everybody within earshot dog's abuse. Unadulterated effs and c's. If you'll pardon my French, Father – being so blunt. And, God above, it's not just pubs. It would curl the hair of your head to pass a primary school getting out these days.'

'Martin – *you* wouldn't say things like that, would you?'

'No.'

'God bless us and save us! He certainly would not – over my dead body,' said Mrs Brennan. 'I just love the innocence of wee children. Isn't it the terrible pity they have to grow up?'

'It is – but that's the way the Lord has planned it. They can't remain in ignorance for ever.' Father Farquharson seemed very definite. He bit decisively into his sandwich.

'Ignorance *is* innocence,' said Martin's mother. 'And it's lovely to see it. That's what I always say.'

'It's not a philosophy you hear seriously espoused these days.' Father Farquharson began to suck at something which had caught between his teeth.

'Indeed Father, I would go so far as to say that it applies not just to – you know what – but to things like doctoring and what have you,' said Mrs Brennan. 'If I have cancer I'd prefer not to know. You're better not knowing a thing about it. That's my theory.'

'A little knowledge is a dangerous thing,' said Mary Lawless. 'A doctor told me once what was wrong with my ear and he might as well have whistled "Blue Suede Shoes." '

'Do you have a toothpick, Mrs Brennan?'

'It's the one thing I don't have in the house.'

'There's those cocktail sticks,' said Martin. He left the room and came back with a cocktail stick and handed it to Father Farquharson.

'Thank you, Martin. Anyway this man in the restaurant – he had asked for a tooth pick. I think it was a well-done steak he'd been having – always a mistake, I say. And the funny—'

'What kind of a steak is a mis-steak, Father?' They all laughed.

Father Farquharson brushed crumbs from his trousers and said, 'Oh you're quick, Mary – far too quick for me.'

'And . . . ?' said Mary Lawless.

'And what?'

'What happened? What was the funny thing . . . ?'

'Oh yes the funny thing was – it broke.'

'What?'

'The toothpick. Between his teeth. It was one of those plastic ones, like an old fashioned pen quill – have you not seen them?'

'No, I can't say I have,' said Mary Lawless. 'But we're nowhere near as sophisticated as yourself, Father. We wouldn't be out dining with this one and that one the way you would be. Bishop this and Cardinal that. Using toothpicks.'

'Anyway,' said Father Farquharson, 'he had to get another toothpick to dislodge the toothpick. A toothpick for toothpicks. It really was quite amusing.'

Martin sat on the floor in front of the china cabinet eating a sandwich. From this low level he could see Mary Lawless's hairy legs. The hairs were pressed flat against her skin inside her nylons or tights. Like wood grain. In contrast, Father Farquharson's legs descended, white and hairless as candles, from his black trousers into his black socks which went into his black shoes. Martin made as if to lean back and his mother shouted at him, 'Don't you dare lean back on that china cabinet, Martin. It's far too fragile.'

'I wasn't going to.'

'Martin – a refill, if you'd be so good.' His mother handed him the teapot.

When he came back into the room Nurse Gilliland said, 'Isn't it great to get to this age with all your bits still functioning.'

'I wouldn't be too sure about that,' said Mary Lawless.

'What? Whether it's great or whether all your bits are still functioning?'

'I think there's bits of me haven't functioned for years.'

'Dare we ask which bits?'

'Aw, now, that would be telling.'

'There's not too much wrong with the tongue,' said Father Farquharson. 'Isn't that so, Mary?'

'I'm saying nothing.'

'It must be the first time that's ever happened.'

'What?'

'You saying nothing.'

'Get away.'

Mary Lawless stirred her tea, the spoon chinging loudly against the china.

'Did any of you ever think of leaving your body to science?' she said.

'God forbid,' said Martin's mother. 'Can you imagine the going over you would get and you stone dead? Aww, no that's not for me at all.' Her cup clicked on its china saucer.

'What does the Church have to say about it, Father?'

'I'm off duty, Mary. Give me peace.'

'It's for the good of others,' said Nurse Gilliland. 'How else would doctors learn where things were – which organ was which?'

'One thing that would worry me,' said Mary Lawless, 'would be Judgment Day . . .'

'Crumbs! That'll worry us all, believe you me,' said Father Farquharson and they all laughed loudly again.

'No – but if you were cut into bits and it came to the Last Day and God had to reassemble you . . .'

'We'll all be reconstituted, is that not the case, Father?'

Father Farquharson put up his hands, laughing.

'Don't ask me,' he said.

'Och come on now, Father,' said Mary Lawless, 'would I come back with all my veins and weight problems or would I come back in my prime? Would I be the fair and flawless Mary Lawless again?'

'With a twenty-inch waist, Mary,' said Nurse Gilliland.

'Like an egg timer.'

'Easy turned upside down.'

'In your prime, Mary – you'll return in your prime. Of that I have no doubt.'

'Then I'll be reunited with my appendix,' said Mrs Brennan.

'Father, when we – you know – pass on,' Nurse Gilliland screwed up her thin face as she tried to phrase her question. 'No, let me come at it from another direction. What's the General Judgment?'

'Oh this is very hard territory.'

'Are you saying I wouldn't understand it, Father?'

'No – no I'm not, but it's hardly the stuff of a pleasant evening with baking as extraordinary as this.' He held up the bread he was eating.

'Go on with you, Father,' said Mrs Brennan. 'It's the same as you get every time you're here.'

'No, truly – it is wonderful.'

'I hate people,' said Mary Lawless, 'who think of bread as simply a vehicle for jam.'

'Bread is bread,' said Mrs Brennan. 'Bread is itself.'

'You're right there,' said Father Farquharson. 'Never spoke a truer word.'

'The General Judgment?'

'If you insist, Nurse Gilliland. The Church teaches that when each of us dies there is "the particular judgement". We die, we come before Our Maker and we are judged accordingly.'

'Ho-ho – that'll be the day,' said Mary Lawless.

'We come into our rightful place beside Him. Or we are turned away. Then on the Last Day there is the General Judgment when Christ will come in all his glory to bring to light the conduct of each one of us and the secrets of our hearts.'

'It'll all be out in the open that day, won't it, Martin?' said his mother. Nurse Gilliland held up her hand as if to stop everyone.

'Given that the Last Day might not happen for some years yet – some few million – what happens in the meantime, Father?'

'Time is not the same for God. It's not a continuum. The best way I can explain it . . . is to think of looking at a map. You can see everywhere at once. Time is two dimensional for the Maker of the Universe. He sees it all from first to last in the blink of an eye.'

'Milton said something like that,' said Martin.

'Milton who?' said Mrs Brennan.

'The poet John Milton.'

'Aw, the growing mind,' said Mary Lawless.

'May I try one of these?' said Father Farquharson, reaching to the angel cakes.

Nurse Gilliland thinned her lips and wrinkled her eyes again. She said, 'It'll be a hard day's work, Father, judging everybody who ever lived in the one day.'

Mrs Brennan laughed.

'You never said a truer word.'

Father Farquharson swallowed his bite of bun and they all awaited his reply.

'Do I detect banter,' he said. Nurse Gilliland smiled and gave herself a little slap on the wrist.

'May God forgive me.'

'Always the stirrer,' said Mary Lawless. 'You were saying earlier, Father, that people drink to relax. I know some people who relax all night long. They become so relaxed they fall down.'

'People nowadays don't drink to relax, Father. When all's said and done they drink to get drunk. The young ones especially.' For some reason they all turned to look at Martin.

'I don't drink,' he said.

'What we need nowadays is the return of somebody like Father Mathew,' said Mary Lawless. 'Get everyone to take the pledge.'

'Was he the man who was the curate in Ballyhackamore in the 1950s?' asked Martin's mother.

'No, indeed he was not,' said Mary Lawless. 'You'd have to go a lot farther back than that, Mrs Brennan. As far back as the Famine, I believe. He formed the Cork Total Abstinence Society.'

'And then they could neither ate nor drink,' said Nurse Gilliland and laughed in her cackling kind of way.

'Seven million of them took the pledge,' said Father Farquharson, nodding his head to agree with Mary Lawless.

'In Cork alone?'

'No, Mrs Brennan – all over. Ireland, England – even the United States. Seven million of them took the pledge.'

'There's a polish called that,' said Martin. 'Pledge. Winos drink polish with ordinary gas bubbled through it.'

'Seven million people drinking that stuff. It'd be some party, eh Martin? God forgive me – making fun of the afflicted.' Nurse Gilliland winked at him.

'Joking about things like that doesn't really help,' said Mrs Brennan. 'Drink always leads to something worse.'

'You never said a truer word,' said Nurse Gilliland. 'Father, have you been a Pioneer all your life?'

'I have indeed.' He thumbed his lapel where the Pioneer pin was stuck. 'Alcohol has never passed my lips.'

'I hope you don't think I'm being cheeky, Father, but what about the wine at mass?' said Nurse Gilliland.

'I'm amazed at you asking such a question.'

'Why, Father?'

'By the time I'm consuming it, its essence has changed.'

'I beg your pardon.'

'I know essences are very difficult . . .'

Mrs Brennan stirred uneasily.

'They keep for a very long time,' she said. 'I have stuff up there in the cupboard for years, and they're as good as new. Vanilla is my favourite. Just one or two drops is all it needs. And almond is good for those wee Bakewells I make. The ones you're so fond of, Father.'

Nurse Gilliland put her head to one side, as if there was something hurting her ear.

'I'm not so sure I know what you mean. Does the consecration take away the flavour of the wine? Or the alcohol?'

'No, it doesn't. And very well you know it. It looks like wine, smells like wine – but it has been changed. To the Precious Blood. In essence.'

'I see,' said Mrs Brennan. 'Are you ready for more tea, Father?'

'I'm fine – fine.'

'But . . .' Nurse Gilliland was still screwing her face up. 'I hate to even begin to suggest this but . . . but could a person get drunk? Would the alcohol still be there? Even though the essence is changed.'

'You're contradicting yourself out of your own mouth now. If its essence is changed, it's not alcohol.' Father Farquharson was beginning to show signs of agitation. He twirled and fiddled with his paper napkin.

'Just while we're on the subject, Father – I hope this doesn't sound cheeky or irreverent but . . .' Nurse Gilliland paused and joined her hands tightly together then turned them this way and that. Palm up, palm down. 'No maybe I shouldn't . . .'

'You're among friends.'

'But don't push your luck . . .' said Mary Lawless.

'It's difficult, Father. Because you might think it's a mockery – and it's not. I'm not mocking anything or anybody, Father. I'm just wanting to know.'

'Unless ye be as little children,' said Mrs Brennan.

'Well?' Father Farquharson tried to refold his napkin to its original creases. 'I don't know what's got into you tonight, Nurse Gilliland. This is supposed to be a night off for me.'

'If a woman – or a man for that matter – had been out early to buy the bread . . . And on their way home they popped into mass and sat up at the front . . .'

'What's coming next?' said Father Farquharson.

'When the priest says the words of the consecration why doesn't . . . what's to stop her bread turning into the . . . Lord, the Precious Body?'

'Holy Frost! Where do you get them. Nurse Gilliland?' said Mrs Brennan.

'Your brains are working overtime,' said Mary Lawless. 'The oul head's going ninety to the dozen.'

Nurse Gilliland shushed the comments, waiting for Father Farquharson to give her an answer. She tried to encourage him, saying, 'The bread is somehow within earshot – it could even be a pan loaf, Father.'

There was a long silence as Father Farquharson considered his answer. He set the neatly folded napkin on his knee and joined his hands together beneath his chin, fingertip to fingertip. Finally he cleared his throat and said, 'Sacerdotal intentionality.' Everyone nodded. 'That's the key. Sacerdotal intentionality.' He looked from one to the other waiting to see if anyone would contradict him. 'The celebrant says the words, This is my Body, and the intention is – and the words are spoken to – what he holds between his fingers – the host. The miracle doesn't leak out, as it were, to bread within the vicinity.'

'Thank you, Father,' said Nurse Gilliland.

'Just as, for instance, now. I said the words of consecration without realising it – in this small room. There are plates of bread on the table. It remains unchanged.'

'Thanks be to God. Who'd want to change Mrs Brennan's baking?'

'You've put my mind at rest, Father,' said Nurse Gilliland. 'It may seem beyond the beyonds, but that one has kept me awake many's a night.'

'I've said it before and I'll say it again – a cup of hot milk,' said Mrs Brennan. 'A cup of hot milk with a spoonful of honey in it – that's the boy to get you over.'

Later as he helped his mother with the dishes he asked her about Mary Lawless and why it was she had hairy legs.

'Never you mind,' she said and made a lot of noise emptying the basin. 'What a terrible question to ask a body. Maybe she doesn't care. Or she's probably too stout to bend over and shave them.'

'Women shave their legs?'

'Or they use special cream. Jesus, Mary and Joseph, what am I doing talking about such things to a boy of your age?'

Just before the bell Wee Jacky, the priest who taught them English, gave back the homework he had marked. He stood at the top desk with the pile of exercise books, glancing down at each name.

'Brennan.' He spun the book through the air to land flat on Martin's desk. 'Coyle.' Another accurate spinning throw. 'Foley.'

Kavanagh opened his book just as soon as it flopped on his desk.

'What did you get?' Martin said.

'A plus plus,' Kavanagh made a circle out of his finger and thumb and held it up to Martin. 'And you?'

'B.'

'By itself?'

99

'I am nonplussed.'

'What about you?' Kavanagh turned to Blaise. Blaise smiled and slid his exercise book into his folder.

Martin disliked this secretiveness in Blaise. He also hated him for making fun of him about the rose window. How should he know a thing like that? He thought Blaise picked on him too much. Last week in the English class they'd been told to sit and read an essay. When he'd finished Martin turned to the Contents page and put a tick beside the title of the essay he'd just read. About four of the essays were already ticked.

Blaise was behind him. After class Blaise said, 'What kind of people tick things off after they've read them?'

'Me.'

'Are you senile? Surely you can remember it without ticking it off.'

'All I did was tick it off.'

'In a couple of years if you come across that essay again and you see the tick you'll say – ah, I've read that. I haven't a clue what it's about but it's fucking-well ticked.'

'You're too smart by half,' said Martin. 'Too weird by half.'

There were many groups sauntering round the track, in both directions. On the left hand side of the Big Field, below the jail wall was a long jump pit of grey sand. There was a narrow run-up track and a take-off board across it, painted white at one time but now darkened. Kavanagh and Blaise were strolling along the narrow runway very close together – almost bumping into one another. When they reached the sand-pit they stepped apart and continued to talk and argue. Martin lagged behind on the narrow track.

'Pray silence!' he shouted. But they seemed to have no intention of doing anything but talking. Martin broke into a run, then hit the board and jumped, yelling at the same time. He landed in a heap between Kavanagh and Blaise.

'For fuck sake.'

'Get a grip, Martin.'

Martin liked this arrangement. A threesome was better than just being with someone else. With one other person you had to keep trying to think of something to say. Conversation was about taking your turn. With two he didn't quite know when it was his turn, whereas with three – it seemed easier. You could butt in. Then duck out again. Things seemed to flow better. And you didn't have to hold the floor.

Blaise said, 'OK, OK I grant you that – but a thing which interests me more is these fucking exams. I was serious the other day: is there any way we can get a look at this year's papers?'

Kavanagh and Martin shrugged. Blaise said, 'The papers are printed. Right? So that means there must be a printing works somewhere – as we speak – grinding out our physics paper. It would seem reasonable to me that the same printer probably does the chemistry and the English. And the A level Sanskrit and Mandarin Chinese.'

'What are you on about?' said Kavanagh.

'This is really interesting,' said Martin, pretending to lean forward, lolling his tongue out, so great was his anticipation.

'Then if you look up the printer in the phone book you discover their premises is at 43 Whittycombe Street or somewhere.'

'So?' said Kavanagh. 'Get to the fucking point.'

'*Our* exam papers will be there. In little piles. Big piles, probably.'

'What do we do? Just go down to Whitty-whatever-ya-callit Street and ask to see the A level chemistry paper for this year.'

'No, we don't. We think.'

'About what?'

'About how to get in there – how to get a look at those papers without anybody knowing.'

'You're mad in the skull.'

'At this moment somebody – who is earning a pittance – is putting them into sealed envelopes. They might be open to a bit of bribery and corruption.'

'Is it so important to you to pass?' said Kavanagh.

'I've spent some time being educated by the inappropriately named Christian Brothers,' said Blaise. 'I've been to Derry and Armagh, to Garron Tower and now this fucking dump.'

'Why were you chucked out of so many places?'

Blaise ignored Martin's question.

'If I louse this up the only place left is somewhere in England,' he said. 'Can you imagine anything worse? My old man says I'm intelligent and that he'll continue to educate me until I pass. Until I succumb to success.'

'But this method of passing is . . .' Martin wasn't sure of the word.

The next day at lunch time Blaise said very little. Martin and he were sauntering along the drive. Boarders were allowed out at lunch time – 'down to the shops,' as they called it. Martin hoped that Kavanagh would soon turn up. He didn't know how to talk to Blaise by himself.

'Where's the big lad?' asked Blaise.

'He's getting dressed. He had last period free and he was practising lay-ups in the gym.'

'What are lay-ups?'

'You know when you run in, bounce the ball off the board. The easiest shot in basketball.'

'And he needs to practise that?'

'Kavanagh does. He hasn't got it perfect yet. He gets it about ninety nine point nine per cent right. But the point one per cent miss rate really annoys him.'

'I hate all that stuff. Somebody should invent a sport without competition. Guys helping each other over the finishing line.'

'After you, sir. No. After you.'

'If I threw this javelin farther than the other guy he'd only be embarrassed so I'll stick it in the ground at my feet. I'm hoping to avoid doing Gym ever again in my life. I told the gym teacher I've had open heart surgery but I don't think he believed me. He wants me to get a note from my old man.' They walked together silently.

After a while Blaise said, 'I made a few calls yesterday.' He sighed heavily. 'It seems the papers – although they are made up here – are printed in England.'

'What?' Martin almost screeched. 'Who did you phone?'

'The Northern Ireland Schools Examination Authority or some such.'

'Jesus – what did you say?'

'Said I was doing a thesis. For a Diploma in Education. Put on a bit of a voice.'

'You don't have to do that.'

'Thank you.'

They got some fish and chips. Kavanagh, running to catch them up, met them coming out of the chippy. His hair was still wet from the shower. He dug right into Martin's paper and pulled out a handful of chips.

'That's all,' said Martin. 'Get your own fuckin dinner.' They waited with him until Kavanagh got his fish supper. The fat girl in the white overalls still blushed but was able to serve Kavanagh.

'Are you OK, Isobel?'

'I'm fine,' she said and laughed in a nervous sort of way as she wrapped his bag and gave him his change. Then they headed back up the road.

'She's really coming on,' said Kavanagh. 'Speech. Who knows what'll be next.'

'It's because you used her name.'

'Do you want me to call her somebody else's name?'

'This mad bastard,' said Martin pointing to Blaise with a chip, 'phoned the Northern Ireland Schools people and said he was doing a Dip.Ed. and found out the papers are printed across the water.'

'By confidential printers,' said Blaise. 'It's so fucking typical.'

'Of what?'

'Our luck.'

'They must ship them over here at some stage,' said Kavanagh.

'Last year they arrived about two weeks before the exams started,' said Martin.

'You saw this?' Blaise's voice went up an octave and he cocked his head to one side.

'Yeah. Everybody knows this. I was hanging around and this man comes along with all the brown envelopes, on a wheely thing. He got Joe Boggs to give him a lift with it up the stairs. They store them in that room beside the chapel. Where Joe Boggs keeps his cleaning stuff. Very hush-hush.'

'Shit the bed,' said Blaise. 'When did you say this was?'

'A week, maybe two, before the exams.'

'It would be nice to know exactly *when* they arrive this year.'

'People from outside school invigilate,' said Martin. 'They

come in here half an hour before and pick up the exam papers for the day, then they go to the gym or wherever the exam hall is.'

'I say, Philip,' said Kavanagh. 'I feel an adventure coming on. Shall we bring a length of rope and Lucy-Ann?'

'Not forgetting Kiki the parrot.'

5. Forty Minutes

Martin sat at the back of the study hall trying to think of another sentence or two to add to his unfinished homework. But what was the point? He'd written only about half a page – about how Milton found it easier to create Satan than God – based on the quote: 'But O how fall'n! how changed . . .' He hated Milton. Organ-voiced Milton was a complete bollicks. He'd cobbled the half-page together from a critical book out of the library and his own puny efforts. Last night he'd sat for over an hour squeezing out one awkward sentence after another until he'd got a paragraph. Then he was so disgusted he gave up. He didn't want to write more drivel, so he wrote nothing.

'This great epic poem is characterised by a sonorous nobility of expression and a compelling moral fervour. It was written by John Milton at the height of his career as a poet even though he was blind. Often blind people can see the truth better than the rest of us. For his material he picked the fall of man, the fall of the whole human race since Adam and Eve began it. Or begat it, maybe. And the picture was further complicated by Milton's intense conviction that his poetry must teach.'

He closed the exercise book. He would have another go at it tonight. Tonight he would get it finished.

Why did students have to put up with this? If you lined up everybody in Ireland and pointed a gun at their head and said *How important is it to be able to discuss Milton's Paradise Lost with a modicum of intelligence and insight?* and there were two boxes marked IMPORTANT and NOT VERY IMPORTANT. If you shot everybody who ticked NOT VERY IMPORTANT it would be a lot worse than the Famine. In fact it would be a total fuckin wipe-out. The only ones left would be English teachers. Ireland would be a country run by English teachers.

In the meantime such a disastrous attempt at an essay meant he had to avoid the English class. Wee Jacky rarely called the roll. Last year Martin would have skipped off but he had made promises to his mother. He *had* to be there at registration. And after registration he had to find a way to keep out of sight for forty minutes. Now in the corridor he looked at the clock. It was only ten past. Thank God it wasn't a double period. He had to have some excuse ready if he was stopped. 'Just going to the toilet.' Or coming from, depending on where he was nabbed. But that wouldn't do if he was sitting down somewhere. He stowed his bag in the old locker room and walked down towards the Wing. This was where Blaise had got in through the window. It seemed like a good place to hole up.

He knew one of the apprentice priests to talk to, Alfie Gribben. His nick-name was the Big Alpha. Martin walked slowly down a narrow flight of stairs which led to the extension. He should have taken a book out of his bag. 'I was asked to bring this to Big Alpha's room.' At the bottom he stopped and listened. Somebody was typing somewhere. He sat down on the last step. If nobody came past he could sit for ages. The Spiritual Director, Father Barry, his room was down here somewhere. If somebody caught him, he could always say that's who he was looking for. 'I need some spiritual direction.'

But he felt restless, so he stood and moved towards the sound of the typing. The doorways on to the street had been bricked up and access to the rooms was from a central corridor which had been driven through the middle of the houses. There were small alcoves leading off the main corridor — hallways of the original kitchen houses. The typing stopped. Martin stepped into one of the alcoves. He heard a door swing open. Footsteps went along the corridor and another door opened and closed. Martin heard the guy taking a piss, heard it going in the bowl, then the flush. The bathroom door opened and closed again and the footsteps approached. There was a terrible strong smell of aftershave. But the guy didn't go back into his room, he came on to the foot of the stairs. It was a red-haired guy whose name Martin wasn't sure of. McGratten or McClatchey or something. Out of the corner of his eye this guy noticed Martin in the alcove.

'Hi – is anything wrong?'

'No. I was looking for the Spiritual Director's room.'

'It's here.' The guy pointed. 'But I know for a fact that he's got a class right now.' They smiled at each other. 'Is there anything I can do?'

'No. Eh – what time is it?' The guy looked at his watch.

'A quarter past.'

'It can't be . . .'

'Maybe I'm just a bit slow.' He looked at his watch again to check.

'Maybe I'll just wait for him.'

'Goodness – if it's later then I'd better be on my way.'

And he was away, pounding up the stairs leaving behind him a wake of Old Spice. Goodness. Goodness – who said goodness nowadays? How quaint. He'd heard a man saying once, 'Dearie, dearie, dearie fuckin me.' And Father Farquharson had an equally strange line in swear words. At different times depending on the scale of his amazement Martin had heard him say 'My stars' or 'My sainted aunt,' and once when he heard about Mamie Doran's first pregnancy at the age of forty-three he said, 'My shattered nerves.'

Martin was going to sit on the bottom stair again but realised that when the door at the top of the stairs was pushed open he was immediately visible. He walked quietly down the corridor looking at the doors. He found the bathroom. It had a small male logo on the door which, when Martin thought about it, was totally unnecessary. He went in and bolted the door. He put the lid of the toilet down and sat on it as if it was an ordinary seat. There were a couple of hairs adhering to the side of the bath. One was in the shape of a music sign he didn't know the name for. 𝄞. He wished he'd brought a book or something to read. So little had been vandalised. There was no graffiti at all but, he supposed, if you can't trust people who want to be priests. On the other hand there had been that business of the guys throwing stones at the greenhouse in Ardglass. He stood up and looked at himself in a round shaving mirror attached to the wall. It could extend on a metallic lattice arm. One side of the mirror was normal, the other magnified. In the dished side his face looked like a giant's and the pimples on his forehead looked ten times worse. It made him think he needed a shave – salt and pepper hairs on his jaw line. Like a cowboy. This was good – he'd fancy one of these at home. He stroked his chin but could feel little. He flipped the mirror over and there he was – changed back to normal again. He wondered what time it was.

There was a frosted window behind the lavatory. Above it was a smaller one which hinged open. He pushed it outwards and notched the bar on to the outermost hole. All he could see was a brick corner and a bit of pavement with some sweety papers swirling around. So much for the outside world. He sat on the edge of the bath and looked down at the lavatory seat. Why he needed to look underneath it, he'd no idea but he found himself lifting the lid. At the back of the bowl it said ARMITAGE SHANKS. That's what he was doing – he was looking for things to read. He was a fucking compulsive reader. Of simple material. Show me a Cornflakes packet and I'm happy. Or a HP sauce bottle if I'm feeling intellectual. *Cette sauce de haute qualité.* Reading was a way of passing time.

There was a piece of white plastic strapped to the inside of the rim of the toilet bowl with a sky-blue brick in it. It had the texture of melting ice. A little of its antiseptic perfume wafted up. What the fuck was he doing? Sitting in an apprentice priest's toilet staring down the lavatory bowl? He'd have been far better off brazening it out in the English class – telling Wee Jacky the truth. I couldn't get it finished, Father. I'll hand it in tomorrow.

Fuckin Milton. In second year they'd been forced to memorise a sonnet which began 'Cromwell, our chief of men . . .' In an Irish Catholic school? He could *still* remember the fuckin thing, 'who through a cloud not of war only, but detractions rude, guided by faith and matchless fortitude to peace and truth thy glorious way hast ploughed.' Cromwell, instead of paying his men for their looting and burning and murdering, gave them bits of Ireland to keep, in lieu of wages. Martin had learned this, not in school, not from the teacher who made them learn off the poem, but from the man who owned the corner shop on the way to the park. He wondered if he could risk having a cigarette. Blow it out the wee window. Maybe he'd be best to wait until break time.

'All over Cromwell, is my name for him,' the shopkeeper had said. 'He was like a plague all over Ireland. In Drogheda he put three thousand to the sword — then when he discovered people hiding from him in a church, claiming — what is it you claim in a church? — men, women and childer — what did he do? He set alight to it. It was "all over" for them, right enough. The wart-faced bastard. The cruelties of Cromwell . . .' and he'd shake his head as if it was beyond words.

For something to do Martin flushed the toilet. He wondered what time it was now. He was failing miserably to pass the time. He was probably the only guy in the school without a watch. But his mother kept insisting, 'You'll get a watch on your eighteenth birthday and not an hour before.'

'How would I know,' he asked, 'if it was an hour before or not? In *Paradise Lost* God sees everything at once — the past, the present and the future. He's the only one around here who doesn't need a watch.'

'Away and give my head peace.'

Sanctuary. That was what it was called, hiding in a church. Martin wondered if he should go up to the college chapel. Nobody would be there. If he was caught, they couldn't do a thing. It would be a matter between him and his God.

'You can't punish me for praying. I was in the midst of a major spiritual crisis. I had to get it sorted out with my Saviour, English class or no English class.'

It would be more interesting in the chapel. Not that it was entirely uninteresting here.

The only problem was the route, the miles of corridor. He had no way of knowing where Condor was, whether he was on the prowl or not. Or he could be nabbed by another teacher who would then report him to Condor. He was safe enough here. He would be safe enough in the chapel. It was the dash from the sand dunes to the sea was the problem. He'd seen this thing about turtles hatching from the sand in their millions and trying to get into the water before being swallowed by seagulls. He could go along the main corridor but then he could take the first staircase. The big disadvantage of this was that he'd have to pass the Reverend Head's door. If he took the far staircase he'd have to pass the staff room on the first floor, which was worse. Teachers were always coming and going and they'd want to know why he was trailing about the place when he should be in English. In all his years at the school he'd only been to the staff room once with a message. The French teacher, Wee Clo, had opened the door.

'*Un moment*,' he said. Behind him the air was blue with cigarette smoke. Father McGrady was leaning over the billiard table, about to take a shot. Wee Clo snapped the door closed. It was like a photo it was so brief – like the door was the shutter. From inside Martin heard the balls click as Father McGrady played his shot.

Once he was past the Reverend Head's room it was all over – straight into the chapel. He would see the time in the main corridor and that would be a help.

Jesus, he was like Hamlet. Why didn't he just do the thing?

'Right,' he said out loud. He reached to unbolt the lavatory door. It was stiff and when he put pressure on it suddenly it snapped back with a loud metallic crack. It sounded like a gunshot. He put his head out and looked all around. Nobody stirred. The place must have been empty. He climbed the stairs back up out of the Wing, then through the door and into the school corridor. This must have been the route Blaise took the other night.

The fucking clock must have stopped. What was wrong with the bastard? It was only twenty past. He had still ages to put in.

There was nobody about. He walked as quietly and as casually as he could. He could hear Ding-dong's voice teaching History to the first-years. Ding-dong had once sent a first-year boy to the office to ask for a new exercise book. Cuntyballs, the school secretary, had slid the hatch open.

'Who's it for?'

'Mr . . . eh Mr Dong.'

'The reason his nickname is Ding-dong is because his name is Bell. Mr Bell to you. Here.' And he handed over the new exercise book.

Mr Dong – forfuck sake.

Martin heard the clack of a pointer on a blackboard from the next room, then Ned Kelly's voice shouting, '*It's about time . . . I do not believe this.*'

Walking along the corridor past the classrooms was like turning the tuning knob of a radio – you heard only bits and pieces. Martin passed another door. There was nothing but silence. Either the room was empty or it was Condor in charge. In his class boys cowered in their desks. You never knew what he was going to do next. You got the feeling that he would slap you down like a wasp if you annoyed him, even slightly. A door slammed somewhere. Footsteps.

Martin climbed the first staircase two at a time and was out of sight before the person turned on to the main corridor. The upper floor was covered with lino and smelled of polish. All along the right hand side were windows. Martin looked down on to the front quad. In the centre of the tarmac was a fenced-off garden space with a weeping willow in the middle of it. A car was turning. How could he have been in the Wing for only ten minutes? It had seemed like half an hour, at least.

The Reverend Head's room was on his left. Martin found himself holding his breath. He was behaving like a first-year kid. He breathed out. Beside the door stood a large trophy case. There were a lot of silver platters and cups, and medals pinned to boards of green plush. The trophy standing in the centre of the case was Gaelic football's biggest school prize, the McCrory Cup. Beyond the case were framed photographs of winning teams, going back to the beginning of the school. A short flight of stairs and he pushed open the chapel door. The place was empty. The swing door closed behind him with a breathing sound. Made it.

He slid his behind on to the bench seat at the back. There was a kneeler, topped with a rubber pad, which ran the length of the row.

'They have it easy nowadays,' was the kind of thing Mary Lawless would say. 'In my day they made you suffer. Good hard wooden kneelers. Toughen up the oul knees – although they were fierce on the nylons.'

'Sure what would be the point, Father,' said Nurse Gilliland, 'of going to Lough Derg to do penance if it was easy?' Father Farquharson nodded and smiled.

'You might as well go and stay at Mrs Kelly's boarding house in Portstewart,' said Father Farquharson. 'Which reminds me, Mrs Brennan, I have a friend from Dublin coming on a bit of a holiday

— he's an Order priest — a Seven Sorrows man. Very quiet. I wonder would you mind . . . it would only be for a few nights.'

'Oh Father. You know we can't . . .' Father Farquharson waited to hear the reason why.

'The parochial house will be full that week. I must get a No Vacancies sign for the window,' he said.

'Now you've embarrassed me,' said Mrs Brennan. Still Father Farquharson stared at her waiting for an explanation. 'You know I'd be delighted. But we don't have the best of facilities.'

'Goodness gracious, don't let a thing like that worry you. This is a man more of the spirit than the body. And, goodness knows, if he wants a bath he can come round to the parochial house, can't he? He is a great fan of the Desert Fathers. Not too much water there. His name is Father O'Hare — Father Estyn O'Hare.'

'Oh, Father Farquharson, before I forget. I have a wee mass card I want you to sign.'

Father Farquharson gave a brief nod and looked, first down at his shoes, then up to the ceiling. Martin's mother stood in the middle of the room her hands dancing, trying to remember where she'd left the mass card. It was as if her body was going back, doing again all the things she'd done during the past hour. Lifting and laying. Then she dashed off to the kitchen.

'When are the next clerical changes due, Father?' asked Mary Lawless.

'There'll be nothing now till next spring, I'm thinking. Thank God.'

'Are you settled here, Father?'

'As much as I'll ever be.'

The door opened and Mrs Brennan came back in again with the mass card. She handed it to the priest. He unclipped a fountain pen from his inside pocket. The lining of his black suit was silk. He opened the card carefully to sign it and a five pound note nearly slipped off into the hearth. His hand barely touched it but guided it into his trouser pocket. He unscrewed the pen top and added his signature to the inside of the card. He blew a little on the scribbled ink, folded it shut and gave it back to Mrs Brennan.

'Thank you, Father. It's very good of you.'

Father Farquharson didn't say anything. He just gave a kind of embarrassed grin and tried to change the subject by answering Mary Lawless.

'This has been a very good parish for me. By and large.'

Martin knelt down on the rubber kneeler. He tried to pray but it was difficult, knowing that he was skiving class – something he knew to be a sin, however venial. He sat up on the seat again, leaned forward and covered his face with his hands trying to think of words to pray in. He knew his prayer was bad when it had a bargaining element. Just let me get through this forty-minute period and I'll never do this again. Protect me God in Your own house. From those that would persecute me. And beat the living daylights out of me. Allow me this small sin and I will be the better person afterwards. Sanctuary. The sanctuary lamp was lit as always and its flame wavered through the red glass which contained it. Ruby. Red for danger.

Father O'Hare was the most seriously weird priest he had ever met. He had arrived to stay when Martin was ten. Martin remembered that because it was just after he had done the eleven-plus and everybody was saying how young Martin was to be doing it, and him not even eleven yet. Martin's mother had lived in a state of suppressed delight before the visit. She was a great woman for priests. Nothing was too much trouble. Meals were a pleasure to cook, errands were run with gusto, jokes were laughed at. The Victorian jug and basin were resurrected from a back cupboard and Martin was made to carry hot water and soap to the priest's room. The priest remained in bed with the covers up to his chin until Martin left the room.

Martin wasn't sure why but he knew there was nothing his mother liked better than the thought of a priest sleeping in the house. Her happiness was obvious as she moved about, humming a hymn – making the bed, folding pyjamas and tucking them under the pillow, carrying his wash bowl down the stairs and emptying it in the sink.

He was a thin, grey man in his early sixties – barely there. Mary Lawless said of him that if he turned sideways he'd disappear. Martin's mother said she thought that Father Farquharson had invited him on this wee holiday 'to get him out of himself'. The old priest would sit in the corner, his elbows resting on the wooden arms of the armchair and leaning his chin on his joined knuckles. He seemed to be staring at nothing. A total weirdo. Occasionally his jaw moved and he made a little clumping noise with his false teeth. He never read a paper or watched TV. Mrs Brennan wondered if it was saintliness or vacancy. In the end she decided it was depression. Nurse Gilliland agreed with her and for months after his visit she added a prayer to the trimmings of her nightly rosary that it would soon lift.

At the back of the chapel was a painting of the Crucifixion with Our Lady and Mary Magdalene standing at the foot of the cross. It was very old and painted on panels – you could see where they joined halfway up the painting. The varnish had dulled but you could still see the feature the artist had made of Mary Magdalene's yellow hair – full of curls and twists, cascades of it falling over her shoulders.

One year when he was doing art, the art teacher Tommy Cooper had given him the key for the book cupboard in the art room.

'Have a look through some of that stuff, see if it gives you any ideas.' Martin flicked through a book on the history of art. There was a statue of David but he was wearing Indian ink bathing trunks. He tilted the face of the page to the light to see if the ink was thin enough to be transparent. It was matt black, opaque and all he could see was the pattern of the brush marks. On other pages whole pictures were obliterated.

'Sir, what's all this?' he asked, showing a black page.

'It's none of my doing,' said Tommy Cooper.

Martin flicked backwards and forwards.

On the next page there was a print of a strange figure, not covered by ink. It was a naked woman but you couldn't see anything because her body was covered in hair. For a moment he thought it was shading, but no, it was definitely hair. She was surrounded by angels – four of them. On the page following she was there again, held up by two angels this time. He looked at the text below the picture

Mary Magdalene borne aloft by two angels.
Press of Gunter Zaimer, Augsburg 1470–73.

Mary Magdalene wasn't hairy. She was a fallen woman. You had to be normal to be a fallen woman – or nobody would have fallen for you. He looked back at the first print.

Mary Magdalene borne aloft by four angels –
Artists Michael Wolgemut & H. Pleydenwurff.
Press of Anton Kobenberger, Nuremberg 1493.

What was this all about? It said nothing about this in the scriptures. She washed Christ's feet, dried them with her long hair and put ointment on them. But it was a big jump from this to looking like a gorilla.

'Sir, why is Mary Magdalene all hairy?'

'Let me see.' Tommy Cooper leaned over the book and looked.

'Maybe it's shading – cross-hatching. To darken the figure down a bit.'

'They could have used Indian ink – like on the rest of them.'

'Nothing to do with me, Brennan. That's the powers-that-be.'

'Hairy Mary full of grace.'

'There's no need to mock, Brennan. If you want to know more ask one of the priests.'

Outside the sun came out. The chapel's stained glass windows were magnificent. He had never seen such intensity in colour. Someone had said that the colour had such quality because it was layered. A double thickness – blue glass against red glass gave an intense purple. Blue sandwiched with yellow gave a voluptuous green. When the sunlight came through the chapel windows it picked up the colour from the glass and laid it on the floor. Undersea blues, intense ruby reds, violets, celery greens were vivid on the parquet tiles. There was a window depicting St Paul on the Road to Damascus. Saul had fallen and was propped up on one hand, shielding his face with the other from the brightness of the rays coming from around the face of the Lord. From persecutor to apostle in an instant. These windows were so highly prized they had been buried during the war.

There was the loud slam of a door and Martin froze. Fuck. Footsteps pacing to and fro on the wooden boards in the sacristy.

Vamoose. Get the hell out. Still he didn't move. It could be Condor or the Reverend Head. Earlier he had thought of a number of things to say if he was caught in the chapel but all of these now deserted him. He would mumble and blush, stammer something stupid. Probably end up admitting that he was mitching the English class because he hadn't done the homework. Why couldn't he be more like Blaise?

'What are you doing here, boy?'

'I'm checking the stained glass for the efficacy of its waterproof seal,' Blaise would have said. 'For a chemistry experiment. The lead surrounds denature in acid rain.' Or some such.

It wasn't that Martin couldn't think the things up – it was just that he couldn't carry them off. He was a totally bad liar. There was no need to attach him to a lie detector. He just gave the game away. He couldn't make eye contact with whoever was question- ing him, his shoulders drooped, his voice shook. His grammar went to pieces and his sentences stumbled and sounded stupid.

Martin stood. The daffs was the only place left. He tiptoed to the back of the chapel past the Crucifixion and as quietly as he could, opened the door and left. He held the handle from the outside to prevent the door making any noise as it flopped back into place. Still the staircase and corridors were quiet. He would need to get a look at the clock, to see how long he had to go before the bell. When he saw that it was just after half past he could hardly believe it. Another twenty fuckin minutes mooching about. Being a sitting duck.

Walking the corridor like this, if anybody pounced, he was going to the toilet. Or going to the water fountain to get a drink because he felt slightly ill.

When he crossed the yard to the toilets he kept as close as he could to the wall. No one saw him. The daffs, when it was empty, was a strange place. Around the walls were toilet cubicles; in a central island stood a bank of full-length upright urinals. Martin went into a cubicle and closed and barred the door. The one most likely to be around was Joe Boggs – but he was no threat. He was a general handyman and one of his jobs was to keep the toilets clean. He had painted the cubicle doors again and again to cover the obscenities but what had been deeply gouged into the wood with knives and compass points still showed through. Big dicks, huge tits.

The toilet seats had long ago been smashed or pulled off and not replaced. There was no toilet roll left so he used the cardboard tube to wipe the delf rim thoroughly before sitting down. It gave him a strange feeling, a kind of nausea, which made him think he was sitting on a toothless lower jaw. Really squeamish guys squatted on top of the toilet like some kind of shitting bird. He had never actually seen a boy do this but he had seen shoe prints on the delf and had seen the disgusting results of a poor aim.

Martin sat on the toilet, his trousers down, staring around him. Every so often, Condor patrolled the daffs, bending at the waist, checking beneath each cubicle door. If he saw you sitting there with your trousers up he would have every right to demand an explanation. So it was better to have your trousers about your ankles.

When the truly weird Father O'Hare had arrived to stay in their house he had said to Martin, 'I believe you're an altar boy.'

'Yes, Father.'

'Will you serve my mass in the morning?'

'Yes, Father.'

'Seven o'clock. An early start – but it leaves the rest of the day free.'

'But for what?' said Mrs Brennan afterwards to Martin.

In the morning Mrs Brennan fussed around in her dressing gown, getting Martin ready. Martin was still distant with sleep: his actions felt unreal, the sounds he heard were indistinct. When the priest finally came down Mrs Brennan pounced on him.

'Here, let me give you a wee brush,' she said. With two or three deft swipes of the clothes brush she rid his clerical black of dandruff. 'I'll have your breakfast ready when you come back. Then, please God, I'll get a wee run out to nine o'clock mass myself.' She held out his black overcoat, angling the arm holes on to the priest's stiff arms as they pointed backwards. She did all but button it up for him like a child. Then she also swiped the shoulders of the overcoat with the brush.

Each morning of his visit the two walked silently side by side through the dark towards the church. At ten years of age Martin didn't much know what to say. It was really always the grown-up's job to keep the conversation going but Father O'Hare didn't seem interested. He was frail but walked with determination. It was a very cold time of year and there was ice on the puddles. Rather than say something Martin put his weight on one of the ice sheets to let the priest hear the creaking noise it made.

'Keep up, keep up,' was all he said.

At that time of morning there was a congregation of about ten or fifteen, sitting here and there, people mostly by themselves. Men in their overalls on their way to work. Mary Lawless was there and, in the left hand aisle, Nurse Gilliland. The church sounded empty because every sound echoed. The door squeaking open and thudding shut. A man's cough answered by a woman's cough. Footsteps coming up the aisle – loud on the marble, different sounding on the metal grilles of the floor.

On the last morning of his stay, after mass Martin had changed and was in the altar boys' dressing room waiting for Father O'Hare to take off his vestments. The previous two mornings they had walked back home in silence. After a couple of minutes the priest came to the door in his black suit and clerical collar. Martin made to edge past him but the priest barred the way.

'A word, Martin.' He indicated the bench beneath the row of hooks hung with surplices and soutanes. Under it were black gym shoes with names written on their canvas insides. Martin sat down. 'I promised your mother I'd have a word.' Father O'Hare sat down beside him and it seemed very awkward. Martin had never seen a priest on this bench. It had been built low for the boys. Father O'Hare's knees were jutting up and his hands were fidgeting all over the place. He looked at his watch. 'Is there an eight o'clock mass?'

'Yes, Father Farquharson is saying it this week.'

'We'll have to hurry so. What age are you, Martin?'

'Ten and a bit, Father.'

'You know – you know how you are unfortunate enough – not to have a room – forgive me, where you can wash – solely for the purpose of washing. A bathroom. Well your mother has asked me . . . Did you ever hear tell of the Feast of the Circumcision?'

'Yes, Father.'

'Do you know what the Circumcision is?'

'Yes, Father. It's the feast – when it happens. After Christmas.'

118

'But do you know what it is?'

'Yeah.' Martin seemed unsure now.

'The ancient Jewish religion demanded that every boy have his prepuce surgically removed – for hygienic reasons.' Father O'Hare's voice sounded funny – like it was shaking. 'And of course Our Lord Jesus Christ being born into the Jewish faith was no exception. So his prepuce was removed. Indeed it is a matter of some embarrassment to Our Holy Mother the Church that there are some eight shrines in Europe alone dedicated to the Divine Prepuce. Vying with one another – because only one of them can be genuine. The official Church nowadays turns up its nose but there is a great thirst among the laity for relics, for reassurance. And what greater relic could there be than the flesh of Our Blessed Lord and Saviour, Jesus Christ. The Turin Shroud, the one true cross, Veronica's veil – all of them pale into insignificance beside this, the actual flesh.' Martin had never heard him say more than one or two sentences at any one time. But now it seemed impossible to stop him talking. And he was talking very fast.

'My mother'll be waiting, Father.'

'You're right, young man.' He looked at his watch again. 'I don't want to become involved in a whole rigmarole. Eh?' Martin didn't know what to say. 'Part of the problem might really be about boys' hygiene. That's what I promised her good self I would do. Say a few words about that. It can be a terrible trap for germs. Do you understand?'

'What, Father?'

'The prepuce,' said Father O'Hare. 'If your prepuce is quite long. I suppose it'll cause you no problems later on with tightness. All you have to do is pull it back and pop the centre out like a little red acorn. That's where the trouble is – smegma – that's where you have to wash every day. You hear me?'

'Yes, Father.'

'But a demonstration is worth a thousand words. Let's go back into the sacristy. For a little examination. There's a toilet there.' He levered himself up on to his feet and made a sweeping gesture, waving Martin through, like a man bowling. Martin walked ahead of him unsure what this was all about. The toilet door off the

119

sacristy had bubbled opaque glass. Father O'Hare opened the door and looked in.

'Empty.' He smiled. An outer door banged and footsteps approached over the boards of the hallway. The sacristy door opened. It was Father Farquharson.

'Good morning, Estyn. Martin.' He clapped his hands together and complained of the bitter cold. 'How are things?'

'Fine,' said Father O'Hare. The old priest turned around and moved towards the outside door. He beckoned to Martin. Father O'Hare held the sacristy door open for the boy.

'What about the toilet, Father?'

'Just go – if you want to.'

'I don't want to.'

'Oh very well.' There was now irritation in his voice. 'Come along – your mother will have the breakfast out.'

'You're leaving today?' said Father Farquharson.

'I am indeed.'

'I'll come round and see you before you go.'

On the way home very little was said. 'I'll tell your mother we had our little talk. It was her, after all, who asked me to tell you. But, the way things are, I don't think you should report any of our conversation. Women are easily embarrassed by these kind of things, by men's personal hygiene. So promise me. Not a word?'

Martin nodded. Father O'Hare handed him a folded ten shilling note.

'Good boy. You wouldn't want to embarrass that dear mother of yours. She's a living saint.'

Martin had never told a soul about the conversation because he was confused about what had been said. At the time he hadn't a baldy notion what the man was on about. He could hardly remember the words. What kind of praying was Pray Puss? But he knew that something weird had just happened. And he never told his mother about the money.

The white tiles and glass roof of the toilets reflected sounds, gave them a sharp echo, like public swimming baths. Every so often there was a violent hissing from the row of upright urinals in the central island as they rinsed automatically then drained away. The cisterns would begin to refill. Clinking and dribbling. Martin thought there was something incredibly lonely in the sounds. Eventually he heard the break bell ring in the distance.

'Thank God for that,' he said and, at last feeling safe, he stood. He guessed there would be a red weal on his backside and thighs in the shape of a horseshoe. He fixed his trousers, pulled back the bolt and went out into the main area. He lit his cigarette to have it well smoked by the time the scroungers arrived. He had another one in a packet in his breast pocket for the afternoon. Very quickly the daffs began to fill. Various groups tended to stand together – the Gaelic footballers, the hard men, the hobbies crowd. Juniors, like Maguire, came in and messed around. Maguire lived near Martin and felt it gave him the right to talk to him even though he was years below him.

'Brennan, give us a drag.'

'If you can't afford them, son, don't smoke.'

But he offered the cigarette to the boy. Maguire inhaled once, and then again quickly.

'Easy – don't make a fuckin furnace out of it.'

Martin took his cigarette back. The others began to arrive and light up. Brian Sweeny lit a tiny butt with a single match which he struck between the glazed tiles.

'Look at the size of that.'

'Hard times,' said Brian. 'Singe the hairs up your nose – lighting it.' The noise level inside the toilet block rose as everybody shouted to be heard above the noise. The air was *filled* with blue-grey cigarette smoke. Martin edged his hip onto a washbasin and tapped his cigarette into it. The ash went black where it came in contact with water. Kavanagh joined them.

'Why did you not turn up at English?' he said.

'I hadn't the homework done,' said Martin. 'I hate that.'

'What?'

'Not being able to say, I'll hand it in tomorrow. He makes you feel like some kind of a brainless cunt if you don't hand it in when he wants it.'

'He's not so bad,' said Kavanagh.

'I have just spent the longest forty minutes of my life. Sitting around in toilets all morning.'

'Did your bowels move?' said Kavanagh.

'Where's Blaise?'

'He's on his way.' The Gaelic football players were making a lot of noise in the right hand corner. One of them, a very small guy called Corscadden, was doing exercises, trying to chin the door frame ten times. The others were counting aloud, urging him on. Blaise joined them by the washbasins. 'Do you see your wee man over there?' said Kavanagh. 'The one chinning the bar? He's so wee that when he went to see the careers officer the guy recommended him for a bonsai lumberjack.'

After the joke nobody said anything for a while. Blaise had his hands in his pockets and he was leaning his back against the tiled wall. He said, 'Compared to Simeon Stylites we're having a ball.'

'Who?'

'Who him?'

'Him – a mad medieval fucker who stood on a sixty-foot pillar most of his life. For the greater glory of God.'

'Are you sure it wasn't Nelson?'

'Or a stand–in for him.'

'No this was a bit before his time. He stood on a pillar as penance. For most of his life.'

'Are you kidding?'

'I kid you not. He said mass up there. People flocked to see him.'

'Did he come down for a crap?'

'Holy men sublimate it.'

'Remember the joke about the oul boy in hospital shitting himself and trying to save face – rolling it up and flicking it round the ward to get rid of it.'

'This is a total non-sequitur.'

'And he offers everybody a ciggie. *If they're anything like your Maltesers you can smoke them yourself.*'

'What has that to do with anything?' said Blaise.

'A boy on top of such a pillar,' said Kavanagh, 'would be well placed to commit suicide.'

'God is the Great Lie,' said Blaise, 'and we are the generation who found it out.'

'You don't believe in God?' said Martin.

'You grasp things so quickly,' said Blaise. He turned to Kavanagh. 'The whole of religion is balanced on a pin point.'

'Which is?'

122

'That it's true. And it's obviously not.'

'How can you prove that?' said Kavanagh.

'I don't have to prove or disprove anything. Nor explain anything. I have no evidence there is a God. I have no evidence of an afterlife.'

'What about geniuses like Thomas Aquinas and . . . and . . .'

'It was the thinking of the time. I mean every genius in the world accepted that things fell at different speeds according to their weight until Galileo came along. Then he said, no – let's drop a couple of things off the leaning tower of Pisa.'

'And what about the scriptures?' said Martin.

Blaise gave a dismissive slow shrug then said, 'It's the believers who have all the explaining to do. Science is about evidence and repeatability. Except when it comes to God. Then you apply a completely different set of rules.' Kavanagh seemed wary about launching into a full-scale argument. Martin knew he couldn't win against Blaise. Nobody said anything for a while.

'Fuck theology,' Blaise said, 'we need to think of a way to get into that store room.'

'Which?' Blaise looked at Martin and raised his eyebrow.

'And then what?' asked Kavanagh.

'Then we'd go to work on how to open the envelope without anybody finding out,' said Martin.

'I've already done that. Last night Condor took study . . .'

'Condor!'

'. . . and he walked up and down all night reading the breviary. He had a bunch of papers and stuff sitting on his desk and I spotted the Greek and Latin past papers. In their original envelopes. So when his back was turned I borrowed one.'

'You did not.'

'Ya bastard . . .'

'It's a water-based gum. So we could easily steam open the bottom of the envelope – not the top, it would be too easily noticed. Get a paper out, maybe get Martin here to photograph it. And we all pass with superb results.'

'This is a bit . . .'

'What?' said Blaise.

'A bit fuckin tricky,' said Martin. 'Morally speaking.'

'Kavanagh?'

'I dunno,' said Kavanagh. 'I agree. It doesn't seem entirely fair.'

'These exams are set and examined by Englishmen,' said Blaise. 'British men from the North of Ireland – it's total fuckin cultural imperialism – all they do is ape the English system. Any Irishman worth his salt would fuck these exams up the bum, if he could.'

'What a weird line of logic.'

'Imagine what would happen if you did really well,' said Blaise. 'Top marks would take you where?'

'Into Oxford or Cambridge—'

'The home of the British establishment.'

'We're at a Catholic school in Ireland but its aspirations are to be an English public school.'

'You *sound* like you've been to one.'

'I cannot help the way I speak. No more than you can. The way you think is far more important – although in your case, Martin, that doesn't seem to make a lot of difference.'

'How do you figure we're like an English public school?'

'We are not *like* it. Far from it. We are only *trying* to be like it. Out of sheer fuckin envy. That English teacher what's-his-name raves about authors like Hardy and Evelyn Waugh and Rupert Brooke – stands the village clock at ten to three? They think they're creating an Enid Blyton world.'

'Don't you dare say anything bad about our Enid,' said Kavanagh.

'We study Latin and Greek. You told me about learning that Cromwell sonnet. Right wing, establishment values. The whole aim of the school is to get one or two people into Oxford or fucking Cambridge. The rest can become Christian gentlemen in the lower reaches of the Northern Ireland Civil Service or Catholic teachers.'

'And what's wrong with that?' said Martin. 'My Great-Aunt Annie said *If you work hard at school, son, you'll get a job in out of the weather.* The ideal job, according to her, was to get something behind a post office counter.'

'For you, Martin, she was over-ambitious.'

'Fuck off.'

'The establishment have a built-in advantage. All we're doing is correcting the imbalance. The establishment have made us feel this way – given us a conscience – to stop us beating them. They want to hold on to the power. The justification is that equality of opportunity does *not* exist. There are guys at public school, guys with extra tuition, guys whose da doesn't get drunk and beat the fuck out of them.'

'That's crap and you know it.'

'Take the Qualifying – the eleven-plus for fucksake – to this day in the North of Ireland if you're not a success at eleven years of age you're a failure for life. Getting a look at the exam papers *beforehand* just evens things out a bit. Some of us are smart enough *and* responsible enough to be able to make up our own rules. Having more money is a way of cheating. I am born with more money than you – therefore I can have more things than you. And it follows I will have more power than you. What idiot says the system is fair? Learning to survive it is more important. What we're doing is exploring an alternative way of passing – a way that requires every bit as much intelligence. And a few other qualities as well. Are you game?'

6.   An Afternoon in the Waterworks

Martin had to stoop to get through the door into the room where the final-year Religious Knowledge classes took place. It was a drab room full of empty cupboards in the oldest part of the school, up a winding back stair. The windows were of grey ribbed glass because they overlooked part of the convent next door. The class was taken by Father Barry, the Spiritual Director. He was quite young, not long ordained. He wore a black soutane and shoulder cape. The Roman collar he wore exposed just an inch of white and it reminded Martin of a baby's single tooth.

They heard his footsteps on the stairway before he ducked into the room and recited the first part of the Hail Mary. The class recited their part. He apologised for being late – he was a little breathless for having come up the stairs at speed. They could see that whatever had kept him late had annoyed him. He paced slowly up and down in front of the class. His hands were joined behind his back. Kavanagh said, 'It's OK Father you can be as late as you like.'

Father Barry didn't smile – as he usually would have – but began, 'You are going to have to leave here and go out to face the world very soon. Most of you will get a job of some sort. And this time next year you'll be working among people of other faiths, other beliefs. It ill behoves us to ignore this fact.' He sat down, put his head back and looked at the ceiling. 'We should be able to defend our Catholic faith. To die for it, if need be. To defend it – not aggressively but quietly and with dignity. So in our last term here we are going to examine some basic tenets of Catholicism with a view to defending them against attack. This will necessarily expose some of you to arguments against our religion which you may not have previously heard. But you're big enough and ugly enough.' He smiled at his own joke. 'Do you think you'd win an argument with a Presbyterian who knew his Bible inside out? Do you know what you'd say to an agnostic? Do you even know what an agnostic is?' He stared down at his polished shoes while he waited for an answer. He pushed his horn-rimmed specs higher on his nose with his finger. 'Would you have any difficulty, Mr Kavanagh?' Kavanagh moved in his seat, as if to speak but nothing came out. 'How confident would you be, Mr Brennan? In a coffee bar perhaps – getting into a debate. Would you be able to acquit yourself well?'

'It would depend on the question, Father.'

'OK. How would you convince a man – be he Muslim, Hindu, Jew or Baptist – that the Catholic Church was the one, true Church?' Martin sat there, staring ahead. He hadn't a clue where to begin. 'Anybody?' The Spiritual Director looked around the class then gave an audible sigh.

'Or could you, for instance, prove to anyone's satisfaction that the present Pope, the Vicar of Rome, is Christ's representative on earth?'

Martin had been thinking of ways to answer the first question – and this second question threw him. He knew that if he tried to answer there would be those in the class who would laugh at his efforts. *The gaper*, indeed. He closed his mouth and tried to formulate the beginning of a sentence.

'Anybody?' Father Barry looked around the class, as if his head was on a tripod. Panning to the left, then all the way round to the right. 'How is it, in this school I see boys talking all day long – they even talk behind their hands in class – why is it then, when you ask them to talk *officially*, they clam up? Not a word when it comes to Religion? Not a word when it comes to moral issues. Classes like this make me despair.' He gazed directly at Martin and said, 'You're all old enough to know what we're here for. You're all old enough to know that there are problems and philosophies that need to be talked through. You're an intelligent bunch – the *crème de la crème*. Why won't you do it here? I bet you'll do it after class. In the daffs.' Everybody smiled at him using the school word.

There was the sound of footsteps on the stairs and a knock at the door. Father Barry strode to open it. It was a first-year sent to fetch him for a phone call.

'I will not be long,' said the Spiritual Director. 'I want you to conduct yourselves with decorum in my absence. In other words – act your age.' And he was away clattering down the stairs.

The boys heaved a sigh at the prospect of a semi-free period. They fell into relaxed poses and yawned. Some put their feet up on the desks. Different groups started up conversations in different parts of the room. Sometimes in moments of silence things were said between groups. Boys kept looking at the time as the period ticked away.

'There's hardly any time left.'

'Ya beaut.'

'What does he think we could get up to?' said Kavanagh.

'Blow the place up,' said Sharkey. 'Like Nelson's Pillar.' He mimicked an explosion with his mouth. 'Wasn't that brilliant to bring it down like that – in the middle of O'Connell Street.' There was a lot of agreement and chuckling.

A voice said, 'It was stupid.' They all turned to look. It was Blaise. 'Somebody could have been killed.'

'Fuck off. It was brilliant,' said Sharkey. 'The IRA are geniuses at that kind of thing. Ireland needs more people like that. People who aren't afraid to commit themselves to getting rid of the British. What we need here is a just war. Like Cyprus.'

'Get a United Ireland,' said the bonsai lumberjack.

'Nobody *seriously* talks about such things any more,' said Blaise. 'Nationalism helps no one. Violence helps no one. You're going back to the Dark Ages.'

'This province was hatched in the twenties by Pro British, Unionist-Orange violence.' Sharkey was becoming intense. 'So, it follows that the only way to end it is by the use of force – the more the better, and the sooner the better. The second-class citizens should become first-class warriors.'

'What grown-up did you hear saying that?' said Blaise. 'A United Ireland is not worth a single fucking life.' Sharkey turned to stare at Blaise and curled his lip. 'As Dr Johnson said, "Patriotism is the last refuge of a scoundrel." ' As Blaise said this he was fiddling with his fingers. He pretended to fold them away but left two of them extended in Sharkey's direction. He motioned them slightly upwards. Sharkey half rose out of his desk.

'Is this how we conduct ourselves?' said Martin.

'And so, folks, the discussion ended with blood on the floor,' said Kavanagh putting on the voice of a commentator and holding up a pretend microphone to his mouth.

'And I know whose,' said O'Grady, one of the Sharkey camp.

Footsteps on the stairs prevented Sharkey getting right out of his seat. He stared at Blaise and Blaise stared back. Father Barry bowed his head and came back into the room.

'Where were we?' Nobody answered. 'Yes, that reminds me. I was just decrying your inability to contribute anything to our debate. In the little time left to us today is there anything of a spiritual nature *you* would like to discuss?'

There was a long tense silence. There was still an atmosphere of threat in the air. Sharkey was looking round at Blaise. Blaise raised his eyebrow. Father Barry allowed the silence to continue in order to embarrass someone into saying something. He pointedly sat down on his chair as if to say I can wait for ever. But everybody was hiding, looking down at their desks. Father Barry leaned back, put his hands behind his head. Then somebody cleared his throat and began speaking.

'Father, why not begin at the beginning.' It was Blaise.

'A good place to start. To whom am I talking?'

'Blaise Foley, Father.'

'That's right. You're welcome. And you were saying?'

'We were talking about this earlier. In the daffs. If we begin at the beginning and discover that there is *no* God then that'll save us a lot of work.' There was an amazing silence in the room. Somewhere distantly a door slammed. In the convent somebody was washing cutlery. Martin looked at Kavanagh. Kavanagh looked at Martin and made a face which said, I cannot believe he just said that.

'Go on,' said the Spiritual Director.

'And if there is no God then we can just dismiss the rest of it.' Father Barry's lips seemed to have got thinner. He took his hands from behind his head and placed them on his knees. Blaise paused a long time before he spoke again. 'It seems to me that there are two ways of thinking in this school. There is the scientific way — we go into laboratories and do experiments — we measure and weigh. We gather evidence. Science is about evidence and observation. Science is about repeatability. But in the same school we walk from the laboratory to this classroom and the approach to everything changes. In here we speculate and wonder. This is called metaphysics. And we've just come from physics. We can't measure God and the reason why we can't measure God is because he doesn't exist.'

The Spiritual Director took off his glasses and began polishing them with his white linen hanky.

'Anybody?' he said.

Nobody moved. Nobody spoke.

'Measuring God is a nice idea. But God is not for the measuring, He's for worshipping. An entirely different proposition. An entirely different dimension. It's like trying to measure how loud a sound is with a weighing machine. Or measuring the amount of love we have with a ruler.'

Blaise was trying to speak but Father Barry went on. 'Descartes – one of the greatest minds of all time – said that the human body may be regarded as a hugely complicated machine but it only becomes a person when it is joined to an incorporeal soul. The body bit we can measure; the other we can't.' Blaise opened his mouth but Father Barry was not finished. 'But I suppose in a way you are right. Kant would say that there is no rational argument to prove the existence of God. "I had to remove *knowledge* to make way for *faith*," he says. The spiritual derives not from deductive logic but from personal experience – a kind of Christian existentialism – which you, Foley, are obviously and sadly lacking . . .'

In the distance the bell rang. 'Another day, Mr Foley, we shall discuss this at greater length. And I would appreciate it if the rest of you could think of something to contribute to the arguments.' He stood up and swept from the room, almost forgetting to duck his head on the way out.

It was lunch time. The classroom began to empty. Sharkey coincided with Blaise going through the door.

'Poncy cunt.'

'That's a good argument,' said Blaise. Sharkey pushed Blaise's shoulder, thrust him back against the jamb of the door.

'Hey – fuck off,' said Blaise.

Sharkey cocked his fist but Kavanagh grabbed it and pulled them apart. Kavanagh's height and weight meant he was in charge. He pushed Sharkey on ahead, down the corridor and held

Blaise behind him. Sharkey sneered at Blaise, 'You watch yourself, ya poncy cunt. You have it coming to you. Your mates won't always be around.'

Blaise had gone ashen. They walked out into the sunlight of the yard.

'That always makes me so angry.' Blaise sat down on the ground with his back to the wall and knotted his fists in front of him. 'Violence always wins in the short run.'

'Sharkey is a complete wanker,' said Kavanagh.

'Are you OK?' asked Martin.

'Yeah.' Martin and Kavanagh hunkered down beside Blaise, one on each side.

'Hey, it's really warm.' Kavanagh closed his eyes and put his head back.

'Sharkey's a fuckin tit,' said Martin. 'Take no notice of him.'

'It's nice to know he considers us mates,' said Blaise. He made a chicken-like gesture with his elbows, hitting both of the boys at once. They elbowed him back. 'You know what I think,' said Blaise. 'I think we should take the rest of the day off. Stroll out into the world. Leave this place to get on with the business of indoctrination.'

'Sounds good to me.' Martin also turned his face up to the sun. 'Yeah — into town?'

'Naw, town is crap,' said Kavanagh. 'What about the Waterworks?'

'That's very close to my home base,' said Martin. 'My ma or some of her oul biddy friends might see me. And I gave her my word I'd work my bollicks off.'

'Nobody'll see you.'

'Maybe we could do some work?'

'Aye — that'll be right.' Kavanagh laughed.

It must have been the fat girl's day off. Or else she was out the back peeling spuds. They got sausage suppers and walked up the Antrim Road eating them out of bags. Martin led them to the side of the road farthest from his street. He kept ducking down into his collar and staring at the ground. Blaise laughed at him.

'Your mother must be some machine,' he said.

'It's too near the exams,' Martin said. 'And I'm on my word of honour.'

They made it to the Waterworks without meeting anyone who knew them. It was a park but not a park, an old reservoir open to the public. Inside the gateway was a large noticeboard displaying the Bye-Laws. Blaise stopped in front of it – his head back, looking up. Every line of its small print began with DO NOT. There were two hundred and forty-eight things you couldn't do.

'It's like school,' said Kavanagh.

'And that doesn't include the serious things, like calumny and murder,' said Blaise.

'No mention of open air wanking, is there?' said Martin.

'Why? Do you want to indulge?'

'Fuck off.'

'Did you hear about the complete wanker?' said Kavanagh. 'Somebody stuck a label on his dick – *For external use only.*'

There were three ponds at different heights separated by grassy slopes and waterways. The lowest was more a river than a pond, a sluice disappearing down into a black underground tunnel. Because it was overlooked by the road, old prams and trolleys had been thrown down and remained there as rusting barriers gathering other junk. Martin had frequently seen rats there. They walked up steps to the middle level, a model boating pond – a rectangular expanse of water surrounded by concrete paths. A number of grown men were sailing model yachts from one side to the other. The boats looked good, their white sails at a tangent to the water. The top corners of the middle pond were always full of floating debris: cigarette butts, sweet papers, glass bottles, sticks and grass. In the autumn, sour stolen apples with one bite out of them bobbed in these corners. If the day was windy, brownish foam lathered up from the choppy waves and covered everything in the corners with a frothy scum.

'During the war,' said Martin, 'the Germans thought it was the docks and bombed the fuck out of it – including the houses all round. My mother's area.'

The uppermost pond was large enough to be called a lake. It had fish in it and there was always a big flock of swans drifting about, white against the dark of the water. From a distance their thin necks created intricate patterns, lowering and lifting, looping to feed beneath the surface, turning to preen beneath their wings. Martin loved to watch them take off, running with those flat webbed feet, the splashes further and further apart until there was no splash and the bird was up, its neck arrowing into the air in front of it, its wings creating that whoop sound against the air.

'Have you ever seen them taking off?' said Martin. The two others nodded.

'It's a bit of a slap dash,' said Blaise.

From the top pond the view was of the green hills which surrounded the city. Black Mountain, Divis, Squires Hill, Cave Hill with Napoleon's Nose obvious from this angle – an emperor lying on his back staring at the sky.

There was a tractor cutting the grass at the far side of the lake and the smell drifted across, mixed with the brackish smell of the water. On this side of the pond the grass had not yet been cut: when they walked down to the water's edge it was up to their knees. Kavanagh spread his blazer to sit on. The others did the same. The long grass trapped underneath gave a pleasant springiness to the material when they first lay down. The stones beneath the surface of the water were not like natural stones but octagons and lumpy pentagons, covered with brown underwater moss, like fine hair, which waved as the water moved. The water made continual clucking noises not far from their feet. The breeze rippled the surface. There was a Waterworks guy in overalls rowing a small boat near the swans. They could hear the dull thumping as he shipped his oars at one point. They heard it fractionally later than they saw it. The sun was warm, now that they were down out of the wind. Martin pulled a stalk of grass and began to chew the white sweetish stem.

'Hey, this beats school.'

'Anything beats that place.' Blaise lay flat looking at the sky. A fish splashed not far from the edge with a slap. Martin had noticed about Blaise that he rarely laughed. He said funny and outrageous things but didn't laugh at them. Occasionally he smiled. And it was good to see him when this happened.

'Did you see Father Barry's face this morning when you said – about there being no God,' said Martin. 'He nearly shit a brick.'

'I thought he took it quite well,' said Kavanagh. 'An older priest would have put an arm lock on you and marched you straight to the Reverend Head's room – henceforth to be expelled.'

'Who's Kant?' said Martin.

'A philosopher,' said Blaise.

Kavanagh put on a posh English voice and said, 'He won't be a stewpid facking Kant then.'

'No indeed,' said Blaise. 'A man rowing a boat.'

'So?'

'What's so good about a man rowing a boat?' said Martin.

'It's a good thing to watch. It's a good image.'

'What's it an image of?'

'Nothing. Just a good visual image.'

'I thought an image had to be like something. Like something else. *One of the dominant images in "Macbeth" is of food and feasting.*'

'And?'

'And what?'

'And what else? You said it had to be like something. What is food and feasting like – in *Macbeth*?'

Martin shrugged.

'Normality. Banquo's ghost fucks everything up.'

'*You have displaced the mirth,*' snarled Kavanagh, '*broke the good meeting, with most admired disorder.*'

'OK – it's not Banquo who fucks things up, it's Macbeth,' said Blaise. He too was chewing at the stem of a piece of grass now, biting fragments off it and spitting them out. 'We are all like a man rowing a boat. We have our backs to the way we're going. We can't look ahead, can't see the future. All we can see is the past behind us.'

'Very good,' said Kavanagh. 'But not so the canoeist.' They all laughed.

Blaise joined his hands and cradled them behind his head and said, 'Where do you think we'll be three or four years from now?'

'What a crass question,' said Martin.

'It'll be easier looking back. Three or four years from now you'll say – remember that day we mitched off to the Waterworks.' They thought about this in silence. Clouds covered the sun and their shadow could be seen moving on the hills. The water sounded continually at the lake edge.

After a while Kavanagh asked Blaise, 'So what's it like to be a boarder?'

'The fuckin pits.' Blaise wrinkled his nose. 'The place is full of ganches from the country. They'd believe anything. In the Big Dorm there's supposed to be a ghost cubicle – Number 13 – it's never used. A guy in the 1930s or '40s from Rasharkin, his da was a rich farmer and the boy was gambling too much, getting the day-boys to put bets on for him. Eventually he topped himself – hung himself with his football laces.' Blaise smiled. 'He took his own life while the balance of his bank was disturbed.' They all laughed.

'What's the food like?'

'They've these teapots with a handle fore and aft. They put the sugar and milk in first – it's totally disgusting.'

Just then two young mothers with pushchairs approached along the path. Kavanagh came up off his elbow and Martin's neck lengthened. Both boys followed them with their eyes. Blaise remained flat out. The women were wearing short skirts and both had good legs. They were only a few years older than the boys.

'Hey Blaise, wait till you see this.' Blaise raised his head, bent his neck only.

'Women with prams?' He sounded incredulous.

'The one nearest us is a beaut,' said Martin.

'They're both beauts,' said Kavanagh.

When they had gone past on the path above, the women stopped and the boys clearly heard one of them saying, 'Would you look at the state of that?' She bent over and wiped her baby's face with a white handkerchief. 'I don't know how he does it. A mucky wee pup.' Bending, she bared the backs of her thighs.

'Jesus . . .'

'Fuck me . . .'

Blaise did not move. He said, 'You guys are pathetic.' The women did not even glance at the schoolboys sprawled on the grass by the water.

'Oh I just love that H women have at the back of their knee – like goalposts,' said Kavanagh. 'It's truly beautiful.'

'Yeah, yeah,' Martin laughed, recognising what he was saying.

'The only truly beautiful thing I ever saw was . . .' Blaise waited.

'What?'

'Go on.'

'. . . a boy called McAllister.'

'Steady on.'

'Explain yourself, young man.'

'I was in the gym one day in my last school,' said Blaise, 'skiving as usual – they put you on top of the wall-bars when you have an excuse. Jesus I hate gym. Anyway there was this boy McAllister and he was beside a vault horse – one of those incredibly ugly things, square leather body, four legs, one sticking out of each corner – and sunlight came in the upper windows and hit him. He was blond with brown eyes. He was wearing a white T-shirt. And I think that was the most beautiful thing I have ever seen. Him in the sunlight.'

'Hey, I think we have to be wary of this guy,' said Martin.

'No – no, you've got it all wrong. It wasn't sexy. It was just simply beautiful. If you can't distinguish those two things then . . .' Blaise shrugged, 'you're a dumbfuck.'

'It takes all sorts,' said Kavanagh.

'If you were given the choice of going to bed with one of those women who just went past – the beaut, if you fancied her – or that guy McAllister – which would it be?'

'You don't need to ask.'

'Which would it be?'

'If you have to ask the question,' said Blaise, 'you wouldn't understand the answer.'

'You *are* a homo.'

'Certainly not.'

'Gentlemen, gentlemen,' said Kavanagh. He drew himself up to make a statement. 'There is no man in the world however handsome or attractive I would ever go to bed with. And there is no woman under – say thirty – no matter what state she was in that I *wouldn't* go to bed with – apart from my immediate family.'

'Why?' said Blaise. 'What's wrong with them?'

'Fuck off, Mr Foley.' Kavanagh waved his arms and shouted at the top of his voice: '*Your wives, your daughters, your matrons and your maids could not fill up the cistern of my lust.*'

'Steady on, man. Maybe that's what the H at the back of the knee stands for,' said Martin.

'Hoor?' said Kavanagh.

'Only if you can't spell properly,' said Blaise.

'Holiness, probably.'

'It's not long since those girls were at St Dominic's.'

'Aye, that's probably where they got pregnant,' said Martin. 'My dearly beloved mother says if there were no bad women then there'd be no bad men.' He put on a scrawny voice to imitate her. He plucked a yellow dandelion and looked at the stem. Almost immediately it oozed a circle of milky stuff.

'*Thee* most important event in the life of a young man is the loss of his virginity.' Kavanagh winked at Blaise. 'It certainly was for me.'

'You're taking the piss,' said Martin.

'I am not.'

'Who was it then?'

'It would be ungallant of me to reveal the lady's name.' Kavanagh paused. 'Or names.'

'She had several names?' said Blaise. Kavanagh laughed and shook his head. 'The best loss of virginity story I know also concerns a woman with many names. St Wilgefortis or Uncumber or Liberata — it's not recorded why she had so many names. She was the daughter of the king of Portugal and had taken a vow of virginity. Anyway her old man wanted her to marry the king of somewhere else and she prayed like mad. God's answer was to make her grow a beard overnight. And seeing his fiancée with a beard made the king of somewhere else fuck off back home. Pronto.'

'Nice one.'

'And the king of Portugal was so mad at his daughter he had her crucified.'

'Even nicer one.'

'So if you ever see a crucifix with a bearded woman on it — that's who it is. If you can remember one of her bloody names.'

The sun was hot. Kavanagh stripped off his shirt and lay back. His body was white except for the darker red in a V at his throat. He joined his hands behind his head.

'This is the life.'

'Speaking of hair. Look at the armpits.'

'So?'

'Italian women don't shave under their arms,' said Martin. 'It's weird.'

'I think it's sexy,' said Kavanagh. 'Like going about with a couple of spare cunts.'

Blaise smiled. 'That's what I have to do,' he said. 'Knock about with you two.' They all rolled about laughing in the grass. Martin raised his head and looked for the women with their babies. They had reached the far side and he could still hear their voices faintly across the water and the squeak of the springs of one of the pushchairs.

'How do you know . . . you know . . . ?'

'I'm not with you, young Brennan.'

'How do you know . . . how?'

'How to what?'

Martin nodded at the two women.

'To do it?' Kavanagh chuckled and plucked a stalk of grass for himself. 'Instinct. The old stag in all of us. Nature just takes over — at least that's what I've always found.'

'You're taking the piss.'

'A bit of advice, Brennan, from a more experienced man. When you're doing it don't forget the face,' said Kavanagh. 'Pay attention to her face — and the rewards will be rich.'

'Gee thanks,' said Martin. He made snorting noises and went on chewing his grass. 'Who taught you to wipe your arse?' Blaise and Kavanagh both looked at him. 'It's a serious educational question,' said Martin. 'It was a great-aunt of mine who taught me.'

'She was great if she taught you that.'

'To double over the paper,' Martin went on, ignoring what the others said. 'To wipe up and not down. How many sheets. Did you ever meet anyone who used just the one slice? A single sheet of *Medicated with Izal Germicide*. Of course you never. Everybody always doubles it — folds it over. Are you going to be the one brave enough to say that's strong enough just by *looking* at it. That's safe?'

'Safe?'

'To stop the old finger going right through. Because that's the fear. The brown finger. Aw fuck. And the scrubbing with the nailbrush.' He squirmed and writhed on the grass holding his right hand at arm's length with his left. 'And the staying as far away from the finger as possible. You don't want to be on the same side of the street as your hand for most of the week. Did anybody ever teach you?'

'I can't remember,' said Kavanagh. 'I'm sure my technique has improved since I was a two-year-old. But I don't remember diagrams or anything. What about you, Foley?'

'I haven't passed a motion since I was born.' Blaise didn't raise his head. 'And did you know that Arabs wipe their arses with stones?' He paused for a moment. 'Maybe it's more correct to say "Arabs wipe their arse – singular – with stones." Any Arab has only one arse.'

'Of course the stones would be plural, too.' Kavanagh scratched his armpit. 'As the lad said, who ever heard of anybody using just the one slice of paper.'

'They'd be very hard to flush away,' said Martin.

'Aye, I've done ones like that too,' said Kavanagh.

'Anyway – this was not the question I was asking,' said Martin. 'What I want to know is how do you know about the big one?' There was silence. 'Have you done it yet, Kavanagh?'

'You're always asking me that.'

'Because you never tell me the answer.'

'It's for me to know and for you to find out.'

'Aw fuck – you sound like one of my mother's oul-biddy friends. Blaise?'

'No – whatever it is you're talking about.'

'It's a matter of definition,' said Kavanagh. 'How you define *it*.'

'You know what I mean. For fucksake . . .'

'We've all had a range of experience. The day you first touch mammary, the day you first get your hand on *it*. Did I tell you about the nosy bastard of a priest quizzing me in confession? After I said I touched this girl one night he says, "Was she wet?" nearly panting through the grille, he was. Slavering like. And I says, "No, Father, we had an umbrella." They all laughed but Martin wasn't too sure about what was funny. And he didn't want to ask any more questions. To betray himself.

'OK. I tell you what,' said Kavanagh. 'The night we get it – inside – lock, stock and barrel – we phone each other.'

'So you *haven't* got it yet,' said Martin, pointing dramatically at him. 'You could always start with the fat girl in the chippy.'

'Isobel?'

'She adores you.'

'I think I'll leave her for you, Martin. But I'm beginning to agree with Blaise,' said Kavanagh. 'You just don't listen. After the full works – on the phone.'

'That's probably what I'd have done anyway,' said Martin.

'So the pact is – when you get off her – you get on the phone. Dismount and dial. Within reason, manners permitting. I kid you not. Any time of the day or night – even if it's three in the morning – wherever you are in the world.' Kavanagh kicked Blaise's shoulder. 'Whatever age you may be.'

'I'm on,' said Martin. Blaise just snorted. Kavanagh started laughing.

'I can just imagine the scene. My old man has answered the phone, the mother is in her nightie on the landing, listening over the banisters. *Jesus Mary and Joseph – somebody's dead. Why else would anybody be phoning at this hour.*' He made as if to cover the mouthpiece with his hand and look up at Mrs Kavanagh on the landing: '*It's Martin. He's just got his hole.*

Oh thanks be to God, says the mother.'

'And maybe when *you* phone to tell *me* I'm out and there's one of my ma's supper evenings going on with Father Farquharson and all. *I'm afraid Martin's out* – my mother has a very polite voice on the phone. *Can I take a message?*

Yeah – just tell him I got my hole.

Who'll I say called?

Cardinal Kavanagh.'

Kavanagh interrupted, 'Fuck you. At least give me some credit – His Holiness, the Pope.'

'Would you like Martin to phone you back, Holy Father?'

'Naw,' said Kavanagh. 'I'm saying seven o'clock mass in St Peter's in the morning. I need to get some shut-eye. If he's free, maybe Martin would like to be altar boy?'

'Night on a Bare Mountain Lassie,' said Blaise. He was lying on his back squinting through one eye at the hills. 'It really does look like Napoleon's nose from this angle. The Emperor. So, speaking of pacts – are you gentlemen game for this exam thing? How to cheat the system that cheats you.' Nobody answered him. Martin felt his stomach sink. He didn't want to lose face. He was continuing because he didn't know how to stop continuing.

'Well?'

'Yeah,' said Kavanagh, 'provided we don't get caught.'

'Is there any way we could cover ourselves?' said Martin. 'Make out like it was a joke – a student prank? Maybe write a letter to the authorities and post it just before we do the business. If we get caught we can say it was a joke – we're stealing these papers because we want to point out it's an unfair system.'

'Crap,' said Blaise. 'Then they'd know and they'd cancel the exam. Everybody'd have to re-sit. We'll do it so that nobody'll know a thing about it. Except us. And we'll get good results. We'll get the best fucking results ever seen. Which is no more than we deserve. Being bright boys. Eh, Martin?'

'Quit taking the piss.'

'But how do we get into that room?' said Kavanagh. The sun had gone behind a big cloud. Kavanagh's skin had come up in goose-bumps. He put his shirt back on again but didn't button it.

'How do you get into *any* room?' said Blaise.

'Open the door.'

'You need a key. Who has keys for that room?'

Martin and Kavanagh shrugged.

'Joe Boggs,' said Martin. 'That's where he keeps his cleaning stuff.'

'So what do we do? Pinch that huge big bunch of keys off him? And then stand in the corridor trying each one till we get the right one?'

'I've been in Condor's room. He has a key cupboard on his wall.'

'Tell us more.'

'Every key in the school should be in it.'

'How do we get in there?' said Blaise.

'Fucking Condor's room?'

'He takes you in there to thump you; for smoking. At least he did me. He raided the daffs last year. About ten of us. Up to his room. And . . .'

'Wait till you hear this,' said Kavanagh.

'. . . the bastard lights his pipe and says *I will go on caning you*

141

until this goes out and he walks up and down the line thumping us, puffing away at this fucking Sherlock Holmes pipe.'

'The man's a psychopath. Get to the point,' said Blaise.

'Condor scares the shit out of me – he's a complete bastard and he was working his way round to me. Thump – thump – thump. I remember every fuckin detail. I was *so* angry. The smell of that tobacco – I usually like tobacco but as he was reading us the riot act, giving us the oul fuckin tired dressing down, he was hoaking out the pipe into an ashtray with this wee bloody implement thing he has. Like wet stinking black straw. Fucking stinking. You could smell it across the room. I was staring at the key cupboard, with its wee ordinary key in the lock. Inside all the hooks, numbered and all. I remember he opened his room with a Yale key with a wee yellow plastic cover thing on it.' Martin suddenly spat out his chewed stalk of grass and straightened. 'Does he ever say mass in the mornings?'

'All priests do,' said Kavanagh.

'In school?'

'I don't know,' Blaise shrugged. 'What difference would *that* make?'

'Find out,' said Martin. He became restless at the thought which had come into his head. He stood and moved up to the tarmac path. Here and there the old surface had broken into potholes. It had been loosely filled in with stones. Martin bent and picked up the largest one. He turned and threw it as high as he could into the air over the water. It soared and slowed, then began to fall. When it hit the water it made a muted sound. *Fudge!* He lifted a handful of stones and went down the short slope to the water's edge.

'Thirty-two feet per second per second.'

'We call that a dead man's fart.'

Kavanagh saw what Martin was doing and went up and gathered a handful of stones for himself. Blaise watched them.

'The higher the better,' said Martin. Kavanagh prepared to throw, his body bent back, his throwing hand almost to the ground behind him. He whipped his hand through and the stone disappeared up into the blue. Martin shaded his eyes. Squinting up at the brightness. *Chuff!* The stone hit the water some way out.

The water was fretted enough for there to be no spreading rings — just a little irruption. The little wind died away.

'It's the sound of bursting from one element to another,' said Blaise. 'Breaking the sound barrier.' Martin threw again. Then Kavanagh. Each time the stone made the plunge into the water there was the satisfying noise. The swans began to swim towards them, thinking there was food on the go. The wind had dropped enough for each swan to leave a wake.

'It goes in a kind of parabola,' said Kavanagh.

Martin threw again and said, 'Like shooting an arrow straight up.' They ran out of stones and couldn't be bothered going back up on to the path to get more.

'Did you ever hear of Zeno's paradoxes?' said Blaise.

'Nope,' said Kavanagh. Blaise didn't even wait for an answer from Martin. And Martin was aware of it.

'They're arguments against motion,' said Blaise. He made the other two stand up and placed them a couple of feet from each other, both facing in the direction of the Cave Hill. 'Just say there's a race and you are Achilles . . .' He reached out and put his hand on Kavanagh's shoulder.

'Aw, fuck. My heel.' Kavanagh made a grab for it as if he was in pain. Blaise straightened him up and made him stand to attention. He took two paces and beckoned Martin.

'And you are the dumbfuck tortoise.' Blaise positioned Martin a distance in front of Kavanagh. 'So Achilles is so confident he gives you a start.'

'Does he not have to fall asleep?' said Martin.

'Shut up,' said Blaise. 'When I say Go . . .' Kavanagh was away running, exaggeratedly lifting his knees. 'For fucksake . . .' Kavanagh heard the irritation in Blaise's voice but continued mock running in a great loop over the grass until he came back. Blaise continued:

'When Achilles reaches the point where dumbfuck here started, dumbfuck will have moved on a bit — right?'

'OK,' said Kavanagh. He stopped running on the spot.

'I still think he should be falling asleep and I run past him — not run past him but kind of plod past him.' Now Martin started to make giant steps — his idea of plodding. Blaise punched him on the shoulder.

'Cut it out. You're thinking of Aesop.'

'Every time Achilles gets to here, dumbfuck will have moved on a bit. And so on – infinitely.'

Kavanagh rugby-tackled Blaise and brought him to the ground. Martin, rather than be left out, flung himself on top of the other two. The three of them wrestled on the grass. Martin looked up and saw an old gent carrying a silver-topped cane. He was out walking his dog, a wee Jack Russell. He looked down at the struggling heap of bodies and rolled his eyes. The knot of Martin's school tie was pulled to the size of a sixpence and ended up somewhere below his ear. Blaise's shirt tail came out and, although he was laughing, he called out for them to stop the nonsense. Kavanagh was revving like an aeroplane and Martin was shouting, 'What noise does a tortoise make?'

The old gent moved on, swinging his cane, looking as if he'd like to have waded into the fight and beat fuck out of them all for being out of school at that time of day. Kavanagh got Blaise's head in a lock grip and Blaise's voice was yelling out. It was difficult to know if he was pretending to be angry or if he was really mad.

'Stop it you big cunt. Or I'll fuckin kill you.'

'I'll kill him for you,' said Martin and he got a grip beneath Kavanagh's chin and applied as much pressure as he dared. Kavanagh eventually let go.

'About bloody time, you big –' Blaise stood and undid his trousers and tucked his shirt back in – 'fuckers,' he said. They still couldn't tell whether he was truly angry or not. His face was red and his hair tossed.

Martin loosened off the knot in his tie and began to tie it again properly. They flopped down again on the grass. Kavanagh's chest was heaving. Gradually everyone's breath returned to normal. Nobody spoke. Martin was near the water's edge. He smelled the cut grass and trailed his hand in the water.

'Hey it's nearly warm.' Martin dried his hand on the side of his trousers and lit a cigarette. He spun the match towards the water. He loved the tang of the smell of the sulphur. He lay down. There was also something in the grass which smelled good – a plant of some sort, like pineapple weed or meadowsweet or something. He looked around and the grass was close to his face. He closed one eye. Some of the blades were veined green, others were stalks

– mixed new summer grass which slanted this way and that, creating a pattern that was perfect, with the sky behind it. The blades fitted the sky the way a key fits a lock. Grass green and sky blue. Those were the colours – they were what was being referred to. Adjectives and nouns. Grass and sky, green and blue. The sun was warm on the black material of his blazer. He inhaled his cigarette and felt a jag of pleasure, in his lungs, between his fingers. For a moment his head felt light. Everything combined to give him a rush of intensity at the rightness of things. The key turned in the lock. The liquid went clear with the addition of a single drop. Everything else he thought of only added to the feeling. The water at the edge of the lake was warm and silky on his fingers. His best friends were here, he was sure he would pass his exams this time. He identified the upward rush as happiness. He was sure he would never die. And he was sure he would remember feeling this for the rest of his life. It was like the feeling he'd had in Ardglass when he decided not to be a priest. He wondered if it had anything to do with lying down. Then, he'd lain on a wall, now he was on the grass. He knew it was a daft conclusion – like the kid who thought the wind was created by the waving of trees – but it was funny and the fact that he thought it was funny only added to the rightness of things. Suddenly there was the sound of swans lifting and flying overhead. Moving from one stretch of water to another. The sound of moving from one element to another. The stone falling from air to water. The swans from here to there. Love was in it somewhere but he couldn't tell where or with whom.

Instinctively around about four o'clock all three stood up and gathered their things together. They began to walk slowly along the path with Blaise leading the way.

'Why're we walking in this direction?' said Martin.

'I want to call in home,' said Blaise, 'before I go back.'

'Where's home?'

'Over there,' Blaise said nodding in the direction of the Cave Hill.

'In a cave?' said Martin.

'About half a mile that way,' said Blaise. 'I want to see if I've got any post.'

'Post? Do you get post?' Martin sounded incredulous.

'Yeah – don't you?'

'Never. Except exam results.'

They walked down to a gate at the side of the Waterworks but it was locked. It was of iron bars with viciously sharp points. Kavanagh knew a way up on to the pillar which held the gate and with his big stretch was able to climb over with little trouble. Martin interlocked his hands and made a stirrup for Blaise.

Blaise put a foot on the cross-strut of the gate then shouted to Martin, 'Don't move.' Martin did as he was told and felt Blaise's shoe press down hard on his shoulder. Then Blaise was up on to the pillar. Kavanagh helped him down on the other side. Martin tried but he couldn't follow the route the other two had taken. He stood looking through the bars.

'Use the other gate,' said Blaise, pointing up the road. Martin turned to run but just at that moment the old gent with the wee Jack Russell appeared. He was taking a bunch of keys from his pocket. The old guy took in the situation at a glance. He tucked his silver-topped cane under his arm like a newspaper and inserted the key. The gate clanked open but the old man barred the way. He whistled to his dog. The wee thing ran through and stood outside beside Kavanagh and Blaise.

'Do you want out?' said the old guy.

'Thanks,' said Martin. He sidled out through the open gate then the old man locked it again and stowed his keys away in his pocket. The three boys began to stroll. When they were out of earshot Martin said, 'Why has that oul bastard got a key?'

'It used to be private or something,' said Blaise. 'Everybody in the club had a key.'

'Then they let the hoi polloi in,' said Kavanagh. 'Scum like you, Brennan.'

'I thought the hoi polloi was the posh ones?'

'You're probably thinking of hoity toity,' said Kavanagh. 'Is it not really odd to be a boarder with your house so near?'

'Yeah.'

They walked for a while through tree-lined avenues. Then Blaise nodded towards a driveway almost hidden behind a high hedge. There were trees and rhododendrons in the garden.

'Thar she blows,' he said.

'We'll not go in,' said Kavanagh.

'You mean you're going to hang about out here?'

'Yeah.'

'I'll not be long,' said Blaise.

'Who's in?' asked Kavanagh.

'How the fuck would I know,' said Blaise. 'I haven't been home for ages.'

'Who do you *expect* will be in?'

'You don't have to talk to anybody,' said Blaise.

'Why can't you answer my question?'

'My father's away. There'll just be my grandfather and Susan.'

'Who's Susan?'

'She looks after us – sort of housekeeper cum nurse. The oul boy is beginning to lose the place. Threw his piss-pot through the window one night. Thought somebody or something was coming to get him. But you don't have to meet him – or her. You can stay in the front room. I'll make the tea.'

'I wouldn't mind a cuppa tea,' said Martin.

'Yeah, OK,' said Kavanagh. 'After our labours, a big pot of the old Nambarrie would go down well.'

The house was set back a long way from the main road. Only part of it showed between trees. Grey brick, a window, some ivy. The path to the front door was gravel and cinders mixed and Martin was aware of the noise their feet made in the silence. It had been a long afternoon. Now they seemed to have run out of things to talk about. Blaise took out a wallet of keys from his pocket and selected one for the front door. Inside, the hall was dark, old fashioned. There were glass-fronted bookcases along one side full of poetry books. The floor was brown tiles scattered with rugs to make it seem less cold. Martin noticed that the rugs were rumpled enough to catch anyone's toe. He had never seen such a big hall, or so wide a staircase in a house before. There was a black grandfather clock with a loud tick. Blaise paused at the hall table and was looking through the post.

'When my dad's away, he always gets tons of post. It builds up.' Some of the envelopes were for Blaise. He flicked quickly through them and slipped his to one side – envelopes trimmed with red, white and blue: airmails from America. One from India, one from the Vatican. Martin knew where they were from immediately, from the days when he collected stamps. One brown envelope in particular seemed to please Blaise.

A woman's voice called from a room at the bottom of the hall. 'Who is it?'

'It's me,' shouted Blaise. 'Go in there,' he pointed to a door. 'I'll be back in a minute.'

It was a double room with two fireplaces and two doors and two sets of windows and the most obvious thing about it was the grand piano by the back window, its huge black lid uplifted, like the fin of a shark, making the inner room seem deprived of light. There were several aspidistras and cheese plants by the windows. Martin noticed that there were no religious images anywhere, neither picture nor statue. Beside one of the plants was a metronome. Dark prints hung on the walls. There were one or two abstract paintings, brightly coloured. Martin set his bag by the door and went over and looked inside the piano at all the strings and hammers. He plucked one with his finger and it zizzed a bit, then stopped. Kavanagh put his hands in his pockets and started looking at ornaments of spear carriers on the mantelpiece. Between the two rooms, dividing doors had been folded back, concertina-like against the wall. Martin sat down on the edge of a sofa by one of the fireplaces. The sofa was hard and the material rough to the touch.

'Some place,' said Kavanagh. His voice was hushed so that the criticism would not be overheard. 'Do you think Blaise is OK?'

'What?'

'That stuff about the beautiful boy in the gym.'

'I dunno. Maybe he's bisexual.'

'Did you hear about the guy who thought bisexual meant going to bed with two women?'

'No – what about him?'

'Fuck off.'

The room smelled faintly of lavender. Cars could be heard on the road in the distance. And the ticking of the clock from the hallway. The carpet just in front of the sofa was threadbare. The place where everybody sat, the place where all the feet had shuffled over the years. Straight lines of hessian stuff were obvious where the pattern had worn away. Kavanagh moved up to the top

148

end of the room to see what was outside the window. Martin went to the piano again. The sheet music on the rack was Schubert. He pressed a chord of three notes. Softly. Listened to them resonate.

'They go on for longer if you press the pedal,' said Kavanagh. Martin put his foot on the pedal and pressed three different notes. Their sound seemed a rich mixture of brown and cream that hummed infinitely. The sound fitted the room the way the blue sky had earlier fitted the grass around it. The way a blade fits its sheath. When it was no longer audible he struck the same chord again. And savoured it.

'That's such a mournful fucking sound,' said Kavanagh. Martin shrugged and moved away from the piano to look at a picture above the second mantelpiece. Kavanagh reached forward and touched the metronome into motion. It clacked backwards and forwards quickly. He bent and looked at it closely to read what was written on the scale.

'That's *vivace*.' He stopped the machine and adjusted it. It clacked more slowly. A kind of plodding pace. 'And that's *adagio*.'

'Who's talking about mournful,' Martin said. 'Play the *vivace* again.'

Kavanagh changed the metronome back to the faster speed. There was a creaking as one of the doors opened and Martin looked round, grinning. But instead of Blaise an old man stood there. He was tall, but slightly stooped. He had a white goatee beard and glasses. All his movements were very old – shaky and indecisive.

'How did you get in here?' the old man hissed. He moved across the room and raised his hand to strike Martin but instinctively Martin ducked, not knowing what to say. He evaded the old man. The old man was unsteady on his feet as he turned.

'How dare you!' he shouted. 'Bloody burglars.' He staggered a bit as he looked around for a weapon. Kavanagh started to say something to try and calm the old guy down. 'And you've the cheek to do it in your school uniform.' The metronome was going clack-clack-clack over by the window. There was a brass poker standing up in a companion set on the hearth. Martin saw the old man make a grab for it and that was enough.

'Make yourself scarce,' Kavanagh shouted. 'I don't want to

have to hit this old guy.' Martin picked up his bag and ran down the hall. The door had a Yale lock and a twist handle and it required two hands. He waited for Kavanagh to open the second lock, then they were away running, crunching down the path. As he ran Martin felt his knees shaking.

'Fucking madman,' he said.

'Totally berserk.' Kavanagh was starting to laugh.

'How dare you,' shouted Martin. 'Bloody burglars.'

'And you've the cheek to be in school uniform.' They stopped running when they reached the main road and looked back. Kavanagh put his arm around Martin and they fell about laughing. The old man was standing at the door shaking the poker and shouting at the top of his scrawny voice. From that distance his white goatee was jerking like a rabbit's scut. A danger signal. Blaise was nowhere to be seen.

7.   A Sleepless Night

'No offence, Mrs Brennan – I'm sure you're the best mother in the world – but that boy is *thin*. The only growing he's doing is up. How he does it, living with a baker like yourself, I've no idea. I'd be out like a balloon.'

He hated Mary Lawless for mocking him. He'd been wearing an open-necked shirt and when he opened the door to let her in she pretended to use the cavity between his collarbones as a holy water font. She dipped her finger into the hollow and blessed herself as she entered the house.

She was followed in by Nurse Gilliland who said, 'If he gets any thinner the Cruelty will be on to you, Mrs Brennan.'

Later when the food was being handed around a second time Mary Lawless said, 'I'm on a diet.'

'What for?'

She patted her stomach and rolled her eyes to heaven.

'Martin, do the needful,' said his mother. 'Offer those buns around.'

Mary Lawless refused with her hands up.

'I have had an elegant sufficiency.' She patted the corners of her mouth with her serviette to let them all see she'd finished. It was only then she seemed to notice its colour. 'I'm very fond of the navy blue, Mrs Brennan.'

'Oh thank you.'

'I find the dark colours are *so* attractive,' said Nurse Gilliland. '*So* stylish.' She held her serviette up against the lapel of her navy blue dress and it matched perfectly.

'I knew you were coming,' said Mrs Brennan.

'You're never going to believe this,' said Mary Lawless, 'but – I had a twenty-inch waist the day I was married.'

'You had an elastic measuring tape, as well, if you ask me,' said Nurse Gilliland. Father Farquharson turned in his straight-backed armchair and watched each person as they spoke. He had a face which was always on the verge of smiling.

Mary Lawless insisted, 'No, I had really – twenty inches.' She created a circle by joining her thumbs and index fingers together to demonstrate her size. 'That's twenty inches.' Martin was going to set the plate of buns on the coffee table but his mother made a gesture that he should insist.

'Very like a whale in a wee tin,' said Mrs Brennan. 'You took the sausage rolls.'

'Sometimes I eats like a horse and sometimes I just eats grass. My hunger is now assuaged.'

Martin set the plate down.

'All the more for me tomorrow,' he said.

'Ate up, you're a growing boy,' said Mary Lawless. 'It's hard to believe I used to have an hourglass figure.'

'Aye – always running out,' said Nurse Gilliland.

Mary Lawless joined in the joke then said, 'Fruit is said to be a very good thing.'

'An apple a day keeps the doctor at bay,' said Mrs Brennan.

'I find apples an uphill struggle.'

'Aye, I know what you mean,' Nurse Gilliland nodded. 'It's hard to make a meal of an apple – like you wouldn't get a man coming home from the pub starving and then sitting down to an apple. Dieting also can do strange things to the breath.'

'Are you trying to tell me nicely . . . ?'

'No, I am not, Mary. It's just that I was talking to Peter Faul the other day. He's badly failed.'

'A sight for sore eyes.'

'Is he no better?'

'Naw. Not by a long chalk.'

'As yella as a duck's foot.'

'Aye, they say he's not well at all.'

'The doctors have given up on him.'

'Is that so? But sure the doctors give up on everybody.'

'Now you're talking.'

'Merciful hour.'

'There's something odd about his face.'

'Aye – like somebody sat on him when he was warm.'

'Aw, Mary you've the quare way of putting things.'

'A body could tell he wasn't right. His breath was . . . a bit . . . y'know.'

'There's nothing worse, I always say.'

'Than what?'

'Bad breath. Breath that would knock you down. And the worst of it is — there's no way you can diagnose yourself. Somebody has to tell you.'

'If it was me I'd just work in a bank or the post office. Well away from the people you're talking to.'

'They've glass screens in the Northern Bank.'

'Or a telephonist. That'd be a good job for somebody like that.'

'I believe it comes from the teeth.'

'But cleaning them won't help. I knew a schoolteacher once and he brushed them ten times a day, but he could still wither plants at the back of the classroom when he said "Amen".'

'It's the gums,' said Nurse Gilliland nodding. 'Pyorrhoea.'

'And the tongue,' said Mrs Brennan. 'A coating on the tongue can leave you like that . . . it's just one thing after another.'

'Hawing on people like a dragon.'

'I've told Martin always to scrape his tongue first thing in the morning.'

'A tongue strigil,' said Martin.

'No — a spoon,' said his mother.

'We did that in class once — *Everyday Life in Ancient Rome*. When the Romans got sweaty and dirty they covered themselves with oil and scraped it off with a bit of metal called a strigil.'

'The dirty bastes.'

There was silence for a while after Mrs Brennan's strong language. People smiled politely and looked over at Father Farquharson.

'Why is it?' said Nurse Gilliland, 'that you rarely get rhyming names? It just struck me that somebody with the surname Faul would never be called Paul. Paul Faul.'

'Isn't he Peter?' said Mrs Brennan.

'Aye Peter Faul. But I hear what you mean. Paul Faul? I'm not so sure,' said Mary Lawless. 'Although I once knew a Pete Street. Lived at the back of the Tech.'

'It's OK if there's a Mac in the name,' said Mrs Brennan. 'Alan MacCallan, sounds not too bad.'

Mary Lawless cleared her throat.

'A thing I've always wondered is this,' she said. 'If you had two weighing machines and you put a foot on each one, what would you weigh? Can we just assume that the sum of the two scales would be your weight? Eh Martin, a bright boy like you should know that. What do you think?' Martin smiled and shook his head. Mary Lawless went on without waiting for an answer. 'There's a dearth of places where you find two weighing machines side by side. So I never get the chance to do my wee experiment.' Martin nodded. 'My problem is I think too much. Isn't that right, Martin?'

'You're a holy terror, Mary,' said Mrs Brennan. 'But there's none of us getting any younger.'

'Wait till you hear this,' said Mary Lawless. 'Yesterday I was just coming out of my front door and who should be there sunning herself but Mrs O'Neill . . .'

'She's a lady, a real lady,' said Mrs Brennan.

'Aye, a dinner lady,' said Mary Lawless. 'Anyway I'd been up the stairs and down again and I was out of puff and she says *Mary says she you're getting to be an oul doll*. Isn't that a good one?'

'Getting to be an oul doll,' said Mrs Brennan, screwing up her face.

'Ach, the advance of age,' said Nurse Gilliland.

'I see it in my hands,' said Mary Lawless.

'What, you don't look in the mirror?'

'I do and I don't. But when you look in the mirror you subtract things. Sometimes I be sitting and my hands be here . . .' Her hands rested on her thighs. 'And I say to myself – who in under God owns those podgy hands? Then I pick up the skin and it stays up – like making a meringue. They're the hands of another woman – they're my Aunt Tessie's hands and she was buried fifteen years ago.'

'Och, it's sad right enough.'

'Sad's not the word for it.'

'Sometimes I catch myself in the full-length mirror on the wardrobe and I'm shocked. I say *Merciful God how did she get in here? I never knew there was oul women burglars.*'

'The body is one thing,' Father Farquharson shook his head. 'But did you ever arrive into a room at speed and think, what am I here for?'

'That's the way I am at this very moment,' said Mary Lawless. They all recognised what the priest had said and nodded in agreement.

'The mind,' said Mrs Brennan, 'is a killer.'

'But what about the soul?' said Nurse Gilliland. 'After the body and the mind how does the soul show its age?'

'Aye, I've often heard that said,' said Mrs Brennan, 'the poor old soul.'

'I suppose – in a kind of spiritual wisdom,' said Father Farquharson, assuming the question was addressed to him. 'As we grow older we develop habits of holiness. Ritual is a kind of spiritual keep-fit for the soul, eh?'

'It is – it is indeed, Father.'

'Martin, you're very quiet tonight,' said Father Farquharson. 'Do you do drill at that college?'

'Drill?' Martin laughed.

'Or whatever they call it nowadays. PE or Gym or Sports.'

'Yes.'

'Do you like it?'

'It's OK.'

'What's your favourite subject?'

'Science.'

'A man of the future and no mistake.'

'Did you ever hear that said, Mary?' said Mrs Brennan, talking across the conversation. 'The poor old soul.'

'I did. But I don't think it means the same thing – what we were talking about.'

'Oh excuse me, constable!' His mother became very huffy after that. 'Pardon me for butting in,' she muttered quietly so that everyone could hear.

'Can I go now?' said Martin.

His mother nodded, smiling through him at her guests. As Martin left the room he heard Nurse Gilliland saying, 'The last day you had a twenty-inch waist, Mary, was the day of your First Communion.'

When the guests left Martin's mother asked him for help with the dishes. He grumbled a bit but agreed that she would wash and he would dry. Which meant that she was finished and sitting down before he was. She sat on the chair in front of the fire with her head back. She shouted in to him.

'Thanks be to God to get off my feet,' she said. 'I've been on the go since this morning. Is there anything wrong, son? You're very quiet.'

'Naw.'

'You're in a kind of a brown study.'

'Naw.'

'Have you everything ready for school in the morning?'

'Aye.'

Martin dried and put the last plate away. She had reminded him. He went into the kitchen and walked past her chair to the cupboard. He reached up and lifted down the button box. The box was of black lacquered material with patterns of roses on its side. It had a sliding lid with a scooped-out D for your fingernail to get a grip. He opened it and began raking through the contents. There were shapes and sizes and colours in here he remembered since childhood – buttons like black beetles, ones of mother-of-pearl, a card with hooks and eyes stitched to it, striped tiny buttons, wooden toggles, plain sensible men's buttons with four central no-nonsense holes.

'Must you make so much noise?' said his mother.

'Sorry.'

'What are you looking for?'

'Nothing.'

'Martin, what do you take me for? You come in and make a beeline for the cupboard and get the button box down and start looking through it and you're not looking for anything.'

'Nothing important. Just some ones I remember. Like this one.' He held up a yellowish fur-covered button. 'Remember that?'

'I don't know what that was off.'

'Probably Rupert the Bear.'

Martin saw what he was looking for. A couple of old Yale keys held together by fuse wire. He slipped one into his pocket but went on looking through the button box for some time.

156

'Could you waken me at half seven?'

'Why so early?'

'There's a mass for the exams. In the school chapel.'

'It's good you're taking it to heart this year.'

After about an hour in the dark of his bed he was still awake. At least it seemed like an hour. Maybe it was only fifteen minutes. Time was a bit like Mary Lawless's elastic measuring tape. It could stretch. Be different things under different conditions. Like when he was trying to pass the forty minutes while mitching the English class. In the dark of the bedroom time dragged as well. The whole scheme was fucking madness. And yet he had volunteered for it. Jesus. Did he dare to eat a peach? If he didn't get some sleep he wouldn't be fit for anything. He flinched and turned yet again in the bed. Priests were weird. Far Easts was the rhyming slang for them in school. If he was caught doing what he planned to do . . . it didn't bear thinking about. His mother would be summoned to the school. Fuck, she'd be asked to come in to the police barracks, more likely. If he thought of something boring maybe he would drift off. The supper night he'd just endured – especially the priestly contributions. Father Farquharson was one of the weird-est. He was like two different people – one when he was visiting, another when he was in church.

The making of the Holy Water had been *so* embarrassing. It had been just after Father Estyn O'Hare had stayed in their house. Martin was one of the altar boys for the Easter ceremonies and one of his tasks was to push the container of water up to Father Farquharson at the front of the church. It was a Ladies of Charity tea urn which held eight gallons and it was mounted on small steel castors. It was *so* heavy. When Father Farquharson gave the signal that he was ready Martin had to get help from a man to start it moving. He blushed as he pushed, trying to make as little noise as possible with the steel wheels, which were squealing and chattering over the floor. And every single person in the church turned and stared at him leaning his weight into this stupid thing, his two arms out straight in front of him, pushing for all he was worth. And Father Farquharson standing on the altar steps with his nose in the air and a book in his hands. Then one of the castors caught in the broken metal grille on the floor – there was a clack sound as the wheel socketed in. The water see-sawed over the lip of the urn and some of it hit the floor with a slap everybody in the church heard. Father Farquharson was of no help whatsoever. This was ritual – there was no way he could move to help. He looked away with a little sigh. The fault was entirely Martin's. He'd been warned. 'Take care you don't get stuck in that broken grille.' But how could he have seen ahead? He was behind the bloody tea urn, pushing. One of the men from the St Vincent de Paul stepped into the middle aisle and lifted the urn's castor free of the grille. Martin's ears were red with blushing. His gym shoes slipped on the wet floor but he didn't fall. He got to the altar steps and Father Farquharson began the blessing of the water. Praying over it from the book and putting drops of holy oils in it and some chrism, making crosses in it – and over it – with his finger, sometimes three times. He breathed on it in the shape of a cross and he dipped the bottom of the lit paschal candle in it three times. And each time he said what he said, he said it higher. It was like somebody was squeezing him by the balls. Three, like forty, seemed to be an important number in religion – three persons in God, three Hail Marys, three crosses on Calvary. His mother also used forty a lot. 'She's as cross as forty cats,' she'd say and she was always going for 'forty winks'. If only he could get forty winks now. He'd settle for thirty-nine. He turned yet again in the bed.

The next day Martin and another altar boy, Maginn, had been asked to give out the Holy Water. The thing that amazed Martin was Father Farquharson's attitude, after the seriousness of the performance the night before. People came and went all morning bringing with them an assortment of bottles – blue milk of magnesia bottles, lemonade bottles, flat whiskey bottles that fitted the pocket. The two boys filled them all from the urn and handed them back – Maginn from the tap where the tea would normally come out, Martin from the surface of the water. Any bottle Martin put in horizontally made pleasant glooping noises as it filled. Martin's hands were raw red with the cold dipping in and out the water. About midday Father Farquharson came into the baptistry.

'Hello, boys,' he said, 'How are things?'

'The Holy Water is getting low, Father.'

'Holy smoke! Stupendous. We must have been doing a good trade then?' Father Farquharson moved up and down on his toes. He leaned over and looked into the urn. 'Golly! You're right. An impending drought. Maybe that's because you sloshed so much of it out on to the floor last night, Martin.'

'What will we do if we run out, Father?' Maginn asked.

'Fill her up at the tap, man – at the back of the parochial house.'

Martin looked at Maginn, then at the priest to see if it was a joke. 'It's quite all right – all quite liturgical. Use the bucket – if you can't bring the mountain to Mohammed . . . Martin don't look so worried. You see, it has all got to do with atoms. What you have here is concentrated stuff. It stands to reason we can only bless so much of it on Easter Saturday and yet that amount has to do us the whole year. So we add water. Dilute it, so to speak. To make it go round.' Father Farquharson interlocked his fingers and when he pulled on them they did not come apart. 'Atoms hold on to one another, so to speak. Haven't you done *any* science in school?'

Why couldn't he sleep? Macbeth talks about sleep that knits up the ravelled sleeve of care. What did that mean? The sleeve of your jumper or pullover or something would have had to unravel first, so that it could be knitted up again. Shakespeare was crap sometimes, but he was a hell of a lot better than fucking Milton. Darned – his mother talked about darning socks when she was young. She had a wooden mushroom thing to prove it. She just slipped it inside the sock and the job was so much easier to do. He twisted and turned. He was exhausted trying to get over to sleep. He wondered if he should get up and make some hot milk. His mother's remedy. But at least he was warm now and there were periods when he drifted off into a state of half-sleep where words became weird and repeated and distorted. A word like gwine or murock or feburate – what did they mean? Or pellagera or feculant or mermish. They were like place names signposting a part of the country he didn't know. Why did they disturb him? They had almost a feel to them, they weighed too heavy or too light, they had sandpaper edges or cut his lip like paper when he spoke them and there was blood left on the gummed edge. And his face was too close to the moon – like velvet sandpaper . . . or he was falling. Falling dreams were the worst, where his stomach elevatored in the safety of his bed. He could experience falling, if the brain put out the right chemicals. And he hated it. Like when he was a baby, like when grown-ups threw him up in the air and caught him on the way down. The first time he must have giggled, because whoever it was thought he liked it and threw him up again and again. Each time his stomach swooned as he fell. The uncle or whoever it was added variations – to make the thing seem more dangerous – like clapping hands between the throwing and the catching. Like closing, or pretending to close his eyes when Martin began his fall. Whatever way it was done, Martin was terrified by the game but, perversely, his face showed delight. It was exactly the feeling he was experiencing now. With Blaise. With Kavanagh. But this time the stomach was fine. It was the air. In the pitch black. He felt the breeze. He had to distinguish whether it was the air was moving or him. If it was him, he had to work out whether he was moving horizontally, say, being driven at sixty miles per hour along a road through the darkest night. Or whether he was travelling perpendicularly downwards and the brain somehow had not been told to react in the normal stomach scream way. A bellyful of – was it adrenalin? If he was travelling perpendicularly down he wondered if there was a method of escape. The situation was not yet urgent but at least he would like to reassure himself that, firstly, there was a trapeze or some such thing and secondly, that it was within reach. If not a trapeze, then at least a catcher. But if a catcher caught him, firmly locking hands, the way atoms are supposed to, according to Father Farquharson, holding the wrists for safety, some time could elapse before he realised, or they jointly realised – for he had no way of knowing the mental state of the catcher – that both of them were falling. The safety of the grip was an illusion. Although the sinews and bone and muscle had locked on to his hands, the catcher's wiry legs were not hooked around the bar of anything. The catcher in effect was not attached. But not to worry, there would be safety nets below them. Except that somehow word had been got to him that they were not yet in place. Things had been delayed. Negotiations were not yet finished and the nets were lying flat on the ground and he would die instantly with the pattern of a safety net embedded in his skin. And then people

could use him as a grid for playing noughts and crosses before they
buried him . . .

8.   An Early Morning in School

He woke before his mother and was dressed when he heard her call. He didn't feel like eating anything. On his way down the road to school he smoked a cigarette to calm his nerves. It was the sign of a real smoker, smoking on your own. Not just a social thing. Not showing off.

The clock in the post office said seven minutes to eight. He was in good time. Take it easy – he didn't want to get there too early. But he wanted the maximum amount of time to do the business. Fuck, he was mad. He wished Kavanagh had come along to keep dick. It would be a comfort of some sort. Right now, the only way he could cope with what he was about to do was *not* to think about it. Not sleeping hadn't helped.

The school driveway was empty. Not a soul. Martin walked up, keeping close to the wall and the science buildings. If you kept in close to the wall you couldn't be seen from the main staff corridor on the first floor. He didn't want to have to explain to anyone why he was in school so early. The first thing was to dump the bag. He took his time. There was nobody in the locker room yet. Nor in the corridors. He climbed the stairs and passed the cleaners' store room. The door was dark brown, wood-grained – with its number, 109, painted in faded yellow.

He went up the steps towards the chapel with as little noise as possible. Through the coloured glass doors he tried to make out if mass had started. Then he heard Condor's unmistakably deep voice.

'To prepare ourselves to celebrate the sacred mysteries, let us call to mind our sins. I confess to almighty God . . .'

The boys raggedly joined in but their voices were too quiet. Too shy. Martin turned and walked as quickly as he dared to the corridor entrance of the sacristy. He opened the door and it gave a long unoiled screech. Up two steps and into the robing room. His heart was pounding. The door of the robing room was open. He knew about adrenalin from biology. The effect it had on you. But it was all in the mind. So far, he still could come up with an excuse. I'm just looking around. I left something in here yesterday. He put his head in first. Nobody. There was a smell of daffodils but he couldn't see where it was coming from. Condor's deep voice boomed from the altar beyond the door.

'Lord have mercy.' It was followed by the mumbling which he knew was the boys' version of the response. 'Lord have mercy.'

'Christ have mercy,' said Condor.

'Christ have mercy,' said Martin to himself. Condor must be hammering on. That was the Kyrie over. There were fast priests and slow priests and there were those who could finish exactly on the half-hour. It was a favourite subject of conversation when his mother had people in. Father Blaney was a flyer, Father White could be fast one day and take his time the next. But if you were in a hurry it was always great to see Father 'Twenty Minutes' Toomey coming out on to the altar.

Maybe the flowers decorating the altar were daffodils. Martin looked at the top of the vestment chest of drawers. The discarded pile was there. He'd better get a move on. The pipe implements thing, the box of Swan matches, the pens, the coins, some copper some silver. And the keys. Two long silvery ones, a VW car key with a black pretend tyre around it, three Yale keys, each with a different-coloured plastic cover, like a little shoulder cape. There was a yellow one which was Condor's room. He took a deep breath and lifted the bunch. I cannot believe I am doing this. His rubber-soled shoes squidged and squeaked on the polished boards. He stepped on to a runner of sage green carpet and stayed on it until he was out of the room. The door into the corridor screeched closed with too heavy a clunk as he pulled it after him. Holy Jesus, what am I doing? Whatever it was, he had better do it like fucking greased lightning. If he was stopped and searched now . . . There was no excuse he could give. If you'd like to come down to the police barracks with us, sir, and explain why you are carrying a set of keys belonging to Father O'Malley? But that would never happen – Condor would never call in the police. He hated them so much. The keys clinked in the pocket of his blazer at each step. But who would stop and search him? He looked perfectly innocent. It was all in the mind. He was now in the staff corridor overlooking the driveway. Still nobody – in either driveway or corridor. Distantly he heard the Sanctus bell. Fuck – it's getting late. Condor must be going like the clappers. And it was only about ten past. Things were going too fucking fast. The corridor windows looked like they had just been cleaned – everything outside was crystal sharp. The early light slanted in and squared the cream walls with brightness. A bird was singing but he couldn't see where it was perched and he certainly wasn't going to stop and look. He could see down on the bald crown of the willow tree in the quad. His right hand was in his pocket to dampen the noise of the keys. With his fingers he sought out the Yale – glanced down and saw it was the one with the yellow plastic. He held it poised, horizontal – ready to go in the lock, but still inside his pocket. Round the corner, past the glass trophy cupboard. Still, not a soul about the place. Then he heard a noise – a kind of rattle. Joe Boggs came from the far end of the corridor carrying a mop and bucket. Martin kept walking and staring out the windows. No matter what was happening in the school Joe Boggs never interfered. He was kind of a zombie. They nodded to each other as they passed. You could tell the mop bucket was empty by the way he carried it, tilted. The shaft of the mop leaned lightly against his shoulder. Martin continued past Condor's room listening to Joe Boggs's feet. He heard them turn the corner and he spun round and retraced his steps. He stopped at Condor's door and raised his hand as if to knock. But from his hand produced the keys, like a magician. The key fitted smoothly: its little serrations rippled into the centre of the circular lock. Then he glanced both ways. His hand turned and the door swung open. Oh, so simple. And he was inside. He realised he hadn't breathed for some time and now with the door shut he exhaled.

'Jesus.'

The room was as he'd remembered it. There was a large, almost black, oil painting of St Ignatius of Loyola above the fireplace. The mouth of the fireplace was blocked with hardboard. To one side of the door above a bookcase was a black and white picture of Christ, the Saviour of the World. He had a staff in one hand and a ball surmounted by a cross in the other. His eyes were turned to heaven in a kind of *who's making that noise upstairs* look. He had seen pictures of Christ where his eyes followed you round the room. That was from first-year Art: if the eyes were dead centre then that was the illusion. Stupid bastards were impressed by this. They thought it was what art was about. The room smelled heavily of pipe smoke, aniseed and dust. On the mantelpiece half a dozen pipes stood in a rack with their mouthpieces in the air. The rack was supposed to be a rustic five-barred gate. Several dark green packets of tobacco labelled CONDOR were stacked behind. There were papers and files everywhere. On the windowsill were a couple of unwatered terracotta pots each containing a dead, pale brown, feathery plant. One hung on to a length of thin bamboo. It was so strange – the emptiness. The silence. He went to the desk and bent over to see the paper pinned to the wall above it. The letters and numbers seemed to jump about before his eyes. Because his head was tilted he couldn't trace the line across the page. He tried to follow it with his finger. It was shaking badly. Christ, what a state he was in. There was an ashtray beneath his face. It was reeking of half-smoked tobacco, scraped from the pipe bowl, like soggy blackened straw. Just the same smell as the day he'd been thumped for smoking. There could be no excuse *whatsoever* now, if he was caught. This was burglary. Of the Dean of Discipline's room. Instant expulsion. Thou sure and firm-set earth, hear not my steps, which way they walk, for fear the very stones prate of my whereabout. His mother weeping – at the foot of the cross. A life destroyed. Two lives destroyed. Fuck – stop thinking. Start doing. And get outa there. He wasn't sure . . . couldn't be sure that the number was the correct one. A clear plastic ruler stood up in a tin of pencils and pens. He lifted it and held it firmly and as horizontally as he could against the page beneath **Cleaners Store** without the apostrophe:

Cleaners Store 109...**M7**.

He went to the glass-fronted cupboard. He was speaking to himself, 'M seven, M seven.' The cupboard was locked with a small baby-like key which was left in the lock. Martin turned it. The cupboard door swung open. The glass was old, and looking through it towards the window everything became wibbled and wavy. On the cup hook marked M7 hung a ring of half a dozen keys. Martin checked that the saw teeth were the same on the shank of each key by holding them together so that the mountains and valleys matched. He slipped one key off the ring and substituted his own key, the one he had rummaged out of the button box.

There was a knock at the door.

Holy fuck. His heart pounded. He nearly dropped all the keys. In the name of Jesus, who was it? What should he do? He silenced the bunch of keys by holding them tightly. There was a thin strip of light beneath the door. Someone's shadow interrupted it. Two shadows, two feet. Martin breathed through his mouth so's he wouldn't make the slightest sound. He looked around slowly as if the noise of moving might give him away. He wanted to pray – but how could you pray on such a mission. How could he ask for help when he was up to no good? Please God help me – I have just stolen a key so's we can steal another key so's we can steal exam papers and undermine society as we know it. Whoever was outside knocked again. Everything seemed to be happening in the slow motion of extreme danger. Three raps of the knuckle. Knock – knock – knock. Here's a knocking indeed. The same sound pattern as the first knock. *Vivace*, almost. Like the metronome. A metronome registered time unscientifically: instead of milliseconds and seconds it used stupid Italian words. The door shuddered a little in its frame. Then – suddenly – Martin realised he was going to shite himself. He had to tighten his sphincter, pinch the muscles and hold on as tight as he could. Once, in bed he had pissed himself – but he had been a kid, a wee child. It had been during a dream – he'd been dreaming that he was actually at the toilet. So it wasn't his fault in a way. He had an excuse. That was nothing in terms of awfulness compared to the possibility of him shiting himself in Condor's room. He held on. It was as if his arse-hole had sucked a lemon. He daren't move until the shadows at the door gave up and went away. Whoever it was stood on and on. Martin looked up at the ceiling and when he looked back again the strip of light beneath the door was clear and uninterrupted. They had given up and gone. If Condor lived here, there must be a toilet. Martin looked around the room. There were three doors. Still he held on. He held on and walked and tried the first door. It was a wall cupboard filled with shelves of glasses and bottles –

green gin bottles, whiskey bottles. The next door was a bedroom. Off the bedroom, reflected in a mirror, he could see a lavatory through an open door. He put his hand to his bum, pressed hard and walked carefully. He dropped his trousers and sat down and let go. Fuck, what a noise. It sounded like he was having a piss, it was so watery. He gave a loud groan and put his head in his hands. That's where the word had come from. Shit scared. He was shit scared. He looked over his shoulder into the bedroom. Condor hadn't made his bed. On the floor of the lavatory were piles of *Golfer's Weekly* and *Time* magazine. There was a small wooden bookshelf filled with books and the first spine was an Enid Blyton adventure. She knows nothing about it. Nobody shits themselves in her books. And why in under God had Condor got a book like that on his shelves? That was a question that had to be asked. From where he was he could see the alarm clock on Condor's bedside table. Sixteen minutes past. Maybe he kept it fast all the time so's he would be punctual – have time in hand. For thumping those pupils who were actually late. His mother did that – always kept her alarm clock fast. He whacked off a spool of paper and folded it over and over again and wiped himself. And repeated the process. The stink was something awful. That kind of sick-arse smell. Not at all like an ordinary crap. Condor would know, the minute he came back, that somebody had been in his toilet. Martin jumped to his feet and did himself up, looking over his shoulder. The liquid at the bottom of the bowl was a dreadful colour. He flushed the toilet – a chain pull with a delf handle. He opened the lavatory window, pushed it out as far as it would go and latched it there on the last notch. He took a towel from a rail and gave it a couple of flaps in the direction of the open window. He glanced at the clock on his way out of the bedroom. Almost twenty fucking past. He was cutting it fine. A glimpse of himself in a full-length mirror startled him. He'd forgotten he was in school uniform. Then he noticed something else. There was a white Roman collar, half in, half out of the neck of a priest's black vest on a bedside chair. Martin noticed some coloured writing on the inside of the collar. There was something very familiar about it. Then he knew. The remnants of the familiar script of the words *Fairy Liquid*. Condor's white collar was white plastic cut from a Fairy Liquid bottle. Jesus – how cheap could you get? It was hard to believe. He closed the glass key cupboard door and locked it. There was a noise at the door. Not a knock. A swishing noise. He looked at the strip of light. Something was moving outside. Rhythmically. To and fro. Again he was reminded of the metronome. It stopped and he listened so much he could hear white noise in his ears. Then the gurgling of water. Then the rhythmic swishing again. It was fucking Joe Boggs. Mopping the corridor. He heard the clank of the mop bucket handle. Joe Boggs might be a fucking zombie but if he saw Martin coming strolling out of Condor's room . . . So Martin waited. There was nothing else he could do. And as he waited he trembled. His knees were actually shaking. The backwards and forwards swish of the mop was like the sound of somebody breathing in and out. How long did it take to do a corridor? He moved to where he could see into the bedroom again. A minute had passed. No shadow was moving outside the door but he could still hear the mopping. What he didn't know was whether Joe Boggs was mopping *up to* or *away from* the door. If he opened the door quietly and Joe had his back to him that'd be OK. He could slip out and never be noticed. But if he opened the door and Joe was facing him . . . It was too much of a risk. All or none. If it matters at all it must matter completely. Martin knelt and put his head to the board floor to try and see under the door. He could sense movement but that was no help: people mopped backwards – nobody mopped forwards and walked on the floor they had just cleaned. He could see the shine of wet but had no idea which direction the janitor would be facing.

The black phone on the desk rang. The fucking phone rang – scaring the shite out of him. Again. It went on ringing and ringing and ringing and ringing. He had a great temptation to lift it – to silence it. Lift it and say nothing. Just stop the fucking thing ringing, just stop it driving him mad. Pairs of rings. Ring-ring. Ring-ring. Ring-ring. It was physical. In his temples. Belling in his eyes. In his empty stomach. Then – thanks be to Jesus – it stopped. He got up off his knees. Then he heard a clank of the mop bucket handle and it sounded like it was very far away. Go. Go for it now. He moved quickly towards the door. Fuck it – the bathroom window. He ran in through the bedroom and closed the window – left it as he'd found it. Some of his stink was still in

168

the air but it wasn't as bad. Then back through the bedroom –
twenty-five past – and he was out to the door. He tapped his
pocket to check that he had Condor's bunch of keys. He opened
the door and put his head out. Nobody. He stepped out of the
room and closed the door. Joe must have gone to change his
water. But the floor was wet. He only noticed it was wet
underfoot when he had taken about five steps. He looked back.
There was actual evidence – his footprints coming out of
Condor's room. And the soles of the shoes he was wearing had
such a distinctive pattern, full of weaving and zigzags. Aw fuck. It
was as plain as a burglar's footprints in the snow. He would have
to confuse the issue. So he walked back and overlapped his own
prints, walked down the hall to where the floor had dried or
partially dried. The surface was drying unevenly, revealing swathes
and sweeps of the mop. Then he walked back up the corridor
again, criss-crossing over his own prints. When he turned the
corner into the unwashed part of the corridor he left wet
footprints on the dry lino. Christ, what a mess. What a fucking
dunderhead he was. A dumbfuck, a complete and utter dumbfuck.
He was cutting it very fine. He had to have Condor's keys back
before the end of mass, before he came off the altar. Now he
could see the clock at the end of the corridor. It was twenty-five
past. Condor *did* keep his fucking clock fast. He might have
known how else did he get down to the head of the drive every
morning on the dot of nine? Martin wanted to run, but he
walked. Because just as soon as he started to run some teacher
would step out from nowhere – you boy, stop running – and he'd
want to know why you were running and where were you
running to and had you never heard of self-discipline and how
easily accidents can happen and whether or not he had ever
considered the possibility of bowling someone over and fuckin
crap and more fuckin crap. So he walked. He could be into the
sacristy and have the keys returned before Condor had even
finished communion.

Then the Reverend Head walked round the corner.

'The early bird,' he said.

'Yes, Father.'

'What particular worm are you out to catch this morning,
Martin?'

'None, Father.'

'So tell me — how is your repeat year going?'

'Good. Good enough.'

'And the exams. How are the preparations going?'

'Good.' But he had already said 'good' twice. He had better add something to sound like an intelligent human being. 'Well. They're going well.'

'Are you putting in the hours at home?' Martin didn't want to sound like it was all plain sailing — didn't want it to seem that he was dying to get away from him.

'It's hard to concentrate.'

'I know. I know. But it'll come. What subjects are you doing?'

'English. Chemistry and Physics. And O grade Latin.'

'Slightly strange combination.'

'It's what you said I should do.'

'Did I indeed? I must have been thinking ahead to the job market. Any signs there, Martin? Any indications? Made up your mind yet?'

'No, Father.' Inside his pocket Martin held the bunch of keys tightly in his hand. The big chrome ones dug into him. The sharp jaggedy part, the part that turned in the lock. So much so that he thought they were going to cut him, to produce blood. Why did you bring these daggers from the place? Also he could still sense that his knees were shaking inside his trousers. If the Reverend Head noticed, he'd be sure to ask about it. You're not afraid of me, Martin, are you?

'You've thought about a vocation?'

'Yes.' The Reverend Head raised one eyebrow. 'I mean, Father, I've thought about it. But I don't think . . .' Martin tried to position his legs inside his trousers so that his trembling would not touch the grey material and broadcast his state to the outside world, in particular the Reverend Head.

'What? Finish your sentences.'

'I don't think I have a vocation.'

'Did you go to the Retreat in Ardglass this year?'

'Yes, Father.'

'And how did you find that?'

'It was good. I mean it stretched you. Made you think.'

'If you want to talk about it any further, feel free to come and see me. It's what I'm here for.' He talked on about his faith in young men, about how they could be trusted to do the right thing. Some people were dismissive of the younger generation, but not him. No, sir-ee. The young ones came up trumps every time. The Reverend Head questioned him further about his mother and about Father Farquharson. Martin wanted to be dead. The clock in the distance now said 8.30. His guts had gone to water again and he was having to tighten and pinch the muscles of his arse. He felt he badly wanted to go again. Then in the distance above his head he heard the rumbling of people rising and the clattering of feet and raised voices as the boys poured out of the chapel.

'Is that the time?' said the Reverend Head looking at his watch. 'Father McMullan must have had his foot on the accelerator this morning. Are you all right, Martin? Is there something biting you?'

'No, Father.' The keys were gnawing into the flesh of his hand.

'Carry on with the worm search.'

'Pardon, Father?'

'The early bird.'

'Oh . . .' The Reverend Head continued on his way to his room, his hands behind his back. Martin walked towards the sacristy. What the fuck was he going to do? Condor was, at this very minute, getting out of his vestments.

He went into the altar boys' room. There were two servers there. First-year boarders. One of them was a wee McKelvey from Cookstown – there seemed to be one of them in every year.

'Where's Condor?' Wee McKelvey waved his thumb at the next room. Martin stood not knowing what to do. He was still trembling, still shaking. Then he heard Condor's deep voice.

'Anyone seen my keys?' Condor came to the doorway. Then into the altar boys' dressing room, where he stood with his hand on the jamb. He was by now in his soutane with the shoulder cape.

'No, Father,' said McKelvey. It was only then that Condor noticed Martin.

'Brennan – what has you here?' Martin didn't say anything because he knew his voice would shake and give him away. He didn't know where he got the idea or the strength to put it in motion but he pushed past Condor into the sacristy and began as if looking for the keys. As he passed the priest he got a whiff of tobacco. His movement was so definite that Condor and the two altar boys followed him. The altar boys looked around. Martin went to the far side of the robing table and squatted down. There was a dark green metal wastepaper bin.

'Is this them, Father?' Martin rattled the bunch of keys against the metal and held them up.

'Good man.' Condor took the keys from him and slipped them into his pocket. He then picked up his other paraphernalia – coins, which he pulled towards himself like a poker dealer, his pipe cleaner and stuff. 'We don't often have the pleasure of your company at this hour of the morning, Brennan.'

'No, Father. I'm turning over a new leaf.'

'What has you in here?'

'I wanted to ask McKelvey something.'

'Come on boys – get a move on.'

And Condor was away. The sacristy door slammed. Martin exhaled.

'Jesus.'

'What did you want to ask me?' said wee McKelvey.

'Knock, knock.'

'Who's there?'

'Doctor.'

'Doctor Who?'

'How did you know?' Martin walked away and headed for the toilets.

He checked through the cloth of his pocket that the key had not disappeared. It was still there. He couldn't wait to show it to Blaise and Kavanagh.

It was still very early. There were a couple of first-years hanging around in the yard outside kicking a tennis ball against the wall. Martin had to hurry the last few steps into a cubicle. He chose the same one as he'd sat in when he'd been skiving off from Wee Jacky's English class. It was becoming quite a home from home. He got his trousers and drawers down in the nick of time. He sat there and let what was left in him drain out. His head was in his hands and his elbows rested on his knees. But where on earth was it all coming from? He'd only had a sausage roll and an egg and onion sandwich in the last twelve hours. His appetite had disappeared because of his nerves. He couldn't afford this. He was skinny enough, without all this loss. If only he could eat more, exercise more. He'd thought of doing muscle-building exercises – of sending away for Bullworkers he'd seen advertised – but that was as far as it went. They were far too expensive.

He heard voices and smelled cigarette smoke. Boys coming in for a quick puff before class started. The five to nine warning bell went. Martin looked around and saw that there was no paper. What a fucking place. When he needed it in an emergency. Then he realised he had never crapped in school before, in all his years there. And he was doing a year more than most. His bag was in the locker room so he couldn't tear a page from a jotter. He began to go through his pockets. On his bare thighs were two round red marks where he had rested the points of his elbows. The only thing he found in his inside pocket was a slip of paper his mother had given him, and made him promise to carry with him at all times. It said 'In case of an emergency please notify a priest.' But it was too small. He found a softness at the bottom of his blazer pocket and pulled it out. A serviette, navy blue and bunched up.

'Thank you mother.'

At lunch time when they reached the row of shops Kavanagh protested. Blaise said Kavanagh was the tallest and therefore looked the oldest. Martin agreed that Kavanagh looked the most responsible. Kavanagh said the Car Accessories people weren't stupid – they knew the age of guys in school uniform.

'Schoolboys get keys cut too,' said Blaise. Eventually Kavanagh went in and got the key cut while the other two waited outside.

'What we need to know now,' said Blaise, 'is *when* the papers will arrive. Maybe I should make another phone call. What do you call the guy in the school office?'

'Cuntyballs.'

'No, his real name. I can't phone up the Ministry of Education and say *My name is Cuntyballs.*'

'I don't see why not,' said Martin. 'Maurice Collins, I think.'

'Mistah Collins.' Blaise spat the name out in a military manner.

Inside the shop they could hear the metallic saw-whine of a key being cut.

'Have you got money for the phone?' said Blaise. Martin handed over what change he had in his pocket. There was a phone box further down the road on the same side.

'Will we wait for the man?' said Blaise.

Martin nodded. Kavanagh came out with two keys lying flat on his palm. One of them was bright and new. Blaise took charge of it. The other he turned over to Martin. Then he dusted his hands with some satisfaction. Martin slipped the key into his trouser pocket.

They walked down to the phone and waited outside. There was a woman in the box which meant at least the phone was working. When she hung up the three boys crowded in. Blaise produced a small diary and set it on the shelf. He put in Martin's money, then dialled. They all listened to the purring of the dialling tone.

'Yes, thank you. Mr Livingstone, please?' Blaise covered the mouthpiece with his hand. Kavanagh was laughing, but trying not to do it out loud. Blaise rolled his eyes, told them in a hissing voice to shut up. A voice came on the line. Blaise stated the name of the school and asked when could he expect delivery of this year's examination papers. The tiny voice in the earpiece said,

'Who am I talking to?'

'Cunt . . . Collins, Mistah Collins here,' said Blaise. Martin bent over and started biting his finger. Kavanagh's tall body jack-knifed but still he didn't make any noise.

'Just a moment . . .' There was a pause. Blaise smiled and moved his eyebrows. He said to Kavanagh 'Cuntyballs is a nice man — everybody likes him. Hello?'

'Yes, hello. They should be there on Tuesday the 25th. In the morning some time.'

'Can you not be more precise than that?' Kavanagh was still in fits and shaking his head furiously, telling Blaise to get off while he was still ahead. Blaise went on, 'I'm a busy man and if security is to be a priority I'm going to have to be there — ready and waiting — to uplift the said papers on their arrival.'

'I can't be that precise. But mid to late morning is the best I can do.'

174

'Very good – thank you Mr Livingstone. Thank you for all your help.'

When he put the phone down the noise of laughter was deafening. They were all howling in the confined space. Blaise was trying to say that he almost told the Ministry of Education that his name was Cuntyballs. While Kavanagh was trying to point out that Blaise had, as near as dammit, admitted to the man his name was Cuntyballs. And Martin was screaming that Blaise told the man his name *was* Cuntyballs. There were bite marks and blood on the knuckle of Martin's finger.

On the Tuesday morning they had a class in Jacques Cousteau's room which overlooked the driveway. Martin sat on a stool by the window and watched the comings and goings. After eleven, a navy van drew up and the driver disappeared out of sight in the direction of the front door. There was another guy in the van. Martin could see a bare forearm resting on the rolled-down window. The guy was flicking the ash from his cigarette. After a while Condor and Cuntyballs came from the direction of the office behind the willow tree. There was a trundling of metallic wheels and Joe Boggs arrived from a different direction with his railway porter's trolley. Martin gave the thumbs up to the others and asked to go to the toilet. Cousteau just sighed and nodded.

Martin headed down the stairs towards the front door to see what he could see. Condor stood in the corridor his feet astride, his hands in his pockets, making the black bell of his soutane as wide as possible. Behind him, round the corner, Cuntyballs and Joe Boggs struggled up the main stairs with the railway porter's trolley loaded with brown paper packets. Joe was higher up the stairs, Cuntyballs stooping below him, hoisting the wheels up the treads of the stairs, the way he would help a woman up steps with her buggy.

'Where do you think you're going?' said Condor. His voice echoed deeply in the empty corridor.

'The toilet, Father.' Martin looked closely at his Roman collar. It seemed perfectly normal.

'You know the reason we have a break?' He swung the arm out to expose his watch. 'In ten minutes' time?'

'Couldn't wait, Father.'

'Are you some kind of oul woman? Couldn't wait ten minutes?' He waved him by. Martin went across the yard into the toilet. He stood listening to the mournful sizzling and swishing of the urinals and when he thought sufficient time was up he went out again. He went up the back stairs and looked down the length of the upstairs corridor. The door of the cleaner's store was open and Joe Boggs was coming out with his trolley. It rattled even more now that it was light. He and Cuntyballs were laughing at something.

'Look, where I bit myself in the phone box the other day.' Martin held his finger out for them to see. There were ripples of laughter still running through the three of them as they sat in the locker room. It was empty at this time during the lunch break. Everyone had gone to the canteen or down to the shops or over to the daffs for a smoke.
    'Oh I forgot to tell you,' said Martin, 'about Condor's collar.'
    'What about it?'
    'Next time you see him take a good look at his collar.'
    'Why?'
    'It's not all it seems.'
    'What do you mean?'
    'It's cut from a Fairy Liquid bottle.'
    'You're taking the piss.'
    'I am not. I saw it with my own two eyes. In his bedroom.'
    'Fuckin skinflint.'
    'Turn-collar,' said Blaise. 'So what's next?'
    'It's over to you,' said Kavanagh. 'The next move is yourn.'
    'Did you remember the torch?' Kavanagh produced a torch from his bag and shone it in Blaise's face to prove it was working. 'Nobody, but nobody should get to know about this.' Blaise looked from one to the other. Martin and Kavanagh nodded. 'If word gets out – we're fucked.'
    'I want that back. It's the light of my life.'
    'You'll need something like a draught excluder for the light under the door,' said Martin. 'Just in case somebody's passing.'
    'At four in the morning?' Blaise sounded scornful. Then he paused. 'Hey maybe create a diversion. Shoot a racehorse or something.'
    'Where would you get a racehorse at four in the morning?'

'Shooting it would wake everybody.'

'Shoot the Sexual Athlete when he's having a wank on the track.' They all fell about laughing at the thought of being shot in mid-wank.

'But how are you going to wake at four?' said Martin.

'The same way I wake at eight.'

'Thanks.'

'Bang your head on the pillow eight times or four times before you go to sleep. That's when you wake.'

'If you get caught, swallow the poison,' said Kavanagh.

'And tell them I had nothing to do with it,' said Martin. 'Any of it.'

His nose was cold. And his eyelids. He kept twisting and turning in the bed, hoping that he would fall asleep on the side he was lying on. Then giving up and turning on the other side. He tried to imagine what Blaise was doing. He had never been in the boarders' dorms, so he found it hard to picture. It couldn't be four o'clock yet. His school diary said that sunrise was at 0452. Blaise was such a madman. He'd asked Martin if he knew anyone who would like to buy a thing signed by W.B. Yeats. He showed it to him – a handwritten document of about three pages. It was an introduction to something called *Geetanjali* by Rabindranath Tagore.

'I read it,' Blaise said. 'It's crap but it might be worth a few quid.'

'How did you get it?'

'It came into my possession.'

Another day the Spiritual Director had been telling them about some king of England who was a bit of a lame duck.

'Why do you call him that?' Blaise had said.

'What?'

'A lame duck.'

'Because he was that kind of person. A total disaster.'

'To be a lame duck is fairly OK. Ducks fly. Ducks swim a lot. To be lame is only a minor irritation for a duck.'

'It's a term of speech, Foley. No matter what its origins are, it means to be seriously disadvantaged.'

'A king?'

'In some departments. He was a born loser. People use words to mean what they want to mean.'

'If it was a hen, sir, it would work better. A lame hen.'

Maybe it was something to do with his saint's name but he did have a thing about animals. Normally he would have been all for disruption on a grand scale but one day, during the morning break, a black mongrel strayed up the long school drive. Jimmy Flynn from Martin's year went over to it and made friends with it. He enticed it through the corridors, its claws clicking and padding over the floor, to the inner school yard. It was a poor-looking thing like one of those beach dogs – excitable and quivery – who would run after anything thrown for it, would skulk if scolded – a complete underdog of a dog. It ran this way and that in the crowded playground almost berserk with the amount of attention it was getting. Guys fed it bits of their lunch, threw gym shoes for it to fetch. When the bell went Jimmy Flynn brought the dog to heel and said, 'We'll get a bit of mileage out of this. Bring it into English.'

But Blaise intervened. Without saying a word he took the dog from Flynn. He stooped and held it by the hair at the back of its neck and walked it to a side door behind the kitchens. It was a door within a door. A gate. He opened it and let the dog out into the street. He made a joke of it, saying, 'It's too intelligent for in here. If we let him stay, he'd only get dog's abuse.'

Another time in the Religious class the teacher asked for an example of something they thought immoral. Blaise said, 'Horses in bullfights – the picadors' horses – the ones with the quilted sides – that are terrified of being gored. Well, they have had their vocal cords cut so their screams won't be heard. Because it would disturb the crowd.' There was silence for a long time after that – as people thought about it.

He hoped that Blaise would chicken out of stealing the exam papers. That way Martin would be in the clear. He had got into Blaise and Kavanagh's good books for getting into Condor's room and nicking the storeroom key but if it was Blaise who chickened out that would suit fine. There would be no more to be said. It would be one hell of a big relief. Maybe Blaise was all bluster.

When it came to the crunch he might not be up to it. Martin imagined him coming along the corridor in the morning.

'Well?'

'It's off. I got up last night but it was just too dangerous.'

'Too bad.'

'I don't think we should go ahead with this. It's too risky.'

Martin would probably bluster a bit: 'What the fuck did I risk my neck for – getting into Condor's room?' But after a while he could come down to a more mousy position and shrug and say 'I suppose it suits me.'

Martin wondered if Kavanagh felt the way he did. But Kavanagh usually spoke out. He wouldn't be mealy mouthed about it. He would have said something like, 'We will proceed no further in this business, Mrs Macbeth. The whole thing's a bad idea.' Or could it be that he, too, was the undercow of Blaise, that he, too, was in thrall to him. Maybe Martin just imagined Kavanagh was strong willed, strong minded. Maybe Kavanagh was like Martin – do I dare to eat a peach? Maybe Kavanagh was the catcher of his falling dream. Attached to nothing.

He tried to hold his nose to warm it up – put a warm fingertip on each eyelid. It must have worked because he remembered nothing else until he woke in the morning with the words of his dreams repeating in his head, words which he was convinced would solve everything. Garabandy. Milkquistic. Fockuental.

9.   A Photographic Evening

He met Kavanagh at the top of the road and they walked to school through the drizzling rain.

'Well?'

'Do you think he's done it?' said Martin. Kavanagh shrugged and screwed his face up against the rain. They didn't mention him again.

They had the first two periods free, but they had to be in school at nine like everybody else. If they were late Condor would thump them just the same as any other day – except that he would shelter from the rain in the Science archway. Free periods had to be spent in the study hall, studying.

Martin and Kavanagh went straight there. A strong smell of wet blazers was everywhere and the windows had steamed up on the inside. Overlooking the rows of desks was a life-size statue of the Curé d'Ars with one arm extended. He had a bald head and grey locks and the two purple tabs of his priestly French garb hung out over his collar. The boys always put something in his right hand. This morning it was a Coke bottle. Every boy in the school referred to him as 'this curio of ours'.

Martin and Kavanagh sat on the desk tops with their feet on the seats, talking. It was not nine o'clock yet, so nobody had turned up to supervise. Free periods depended very much on who was supervising. It could be dire silence with somebody like Condor, forced to sit there reading and rereading the same line for forty minutes. Maybe turning a page just in case he was keeping an eye on you. Or it could be easy going, a bit of chat here and there, with Wee Clo or Cousteau.

Blaise appeared in the doorway. He walked towards them. He was carrying a leather briefcase. This was unusual because, being a boarder, he carried only the books he needed for the next class.

'Well?' said Martin.

'Well what?'

'Come on – fuck ya,' said Kavanagh. 'How did it go?'

'I found it difficult to sleep . . .'

'Me too . . .'

'But when I did get up at four there was some bastard moving around. He was a prefect – I could hear him pissing – boy, could I hear him pissing – like a man on stilts.'

'So?' Kavanagh said.

'I went back to my bed.'

Martin and Kavanagh looked at each other.

'That's not so hot,' Martin said. 'The rest of us risk our lives . . .'

'But when the dorm settled I got up again.' Blaise began to unzip the top of his briefcase. 'And I went downstairs with the key you so generously provided, and my torch and my bath towel. And I got these.' He looked all around, but seeing only first-years trying to finish homework, he produced a brown envelope with a cellophane window. He offered it – held it out in front of him while he looked down into his briefcase. Kavanagh out-waited Martin. Martin took it and looked at the cellophane window. ADVANCED LEVEL CHEMISTRY pale green with this year's date on it, so many days hence.

'Fuckin hell.' He felt weak. His insides sank. But Blaise was handing him another envelope. ADVANCED LEVEL PHYSICS. Pale pink.

'Jesus.' And ADVANCED LEVEL ENGLISH LITERATURE and PURE and APPLIED MATHS in pastel shades of blue and cream and yellow. Martin was in a kind of daze, just taking each envelope as it was handed to him.

'Holy fuck, Blaise,' said Kavanagh, angling his head and reading the titles in the cellophane windows.

'Fuckin hell. Get these out of sight,' said Martin as if he had suddenly become aware of the danger. He grabbed his bag and slid the envelopes down behind a ring binder marked English Notes.

'Relax,' said Blaise. 'And here – did somebody not mention O grade Latin as a requirement for something?'

'Shit the bed.'

'I was the best part of half an hour in there sorting through this stuff.'

'Why are you giving them all to me?' said Martin.

'It would be very dodgy for me to attempt steaming them here – in the school dormitory,' said Blaise. 'I don't even have access to a kettle.'

'Access to a fucking kettle.' Martin didn't know what he was saying.

'Will these not be missed?' said Kavanagh.

'Nobody'll miss an envelope until the day of the exam,' said Blaise, 'and by that time we'll have put them back.' Blaise was still holding out the O grade Latin papers. Martin seemed frozen.

'There's no point in having two stashes,' said Kavanagh. 'Twice as easy found. You take them all, Martin.'

'Gee thanks.' Martin took the Latin papers and slid them down into his bag with the others.

Over the day the quality of the rain changed – but it never stopped. It went from drizzle to showers and it rattled against the windows of each classroom they went to. Martin watched the droplets on the pane beside him quiver and run into one another. In one classroom there was a wire grille protecting the window and the rain dripped and zigzagged from one level to the next. The drainpipes clunked and spluttered. And all day the papers burned there in his bag. He barely let the strap slip off his shoulder, did not dare to be parted from it for an instant. In Physics, after he took his textbook out he fastened up the buckle straps to their shortest and set the bag on the walked-over wet floor. He made sure to place the leg of the stool inside the loop of the shoulder strap and never to take his behind off the stool. Somebody, acting the maggot, could just pinch it for a laugh – throw the bag around the wet playground, then where would he be? During English the rain stopped and the sun even came out for a bit. There was homework to be handed in and Wee Jacky came round the desks gathering the exercise books. Normally the boys set them on his desk at the end of the period on their way out but today, of all days, he came down among them.

'The results of your labours, please, gentlemen.' Martin opened his bag and dug for his orange English exercise book. Wee Jacky stood waiting, a pile of a dozen exercises already in his hands. The brown envelopes could be seen. And he was sure Wee Jacky saw them – but there was no recognition of what they were. Martin refastened the buckle straps, his heart pounding.

The last bell of the day rang and everyone headed down the driveway. Kavanagh was staying on for something energetic – pole vault or basketball practice. They had planned to meet later at Kavanagh's place. And do the business. Kavanagh said on Wednesdays his people went out to the Old Boys and his sisters were *never* in.

Martin turned for home outside the school gates. After the rain everything looked rinsed – trees, pavements, even the red buses looked clean. His bag bulged with camera equipment he'd borrowed. He kept to the inside of the pavement. Less risk there. He could hardly believe the way he was thinking. If a lorry careered off the road and hit him, he'd be brought to the hospital. The police would be called in and they'd have to sort through his bag for proof of identity. And find the exam papers – like finding a copy of the worst wank magazine in the world. One day at a bus stop he'd found one in the waste bin. He couldn't stand there at the bus stop flicking through it – he wanted to have a good look at it – so he slid it into his bag. If he'd been knocked down that day his mother would have been mortified in front of the hospital staff.

'Mrs Brennan, we're obliged to return Martin's effects. I've looked through them. I'm dreadfully sorry. Of course he may have just found this filthy magazine in a waste bin at a bus stop. And the bus hit him *before* he could get round to having a wank. Of that we're definite. So he's probably in heaven.'

'Thanks be to God for small mercies.'

Even though he had been to Kavanagh's house several times he could never remember which of the doorbells worked. The Victorian one looked useless. The white push-button on the porch door sounded dully somewhere at the back of the house. At half eight, it was still bright and birds were singing. The porch door was of stained glass and he saw Kavanagh's shape coming to open it. The hallway was large, big as a room with a wide staircase. Kavanagh put him in the sitting room and went off somewhere. Martin unslung his bag and sat on the sofa staring at the ceiling. The room was so quiet traffic could be heard from the main road. The large bay window was cloaked in heavily patterned curtains which were held back by tasselled cords. The pelmet had a gold fringe. It was all heavy duty stuff with flock maroon wallpaper in a fleur-de-lys pattern. He liked to brush his fingers over the upraised flowers. There was too much to look at in the room and yet there was nothing to look at. It was about ten times the size of the parlour at home. And the pictures on the walls were terrible – scenes of cattle drinking beside a cluster of framed certificates belonging to the sisters – both older. One had done dentistry, the other psychiatry. And his da. Kavanagh's old man was a doctor, not a GP but a hospital doctor. There was also a brass relief of Whistler's mother. A clothes brush with a matching brass handle attached to it. From somewhere else in the house he could faintly hear music. Country and western. It sounded like 'The Padre of Old San Antone'. He thought of the papers in his bag. And suddenly, for no reason he could think of, he felt hopeless. Infinitely sad. Even the material of the sofa beneath his hand felt wretched. The feeling was so intense it clenched his stomach. He closed his eyes and waited for it to disappear. Kavanagh stuck his head around the door.

'How many sugars?'

'But I'm just after my own tea.'

'You could force down another one.'

'Two sugars.'

Kavanagh's head ducked out, leaving him alone again. Still the mournful tune went on. And the traffic. And the disaster they were about to get involved in. His limbs felt weighed down so that he could not move. His muscles had turned to lead. Gravity had increased its hold on him and wanted to drag him down through the sofa, through the floor. Fuck, what a . . .

Kavanagh pushed the door open with his foot and came in bearing the tea. There was a slice of cake each. They drank their tea from china mugs.

'That's German cake,' said Kavanagh.

'It's good,' said Martin. He rubbed his fingers free of the icing dust.

Mrs Kavanagh, obviously dressed to go out and looking great in a red dress, silvery stockings and sling-backs, came in to say hello.

She stood at the doorway as if not wanting to intrude. Her feet were apart on either side of the door and her hands rested on the inside and outside handles. Looking at her, he felt the bad feeling draining out of him.

'That's what I like to see – feeding the brain cells,' said Mrs Kavanagh. 'This year of all years.'

'Uh-huh.'

'How d'you think you'll do?'

'Haven't a clue.'

'Do a bit of work,' she mock-scolded. 'You can't leave it all up to the Man Above. Prayers are all very well but there's no substitute for the studying.'

Kavanagh sat silent, not joining the conversation, his head down. Martin remembered the day Kavanagh had taken the soup in his house. He'd been embarrassed about his mother but there was no need for Kavanagh to feel that way. Mrs Kavanagh was old but kinda sexy at the same time. She played with the door, moving it slightly between her feet.

'What are you going to do next year?'

'If I get enough marks I'll go to the University.'

'To do what?'

'A degree.'

'Good for you. In what?'

Martin was in mid shrug when the phone rang in the distance. Mrs Kavanagh said, 'That's me,' and Martin heard the click of her high heels on the tiled floor as she ran. Kavanagh rolled his eyes. Martin contradicted him.

'Naw, naw. She's OK. Every time I come here she looks younger.'

Kavanagh snorted.

'My ma's old,' said Martin. 'Like Whistler's mother.'

'Who he?'

'The painter – there on your wall.'

Kavanagh stood up and closely inspected the brass plaque.

'I never knew that was anybody's mother – just thought it was some oul woman.' He paused and pulled a face. 'Fuck, this is desperate.'

'Yeah – I've never been this jumpy about anything.'

They climbed the stairs to Kavanagh's bedroom. There was a

radiator on the landing with about ten pairs of flimsy knickers on it. Martin stared. In the bedroom they didn't say anything. Martin picked up a pack of cards and began laying out solitaire on the carpet. After a while they heard the slam of the front door.

'Hold on,' said Kavanagh. Martin heard the car pull away and gather speed. Kavanagh went downstairs for the kettle. Martin sat looking around, saw himself reflected in the wardrobe mirror. The style of the room wasn't as bad as downstairs. Kavanagh must have exerted some taste. There was a small wooden crucifix above the bed. An old-fashioned fireplace was painted white. A desk and a chair by the window. On the wall above this desk was a year calendar with each day of the past Xed out in black. Some dates in June had been enclosed in red boxes, each with the subject of the exam written above.

Kavanagh had photos of himself in frames on the wall: an action shot of him soaring over the bar in mid pole vault – various basketball teams since first year – early ones in baggy white gym kit, later ones of the school team with their green and yellow strip. In each picture Kavanagh sat in the middle with his arms folded and his knees open and a big grin on his face. Say cheese. And everybody said 'Fromage'. He always wore number 9.

'Who took the pole vault shot?'

'A guy from the *Telegraph*. At the Interschools.'

'I'll take some of you. Maybe this year.'

Martin set up his gear. The tripod – the legs hardly extended at all – on the desk holding the camera *beneath* – shining the desk lamp down on the paper – the cable release – the light meter. When it was all done he went to the window and stood looking down into the street. There were trees growing out of the pavements on both sides of the road. Roots were heaving up, here and there. The leaves looked washed and bright green. A black taxi cab pulled up. It took a long time before anybody got out. The engine was still running, the cab shuddering. The back door opened and Blaise stepped down carrying his briefcase.

'Fucksake . . .'

Martin heard the doorbell and the voices coming up the stairs.

'But how did you know where I lived?' Kavanagh was saying.

'I asked Cuntybollicks.'

'Cunty Balls. His second name is not Bollicks. Look who's here,' Kavanagh shouted ahead to Martin.

'Hi,' said Martin. Although he said a lot of hurtful things, Martin somehow felt better with Blaise there. Safer in some way.

Kavanagh hunkered down to plug the kettle into a wall socket. It began to rattle and bubble almost immediately. 'So what brings you here?' he said.

'I didn't want to miss the fun.'

'There's no fun yet. Just wait till we build up a head of steam here.'

'That's another reason I came.'

'What?'

'I'm not happy with the steam idea. When I tried it on Condor's envelope it didn't look good. It wrinkled and stained a bit. Even when it dried out, it looked tampered with.'

'I thought you didn't have access to a kettle,' said Martin.

'Don't be so tiresome, Martin.'

'No, really. Where did you do this?'

'There are kitchens in the school.'

'So how do you propose opening them?' asked Kavanagh.

'A knife – anything.'

Kavanagh and Martin looked at each other, not understanding. Blaise produced a sheaf of large brown manila envelopes from his briefcase.

'After school I went into town. Her Majesty's Stationery Office. With Condor's original. And I asked them for the nearest thing to it.' He held them out to Martin. 'Compare and contrast.' Martin opened his bag and took the exam envelopes out. It was as if they'd been taken from the same ream of heavy duty brown paper.

'A man on a galloping horse . . .'

'Blaise – you're a fuckin genius.'

'They're not cheap,' said Blaise. 'I'll be looking for a contribution.'

There was a shiny letter opener in the shape of a sword on Kavanagh's desk. Blaise picked it up.

'Here goes,' he said. 'What'll we start with?'

'Highest card chooses,' said Martin. He pulled the wrecked game of solitaire together and began to shuffle the cards. He stood and imitated a drum roll, then dealt a card to Kavanagh. When he flipped it over it was the seven of hearts. The drum roll continued and he dealt a two of clubs to Blaise. They all laughed.

'Cheat.' The noise Martin was making rose to a climax as he dealt himself a Queen of Diamonds.

'A charlatan and thimblerigger.'

'English – we'll take a look at English first,' said Martin.

'Sell – fish.'

Blaise looked through the cellophane windows and selected the correct envelope. He slid the miniature sword beneath the flap. Martin felt it like a stab in himself. The bad feeling began to fill him again. Blaise made little sawing motions, leaving a smooth slit. As he did so he bit down on his lower lip.

'Wait,' said Kavanagh. 'I don't want to sound melodramatic – or like it was in a movie – but what's the state of fingerprinting at the minute?'

The other two shrugged.

'It might be wise to assume that they can detect them on paper,' said Blaise.

Martin was again full to the brim with misery. He couldn't say anything for a while.

'Certainly on cellophane,' said Kavanagh. 'They can find as many prints as they like on the *outside* of the envelopes – but not on the papers.'

'You might be right,' said Blaise.

'Hold everything.' Kavanagh got up and went downstairs. During the whole time he was out of the room Martin and Blaise did not speak. Kavanagh came back in, slightly out of breath, with a blue box, like a tissue box. From a slit he plucked a glove made of clear cellophane-like stuff and handed it to Martin.

'Better to be safe than sorry, Monsieur Poirot. Remind me to put the box back.' He put on a voice of a fairground salesman: 'One size fits all. Left or right – it'll be all right.'

Martin felt that his silence would be noticed. He had to say something soon. The cellophane gloves, when he put them on, seemed to shrink and cling to his fingers.

'They're sexy,' he said.

'Let me at them,' said Kavanagh. They all put them on. They made faint rustling noises. Blaise pulled out the batch of pale blue exam papers. The other two couldn't wait and leaned over his shoulder trying to see.

'What's on?' they both said. Blaise handed them a paper each and turned to the first page.

'*Macbeth*,' he said.

'Fucksake we *know* that – we've been studying it all year so it *would* be on. What's the question?'

'Imagery . . . How does the imagery contribute . . . A quote from Caroline Spurgeon . . .'

'I can do this one,' said Martin. 'I've already done an essay on this. Ill-fitting clothes and all. Who's on the poetry?'

'Ummm – John Donne – Milton – Hopkins.'

They talked and laughed their way through the whole exam paper, then began to open the others.

'Come on, lads,' said Kavanagh. 'A bit more systematic. A bit of self-discipline is needed here. Photos, Brennan.'

The English paper was laid flat on the desk and Martin took a reading with his light meter.

'No walking about,' he said. 'It'll shake the floor.' He released the shutter and at the noise the other two stood in exaggerated attitudes – like a game of statues. Martin ignored them and counted the seconds aloud: 'Fuck the Queen – one. Fuck the Queen – two. Fuck the Queen – three.'

The statue joke wore off after a while but Martin continued to count the seconds in the same way. Even when it was into himself.

When the English paper was photographed Blaise took one of Her Majesty's Stationery Office envelopes, its fresh gum shining, and slid all the papers back into it. Kavanagh had brought a dish of water and a sponge from the bathroom. The gummed flap was wiped and the envelope sealed. It looked perfect.

'What more could you want?' said Blaise.

'A big girl lying on her back,' said Kavanagh.

'Ask and you shall receive.'

'What? What do you mean?'

'Maybe not the real thing,' said Blaise. 'But a picture of the real thing. Lovely ladies and gentlemen showing their wares.'

'In your dreams,' said Kavanagh.

'In your wet dreams,' said Blaise.

189

'Porn?'

'If that's the case, I can do without the pictures of gentlemen,' said Martin over his shoulder.

'How much are they showing?'

'Everything you're interested in – they show *more* than their wares.'

'Where is this stuff?'

'Don't fucking scoff. I can get it – for you.'

'Well, do then. Share that kind of thing around.' Martin looked hard at Kavanagh to see if he was serious. 'Just curiosity,' Kavanagh said to Martin. 'It's all part of our education.' He hung his tongue out like a dog. Martin turned up his nose.

'That kind of stuff. I don't know . . .'

'Martin sounds like he disapproves,' said Blaise. 'But I knew he would. You're so steeped in establishment values. Pornography is all about class. The people at the top tell the people at the bottom what they can look at, what they can read. It's OK for the censor, who sits and views this material day in day out without being corrupted, but just show it to a working-class chap and he'll be utterly destroyed by it. How dare they?'

'Pornography just makes you want to wank. And that can't be good.'

'There's nothing wrong with wanking,' said Blaise. Martin rolled his eyes and laughed. As if he couldn't believe what he was hearing. The shutter whirred and clunked. 'Everybody does it, so it can't be wrong.'

'Every man for himself.' Kavanagh was laughing. 'Do you think girls wank?'

'Naw – how could they?' said Martin. 'They don't have a cock. Or so I'm led to believe.'

'Such vast anatomical knowledge,' said Blaise. He too was laughing. He began speaking directly to Kavanagh. 'In England the people in charge are the upper classes. Here in bog Ireland it's the clergy. They make the rules. St Patrick would have been far better employed if he'd driven out the priests, instead of the snakes . . .'

'They *are* the snakes,' said Kavanagh. 'Blacking out pictures in art books. They say it was Condor did that personally – sat up all night doing it – the Indian ink bathing trunks.'

'Remember second year?' said Martin 'The biology books with the twenty pages guillotined out.'

'Human Reproduction,' Kavanagh told Blaise. 'They thought we were so stupid we wouldn't look up the index.'

As the other two talked Martin worked his way through the other subject papers methodically, turning pages, flattening the centre fold with a rub of his gloved finger. Each time the shutter mechanism worked it made a satisfying clunk. Turn the page. Martin said he felt like a doctor, what with the clear gloves and the hypodermic feel to the cable release each time he pressed it. Blaise lay on the bed and Kavanagh was on the floor with his feet in the hearth.

'I should get somebody to write out the answers for me beforehand,' said Blaise. 'On blank answer books – and bring them in. One of you guys could do it for me.'

'I'm no good,' said Martin. 'If I did it for you you'd probably fail. Even knowing the friggin questions. And a handwriting expert would put us in jail.'

'He wouldn't have to be an expert,' said Kavanagh. 'But why wouldn't you do them yourself?'

'I'm a lazy bastard.' They all smiled and nodded. 'And I'm a dumbfuck speller.'

'It'd be just an extra risk,' said Kavanagh. 'You'd get caught going in with it.'

'I need a piss,' said Martin.

'Third on the right,' Kavanagh told him. 'Don't forget to take the gloves off.'

'If I was you, I'd keep them on,' shouted Blaise.

In the bathroom Martin wondered if he *should* take them off. At least the right hand one. In the end he decided not to. The glove material made whispering noises as he unzipped. The bathroom shelves were crowded with bottles of shampoo and conditioner, lotions and moisturising creams, deodorants and perfumes; the waste bin was full of bundled tissues with make-up on them; nail files and waxing strips, a jam jar of soft brushes and powder puffs, packets of sanitary pads and tampons sat openly on the shelf beside the toilet. Utterly mysterious. Spells and potions. When shall we three meet again. There was a separate shower as well as a bath. He took a tampon out of the box and looked at it. Like a little white cardboard tube with a string. A little stick of dynamite. He didn't want to think too much about it and replaced it carefully just as he'd found it. No incriminating fingerprints. Before he pissed he lifted the seat. When he finished he put it back down again. The toilet flushed with a stainless steel lever. He was going to wash his hands, then remembered he was wearing gloves. It would be *so* great to have a bathroom like this.

When he went back in to join the others he felt they had been talking about him. There was a long pause before Kavanagh said, 'Would anybody pay good money to know what was coming up?'

'Don't even think it,' said Blaise. 'It would be round the school in two minutes – and somebody'd shop us. This is definitely just for the three of us.'

'We must be very careful not to do too well,' said Kavanagh. 'If three of us were to end up getting ninety-eight per cent they'd smell a rat.'

'If Martin got fifty-eight per cent,' said Blaise, 'they'd smell a rat.'

'Fuck off.' There was a lot of nervous laughter going on – Kavanagh and Blaise were on a high. Martin was trying to be in the same sort of mood but was failing.

'What's up Brennan?' said Kavanagh.

'Nothing,' said Martin. He hated being slagged at any time, but couldn't bear it now when he was feeling so iffy. About the cheating. About everything. He wanted to cry more than laugh. All the time his innards were falling, like in a fast elevator.

'There *is* something getting up Brennan's nose,' said Kavanagh.

'No, there isn't.' He went on turning the pages, pressing the remote cable, counting his seconds. But he knew he was on a greased slope and there was nothing he could reach out for to stop his slide. A slope was gravity sideways – Galileo's inclined plane.

In school the next morning Martin and Kavanagh knocked on the staff room door and asked for Jacques Cousteau – by his real name. They told him they had a free double and they wanted to develop some film. He lent them his key. The darkroom was a walk-in book cupboard, off the physics lab. They thought it better if Kavanagh sat outside – a lookout to put anybody off the scent if they came into the lab.

Martin sat inside, where the darkness was total. Pitch black. He had seen pitch being poured on the roads – oily treacle. But the word was not accurate because pitch shone, was glossy, whereas the dark of the darkroom had nothing shiny about it. Like it was fur. In the Hopkins sonnet: 'I wake and feel the fell of dark not day'. *Fell* was a covering of hair. Hopkins, in his despair, felt his face was being pressed into it. But even fur and hair could have a sheen to it. The dark of the darkroom was matt black – a quilted coffin with the lid screwed down which had been put in the earth and covered by five feet of soil. No chink of light, no pinpoint. No shape. Shape totally disappeared and could only be re-established by touch. It was as if the blackness was wrapped around him – it was flat, one dimensional. To get any sense of it not being flat he had to reach out and touch something. He found and saw things with his fingers. This must be what blind people experience. Dark, dark, dark amid the blaze of noon. That fucker Milton again.

He loaded the two films into the developing tank and accurately poured in the developer, guided only by his sense of touch. He agitated the round tank in his hand, hearing the gurgle as he did so – listening to the ticking of the timer. As he waited in the dark he always turned his face up, like some sort of a flower.

What the fuck was he going to do? Nothing about this whole scam felt right for him. He wished he could think himself into Blaise's position of justification – but he was never any good at that kind of argument, he couldn't argue to convince *himself*. The thoughts he had wakened with that morning went on repeating in his head all day. Last night in the first rush of enthusiasm he had seen the English paper. And he couldn't forget it – that was an impossible thing to do. But he hadn't looked at any of the others – the Physics or the Chemistry or the Latin. He had photographed them, yes, but he had only looked at their surfaces – he was blind to what they said. He had made sure the print was in focus, but had not actually read the meaning of the text. He had been absorbed in getting the photography right while the other two had talked and taken notes about what questions had actually been set.

Martin made up his mind that after he had developed the negatives he would hand them over to Blaise and Kavanagh and tell them he was having nothing more to do with it. But what if

Blaise was right? That the whole establishment was corrupt and doing something like this would help bring about its downfall? It could only be changed by an accumulation of such acts. He'd read that the photographer, Dorothea Lange, had given up on the idea of the single picture – the bull's eye theory of photography – that somehow it could all be captured on the one piece of paper. A collection of pictures was better, a lifetime of pictures even more so. To simplify was to falsify.

Last night they had agreed that Blaise would take the resealed envelopes back to school with him. It was Kavanagh who suggested that Martin take an extra roll of film as a cover, just in case somebody, like Cousteau, asked awkward questions. Let's see the film you just developed, boys. And that was them fucking dead. So they sat around and made faces and Martin snapped them. He used the delayed action to get into some of them himself. The flash seemed to burn the centre of his vision to a black hole. Once the negatives had been developed and were seen to be OK the exam papers, snug in their new envelopes, could be put back in the store room at the first opportunity and nobody would be any the wiser.

The alarm bell on the timer rang, startling him. He changed the developer for the stop bath. He knew that Kavanagh could hear the bell outside. He'd be wondering, is it OK? Did the light get in, somehow or other? While the films were washing, Martin went out and gave Kavanagh the thumbs up. Kavanagh came in. Martin wiped the hanging strips with squeegee tongs and finished them off with a blow from the hair drier. He tore a page from a jotter and folded it over so that it formed a wallet of sorts for the finished negatives. He put them carefully in his inside pocket. He did the same for the negatives of the three of them larking about.

'To the daffs, for a smoke.'

The break bell had already gone and they walked across the crowded quad.

'What was Blaise rabbiting on about last night while I was working my back out taking the photographs?'

'The usual pomposities.'

'For instance?'

'Shelley, for God's sake. *Nothing that my masters knew or taught I wanted to learn.*'

'Shelley?'

'Blaise thinks it's a reasonable assumption: to say whatever we've been taught is wrong.'

'Do you believe that?' said Martin. 'Surely that's bollicks.'

'Yeah it is – he says things just to test you – just to make you think.'

'Just to annoy you.'

Inside the daffs they shouldered through the others to their corner. A moment later Blaise arrived. He was smiling.

'Any developments?' he asked. He had an eyebrow which would arch and loop as he spoke, or when he would listen. If Martin said something and Blaise's eyebrow went up he knew he was beaten.

'Ha-ha.' Martin patted his inside pocket.

'Good.'

'Did you put the papers back last night?' said Martin.

'No. I wanted to be sure the negatives were OK.' Martin's face must have betrayed how he felt. 'It'll be OK, Martin. Trust me. Stop worrying. I'll put them back when the time is right. Then we've won.'

'But not until then.'

'Where are they now?' asked Kavanagh.

'Not *in* but *under* my drawer. In the dorm.'

'What do you mean?'

'It's a good place – that space *beneath* a drawer. It's where I kept these.'

He produced a flat brown envelope and handed it to Kavanagh. Kavanagh opened it and peered in. He inserted a hand and pulled a small photo out. He turned it around trying to make out what he was seeing.

'Jesus.' Just then Sean McMahon, one of Sharkey's Republican crowd was passing. He saw better what the photo was from a distance.

'For fuck sake,' he said and reached round Kavanagh and snatched the photo out of his hand.

'Who's messing?'

'Where'd you get this?' shouted McMahon.

'It belongs to Foley – give it back.' Kavanagh made beckoning gestures. 'I haven't even had a chance to look at it yet.'

'It's a big cunt – like you,' shouted McMahon. He was backing away to where Sharkey and his crowd were, over by the right hand cubicles. Kavanagh was following him. McMahon reached out and gave the photo to Sharkey and made a grab for the envelope in Kavanagh's hand. It wasn't a fight. Everybody knew when a fight was starting – the way the crowd moved. This was different. This was pure codology – messing. Martin was close behind Kavanagh.

'What's going on?' Nobody seemed to know. Blaise elbowed his way into the mêlée.

'Dirty photos.' There was an outcry.

'Let's see.' Kavanagh snapped the picture back from Sharkey. 'Who is it?'

'Is she wearing any knickers?'

'It's your big sister, Foley.'

'Can you see her nipples?'

'Fuck her nipples, can you see her tits?'

Blaise was shouting for people to get back – he was using his elbows to fend guys off, trying to clear space for himself. Kavanagh's bulk shielded Blaise from the mob of guys who were pressing in. Both of them blocked the cubicle doorway.

'It's nothing,' said Blaise. Kavanagh dropped his voice.

'What are they?'

'Just some pics. *Get back.*' Blaise made to kick out at the press of bodies. Kavanagh helped him.

'Rabble – begone,' he shouted and shoved them back. 'You blocks, you stones. You worse than bollicks.'

'What's going on?' shouted Martin from behind. Kavanagh, still holding tightly on to the brown envelope and the picture he had snatched back from Sharkey pulled Martin and Blaise into the cubicle and slammed the door shut. Those left outside slapped the door with the flat of their hands. Somebody shouted, 'They're away in for a wank.'

'Give us Barabbas.'

Kavanagh reached into the envelope and produced a small pile of pictures.

'What have we got?'

'They're actual prints. This is not your Health and Efficiency,' said Blaise.

The pictures were black and white. Blaise rested his foot on the delf rim of the lavatory as the other two boys looked. Martin had his hand out waiting for Kavanagh to pass the next one on.

'Hey,' said Kavanagh. Martin looked at what he'd been given. At first he couldn't make it out. Then he realised it was a naked girl. She had her legs in the air.

'She's got tits on her like pouches,' said Martin.

'Have you got a magnifying glass?' said Kavanagh.

'Not every day you see stuff like that, eh? You wouldn't get that in *Playboy*,' said Blaise. Kavanagh was leafing through them. Another girl had her legs wide open. Others were close-ups. No faces. Guys were still banging on the door and shouting.

'Hold it,' said Martin, not sure what he was looking at. 'Who took these?'

'A gynaecologist,' said Kavanagh.

'What's she doing?'

'How would I know?'

'And what is that?'

'They're not very good quality,' said Martin.

'Fuck off, Cartier-Bresson,' said Blaise. 'What does that matter?'

'If they were good quality you could see more.'

'It's less I want to see,' said Kavanagh. 'Jesus, Blaise. Where'd you get this stuff?' Blaise shrugged. Martin unbolted the door.

'Where are you going, Martin?' said Kavanagh. Martin handed Kavanagh what pictures they had looked at. Kavanagh put them back in the envelope.

'After those I need another smoke.' Martin couldn't get out of the confined space until Kavanagh moved. Kavanagh looked down at the remaining couple of photos he hadn't looked at. A girl squatting over a basin and she was looking straight at the camera and grinning. Whatever was coming out of her was in droplets.

'Fuckin hell,' he said and screwed them up and threw them into the toilet.

'What did you do that for?' Blaise made to try and retrieve the pictures but thought better of it. There were brown streaks in the toilet bowl. His lips pursed in disgust as he bent over. Kavanagh reached out and pulled the chain. The toilet flushed with a roar.

'That was my property,' Blaise said.

'You can have it,' said Kavanagh. He handed the envelope with the pictures to Blaise. Martin swung the door inwards and Kavanagh pushed Blaise out into the crowd. They eased themselves out after him and struggled through the mob who were clamouring for a look. When Martin got back to the washbasins he lit his last cigarette.

'I was saving this one for the afternoon.' He crushed the packet and threw it away. Kavanagh shook his head.

'You couldn't even use that stuff for a wank.'

Blaise put his shoulder down and bored his way out through the crowd, pursued by guys still shouting for a look.

10. Days of Inquisition

In the afternoon during a double period of Physics the door opened and Condor came in. He spoke in whispers to Cousteau, who looked suddenly solemn and turned to face the boys.

'The Dean of Discipline would like a word.'

'Has he rumbled us?' said Kavanagh over his shoulder to Martin. Martin swallowed. The negatives in his inside pocket were burning into his ribs. The Dean stood in front of the class and eyed each boy briefly before saying anything. His head moved as he took in each row. He really did look like he had some terrible news for them. Like the Kennedy assassination. When he began to speak he addressed his words to the floor.

'I have been teaching – oh for twenty years now – I've been around boys for that length of time – and longer, if you count my own boyhood. And I enjoy it. Thoroughly. I like boys. I have the utmost respect for them. They make me proud to be associated with them. But sometimes something happens to . . . make me doubt. And when I have doubts about something as basic as my admiration for young men it is a very serious matter indeed. Something is going on in this school – a Catholic grammar school – which is worrying me deeply. I am distressed – and when I get like that, alarm bells should sound. Because I know I will pursue a matter of such magnitude to the ends of the earth.' Martin didn't dare move. He wanted to say to Kavanagh that the game was up but Condor knew every trick in the book, the hand to hide the mouth. He could hear the slightest whisper. Martin was quaking but wanted somehow to communicate it to Kavanagh. It occurred to him to write something on the page in front of him for Kavanagh to see – something like *he knows*. But Condor would be down on top of him like a ton of bricks: *what is it Brennan is choosing to write just at the moment when I most want his attention?* It was crazy. *And what exactly do I know?* So Martin just sat and stared down at the desk top.

'I will leave no stone unturned. No matter what kind of vermin scuttle out from under it. I want to see every senior boy in my room. One at a time. Alphabetical order. Brennan – you're first.' Shit the bed. Condor didn't turn away from him, but kept staring at him. He swung the classroom door open and gestured with his arm to usher Martin out. Martin walked down the aisle between the desks and out into the corridor. There was no opportunity to get the negatives to Kavanagh.

They walked the length of the corridor in silence. Condor was half a step behind him. His soutane swished as he strode along. Martin thought he could maybe drop back and stash the negatives behind a radiator. He touched them in his inside blazer pocket but at that moment Condor said,

'Put an inch to your step, Brennan. We haven't got all day.' As they climbed the stairs Condor moved ahead of him. Could he drop the negatives over the banisters without him noticing? If he was seen doing it, then it was all over. *What are those? Let's have a closer look.* He might as well jump over the banisters after them. Head first. Fall with a squish on to the terrazzo floor.

Outside his door Condor reached into his pocket and produced his bunch of keys. His shoes made squeaking noises on the lino. He selected the key with the yellow cover and as he reached to unlock the door he leaned towards Martin and sniffed. Martin stepped back.

'You're a smoker, Brennan?'

'No, Father.'

'Don't give me that. I can smell it a mile away. Didn't I punish you in this very room for it.'

'I've given up, Father.' The only thing Martin was glad about was that he hadn't any cigarette evidence on him. The priest opened the door with a clash and swish of his keys. He pocketed them and switched on the light.

'You're the photography man, I believe.'

'In Hobbies, Father.' Condor sat down in the office chair behind his desk. Martin stood facing him. He had to keep a tight grip on his bowels again. The bastard knew. He felt what was inside himself turn liquid. Condor swayed in the chair. With his weight it gave off little ticking and clinking noises, like a spring being compressed.

'Inspection time,' the priest said.

Oh fuck – how did he find out? Somehow or other he knew. Had Blaise turned informer? Martin turned out his blazer pockets. A hanky, none too clean, a book of paper matches.

'So you've given up?'

'It's just a book of matches.'

'I'm not after smokers today. It's more serious than that. What's in the trousers?' Martin put his hands into his trouser pockets. There was the chink of change. He pulled out some copper and silver coins and there – fucking hell – in the middle of his hand was the Yale key to the store. He set the handful of stuff on the desk. Condor scrutinised it briefly. The key looked like every other Yale key in the country. The priest then waved a finger at his pockets. Martin pulled out the linings. He knew where the toilet was but that would give everything away. Showing he was shit scared. Knowing where the crapper was, beyond the bedroom.

'Fine,' said Condor. Martin scraped together the key and his coins and repocketed them. 'What about the inside pocket?' Martin tapped it vaguely. He'd been grassed, right down to which pocket. 'Anything in there?' Martin shrugged, kept a tight hold of his muscles. Condor got to his feet as if he was actually going to search him.

'Just some negatives – I developed them this morning, Father.' He was trying to keep the shake out of his voice. At the same time sucking his sphincter in.

'Negatives! Let's have a look.'

Martin drew the folded jotter pages from his inside pocket and set them on the desk. His knees were trembling but not so much that they could be seen. Condor leaned forward. He unfolded one page and saw the celluloid strips. He reached to pick up the top one.

'By the edges, Father.'

'I know.' He sounded irritated. He lifted the strip, his fingers on each side of the sprocket holes and held it up to the light of the window. 'What are these?'

'Pages of a book.'

'What book?'

'A thing on *Macbeth* – by Caroline Spurgeon. An essay.' Condor stared at him with a baleful look of disbelief. 'It was a library book – which had to be left back.' Condor sat down again. His chair made noises, at the redistribution of weight. He looked away from Martin's face and picked up another strip – clear rectangles with black indecipherable squares. He doesn't know. He fucking doesn't know what he's looking at. He hasn't a clue. Condor shuffled among the negatives, opened the second folded page and saw negatives that were different. He leaned forward.

'What are these?'

'Just snaps. Messing, Father.' Condor switched on his desk lamp and held the black strip close to the bulb. He stared at the dark faces.

'Who of?'

'Kavanagh. Foley.'

'Are you friends with the new boy?'

'A bit. Not really. He hasn't been here very long.'

'Who's the third one?' Condor was tilting his head this way and that trying to make out what he was seeing.

'That's me. I'm in some of them. The camera has a self-timer button.'

'Don't try to blind me with science.' He lowered the negative and looked at Martin for what seemed ages.

'It just means you can run round and get in the photo yourself.' Condor continued to stare at him. 'There's a wee red light comes on.' Condor replaced the negative in the folded paper with the others. When he'd examined all the strips he leaned back in the chair. The noise was like the crinkling of silver paper. He reached into the slit of his soutane which led to his pocket. He brought out a clear polythene bag. Inside it was another brown paper bag. There were dark patches of damp or grease on this inner bag. He took it out and set it on the blotter pad on his desk.

'If you are a smoker – which I know you are – you will have been assuaging your craving in the toilet block at morning break – am I right or wrong?'

'I went over at break time, Father. To see some of the boys. The smoke gets on your clothes.'

'So who was smoking then?' Martin shrugged,

'Didn't see, Father.'

'Did you see anything else? Was there anything unusual going on?'

Martin shrugged and shook his head. 'Was there a rumpus?'

'A what Father?'

'A fight, a squabble?'

'No, Father.'

Condor pulled open a drawer in his desk. He raked through it, pens, pencils, paper clips until he found a pair of laboratory tweezers. With one hand he reached forward and opened the paper bag. Then with the tweezers he extracted a piece of crumpled toilet roll.

'I was doing my rounds when I came across these. Did you ever see anything of them before?' He folded back the layers of tissue paper with the tweezers. Inside the toilet roll were two creased and damp black and white photos. The fucking things mustn't have flushed away. Martin tried to be nonchalant. He leaned forward from his waist.

'What are they?'

'That's enough.' Condor covered them up with the toilet paper before Martin could see any details. 'You've never seen photos like these before?'

'No, Father. I didn't see . . . What are they of?'

'Never mind.' Condor looked hard at Martin. His eyes moved, all over the boy's face, testing him for the truth. Martin tried not to flinch, tried not to blush. He found difficulty knowing where to put his eyes. He was so bad at this. He decided the best thing was the most dangerous thing and stared at the toilet paper on the desk as if he was curious about it. Condor bit his lip, then said, 'If somebody had been flashing these things you would have noticed . . . wouldn't you, Brennan?'

'Yes, Father. No, I mean – maybe not.'

'Well?'

'I don't know what you mean, Father. I don't know what it's about.'

Condor leaned forward and rested his elbows on the desk. The tone of his voice changed. He was trying to sound, not like a teacher, but like he was Martin's friend.

'I'm not talking here about . . . a misdemeanour. I'm talking about something *so* serious that . . . I cannot find the words. I'm talking about . . . the immortal soul. No – I'm talking about *more* than that. I'm talking about the immortal souls of five hundred and sixty-two boys. Do you get my drift?'

Martin nodded. But he was trying to look confused, to convince Condor he knew nothing about it.

'It's not a matter of being an informer. It's a matter of souls for all eternity.'

'I've no idea, Father.' Using the tweezers the priest began to replace the photos in the brown paper bag again. 'I really don't know.'

'I don't want you to mention this to *anybody*. You hear me, Brennan?'

'Yes, Father.'

'But if you get a whisper of anything, I want to know. There's no reward – just the satisfaction of knowing you've done a good thing.' Condor slid both hands into his pockets and leaned back in his chair. 'I believe Father Farquharson is a regular visitor at your house?' Martin nodded. 'Your mother is a woman on her own – it would be awful for her to find out that you were involved in something like this.'

'But I'm not.' Condor stared at him for a very long time – so long that Martin began to count into himself: fuck the priest one, fuck the priest two, fuck the priest three . . .

'Back to class now and send me the next man.'

Martin looked out the corridor windows as he hurried back to class. A flock of seagulls stood in the centre circle of the Wee Field all facing the handball alleys. A few rose and circled the goalposts. Even through the glass of the window he could hear their mechanical screeching. He wondered how it was going to look when he went back into class. Coyle had been off for a week. If he said, 'Foley, he wants to see you', everybody would think he had squealed, everybody would be convinced he'd done the dirty on Blaise.

When he opened the door all the heads which were down working came up. All eyes were on him. He could still hear the seagulls in the silence of the classroom. He went up to the teacher and said, 'Whoever's next.' Cousteau consulted his register.

'Coyle.'

'Not here, sir.'

'Foley,' he said. Blaise got up from a bench at the far side of the class and left the room. Martin slid into his desk. Kavanagh half turned and raised an eyebrow.

'After,' Martin mouthed. There was only a couple of minutes of the period left. The bell went. Everyone headed outside into the corridor. Kavanagh could hardly wait.

'So what did he want?'

'The dirty photos.'

Kavanagh whistled.

'Not the exam papers?'

'No but . . .'

'What does he know?'

'He fuckin had them. Right there. In his pocket. Wrapped in toilet paper – although where he got the fuckin toilet paper I've no idea. There's *never* any toilet paper over there. They must have floated. Not flushed away.'

'Holy fuck,' Kavanagh shook his head.

'But you're not going to believe this. He searched me. Every pocket. And the bastard saw the negatives of the exam papers. But he didn't fucking know what he was looking at.'

'Jesus.' Kavanagh was pretending to faint.

'Holding them up to the light.' Martin mimed the gesture.

'And he didn't twig?'

'No.'

'Which of the dirty ones did he find?'

'I couldn't see. But I presume they were the ones you threw down the toilet – they were wet. He must have gone diving for them.'

'Cousteau the Second,' said Kavanagh and whistled. They both headed for the staircase Blaise would come down from Condor's room.

'Those photos were the pits. Christ, he'll go spare.'

'Totally ape-shit.'

'You bet.'

'Things'll become savager by and by.'

'Can you imagine him finding them, floating face up?'

'Cunt up, more like.' They both laughed. They became serious again.

'Do you think Blaise will be OK?' said Martin.

'Yeah — but I'm not so sure about other people.'

'Who?'

'There were a lot of people around. Everybody saw.'

'But who would tell?'

'Sharkey and his crowd are none too keen on Blaise.'

'But they wouldn't squeal.'

Kavanagh shrugged.

'Maybe. Maybe not.' They sat on a window ledge at the foot of the staircase and waited. Martin stared down at his scuffed shoes. There was a creak on the stairs and they both looked up. Blaise was by himself. He came down, his hand trailing lightly on the banisters. Martin and Kavanagh waited.

Blaise said, 'The man's a complete dumbfuck.' He turned at the bottom of the stairs. All three headed along the corridor. 'He threatened me with eternal damnation. Then when that seemed to have no effect he tried the police. Like the way you would threaten a child with a bogeyman. Thought I was behind it — because of my record.'

'Well, he's right, isn't he?'

Blaise ignored Martin.

'I know for sure,' said Blaise, 'the last thing he would *ever* do would be to bring the RUC in here. Can you imagine him doing that? Inviting that crowd of Orange bastards in here to investigate? Giving them the run of the place? That'll be the day.'

'Did you have any of that dirty stuff on you? Did he search you?'

'Don't be stupid.'

'Where did you put it?'

'With the exam papers.'

'When?'

'At lunch time.'

'Fuck.'

'What did he say?' asked Kavanagh.

'Nothing of importance.'

'Did he ask anything about my negatives?' said Martin.

'No.'

'So he knows nothing.'

'How could he?'

'They might have found the papers were missing.'

'Don't be so stupid,' said Blaise. 'Two dumbfucks under the same roof . . .'

'Be sure − you've got to put the envelopes back tonight.'

'Yeah. He's right,' said Kavanagh. 'We'd all sleep a lot easier in our beds.'

'What else did he say?' said Martin. Blaise shrugged.

'Are you interested in what I said to him?' They nodded.

'I said I am innocent of this particular accusation but often, when it comes to the rotten apple in the barrel, I'm proud to be it.'

'You did not.'

'Fuckin liar.'

'And then I went on to say "All the other apples conform, the rotten one teaches them to think for themselves. And if you continue to sit like that on your fat arse I will give you such a fucking punch in the teeth that you'll never eat another apple in your life . . . " '

Kavanagh and Martin laughed. Blaise smirked and said, 'He wants to see Gallagher next. Any idea where he is?'

That night, at tea, Martin's mother stared at him.

'Is anything wrong?'

'No.'

'You're too quiet by half.' He shrugged and went on chewing. 'You'll need to get at the studying − get the sleeves rolled up − it can't be too long now.'

'I was going to.' He hated when that happened − when he decided to do something and then she told him to do it. And it was always happening. It looked like he was doggedly obeying her. 'Do you want me to do the dishes?'

'No, there's just a few things,' she said. 'I'll do them myself. You get on with the work.' He drained off as much of his tea as he could without getting a mouthful of tea-leaves and stood up from the table. She sat on, watching him.

'Excuse me,' she said.

'Excuse me,' he said. He wanted her to know he was irritated. 'It's just us. You can see I'm finished.'

'A true gentleman uses the butter knife even when he's by himself. *Especially* when he's by himself.' She looked up at him in a sniffy kind of way. 'And what, may I ask, are your plans for this evening?'

'Studying.'

'Where?'

'Here.'

'Thanks be to God. There seems to be nothing but girls to distract you down at that library. Do you ever say the prayer I gave you?'

'Yeah.'

He gathered his books and set them on an old drawing board and carried them into the parlour to the chair Father Farquharson sat in when he visited. Because it was the most upright, he said. It was beside the china cabinet and had a straight back and wooden arms. Martin sat down. He rested the drawing board across the arms and became like a baby in a high chair. The surface of the drawing board was scarred with lines. It'd been used frequently as a cutting board. The ruts were so deep he always needed a pad to lean on to stop the lines coming through and interfering with his writing. His mother's prayer was at the back of his homework jotter. When he took it out, it too was warped to the shape of his backside. He didn't particularly want to read it – because if he did, it would just be obeying her again – but his eyes moved over the words.

Students' Prayer to St Anthony
Glorious St Anthony divinely filled with the science of the Saints, I place my studies under thy protection. After thy example, let my knowledge be grounded in the heart of Jesus and in the heart of Mary. With the aid of thy prayers I purpose to perform my studies as a matter of duty with a pure intention and in the spirit of penance. Implore the Father of Light to grant me a ready understanding, a sound judgement and a faithful memory. Obtain for me the grace to work with method, constancy and patience to develop the gifts I have received from God and use them as always for His greater glory. Pray God to bless my efforts

208

so that I may succeed in my examinations, and in the midst of success remain ever humble. Amen.

Why were prayers full of *thy's* and *thee's* and *thine* – *let* this and *let* that – words like *implore* and *obtain* and *grant* that were never used anywhere else? The G of 'Glorious' was huge and ornate and coloured like something out of the Book of Kells. He thought about copying the entwining pattern. It was difficult – a kind of latticework mixed with vine leaves. He made a couple of pencil strokes. But it would need different colours to make one stand out from the other. He pulled himself up short. This bloody prayer was keeping him back from his work. With some determination he put it back into the last page of his homework diary. What next?

He knew there was definitely a question coming up on *Macbeth*. Earlier in the year he had written an essay on the play's imagery and got a B^{++} for it his best mark ever so the Caroline Spurgeon question was playing right into his hands. He began reading this answer again hoping it would go into his head and he could reproduce it in the exam word for word.

Lady Macbeth is the villain of the piece. She puts Macbeth up to it. She says 'fill me, from the crown to the toe, top full of direst cruelty.'

He would have to write essays for the Milton and Hopkins questions. But what was the point? He couldn't judge whether they were crap or not. If he showed his efforts to the English teacher to see if they were any good or not and all the questions subsequently turned up on the exam paper it would look really suspect. *Do you have a crystal ball, Brennan?*

He was useless at studying anyway. He would read the same sentence over and over again. But he was determined it was not going to happen tonight. He picked up a ballpoint pen and tested it to see if it was working. It was. It left a blue wiggle on the top of his page. He got out his copy of *Macbeth* and began to leaf through it. But he didn't know where to begin. He went back to the wiggle and extended it fore and aft until it became a scramble of barbed wire. Gradually it became something more interesting. He filled in bits of it, added triangles and shadows. An abstract thing grew slowly in the corner of his page. He began to put in other colours, the black lead of pencil, the red ink of biro. He had a green biro in his plastic pencil case. When it was finished – although he never could say when a doodle was finished – you could always go back to it – he told himself he should make a cup of tea before he started. He'd start after the tea. The tea would focus him.

'What in the name of God are you wanting tea again for? Aren't you just after your own tea?' He made a fresh pot and poured himself a mug and carried it into the front room. He took a drink from it to lower the level, but it was hot and could not be gulped. He was well practised at the manoeuvre of getting into the armchair.

1. Set mug on drawing board amongst books and papers making sure not to slop over and stain work.
2. Lift board carefully.
3. About turn slowly.
4. Reverse and lower self into armchair, holding board level with cup balanced thereon.
5. Sip tea.
6. Resume study.

He had the determination that this time something was going to be achieved. Something was going to sink into his thick skull. Obtain for me the grace to work with method, constancy and patience.

He found that underlining stuff in books helped. He used pencil so that it could be rubbed out later if the book had to be handed back. But then he found that sometimes he underlined nearly the whole page. And that was useless. Because his eye was drawn to the bit that wasn't underlined. The bit that was unimportant. And he was back where he started. Nevertheless, he did some underlining at the back of the *Macbeth* book, where there were essays. After a while he turned again to his own handwritten essay. The script was ugly and backhand. His elbows were on the board, his head was in his hands staring down. The words seemed to be on the bottom of a stream and writhed in front of his eyes. Stealing the exam papers was at the forefront of his mind. It felt bad. Out and out cheating. For safety reasons they'd agreed that nobody should write down any of the questions. They could be read by projecting them or by using a big magnifying glass. He'd given the negatives to Kavanagh for the night. That gave him a bit of breathing space. Tonight should be devoted to studying. He finished off his tea and tried to concentrate.

Lady Macbeth is the villain of the piece. She puts Macbeth up to it. She says, 'fill me, from the crown to the toe, top full of direst cruelty.'

His eye drifted off the page. He started looking at the pattern of scars on the drawing board. They all seemed to be in parallel. He tore a page off his jotter and laid it on the board. With a lead pencil he did a rubbing. The lines definitely showed through. He lifted the paper and looked directly at the cuts. Paint had been used on the board at one time or another. Several colours of paint. Magnolia and sky blue. He dragged his eye back.

Lady Macbeth is the villain of the piece. She puts Macbeth up to it. She says 'fill me, from the crown . . .

The dirty photographs came back into his head. The woman must have been doing a pee. All those tuftys and breasts. And the shaved ones. They looked odd. Like somebody with ringworm. They'd been really amateur pictures. Badly lit, some of them grainy. It was hard to think of girls posing like that. But the evidence was there – they had done those things. And the camera had recorded it. He was becoming horny – felt it unfurling. That was bad. If he got going in that fashion he'd get no work done at all. In Father Farquharson's chair, too. Grant me a ready understanding, a sound judgement and a faithful memory. He had to do something to distract himself from his groin. He began to enlarge the west side of the doodle by adding a shape to it which resembled a pyramid. Methinks it is like a camel. Or was it a weasel? Was that *Hamlet* or *Macbeth*?

Lady Macbeth is the villain of the piece. She puts Macbeth up to it. She says 'fill me, from the crown to the toe, top full of direst cruelty.'

A lorry went by outside and something in the china cabinet vibrated momentarily. His eye slid down to the bottom shelf. Did the noise come from the Royal Doulton or the Wedgwood? It could have been the plates standing upright at the back, or the stacked saucers and cups rattling at the front. His mother took great pride in her china cabinet. It was a round-shouldered piece of furniture spun out of air and glass and thin slivers of walnut. The wood was in the shape of a four leaf clover – inside, the back panel was lined with yellow silk in jagged lightning patterns. All the shelves were of glass. The top one held her collection of Belleek, stuff so thin that you could see the shadow of your fingers through the china – 'spit-through porcelain' as Mary Lawless called it. It had little green shamrocks, here and there, all over the surface. The middle shelf was where she kept her glass. There were 'Vaze, voz, vazes' and some Venetian goblets with purple barleysugar stems, one or two pieces of Waterford. It was all about display. She only used *some* of these things on supper nights. Once every couple of years the contents of the china cabinet were taken out and washed. He washed and she dried. Only one item in the basin at any one time was the rule. He remembered once as he put the items back clashing two Venetian goblets together. It sounded like a bell and his mother came running in with her hand over her heart and said, 'Jesus, Mary and Joseph – I thought they were goners.'

Lady Macbeth is the villain of the piece. She puts Macbeth up to it. She says, 'fill me, from the crown to the toe, top full of direst cruelty.' Macbeth himself is not exactly innocent because he said earlier 'Stars hide your fires let not light see my black and deep desires.'

Black and deep desires. His were not of murder but of reaching out and handling those small breasts he had seen in the photos. And if she permitted that then she might permit him to touch her between the legs. What would that feel like? His erection came back. Maybe if he went out to the lavatory and had a wank he could then come in and concentrate and get some work done. God might forgive him because it was such a *practical* and *good* reason for a wank. But he only used that dark and damp place as a last resort. He'd wait and take some tissues to bed with him. But that was worse – that was premeditated. What if Blaise was right and there was nothing wrong with it? God made guys and gave them the most pleasurable piece of apparatus imaginable *and then left them alone with it*. I mean, what did He expect? He must stop thinking about dirty things. He was getting nowhere.

How was all this about the bloody exam papers going to end? He would be a goner if anybody found out. He was like the man rowing the boat. His back was to where he was going. He was facing the past, turned away from his future. Afraid to look. He could see his mother sitting across the desk from Condor, her face white and drawn with worry. This was awful. He needed another cup of tea.

His mother was sitting watching TV, her feet propped on a pouffe. He switched on the kettle.

'More tea already?'

'Yeah.'

'Are you getting much done?'

'A fair bit.'

'Good man. That's what I like to hear.'

'Do you want a cup yourself?'

'No thanks, son.'

He made and poured the tea. Going through to the parlour he paused and watched a bit of the news programme, sipping from his cup.

'You could drink tea till it came out your ears,' said his mother without taking her eyes off the screen. He slid his backside on to the arm of the armchair. 'None of that now. Back you go to the work.' After a while he stood and returned to the parlour. And methodically went through the six-step procedure to end up in the chair with the board across his lap sipping tea and resuming his studies. Obtain for me the grace to work with method. He addressed his essay again with renewed determination.

'fill me, from the crown to the toe, top full of direst cruelty.' Macbeth *himself is not exactly innocent because he said earlier 'Stars hide your fires let not light see my black and deep desires.'*

It would be good to get the English paper under his belt. He hadn't decided whether he would look at the questions on the

Physics and Chemistry papers. He could worry about the Latin some other time.

Lady Macbeth is the villain of the piece. She puts Macbeth up to it. She says, 'fill me, from the crown to the toe, top full of direst cruelty.'

Martin took another sip. He wondered if there was anything on the radio. A bit of background. He rejected the idea. It would only put him off his stride. It would break his concentration.

Lady Macbeth is the villain of the piece. She puts Macbeth up to it. She says 'fill me, from the crown to the toe, top full of direst cruelty.'

Lad yMac beth isthe vill ainof the piece. She pu ts Macbethup toit. Sh esays 'fillme, from thecrownto thetoe, topfullof driest ruelty.'

LadyMacbethisthevillainofthepieceSheputsMacbethuptotShesays 'fillme, fromthe thecrown crownto tothetoe toetop topfullof fullof dressed direst c rue lty.'

Remember o lord in the midst of success to remain ever humble.

11. A Time of Reckoning

Blaise was nowhere to be seen during the first two periods. He came in late to the double before lunch and sat near the door away from Martin and Kavanagh. Martin tried to catch his eye. When the lunch-time bell rang and the classroom emptied both Martin and Kavanagh descended on him.

'Where the fuck have you been?'

'On business.'

'Well – did you leave back the envelopes?'

'Shut up.' He looked around at the open door. 'Let's go up round the track. We can talk more easily.'

It was a grey day. Not raining, but with the smell of rain in the air. The boys strolled but their faces were tight. Martin and Kavanagh didn't say anything.

'You're not going to believe me,' said Blaise. 'But I slept in.'

'You haven't left them back?' Martin's voice was a screech. He checked how near the next group of boys were. 'Fuck me – how relaxed can you get?'

'It's not as easy as you think,' said Blaise. 'There are other people in the dorm. I couldn't set my alarm for four in the morning – it would waken everybody. They would all want to know where I was going. And why the fuck was I carrying packets around the school at four in the morning? And what was in the packets? So I didn't set my alarm. And I didn't wake up. It's as simple as that.'

'Aw fuck would you look who's here.' Kavanagh nodded ahead. The Gaelic team, in their green jerseys and yellow shorts, were doing a lunch-time training session, standing around the goal mouth in the Big Field. Condor stood between the posts coaching them. He wore a black overcoat on top of his soutane and was clapping and wringing his hands. The Gym teacher did all the other sport in the school but only Condor had control of the Gaelic team.

'Would you look at the state of Condor – in the boots,' said Blaise.

'Take a look at his collar, if you get close,' said Martin.

'He was a county player, you know. Played for Tyrone.'

'That's really put him on a pedestal for me now,' said Blaise. 'A County Tyrone Gaelic football player. The absolute pinnacle of dumbfuckery.'

Condor's deep voice floated across to them.

'One lap jogging. Go!'

The team jostled and began to run around the perimeter. Martin said to Blaise. 'You fucking *must* wake up tonight. I hardly slept at all last night. I lay there staring at the ceiling thinking about what you were doing. What could go wrong for you? I was worried about you and you were fucking sound asleep.'

'That's quite touching.' Blaise's eyebrow went up. Disbelief that there could be any worry about such a small issue. 'But don't panic.'

'I'm beginning to get black bags under my eyes too,' said Kavanagh. 'Do it tonight, Foley. For fuck sake.'

'OK.'

They had reached the track and the Gaelic team passed close enough for them to hear their pounding boots and panting breath.

'Keep it going, lads,' shouted Kavanagh. The three boys found a place on a bench by the tree walk and sat and watched the training. Not really watched – it was something that was happening in front of their eyes. The sun came through the grey but was weak and milky and there was a chill in the air. They talked between themselves in low voices about the things that had come up on the Physics and Chemistry and Maths papers. Martin kept quiet, tried not to listen too hard, tried not to remember. The running finished and Condor moved in among his team. They squatted or sat and he talked.

'I bet you he's not talking football to that crowd,' said Kavanagh. 'It's still the Inquisition.' When he had said all he had to say Condor threw a ball in amongst the team, told them they could have a ten-minute kick-about before canteen. They began shooting in but without much interest. Condor turned and walked towards the three on the bench.

It looked like he was going to pass them with a nod but he came right up to them.

'I've just been telling the team a thing they didn't know.' He put his head to one side and stared down at them. 'Where were the first organised games in the world, boys?'

'The Olympics?'

'In Greece?'

'No.' Condor shook his head slowly. 'It was in Ireland.' The three boys laughed. Condor said, 'The original Olympics based itself on the Tailteann – the Ancient Irish Games. Most nations look over their shoulders at a sister nation. The Greeks had their eye on Ireland. So the crucible of Western civilisation had to do its homework when it came here, boys. Does that not give you a wee lift? Brennan, does it not make you proud? Mr Kavanagh?'

'Aye, a bit.'

'Before the English were out of their beds, historically speaking. The Greeks were learning from us.'

'Is there a Greek hurling team, Father?'

'Always the smart answer, eh Foley.'

'If it was anything, Father, it was a smart question,' said Blaise. Condor stared at him, refusing to smile. 'I forgot to ask you yesterday, Foley – where is your father at the moment?'

'Iowa State University. I think it's a town called Ames.' Martin looked at Condor's football boots beneath the hem of his soutane. The priest was making vague attempts to clean the mud from the sides of his boots in the long grass. As he turned the boot sideways the aluminium studs on the sole gleamed.

'So – gentlemen,' he said. 'Any word of anything?' All three shook their heads. 'I have enough respect for you and your families to know that you wouldn't be involved in a thing like this. So I will not ask you again. *I* know that *you* know.' He paused, then hitched up the front of his soutane and put his foot up on the bench where they were sitting. A kind of nonchalance. He leaned his elbow on his knee. Martin felt it was a gesture that showed he was trying to get in with them. 'All I'm saying is that I wouldn't be too dismayed if who-ever-it-was ended up getting what he deserves. A doing. Not just a little doing but a good doing. The kind of a doing this particular gentleman deserves. And I'd be looking the other way. On a particular day at a particular time I would be otherwise engaged. Do you get me?' All three of the boys nodded. 'We can police our own outfit here. Despite what I said to you yesterday, Foley.' Condor was wearing banded green and white football socks with his black clerical trousers tucked in, as if he were riding a bicycle. 'Good day to you, gentlemen.' He walked away, his hands joined behind his back, printing the black ash of the track with his studs. He had the wide straddled walk of a man who worked on boats. He looked back once to gauge the effect of what he had said. There was a sort of knowing smile on his face.

When he was out of earshot Kavanagh said, 'This is serious.' All three boys looked at the Gaelic team. They were still shooting in, not caring whether they scored or not. Those who weren't directly involved in the action stood with their hands on their hips looking in the direction of the three boys on the bench.

'That cunt has just set me up,' said Blaise. 'If he said it to us, he has said it to them.' There was silence as they considered this.

'Maybe we should make ourselves scarce,' said Kavanagh.

'I hope he's not accusing *all* of us,' said Martin. Kavanagh looked at him. Blaise's eyebrow went up. 'I need a smoke.'

In the daffs they stood away from the door behind the central island of urinals. Martin offered Blaise a cigarette but he refused. Then he changed his mind.

'The calming properties of nicotine,' said Martin. He lit Blaise's cigarette. 'It's not a matter of taking sides. I'm just not into that kind of stuff.'

'What kind of stuff?'

'Dirty pictures.'

'Do you think I am?' said Blaise. 'I have as much interest in them as I have in attending . . . a vicar's tea party.'

'I fuckin hate that too,' said Martin. He inhaled deeply.

'What?' said Kavanagh.

'That vicar's tea party stuff. Clichés. Cunts who prophesy doom.'

'I'm sorry,' Blaise said, 'it just slipped out. I wasn't thinking.'

'*If Condor starts a war it'll make Vietnam look like a vicar's tea party.*'

218

Martin put on what he considered a newspaperman's voice. 'I hate that.'

'Small cucumber sandwiches and tea and tea strainers and some cakes with red cherries on the top.' Kavanagh tried to think of other suitable items. There was an unfamiliar sound.

'It would be good if you ever *did* get invited to a vicar's tea party,' said Blaise, 'to go along with a machine gun up your coat and your pockets full of hand grenades and kill every old woman wearing a hat by hacking her to death with a machete and piss on all the dead bodies and napalm them and blow the fuck out of them and then run around shouting *I'm trying to make this vicar's tea party look like Vietnam because I don't want to accuse the press of cliché-mongering.*' The unfamiliar sound came again. Like metal on stone. Over and above the singing and sizzling of the water rinsing the urinals.

'Rape and pillage,' said Kavanagh. 'Never pass up an opportunity. The younger ones at least.' Some guys from around them began to drift away.

'I prefer to think of rape as unrequited sex,' said Blaise. '*A journalist spokesman today was at a loss to describe the scene, the vicar's tea party having been removed from his repertoire and rendered redundant. It was as if the sharpest arrow had been removed from my quiver, he complained.*' Blaise, when he did smoke, held the cigarette delicately between his long white fingers and closed his eyes when he inhaled. Now there was just the three of them standing in the corner laughing at their own jokes.

Still the unfamiliar sound persisted. It sounded faintly like horses' hooves. A rattling. A sound as of something hard moving over cobbles.

'What's that?'

'I dunno.' They stopped talking to listen. Then realised that they were on their own. Sharkey, still in his football strip, stepped out from one side of the urinals. O'Grady came round the other side. It was clear now what the noise was. They were still kitted out as they had been on the field. The sound was their football boots on the floor. The metal studs rippled on the terrazzo as they moved. Now there were six or seven of them.

'Here comes the fucking militia,' said Blaise. Sharkey, his face pale, gestured to Martin and Kavanagh.

'You two – c'mere.'

'What are you on about?' said Kavanagh. Sharkey beckoned with his head. Kavanagh went over to him. Martin followed but out of the corner of his eye he saw a streak of green and yellow as O'Grady lunged at Blaise. Sharkey was past the both of them in an instant. He kicked hard at Blaise and Blaise let a small scream out of him. 'What on earth . . .' Other guys in the team were holding Kavanagh and Martin. Somebody had an arm round Martin's throat, tight enough to crack his Adam's apple. The daffs was filled with the rattle and clack of studs on the floor. A toilet door banged open as Blaise fell against it. People were shouting. 'Hey! What . . .' 'Fucksake.' Kavanagh wrestled two or three bodies in their football shirts. Martin fell and the elbow of his blazer went into the drain of the urinal. The water sluicing through the trough was cold. For Martin everything had gone into slow motion. Blaise was half yelling, trying to rationalise, trying to calm everyone down. From his position on the floor Martin saw someone kick Blaise in the chest and he went down, backwards into the cubicle. Momentarily Martin saw it – saw Blaise's head jerk as it bounced off the rim of the toilet bowl. The arc of his descent jigged as he hit on the way down. There was a sickening sound of bone on delf. Everybody heard it – over the sound of the studs. Guys in jerseys were scrumming in now, having a kick.

'Not his face!' somebody shouted. Kavanagh was trying to haul them back, yelling his head off. Sharkey told the team to stop. And within seconds they were all away to get dressed and the place was empty. The urinals flushed and the only sound was the sound of water as it ran into the drains. Kavanagh had been hit on the face and there was a wisp of yellow snot and blood across his cheek. There was mud streaked on his neck and the collar of his shirt. His school tie had been pulled so tight it looked like a striped noose. Kavanagh hunkered down.

'Come on, Blaise,' he said.

'Is he OK?' said Martin. He hated having had his sleeve wet with piss and water. Kavanagh tried to assist Blaise to his feet but his body just lay down again. Martin was frightened by Blaise's ashen colour. With his eyes closed his pale eyelashes seemed longer.

'He's out cold,' said Kavanagh.

'Let me see.' Martin tried to lift Blaise by the shoulders. His head lolled. He tried slapping the pale cheeks lightly like he'd seen people do in films. Kavanagh's face was also chalk white.

'Maybe we shouldn't move him,' said Kavanagh. 'In case there's something broken.'

'Put this on the ground.' Martin took off his blazer and folded it into a pillow. He rubbed dry the damp patch on his forearm and elbow. 'Maybe we should get a doctor . . .'

'I think he needs an ambulance.' Kavanagh was touching Blaise's wrist looking for a pulse. 'Go to the office. Tell Cuntyballs.'

Martin started to run. There was a crowd outside the daffs waiting to see what had happened. Some guys resisted Martin, pushed back at him. He flung himself into them and seeing the look on his face they opened up. Martin ran. If it was serious he was glad to be away from it. He was scared shitless by what had happened. The rest of the quad was crowded and he had to cleave his way through, pushing and half running.

'Watch it – outa the way.' He struggled through the corridor, which was also crowded. He pushed open the office door and the first thing he heard was Condor's voice coming from behind the partition. Martin rapped the frosted glass window in the hatch. Nobody answered. Cuntyballs said something to Condor. Martin rapped again – this time much harder.

'Take it easy, boy.' The window was drawn back with a little ball bearing snarl and Cuntyballs peered out. Condor stood leaning on the mantelpiece.

'There's been an accident. Foley's hurt. He's over in the da . . . toilets. Maybe he needs an ambulance.'

'What? What are you on about, Brennan?'

'It's Foley, Father. He's just lying there.' Condor looked at the colour of Martin's face – at his shirtsleeves, saw the urgency.

'God above.' Condor came out from behind the partition and shouted, 'I'll use my car if necessary,' and with that he ran through the outer door. At the sight of Condor running, the crowds of pupils parted to let him through. Martin followed but lagged behind. He was afraid that Blaise would be dead by the time they got to him.

Kavanagh and Martin were in an empty classroom. The last bell of the day had gone ages ago and it only took the school a couple of minutes to empty. Kavanagh had just come back from the hospital where he'd spent the whole afternoon. He gave Martin his blazer back. He sat on the top of the desk with his feet on the seat and his head in his hands. Martin sat sideways in a desk across the aisle from him.

'What do you think?'

'I dunno,' said Kavanagh.

'Jesus.'

The board hadn't been wiped for days and there was an accumulation of stuff on it. *To earnestly try. Thomas a Becket. Up yours. Fiat lux.*

'D'you think he's gonna be all right?'

Kavanagh continued to stare down at his feet.

'Yeah – sure.'

'He didn't say anything?'

'Naw. He just lay there. His pulse was going. Then Condor came in and cleared the place – he took one look at him and starts saying an Act of Contrition into his ear. He told me to stay with him and keep saying it. Then he ran for his car. Where the fuck did you get to?'

'He said nobody was to go in.'

'So you did what you were told. Good boy. Full marks. I didn't think he should have been moved but Condor scooped him up. I had to stay in the back of the car with him. Condor drove like a fucking maniac. He kept shouting that he'd anoint him as soon as we got to the hospital.'

'Which one?'

'Next door. The Mater.'

'Did the doctor say anything?'

'No.'

'Did Condor say anything?'

'No. He didn't say a dickie bird.'

'Did you tell him what happened?'

'No. I think he knew what happened.'

Martin's stomach felt tight. It was like there was a hand inside him squeezing his gut. He didn't know how to say things. If he said things it would let some of the tightness out.

'You know what this means,' he said.

'What?'

'We're going to have to find those exam papers and put them back.'

'Yeah, I thought that in the back of the car. Fuck. Aren't we awful?'

'What do you mean?'

'To be thinking that way – at that time. The guy may be dying.'

'We better do it quick, before somebody else finds them.' Kavanagh seemed very big and hunched and stunned. It was almost as if he was going to cry. Martin didn't know what to do. He said, 'It'll be OK. It's just the shock. He'll be back tomorrow, as right as rain. And we can tell him we put the papers back.'

'I didn't like the look of him.'

'He'll be OK. He'll wake up and call the doctor a dumbfuck.'

'What if he doesn't wake up?'

'Don't be so bloody morbid.'

They sat for a long time saying nothing. Martin was trying not to panic, trying to figure out what to do for the best.

'There's no harm done if we leave the papers back.' Kavanagh didn't react. Martin stood and moved towards the blackboard. There was a duster sitting on the ledge – a block of wood with a piece of felt stuck to it. He began wiping off the writing. 'There'll be another inquisition, especially when Blaise's old man finds out. They'll come looking for his stuff. And find the porn. And the exam papers.'

Kavanagh raised his head. 'What is there to involve you and me in it?'

'Not a thing. But if they find the porn and the papers they'll come to us – because we were the only mates he had.'

'And we can say we know nothing about it.'

The classroom filled with chalk dust. Martin felt it dry in the back of his throat. He began patting the duster against the board, leaving slightly overlapping impressions of itself. He could taste the chalk.

'If there's a whole investigation into this,' said Kavanagh, 'that's my chances of doing Medicine fucked.'

'That's your chances of doing *anything* fucked.' The sun came

223

out and beamed through the window making the swirling chalk dust seem flat. 'But we have to do it for *his* sake.'

'What?'

'Tidy up.'

'We have to do it for *our* sake. Self-protection. Future prospects? Fucking zero. Can you tell lies?'

'I'm useless at it,' said Martin. Distantly, in the corridor, they heard the sound of running feet.

'The two things must be kept absolutely separate. No fucking way must porn and exam papers be mentioned in the same breath. In fact nobody, but nobody, must mention exam papers. If Condor threatens to put hot needles up your cock – you *still* know fuck all about exam papers.'

Doors were slamming.

'That's the boarders going for their tea,' said Martin.

'The ganches – the country ones getting their noses in the trough.' Kavanagh slid down off the desk. 'Right – let's get one.' They walked towards the dining hall and pulled a first-year aside.

'Where does Foley sleep?'

'The Wee Dorm.'

'Show us.' The boy led them upstairs and showed them cubicle 17. Then they chased him. They had to move with stealth because this place was out of bounds to day boys. If anybody saw them there'd be a whole interrogation.

'I'll keep an eye,' said Kavanagh. He stood by the door looking up and down the corridor. But he also tried to keep out of sight. He waved Martin on. The place was huge and smelled of feet and body odour mixed with disinfectant and carbolic – there were red blocks of Lifebuoy on the washbasins around the perimeter. There were about thirty wooden three-sided cubicles, like in the Retreat House in Ardglass. Martin moved as fast as he could without making noise. In each cubicle was a bed and a hospital green metal locker. There was a glass of water filled with bubbles on the one in Blaise's cubicle. The partitions did not go right to the ground and Martin stooped to check that there were no legs or feet to be seen anywhere. Suitcases lay under each bed. Martin pulled Blaise's case out and flipped the lid open. From a distance Kavanagh shook his head.

'No.' He pointed to the locker. Martin pulled out a wig the

same colour as Blaise's hair and held it up. He frowned. Again Kavanagh pointed. Martin went to the locker beside Blaise's bed. He pulled open the top drawer. Some of the bubbles in the glass rose to the surface. They fell upwards. The drawer was full of socks and underpants, things folded tidily. He took the drawer completely out of its recess and set it on the bed. Beneath it he found a handful of envelopes, including the one containing the dirty photographs. They lay flat where the drawer had been. Kavanagh was making urgent noises from the doorway. He gave up his lookout post and came to Martin.

'Where's the key for the cleaner's cupboard?' said Kavanagh.

'How should I know?' Martin's head was turning this way and that looking back at the door. 'Maybe Blaise has it – in his pocket.'

'That's just fuckin lovely.' Kavanagh raked through the drawer in the locker looking for the shiny newly cut key beneath the socks. 'You must have the original.'

'Yeah.'

'Well why didn't you *say*.'

'Because you didn't fuckin *ask*.' Martin took the key from his trouser pocket. It was the first time he had seen Kavanagh look panicky. Kavanagh replaced the drawer in its recess and slammed it shut. Martin handed him the envelopes.

'We're in deep shite and no mistake.'

'It's OK. It's OK, we've got the stuff. Come on.' Kavanagh looked at the envelopes in his hands and hesitated. 'Hide them.' Kavanagh slid them under his armpit and buttoned his blazer. They began walking to the stairs. 'Let's go past. See if there's anybody about,' Kavanagh said.

'You take these.' He handed him back the envelope with the dirty pictures. 'And destroy them. Completely. Incinerate the bastards.' The envelope was too big to fit in his inside pocket so Martin folded it in half and pushed it down so that not even a fringe of it could be seen. He buttoned his blazer.

They headed for the chapel corridor where the store room was. With all the boarders in the ref, the place echoed – sounded like what it was – an empty school.

'I don't like this. It's so bloody risky.' Kavanagh was

whispering. They were both walking warily, trying to make as little noise as possible.

'What else can we do?' Martin looked round behind him but there was no one in the corridor.

When they came to the door marked 109 Kavanagh stopped. 'You or me?' he said.

'You've done fuck all so far,' said Martin.

'Don't be such a pain.'

'I've got the porn to get rid of.' Kavanagh looked around warily.

'The key?'

Martin handed it over and went on ahead to where the corridor turned at right angles. Round the corner was empty. Martin felt OK. It hadn't felt this way when he'd been on his own in Condor's room, nearly crapping himself. Now it was different somehow. Kavanagh's involvement made it seem like nothing could go wrong.

He nodded to Kavanagh. Kavanagh looked in the other direction, then raised his arm, inserted the key and opened the door. Martin began to count. A light came on in the store. Shit the bed one – shit the bed two – shit the bed three.

'Come on, ya girny bastard.'

On the count of shit the bed fourteen the light went out and Kavanagh emerged. Martin heard the door of the store snap shut. Kavanagh came striding up the corridor.

'Let's go, wee man,' he said.

Martin set off beside him. They went down the stairs, at speed, barely touching the treads. Along the corridor and out into the quad.

'Should we maybe go and visit him? On the way home?'

'Naw,' said Kavanagh.

'Was everything OK in there? In the store?'

'Yeah.' Martin was breathing faster with the effort of keeping up. He was nowhere near as fit as Kavanagh. When they reached the top of the drive Kavanagh looked round at the school building.

'Jesus.'

'What?'

'Don't look. Just keep walking.'

'What?'

'Condor's watching us.'

Martin stared ahead, still walking.

'Where?'

'Upstairs.'

'Fuck. Did he see us, d'you think?'

'He'd be blind if he didn't – we're the only ones here.'

'In the corridor, I mean?'

'Naw – you would have seen him,' said Kavanagh. 'He's just looking out. Having a wee nosy. It's a nice evening.'

They continued to walk, to act natural. Martin hitched his bag into a more comfortable position on his shoulder. It was a thing guys did naturally.

'Maybe we better keep talking,' said Martin.

'Yeah, until we have our backs to him. Think of something.'

'Have you had a flutter recently on the relative velocity of either an equine or canine quadruped?'

'Indeed I have not,' said Kavanagh. 'For it is not my wont to speculate in such a fashion. Had I shekels aplenty I would spend them otherwise.'

'You bewilder me, sir. I had been led to believe by others that you would hazard your very soul on the speed of an animal. Relative to its peers. Is he still looking?'

'I don't know,' said Kavanagh. 'I don't want to look round.'

By now they had turned into the driveway and had their backs to the school.

'Oh happy horse to bear the weight of Anthony.'

'The devil damn thee black, thou cream faced loon.'

'It's OK. Cut it out.'

They walked in silence for the fifty yards down the left side of the drive. Then they heard a car engine behind them, the distinctive sound of a VW. Kavanagh turned.

'Aw Jesus.'

It was Condor. The priest leaned across the front seat and rolled the passenger window down.

'Are you boys for home?'

'Yes, Father,' said Kavanagh. Martin was aware of the envelope of filthy photographs in his pocket. He hesitated.

'Maybe I should just walk . . .'

'Jump in,' said Condor. 'I'll run you up.' Condor opened the passenger door and gave it a little push outwards. When he straightened up behind the wheel he couldn't see their faces. The boys looked at each other. Martin climbed into the back seat, Kavanagh sat in the front.

'It's been one of those days,' said Condor and gave a heavy sigh. The boys nodded. 'The seat belt.' Kavanagh looked around him and pulled the belt and clicked it into place. Condor put the car into gear and they moved forward. The indicator winked to the left. The car smelled of stale pipe. The tray by the gearstick was grey with spilled ash. A green pine tree swung from the driving mirror as the car idled waiting its chance to move into the roadway. A hanging tree.

'I'd just like to thank you boys for all you did today.' Neither Martin nor Kavanagh spoke. Both boys were looking this way and that waiting for a break in the stream of traffic, hoping the journey would be over as soon as possible. What was Condor hoping to get out of this? He had never given anyone a lift in all the time Martin had been at the school. 'I'm just off the phone to the hospital and the news is not good. They say they might have to operate. If there is evidence of internal bleeding. Anything to do with the brain . . .' He tut-tutted and shook his head. Suddenly the road was empty and they moved out of the driveway. 'But please God everything is going to be all right.' Martin listened to the gear changes and the rising engine note. He had never before seen Condor from this position. He wondered if he could see the Fairy Liquid writing from this angle but there was no sign of it. The back of Condor's neck was like the school noticeboard – like someone had pierced it with drawing pins. And some of the holes were occupied with blackheads. But he couldn't be blamed for this – how could he see the back of his neck? Blaise had told them of the ludicrous ritual of having to submit to an inspection by a dorm prefect after they had washed at night. Why hadn't they told Condor he had blackheads in his neck? Maybe it was a skin disease? Martin tried to look away. You should not allow how somebody looked to influence what you felt about them. He looked at Condor's hands on the steering wheel, the black tufts of hair on the joints of his fingers, the memory of pouring water over them serving his mass.

Blaise might be dying at this very moment. That was what he couldn't think of.

Now that they were in the main stream of traffic Condor felt he could talk more easily.

'So, what happened?' Both boys shrugged.

'I was on the other side. I'm not sure.'

'What about you, Martin? Did you see what happened?'

'Not really.'

'Any reason? Come on, boys – this is now a serious matter.'

'Not that I can think of.'

'Nor me.'

'Boys – there comes a point when you have to cease to be schoolboys. We leave all that kind of thing behind us.' His voice was pitched somewhere between wheedling and reasonableness. 'There was an accident in the toilet block – that much I do know. What I want to know is how and why?'

'There was some bad feeling – after an RK class.'

'Was there a fight?'

'Musta been.'

'Foley fell.'

'Who was the bad feeling with?'

'I'm not sure.'

Condor gave a sigh.

'What was the bad feeling about?'

'I'm not really sure.' Condor shook his head in disbelief.

'It's like the Mafia talking to you boys. Different tack. How well did you know Foley?' Kavanagh looked over into the back seat at Martin. He made a downturned mouth.

'Not well, but . . .'

'He didn't seem to know anybody,' said Martin, 'when he came into the school. He hung about with us – a bit. When there was nobody else.' Martin could see Condor's eyes watching him. Condor's eyes in the driving mirror were like somebody looking out of a dark letterbox. The eyes flicked between watching the back seat and the road ahead.

'Boarders and day boys don't mix much,' said Kavanagh. Condor half turned to him in the passenger seat and said, 'But *he* was a day-boy inside his head.' There was a long silence.

How utterly fucking crass to mention the inside of Blaise's

head. Martin felt like rabbit-punching the back of Condor's neck. 'We haven't been able to catch up with his father yet. God knows what he'll say. That's one of the worst things a priest has to do, boys – is to be the bringer of bad tidings.' Condor shook his head. His hair was black and wiry. 'That a rough-house in the toilets should lead to such an accident. Frail boys are much more vulnerable when it comes to something like this. He was a strange boy – didn't play any sport. Did he find it hard to make friends?' Again both boys shrugged and were silent. 'What I said earlier . . . Up at the field. I'm sure that had nothing to do with it. Foley wouldn't have been involved in any such thing.'

'No, Father,' said Martin.

'He just wouldn't,' said Kavanagh.

'It's doubly sad, then. Some rotten apple thinks he's got off scot free . . . But there will be a time. A time will come.'

They were approaching a pedestrian crossing. A girl and her mother hovered waiting to cross. Condor slowed down and stopped the car. He smiled at them as they crossed slowly. When they were off the crossing Condor looked both ways, making sure no one else wanted to cross, before he drove on.

'Up at the field at lunch time – I was talking through my hat. What I meant was that somebody who infects a barrel of apples *deserves* to be punished. Am I not right about that, boys?'

'Yes, Father.'

'*Better a millstone* and all that.'

'This'll do me here, Father, on the right,' said Martin. 'This is my street.'

Condor indicated to turn right and waited in the middle of the road.

'What number?' Martin told him and he pulled up in front of the door. 'There you go. Door to door service. No tip expected.' Kavanagh got out and angled his seat forward, then Martin got out. 'Thanks again, Martin, for everything,' shouted Condor bending low over the steering wheel to see him. 'And a few prayers wouldn't go amiss.' Kavanagh got in again. Condor waited until Martin had opened his front door, then saluted.

'Is that you, Martin?' his mother's voice came out from the kitchen. He touched his inside pocket to make sure the envelope was still completely out of sight. Then went in to face her.

'Very stylish indeed,' she said.
'What?'
'The blazer buttoned.'

He went outside to the toilet and bolted the door and had a look at the pictures again. Even though the light was poor – he could hardly even see them – they were still not sexy in the way the magazine he'd found at the bus stop was sexy. Anyway how could he do a thing like that with his friend lying in the hospital. Him doing it at the same time as Blaise could be dying. The photos were disturbing. They made him feel like an intruder. He'd have to get rid of them as soon as possible. In school, flushing them down the toilet hadn't worked – indeed it had started the whole fucking mess. Going out a walk and throwing them in a bin somewhere would mean that somebody else might get their hands on them. Some kid, maybe. *Better a millstone.* He'd definitely have to burn them. But his mother was in and out the kitchen all the time.

'Can I light a fire in the front room? Do a bit of studying.'

'I've very little coal left and he doesn't come till Tuesday. I'm trying to eke it out. Just go upstairs and use the electric fire.'

He went to his room and lay down on the bed. Downstairs, with his mother, he'd wanted to cry, like when he was a child – when he'd fall or get hurt in some way and run home, holding everything in until he got in through the front door. Then the floodgates would open and his mother would come to him to see what it was all about. But now he was too old for all that. He hadn't even told her what had happened to Blaise. She wouldn't understand. She'd ask stupid questions or questions that couldn't be answered they were so embarrassing.

'But *why* did they knock him down? *Why* don't you go and tell the Headmaster what you saw? Was he a *good* boy? The best thing you can do now is to say a prayer for him.'

He lay on the bed covers, his hands joined behind his head until she called him for his tea. After that he went back to his bedroom. His mother watched television. He found it almost impossible to read a single line of anything. From downstairs he heard the signature music for each of her programmes. He didn't feel like going down and watching with her. When they watched television together she was always on eggs, prepared for anything 'iffy'. Then she would switch channels.

'What's on the BBC?'

If there was something 'iffy' on the BBC as well she would switch off.

'That's quite enough viewing for one evening,' she would say.

He tried to read his chemistry notes. Again and again he saw the bounce of Blaise's head, heard the loud rap of bone against the rim of the bowl. He stared down at the page as if he was hypnotised. And could only get rid of the image by shaking his head. The words bounced off his consciousness as if there was a guard in front of it – a glass wall. He would fail his exams again if this was the way he was going to study.

Before bed he went down for a cup of tea and a sandwich.

'Still wearing the blazer?'

'It's not warm up there.'

On the late night local news there was nothing of any interest. He wanted there to be an item about Blaise. His mother yawned and said, 'Will you slack the fire for me?'

In the kitchen they had an all night grate. A Sofona. He pulled the curtains back to let some light into the yard and went out into the coal house. He covered the fire with a shovel of coal. Then covered the coal with fine slack. He set the shovel outside. When he came back in, his mother was damping down the fire. Pouring on wet tea-leaves and potato peelings saved from the plastic sink tidy, slapping the slack flat with the dainty hearth shovel. He hated her doing this. It was as if he did the labouring part of the exercise, but she was the only one who could do the intelligent part of the job properly. She oozed a sense of satisfaction that things that would normally be thrown in the bin were helping to reduce the fuel bills. She put up the front of the grate and closed off the draught until there was just the slightest wisp of smoke rising from the black and shining slack.

'Bed,' she said.

'Night.'

'Don't forget to say a mouthful of prayers.'

'No.'

He went up to his bedroom and considered whether or not to get changed. If his mother came up it would seem strange to see him sitting there in his blazer at two in the morning. So he changed into his pyjama bottoms and slung his blazer over the back of the chair at his bedside. He was inches from the photographs in the pocket. He turned his pillow upright and got into bed.

Fuck the prayers. He wasn't in the mood, didn't believe they were of any use any more. He lay with the light on, staring ahead.

Half an hour passed. He could hear no sound. He got out of bed and opened his door and listened. His mother always left her bedroom door open, so that if he was out late he'd have to present himself on his way to bed.

'Nice night?'

'Yes — a few pleasant burglaries — in the last one I got a full bottle of vodka, so I'm thoroughly and completely pished.'

'Oh that's nice for you dear. Don't vomit too loudly. Night-night.'

She was not a loud snorer but he could hear sleep noises coming from her bedroom. Rhythmic breathing, mouth smacking. He went to his blazer and took the envelope from the inside pocket. He knew he could be caught sneaking down the stairs so he put on his pyjama jacket and stowed the envelope under his arm. He clamped his arm to his side and began to go quietly down the stairs. He passed her open door and heard her regular deep breathing. The light switch in the kitchen always gave a loud click so he had to ease it up soundlessly until the light came on. He closed the door with extreme slowness because it had a ball catch, and could give out a loud snap if closed quickly. The fire irons were set upright beside the hearth. He took the poker and opened down the fire. The layer beneath the black smoking slack was red and glowing between the bars. The envelope had stuck to the skin of his ribs. He untacked it and it gave him a sticking plaster sensation as it pulled away. He took out the first photograph and slid it between the bars of the fire — pushed it in further with the poker without looking at it. Pictures in the fire. A game his mother liked to play with him when he was small. The photo glowed and burst into flames. Little fantails of blue ran along the edges. Its shape curled and squirmed. He was burning them. At last. Getting rid of them. The grey-white smoke rising from the slack increased. He pushed a third photo in. The first two had blackened and there were tiny lights winking on and off as the air touched them. The next two he put in together, the women face to face. He stopped. Was that a noise? He stuffed the envelope beneath his arm and listened. He opened the door. The ball catch gave a little ringing sound once it had been sprung. Nothing. He couldn't even hear his mother breathing. But that was a bad sign. She might be awake. The next thing he'd know she'd be standing there in the nightie with the hair tied back.

'What are you doing at this hour of the night?'

'My feet were cold.'

He eased the door closed again and continued burning. Breasts and smiles and open cunts and bare backsides. Eventually he pushed the envelope itself between the bars of the grate. He gave a sigh and closed the fire up again. He was so relieved at having the business finished that he became careless and accidentally dropped the poker with a clatter on the hearth. Fuck. You total dumbfuck.

He went into the scullery and put the kettle on. When it boiled he filled a jar. Upstairs a board squeaked. He heard his mother's voice.

'Is that you, Martin?' He opened the kitchen door.

'It's only me,' he said. He turned out the light and began climbing the stairs.

'What are you doing up at this hour of the night?'

'My feet were cold.'

'Why don't you get yourself a jar?'

'I just did,' he said.

In bed the jar was scalding at his feet so he covered it with a towel and clenched it between his knees. He felt good that he'd finally got rid of those things. And that Kavanagh had replaced the exam papers. It was like the feeling after confession. An unburdening. The only casualty was Blaise. But nobody at school had ever died. It was unheard of. So Blaise would probably be all right – and the three of them would get back together again. And if something awful happened, that would just leave him and Kavanagh. But it was unlikely Blaise would be fit to sit his exams. Martin imagined the gymnasium as it had been last year – the year of his failure – with its coconut matting to protect the sprung maple floor and the temporary clock hung on the wall bars. This year it would have

Blaise's empty desk – like Banquo's seat – with his number chalked on it. It would probably have on it the same unopened booklet of lined paper throughout the examination weeks. He knew the keen boys, the show-offs, despite the clock, would take off their watches and set them on the desk in front of them, Kavanagh included. Unload their equipment of pens and pencils and rulers and rubbers. The sighs and groans of the candidates after they'd been given the signal to open their question papers. The sinking feeling that even though he knew the questions he didn't know the answers. The moist palms. The incredible difficulty of beginning the first sentence. The writing until his fingers were sore and the blood seemed to have drained from his arm. The certainty that he was being processed and graded so that society could utilise him. They were making keys for locks. And by trying his best he was doing his worst. The feeling that the invigilator at any minute would walk up behind him and tap him on the shoulder and say – we have reason to believe that by close analysis of your answer you have had prior knowledge of the question. How could that have come about?

At eleven o'clock and at half past three the sound of tea and biscuits being brought to the invigilator. The scrape of biscuits against the plate, the sound of a spoon stirring tea in a china cup, the bite and closed-mouth munching. All in the silence of the exam room. Last year the invigilator had padded up and down the aisles ceaselessly. At the same time reading a book. Kavanagh, as always, would write non-stop, the paper having to be forcibly removed from him by the invigilator at the end. And Martin himself would refuse to take advantage of having seen the papers and would do his best to pass comfortably but not with distinction. And he did not foresee that he would succeed so admirably in his aim that he barely passed. He imagined what would be said at supper evenings. If he failed they would *not* talk about him. If he passed by the skin of his teeth he could hear Father Farquharson saying 'A pass is a pass. Congratulations are in order. The world record in the high jump was only cleared by a whisker.'

'How does that come about – "the skin of your teeth",' Mary Lawless would say. 'There's no skin on your teeth.'

Nurse Gilliland would smile a sideways smile and say something like, 'There'll not be a word about it in a hundred years' time.'

And his mother would be close to tears because her prayers had been answered. Martin had turned out a good boy after all. Even though he was not destined for the priesthood. He didn't curse, knew what a place setting was, could knot his own tie, wear his hair at the correct length and had no interest whatsoever in sex.

Part Two

A Night in the Lab

The night classes were in the middle of the afternoon because of the Troubles. Martin stood waiting for his slides to stain. When the time was right, he washed the dye off and the sections looked like florets of navy blue cauliflower stuck to the glass. Part of some poor bastard's brain. He picked up the slide and looked at it under the microscope. Another ambulance went screaming out of the hospital. Networks of dark blue nuclei. If only you could stain the thoughts. The sum total of all the thoughts of a lifetime – that would be the soul. He could be looking at this poor bastard's soul. The American sirens were a relatively new thing. Before these recent troubles they'd had to make do with the nee-naw sort. But there was something quite classy about the wailing of the new ones. They put the fear of God into people. A swooping sound – like a sensation in the gut when falling. Up and down like a sine wave. The student technicians looked at one another.

The teacher came back in from his smoke and made an announcement that there *was* something going on. One should be careful about the way one went home. Buses were being burned so it was unlikely that there would be a regular service. Those with cars might offer lifts. North and west seemed to be free and it was advisable to head in either of those directions. But what was the point, Martin asked himself, of heading in those directions if they were not where you wanted to go?

All the classes left together. In the bicycle shed Martin smiled at a girl with blonde hair he hadn't seen before. She was hopping a little, putting on bicycle clips.

'Can I offer you a lift?' he said.

'No, I've got a bike.'

'So have I.'

Why did he always have to make such crap jokes? What was he talking about – it wasn't even a joke. Maybe it got the conversation going – but at what cost? What a weirdo, she'd be saying, afraid to look over her shoulder. She was probably from one of the hospitals because she had a name tag which he couldn't read. He would get to know her. Their bikes would bring them together. Maybe by next week she'd have forgotten what he said. Maybe. She unlocked her bike and when she swished past, she gave a nervous little smile.

The class was made up of technicians from different hospitals, different institutions. The term was almost over. Next year they'd have to do that stupid multiple choice exam. A look at *that* paper before the event would do no harm. And his conscience wouldn't worry him in the slightest.

He got out his own key and fiddled with the lock. His fingertips had been stained dark blue by the dye. This crap they were learning – different methods of staining different bits of tissue to show up certain cells – you could look the whole fucking thing up in a book. But the profession wanted you to pass exams in it. The Institute wanted you to be able to walk into an exam and sit down and regurgitate the sixteen steps it took to stain a cross-section of somebody's pancreas with hematoxylin and eosin. Blue and pink. What was the point? Every technician had a book, the way cooks had recipe books, with the sixteen steps. He could read, he could perform the actions. Well, maybe if you were on a desert island and you were asked to stain some sections of pancreas with hematoxylin and eosin and you had no book with you . . .

Exams were crap. He had passed his A levels – but only just. Of course, Kavanagh had done viciously well. For a brainbox like him to have had help made little or no difference. Martin knew he, himself, wasn't stupid . . . but the kind of questions they asked were hateful. Compare this poem with that poem – why does the writer say such and such? Blaise had once said in the English class that it was a perfectly valid response to remain silent in front of a work of art. All Wee Jacky had said was, 'Try and tell that to the examiner.'

The lock fell open and he put it in his pocket. He mounted the bike and pedalled slowly towards the back gate. He was out for the night and it was the beginnings of a nice evening. He leaned his hands close together on the centre section of his drop handlebars, just taking it easy. He tried to map out a trouble-free route in his mind – down the Grosvenor Road – then over the Boyne Bridge, up Sandy Row and on to University Road. Normally after class he would have turned the bike left, up the road for home. To be fed by his mammy. But tonight he was going back to his job, to the lab in the Anatomy Department at the University. For the first time in his life he was going to work a night shift. To help out fucking Kavanagh. So he turned the bike right. It made him think about handlebars. Last winter had been incredibly cold. Even wearing gloves, his hands had been frozen riding to work in the mornings. He really should try out his idea of central heating. It was just that his mother always had something to say if the bike was brought into the kitchen.

'What are you doing with that thing in here, Martin?'

'Never you mind.'

'Don't you dare talk to me like that, boy. You haven't got the key to the door yet, y'know. You've my heart scalded. God knows what I've done to deserve it.'

Of course he could bring the kettle out to the bike. Upside down on the pavement, and pour the boiling water into the handlebars. Then hammer in the corks. What he didn't know was how far the hollowness of the bike went. Would the hot water run throughout the whole frame – down the crossbar and maybe leak out on to the road? It all sounded pretty dangerous which was probably why he had had never tried it. And what about rust?

'Some day you'll be carried in here dead and I'll not be to blame. I hate that bike. You'd be far better paying the bus fare. At least that way you'd still have your life.'

Sometimes he took her advice and travelled by bus. Those mornings, when he hadn't handlebars to deal with, he solved the cold hands problem with a warm hard-boiled egg shoved down each glove. Then he ate them for lunch.

It was very quiet now – he could hear his tyres purring over the road. There was little traffic. The lights were against him. He pulled up by McGladdery's car showroom. At least, the last time he had been to night class it had been McGladdery's. Now the roof was gone. There was nothing in the window except for a ragged line of glass around the frame. Everything was blackened and rusted and burnt. A mechanical digger was trying to clear up, scooping burnt debris into its bucket, the driver roaring it backwards and forwards to dump the stuff into the back of a truck. A pile of burnt cars was stacked on a recovery lorry. The stink of smoke was still in the air. Burning and wet. Like after a barbecue, when the logs have been pissed on. Metal beams stuck up – wooden beams had burnt black – in a pattern of black squares. Like alligator skin. A guy with a shoulder bag was moving around taking photos with a good camera. A Hasselblad by the look of it. The lights changed.

Martin moved off. It was a strange feeling to be in the world's eye. Things of note were happening in his place – it hardly mattered that they were *bad* things. The pride was in getting noticed. There were pictures of his town in every paper in the world, every TV in the world – the fact that it was pictures of his town being burned or blown to fuckin bits was neither here nor there.

The next lights were green. It was weird – it was rush hour and everything should have been much busier. In fact the nearer he got to the town centre, the less busy it was. Going at some speed he turned right on to the Boyne Bridge. The road was littered with stones and bricks. It was like a waste ground instead of a main road. What the fuck was going on? A van was blazing and the air was filled with the smell of burning rubber. He tried to steer between the debris but bounced heavily over a half-brick. A bottle smashed in front of him. Holy fuck – what was happening? He looked over his shoulder and there in the road opposite was a phalanx of police and Land Rovers. Guys were running up to the brow of the bridge and chucking stuff across the road and Martin was in the middle of the whole fucking war on his bicycle. He spun round and retreated, bumping up on to the pavement where there was less crap lying on the ground. He stood on the pedals and flew down the hill. Something hit him on the back. A half-brick or something – he didn't know what. But he didn't feel it. He sensed it, but it wasn't painful. He turned the corner out of the line of fire and headed towards the City Hall as fast as he could, still on the pavement. Why didn't the fuckers give you some warning? TAKE CARE. RIOT IN PROGRESS. Jesus Christ. He could have been shot, got a rubber bullet up his arse or anything. When he felt he was out of the firing line he applied the brakes. He joined the watching crowd.

'What's going on?'

'A bit a trouble.'

'What about?'

'How would you know? Somebody probably said something.'

There wasn't much happening now – the occasional splish of a glass bottle breaking on the street surface, shouting that was hard to make out, 'Yafuckinbastard' kind of yelling. The police just stood.

Martin looked at his watch. He'd need to be getting on. Now that Sandy Row was blocked he'd have to go the long way round. He had things to do for Kavanagh. And time was crucial, he'd been told. And he had a knife to sharpen. He pushed the bike and mounted it while it was in motion. He pedalled up Great Victoria Street slowly, approached Shaftesbury Square, where the Ulster Bank was with its two Elizabeth Frink statues halfway up the wall. Flying Figures or Falling Figures, it was called. But locally they'd become known as Draft and Overdraft. Traffic was coming from all directions. Fuckers came out of junctions. Straight at you. He negotiated the Square, then stood on the pedals, panting up the incline to the University. Trees, green lawns, birdsong.

He went in the front hallway – wheeled the bike past the porter's lodge but didn't recognise the man on duty, so he didn't nod. He rarely talked to any of them – a crowd of Orangemen. Within a day or two of starting they knew what *he* was. So they handed out the departmental mail in silence. Martin figured the reason he got the job was because the Prof who had interviewed him was from Australia and didn't know or, more likely, chose to ignore, the local rules.

The floor of the entrance hallway was like a chessboard, except that the black tiles had worn better than the white and the white squares were slightly dished. He walked over the unevenness while his bicycle ticked smoothly along beside him. Outside the doors he saw a girl with a rucksack standing in the cloisters. It was always a great struggle getting the bike out. The girl pulled the narrow door towards herself and held it for him. She smiled but he was too embarrassed to smile back because she was too classy for him. And his bike banged and clanked against the door. The edge of the metallic pedal hit his shin. He made a face and started a curse, but didn't finish it. By the time he got the bike out and manoeuvred it in the direction of the red brick Victorian building at the back of the quad, the girl was through the door and away.

The clock above the cloistered walk chimed faintly six times every hour. It was right twice a day. Like now: six o'clock as he walked across the quad. The Anatomy Department was surrounded by trimmed lawns which had been cut in horizontal swathes, yellow and dark green, the colour of a vegetable marrow. Outside the ground floor windows were a number of cherry trees. There was very little blossom left on them. The fallen petals lay in pink drifts along the gutters. To one side, in front of the Theology building, was a laburnum tree growing aslant, propped on a wooden stump to prevent it falling any further. It was the right place for a tree with poisonous seeds – outside Theology.

Martin couldn't be bothered to lock his bike so he brought it inside the basement door and climbed the stairs to his lab. He put on his white coat and inspected his shin: the pedal had drawn blood even through his trousers.

The microtome knife sat in a box like a small coffin. He took it out with great care and laid it on the microscope stage. The magnified edge was pitted and uneven. The bevel of a sharp knife should be absolutely straight. Like looking at the sea's horizon. It would take hours to sharpen. Martin poured oil on to the glass plate then added abrasive powder – the smallest amount possible tapped from the blade of a scalpel. The machine was like a record player only instead of a needle there was the knife. It hissed almost continually against the powder – but every so often the noise stopped as the knife turned over and the other side was honed. Tomorrow it'd be sharp enough to split a hair lengthwise. If he knew any way of doing it. He closed the lid of the machine to reduce the noise. That mad bastard Salvador Dali had made *Un chien andalou* and filmed the eyeball being sliced with the razor before you could look away. Martin hated anything to do with the eyeball – by now it was the only thing he was still squeamish about. Dali was nothing but a showman with a stupid moustache. The more elaborate the facial hair the less interesting the personality. He looked at his watch. Ten past six. Everyone would be gone and the front door locked. He needed to get the timetable Kavanagh had left for him in his room.

On a bench beside the door was an empty bottle. There was no point in taking it because there was no one about at this time. It was all part of his trouble-free way of moving around the building during working hours, talking to this one and that one. He always carried the bottle. If anybody stopped him he was just off to fill it. If he had just filled it then he was heading back to do some work.

In the corridor he walked the central strip of brown lino. On each side were ranks of grey metal lockers, used mostly by males. The females had their own in the ladies' room. His shoes made a rubbery squeaking sound in the emptiness. The summer sun was shining on to the floor at the far end by the noticeboard.

He passed the Dissecting Room and was surprised to see a movement through the bubbled glass of the door. He opened it. Dr Cowie, with his back to him, was gathering his bandoleer of tools and papers together. But Jesus, what was going on with the stiffs? Some of them had their legs in the air. It looked awful – as if they had plunged from the sky and were in the act of landing. The place smelled strongly of formalin, enough to smart the eyes. Dr Cowie turned and looked over his glasses.

'Hello.'

'I thought everybody had gone,' said Martin.

'I'm just off.' The doctor folded his glasses and slipped them into their case. 'Why are you around so late?'

'I'm here for the night.'

'For the jazz in the basement?'

'Naw. I didn't know about that.'

'First Wednesday of the month. So?'

'I'm doing something for Kavanagh's BSc thesis,' said Martin.

'What kind of jazz?'

'The usual. Whatever they play down there – who knows? Are you a fan?'

'I like blues – New Orleans. Some modern stuff is all right.'

'What is it you're doing for Kavanagh?'

'A timed thing. It's going to take all night.'

'And why can't Kavanagh do it? Where is he?'

'Playing basketball. In Dublin.'

'And who's paying overtime for a technician for a whole night?'

'It's a favour. He's a mate of mine. We were at school together.'

Dr Cowie snorted a bit. His white coat looked as if it had come straight from the laundry. You could've cut yourself on it.

'And what kind of a day's work can we hope to get out of you tomorrow?' Martin didn't answer. 'Who does he play basketball for?'

'He's on the university team.'

'He's tall enough for it. Is he any good?'

Martin held the door open. Dr Cowie was edging out when Martin nodded to the nearby tables.

'Why are they like that?'

'Like what?'

'With their legs in the air?'

'Oh, those students are dissecting the perineum.'

'Oh.'

Martin climbed the narrow winding stair to the room where the BSc students worked. Both Kavanagh and his girlfriend Pippa had decided to do the extra year before going on to hospital. Of course it was her decision and where she led Kavanagh always followed. People said it was unusual for a girl to mark time in this way. The attic room was empty. He walked to Pippa's place by the window and looked around. She was very neat. Very Christian. Then he saw a small dictionary among her books. He looked up the word *perineum* (*say* perri-**nee**-um) *noun. Anatomy:* the region of the body between the anus and the urogenital organs. He smiled and put the dictionary back where he found it. It was good to know that such a dirty little definition was embedded in a dictionary belonging to Pippa. And that she had one. Pippa's perineum. He went to Kavanagh's place. The papers he wanted had been left for him.

On his way back to the lab he heard the basement door slam. The sound boomed up the lift shaft and stairwell. Dr Cowie's car started, then drove away. Silence – except for the sparrows cheeping outside. And from an open door the dribbling of a cistern in the Ladies. He had never been in the Ladies before. He pushed on the open door and walked past the cubicles. The doors were open and the seats were all down. In a room there was a Tampax dispenser on the wall and a table surrounded by rows of upright lockers. He touched things with his free hand. Books were scattered about, mostly copies of *Gray's Anatomy*. He touched them. There were some limp white coats hanging on hooks looking like they belonged to no one. He trailed the back of his hand across them. An umbrella and an old-fashioned scarf. A small square mirror on a windowsill. A single emerald green glove. He set his papers on the table and pulled on the glove. It was made of a soft leatherette material. It was very small and cramped his hand, crushed it almost. He stripped it off and put it back exactly where he had found it. His hand expanded. He sniffed the faint perfume which remained from the glove.

One locker had its door wide open, a pair of brown leather shoes, feet together pointing outwards. Comfortable, with shapes of bunions, for the hours of standing on the Dissecting Room floor. There was a bottle of Atrixo hand cream on the shelf. He reached up and unscrewed the top and blobbed a little on to his palm. He rubbed his hands together and inhaled deeply. The broken cistern continued to sing and dribble.

He went down the creaking wooden stairs back to his lab and read Kavanagh's instructions. They were straightforward enough. The first rat had to go at seven o'clock. At the bottom of the page in Kavanagh's big block capitals was –

FAILURE TO CARRY OUT THESE
INSTRUCTIONS AT THE SPECIFIED TIMES
WILL RESULT IN CERTAIN DEATH.

The animal house was in the basement, five poorly ventilated rooms. The ceiling was low. Martin could touch it with the heel of his hand. There was a fire in the central room, still giving off some heat. Dr Cowie called it 'the incinerator'. For fuck sake. A posh scientific word for 'the fire downstairs'.

'Just take it down to the incinerator.'

The grate was very deep and could create a fierce roar up the chimney. It became a frightening sound when the metal shield was held across the opening. The fire would go almost white when you did that – and the chimney breast seemed to throb and vibrate with the power of the up-draught.

Martin had only been in the job a week or two when he'd been asked to take something down to the basement. Maybe Dr Cowie was testing him out – seeing how he'd react. He was really an embryologist and this particular day he'd come into the lab, full of himself.

'Martin, come and see this.' He'd a pad of white gauze in one hand and a scalpel in the other. He wore white surgical gloves. 'It just came in. A lovely specimen.'

He carried his secret to the sink and began to unfold it. The last layer of gauze clung slightly to what was inside and the first thing Martin saw was blood. He tried not to flinch. There was something pale and jellied, the size of a small fist, curled in the middle of the blood. Dr Cowie smiled, waiting for Martin to guess what he was looking at. In places the blood was black.

'Well? What do you think?'

'It's a foetus.'

'Spot on.' Dr Cowie used the scalpel as a probe and lifted a tiny translucent arm on its blade. 'About fourteen weeks. See the fingers. All the details are there at this stage.' He let the arm fall and bent forward. 'See that? Do you know what that's called? Lanugo – foetal hair – it's all over.'

All Martin could see was how defensive it looked. Its stick arms and legs were bent and its fists clenched. It had gathered itself into a ball – the way someone would if he was getting a kicking. The head was huge compared to the body, like some imagined thing from Outer Space.

Dr Cowie produced forceps and picked the foetus up by its cord. Martin said, 'What was wrong with it?'

'Nothing. The mother had to have an emergency operation for something else. Let's have a look inside.' Dr Cowie took the foetus into his left hand, his thumb under its chin. He drew his scalpel down the chest. It fell open easily. 'This is the liver. At nine weeks it's enormous, fills the whole cavity.' Dr Cowie went on talking to Martin as if he was a class. 'Any questions?' Martin had shaken his head. But he'd wanted to seem keen.

'What do you want it fixed in?'

'I've too many at fourteen weeks. Just take it down to the incinerator. You know where the basement is?'

In the corridor with the gauze in his hand he felt a stupid urge to walk slowly. Funeral phrases came into his head. *He was a great lad.* Or *All his life he'd wanted to . . .* None of them applied. He carried the foetus to the basement in its gauze and stood facing the fire which had become grey with ash. But here and there deep down it glowed red.

He remembered the first time he'd noticed a pregnant woman. He'd been with his mother walking in the street, probably holding her hand. This other woman came along with her coat tightly buttoned over a huge bump. When she passed he whispered to his mother 'Did you see her? She had a basin or something up her coat.'

He kept looking back over his shoulder. His mother walked on.

'Shhh. Keep your voice down,' she said. The way his mother's eyes darted about, he knew something wasn't right.

'What's wrong with her?'

'She's going to have a baby.'

'Has she bought a basin for it?'

'Don't be silly.'

'What's silly?'

'The baby is inside her.'

'Oh.'

He thought that very strange at the time. How could a baby be inside her? Was it inside her coat? How could it breathe? Did she take it out for a breath of air at night? Why would she try and smuggle a basin down the street?

Along the walls of each room were tiers of cages – rats and mice, mostly. Some guinea pigs. There was a constant noise coming from the cages – twittering, squeaking, scrabbling. He looked at the reference Kavanagh had written and found the cage, then carried it up to the lab.

From a roll of cotton wool he tugged off a wad and stuffed it into the bottom of a stone jar about the size of a biscuit barrel, then splashed in some ether, darkening and dampening the cotton wool. He smelled the whiff, saw the gas corrugate the air above the jar. The lid was a disc of glass so that you could see what was happening in the jar. He rubbed his nose – he still could get the Atrixo hand cream faintly. The cage of rats was on the bench and it was as if they could smell the ether. They were giving off a panicky noise which increased when he raised the wire lid of their cage. He lifted a white rat by its hairless tail and dropped it into the jar and slid the glass lid back into place. It made a hasp-like sound as it slid. He checked his watch. The rat crouched rubbing its nose and eyes, twitching its white whiskers, sneezing. It panicked and stood on hind legs looking for a way out making tiny scrabbling noises with its claws as it went hand over hand all around the curve of the jar. Black ovals of shit appeared and littered the cotton wool. Yellow stains – like piss on snow. The pink eyes, the whiskers flickering. Very quickly it tumbled over backwards and lay on its side, its flanks pumping in and out. Then the movement ceased. Its eyes became clear jelly – a sure sign that it was dead. Martin lifted it out by its tail. The hairs on one flank, where it had lain on the ether, had gathered into wet, yellowed points.

There was a pile of old newspapers on the bench for working on. He took one and dissected out the left leg from the furry skin. It looked like a tiny uncooked chicken drumstick. He dropped it into a jar of formal saline, labelling it carefully with the time. The remains he bundled in the newspaper and dropped the parcel into the bin. He would incinerate them all later. He was hungry. Often he thought he'd like to eat rat.

One day in school the Spiritual Director had told them about the siege of Derry and how the situation had got so bad that rats were caught and sold for food – sixpence apiece. Kavanagh had put up his hand and asked, 'What's that in our money?'

But these particular rats were clean, well reared. They were tender and lean. He imagined throwing a supper night like his mother's with bits and pieces threaded on wooden cocktail sticks. A pickled onion, a pineapple chunk, roasted rat, tomato.

'Ummm, this is delicious,' says Nurse Gilliland.

'What are these, Mrs Brennan?' says Mary Lawless, 'they're absolutely divine.'

'Oh something Martin cooked up,' says his mother.

'What are they Martin? What are we eating?'

'Rat.'

'Ahhhhhhh Jesus, Mary and Joseph – let me vomit copiously.'

After he'd started this job he'd become aware of the anatomy of things. Like chicken. He'd be eating and be aware of the tendons, the muscle bundles, the blood vessels cooked to black threads. Biting through all this he would come upon the bone glistening and faintly bluish. Lamb chops became ribs. And somehow the knowledge of its anatomy faintly repulsed him. He thought of becoming vegetarian but never actually did.

He reached into his bag, took out the alarm clock his mother had lent him and set it for an hour hence. It ticked loudly.

When he'd been getting ready to leave for work that morning his mother had said, 'I'll miss you.'

'It's only for one night,' he said. She stared at him.

'Martin, I'm joking.'

He wondered if he should fix up his bed. How utterly ridiculous. Here he was thinking about sleeping at seven in the evening just because he was out of his own bed. The last time he'd slept away from home, other than holidays, was about three or four years ago – at the silent retreat in Ardglass.

Kavanagh had got him a Territorial Army camp bed from somewhere – sage green canvas stretched taut over metal rods. It would be OK with his sleeping bag. If he opened it out now and left it on the floor it would just be in his way. He'd fall over it and break something. Nevertheless he opened it up as best he could. It was as simple to put up as a deck chair.

'For fuck sake,' he kept saying. It took him ages. Eventually the whole thing stood a springy six inches off the floor. He unrolled his sleeping bag and lay down on top of it, trying it for comfort – on his back – with his hands joined behind his head. It wasn't bad. He bounced up and down a little. Not bad at all. The canvas creaked, made a sound like moving cabbage leaves. But it was comfy. This was the life. He could be lying down looking up at the stars. He tried to turn on his side. More strange squeaking noises. When he bent his knees they stuck out over the edge of the frame. Since it was a Territorial Army bed he could sleep in the 'Atten – shun!' position. He straightened out and looked at his feet, then put his head back and looked up at the ceiling.

Fluorescent tubes hung from chains. Maybe if the IRA got to hear of it, they'd shoot him for sleeping in a Territorial Army bed.

The knife sharpener hissed on and on, pausing to turn and slap its other side down to grate on the ground glass plate. He unpacked his first lot of sandwiches and walked along the corridor away from the noise. He would eat in the peace and quiet of the tea room.

He lit the Bunsen burner and pushed it under the tripod which held the kettle. He weighed the kettle in his hand. There was enough water for one. He dropped a teabag into the mug he liked best – the biggest. This room was usually full of people. At eleven o'clock and four. Coffee breaks at work were good. Everybody came along: doctors, technicians, students – sometimes the Professor. You could always learn a thing or two from the crack.

Yesterday, Walter Graves, one of the young doctors had said, 'The cyclist's heart – these guys on the Tour de France – their hearts are big enough to pump the blood around an elephant. They die young of cardiomyopathy.'

'What's that?' asked Martin.

'An overgrown heart. A heart which has been over-exercised.'

'Hey, I ride a bike to work,' said Martin. 'Am I going to drop dead?'

'Great Victoria Street is not the Alps, Martin.'

'It's the best exercise you can take sitting down.'

'Naw – that heart of yours'll last you right till the end.'

'Till you're knocked down.'

The death was announced this morning of big-hearted Arthur. His mother used the expression whenever he did favours for people. When he said he was working late to help Kavanagh – for no money – he knew it was coming:

'Huh! Big-hearted Arthur.'

The tea room had bookshelves round the walls. There were copies of working anatomy books but there were reproductions of older volumes as well – Galen and Vesalius. The Vesalius book was great, an artist like Leonardo or somebody. The bizarre figures were in a landscape, upright or leaning on a column, or sitting with fist on chin, their muscles detached and hanging down like undone braces.

There was also a book of photographs – Muybridge's *The Male and Female Figure in Motion*. People running and crawling and jumping and carrying buckets of water and God knows what else, all shot from different angles – but the important thing was that they were doing these things stark naked. He could hardly believe it the first time he saw it. Not a dolly on them. And this experiment was carried out back in the 1890s. In America somewhere. The only thing was, that the photos were very small – twelve or fifteen action shots across a double page – and he had to use a magnifying glass to get any sort of a look at the women. A wee glimpse of their rugs. He had little or no interest in men and their tiny white dicks.

The photographer, Muybridge, seemed to have been a bit of a madman. He discovered that some bastard had banged his wife and he'd become the father of somebody else's child. He was not happy at all and so he went off and banged the guy who had banged his wife. With a gun. Stone dead. He got off because the jury in those days figured he had done the right thing. Your man had it coming to him for screwing another man's wife. It was the Wild West with horses and saloon bars and guns and high-kicking women and what have you.

The whole action photography thing had been started to investigate whether or not a horse, when it was galloping, had all four of its hooves off the ground at the same time. This was important to somebody in those days. And it was as much about time as it was about anatomy. You could actually see the progress of milliseconds. The background to all the photographs was dark with white lines like graph paper. Somebody falling from top to bottom of the picture could be charted, could be timed. The more often he looked at the book the less sexy it was. He began to like it for different reasons. The titles of the pictures: *Woman pouring a bucket of water over another woman, Jumping from stone to stone across a brook* – except that there was no brook there, the model was still in the photographer's yard in front of the graph paper fence. *Turning around in surprise and running away, Kicking a hat, Blacksmiths hammering on anvil, Handspring: a flying pigeon interfering.*

It was all supposed to be scientific but he thought it was just funny. Humour had no place in science – Dr Cowie was living proof of that. Take the flying pigeon interfering: this guy wearing

253

a baby's nappy – he must have been shyer than the rest – just as he's about to do his handspring, into the frame walks this bloody pigeon and it gets its picture taken. It looks round only to see this mad bastard coming towards it about to do a handspring and, quite rightly, it takes off. Freeze frame of take-off. A little moment caught. It should have been called, *Pigeon takes off: mad bastard in nappy interfering*.

He got the feel of the people in the pictures. When he looked with his magnifying glass at the woman pouring the bucket of water over the other woman he could see the shock in the doused woman's face, could see the discomfort in the way she held her body, could see the amusement of the woman standing on the stool emptying the bucket over her. All of this on a day of bright sunshine and hard shadows somewhere in America at the end of the last century. The women thinking is this guy Muybridge crazy or a pervert or what? And how much money are we going to earn from this whole daft afternoon, larking about in our pelts in front of so many cameras? For Chrissake, Mildred, let's go home and get something to eat.

It would have made some picture sequence if it had been his mother's friends who had been throwing the buckets of water. A naked Nurse Gilliland and a bare Mary Lawless. That would have been some show. They'd have to be buckets of Holy Water, to get them to do it without a stitch on. Their rugs threadbare. Sexy as steel wool. *Two women baptising each other*.

The kettle began to boil. He poured some water into his cup and swirled the teabag. He unfolded the packet of sandwiches and saw again his mother's dainty four-way pernicketiness. She'd made him two sets of sandwiches: salad for tea time, ham for supper time.

On the nights when Father Farquharson couldn't make it the talk inevitably got round to ailments. And when Martin was in the room the women would pause. Or would drop their voices. One night Mary mentioned her 'hem region'.

'A bit near the knuckle, Mary.' Mrs Brennan glanced in Martin's direction. 'A little too close.'

'Mary, you should go and see a specialist. I hear there's a very good new man at the Mater.'

'Don't talk to me about him.'

254

'Why? Have you seen him?'

'Seen him?' She looked around the company and paused.

'Martin, get some more milk.'

'But the jug's half full . . .'

'Do as you're told.'

'But . . .'

'They're the same all over – the young ones nowadays,' said Mary Lawless, winking at Martin. 'They've no notion of what to do with themselves – they don't know what to be at next.'

When Martin came back with the filled jug it was Nurse Gilliland who was speaking.

'My bunions have taken off. I've no explanation for it but I can *not* get into a shoe this weather.' She held her foot up for inspection, turned the shoe this way and that. 'At the heels of the hunt I blame all that standing in the wards. When I was a young slip of a thing.'

'Think of bunions as medals,' said Mary Lawless, 'earned devoting yourself to the service of others.'

He poured the last of the milk into his cup and stirred until the tea became a rich brown colour. He fished the teabag out with the spoon and looked round for something to read. *Gray's Anatomy* was on the table in front of him. It was a thick and heavy hardback volume. It fell naturally open at page 168 and there it was. THE FEMALE PUDENDA. The Promised Land. It reminded him of a thing he had seen in a magazine. *The Far East*. His mother had ordered this Catholic publication and another called *The Catholic Fireside*. They had been delivered to the house regularly by the Legion of Mary. Priestly advice had been given from the pulpit that those with young families should not bring English papers into the house, with their salacious pictures, their repulsive morals and pagan attitudes. Instead, rather than leave a gap in the nurture of the minds of the young, they should buy good Catholic Irish publications with entertaining stories and articles written by people who could be trusted. Far be it from the Church to make a suggestion but *The Far East* was as good a recommendation as any. It was full of photographs of priests in their tropical kit – white soutanes, the occasional pith helmet – surrounded by happy black people who had to look very grateful in the company of those called Father Seamus or Father Malachy or Father Finbar. There were articles written by these same priests which could have come from the *Reader's Digest*. It had a children's page – Colum's Corner – containing wholesome and educational games. It was full of photographs of children whose mothers had forced them to send in their photographs and write cute letters. The photos were printed with captions like *Peadar McGrath lives in Main Street, Kenmare but the rest of Kerry is safe enough*. And *Mary Jo, Noel and Philomena O'Leary, Carrigaline, Co. Cork pictured during a pause in hostilities*. This is where Pudsy Ryan's column appeared: 'my diry' it was called. It was supposed to be written by a boy who couldn't spell or punctuate but it was really written by one of the priests. Stuff like, *unkil jorge is here for a koupil of days an he is krossir than a bag ov kats.*

Boys like Pudsy never liked to wash. Oh, what an imp! Pudsy Ryan did naughty things which you were supposed to laugh at. But he never wanked, of that Martin was quite sure. It would have been good to read – *pudsy ryan jerx ov or if you prefair puls his plonker*. To be fair to him, Pudsy was a bit on the young side for that kind of activity.

It was on this fun page he remembered a picture of a slightly balding man with frizzy hair and a frizzy beard – the face was completely surrounded and outlined by hair – and he had wrinkles on his forehead and wrinkles on his chin – a face a bit like a fist – and he was frowning. Definitely frowning. But if you turned him upside down he was smiling. Definitely happy. The same thing was happy and sad. Depending on how you looked at it.

Page 168 of *Gray's Anatomy* had a version not unlike that strange face on the fun page of *The Far East*. Like a mop head. Mysterious, sexy, weird. This was a head-on, spread-thigh view with everything named. URETHRA, ORIFICE OF VAGINA, ANUS, GLANDS OF BARTHOLIN, CLITORIS, MONS VENERIS. The geography of a place he'd never been. Enid Blyton's *The Playground of Adventure*. His eye skimmed down the page and read again 'Each labium has two surfaces, an outer, which is pigmented and covered with strong crisp hairs; and an inner, which is smooth and is beset with sebaceous follicles and is continuous with the genito-urinary mucous tract . . .'

He began eating his sandwich. It was a mixture of crunch and sloppiness. He loved that. It would be awful to eat salad sandwiches if they were freshly made. They had to be seasoned for hours and hours. The bread had to be moist from the tomato which had to merge with the butter and the salad cream, the spine of each lettuce leaf had to stay firm and slightly crisp, the yolk of the hard-boiled egg had to remain dry but the white still had to have a certain slipperiness.

When he finished eating he closed the book and carried his still hot cup of tea back to his own lab. He saw the camp bed laid out and avoided stumbling over it. The hot tea he set on the floor. With great care, so as not to unbalance the bed, he lay down on top of the sleeping bag and stretched out. Before he joined his hands behind his head he looked at his watch. He had twenty minutes before the next rat. His stomach rumbled and he wanted something sweet. Since giving up smoking he'd got this sensation after eating. It used to be a cigarette – now it was chocolate or something sugary. He was getting horny. But there was no time for that kind of thing. He felt very much on his own – isolated. He hadn't felt this way since the silent Retreat. It had been a bizarre couple of days which had been important for him. *If it matters at all it must matter completely.* He'd made an important decision there. NOT to go with the religious life. And that, in its turn, had gradually led him to think – if it doesn't matter completely then it doesn't matter at all.

He thought of the foetus again, of the funeral of himself descending the steps to the basement. He didn't want to pray for it. He wanted to call it something other than 'it'. To burn something without a name seemed wrong somehow. Was it male or female? Evelyn. Some names applied to both sexes. Hilary was the same kind of name. He'd put a shovel of coal on the animal house fire and brought it to a white hot roar with the metal shield. Before he threw the foetus on, he opened up the gauze for a last look. It lay curled up in pink profile. Its tissues were somehow translucent, showing the delicacy of arm and leg bones, of fingers and toes. It had the feeling of a life stopped. Like a photograph. Of a life not started.

He folded the gauze over again – tucked it in – and threw the bundle on the fire. The gauze burned briefly with a blue flame at the edges. He remembered Blaise and the dirty photographs. The way they burned. This is what sex produced. The fire downstairs. He turned and walked away. His legs trembled as he climbed back up the steps.

He could be over to the Students' Union and back before his tea cooled. Buy a Kit-Kat or a Penguin. Maybe a Wagon Wheel. He got up off the bed and checked he had enough money. He took off his white coat, hung it on the back of the door and headed downstairs. The quad was empty as he crossed between the neat lawns. It was a fine evening – the sun had come out and was low in the sky. His shadow was long and diagonal to him. There was still a smell of burning rubber in the air drifting from Sandy Row. He called with the security people and told them he was going to be in the department all night. They said they had already received notification from the Prof.

The Students' Union shop was open until late. He got his Kit-Kat and headed back. The assistant had given him two ten pence pieces in the change. He chinked them as he walked. Then he rubbed their milled edges together. Coins, he felt, were the size of bin lids. There was a cleaner in the Biochemistry Department, Bella, her name was, who had one of these embedded in her. On her day off she'd gone for a cup of tea in town. When a bomb goes off, everything becomes shrapnel. Including a saucer of tips. She survived the explosion but would have a ten pence piece embedded in her pelvis for the rest of her life. It was so close to something vital that the surgeon thought it best to leave it alone. She was told not to overdo things. Thanks for the tip. What was embedded in her mind? Or was the mind incapable of taking in the enormity of what had happened? One second you were blowing on the surface of your newly poured tea before tackling your biscuit, maybe an Empire biscuit, maybe leaning slightly forward in your seat, and a millisecond later you were fifteen feet out into the street having been punched through a plate glass window with both your arms broken and multiple fractures of the right leg and some of your skin ripped off and your other knee sliced open by a soup bowl and a ten pence piece hammered into your pelvis. All for somebody else's Cause. People sitting in the street with their bones sticking out. There were still arguments about who did that particular one. Whether it was the IRA or the

Loyalists or the Brits – what did it matter? It would be hard for Bella to get a night's sleep ever again.

When you heard an explosion – if it was just that – it was bad. Ominous. If it had not been preceded by the nee-naw of fire engines it meant that no warning had been given. There would be casualties. He had heard such an explosion one night in the distance as he walked home. *News at Ten* had said there were five dead. A pub beyond the University.

The girl with the rucksack was still around. She had come into the quad and stood facing the sun with her eyes closed, her hair brightly lit. She looked really good standing like that. Her sunglasses nesting on top of her blondish hair, jeans, a white T-shirt. She had a white wool sweater around her shoulders, the sleeves loosely knotted in the middle of her chest. The shadows of the archways sliced across the flat stone of the walkway. She opened her eyes when she heard his footsteps. The closer he got, the better looking she was. Bare arms, tanned skin. What a good face. Her hair was curled like pine wood shavings or spilled clock springs. He was shy of looking her straight in the eye. He looked down at the flagstones and sort of smiled vaguely as he passed her.

'Hi again,' she said. His heart leapt in his chest. Was she speaking to him? He was the only one there. He looked at her. She had the face of someone it was easy to like. She was smiling and she was definitely addressing him. 'Do you know where the Anatomy Department is?'

'Yeah,' he said pointing. 'Just there. Where I'm going.'

They fell into step. She was exactly the same height as he was. Their eyes were on a level.

'Are you going to the jazz?' she asked.

'No. Maybe later. I don't think it starts until later.' He stammered a bit, didn't know whether he should launch into a whole explanation about working there and all that. Blah-blah-blah. 'There should be a notice over here.'

She was going to walk the whole way to the door with him. Jesus. What were they going to talk about?

'Your accent,' he said. 'Is it American?'

'Naow,' she laughed. 'You don't know?'

'Haven't a clue.'

'Australia. Down under.'

'I thought you were American. Because of the jazz, maybe.'

'Naow. It's just I said I'd meet somebody there. A fellow countryman.' She didn't say anything more. She was leaving it up to him. The thing he'd said about being American because of the jazz was just so fucking stupid. Oh Jesus.

'That's a nice evening,' he said.

'Yeah.'

'You'd need to be careful about where you go in town. There was a bit of trouble down the road – earlier, when I was coming past.' The girl stopped and bent over and stared down at something on the path.

'What are they?'

'Hairy caterpillars. Granny Greybers we call them here.' Two of them were speedily inching and arching their way across the tarmac of the path, brown and bristling between the pink petals of cherry blossom.

'Like a couple of escaped eyebrows,' said Martin.

'In search of a forehead,' said the girl.

It was a blue Gothic door, twin sides meeting at the apex. Each half of the door was plastered with notices and embedded drawing pins and corner remnants left over from previous stuff. She bent slightly forward to read and hummed and hawed. She stretched out her left hand and leaned against the stone pillar of the doorway. The inside of her arm was paler, blue veined. Her hair fell over her face a bit and she jutted her lower lip and blew hard up into her own face. The hair stirred. It moved on her brown temple. How is it that she is not amazed at herself?

'There it is,' Martin said. 'Peetie Red Wallace and His Bald Eagles. Nine o'clock.'

'That's not for ages.' She looked at her watch.

'Would you like a bit of Kit-Kat?'

'You think I'm gonna starve in the meantime?'

'This door should be open soon,' he said, 'the band'll have to set their kit up and all.' He tore off the red outer wrapper of the Kit-Kat and snapped a piece through the silver paper. He peeled back the foil and held the biscuit out to her.

'Thanks,' she said. 'Very polite.'

'It's the way my mother reared me.'

'Well, she sure did a good job. Why do they hold a jazz night

260

in an *Anatomy* Department?' Martin couldn't think of a good answer. 'Do the skeletons dance?'

'It's a good space, the bottom lecture theatre – there's a bit of atmosphere.' He looked at his watch. 'I've gotta go. I don't use this door. I go in the back.'

'What's your hurry?'

'I've to kill . . . something.' Oh fuck – why had he said that? He was afraid of talking about rats. So he hadn't mentioned them. But it had made it so much worse. Her eyes widened – they were so big and dark. 'It's an experiment. Maybe I'll explain later. If I see you at the jazz.' She popped the last of the Kit-Kat into her mouth and licked the chocolate from her fingertips.

'Great tucker, mate,' she shouted after him. He hurried away, almost moaning to himself. You daft cunt, what will she think of you? *I'm off to kill something.*

As he went up in the lift it occurred to him that in the faintest possible way he had made a date. He would see that woman later on.

He slammed the lift gates closed and went up the steps to the Anatomy Library two at a time. If he got there fast enough he could get another look at her as she retraced her steps across the quad. He was glad he'd taken off the white coat to go for the Kit-Kat – he looked such a ganch in it. Nearly as stupid looking as the security staff. The library door squeaked loudly as he pushed it open. He ran to the window overlooking the quad. There she was, sitting on one of the benches, her rucksack on the ground. As he watched her she swung her feet on to the seat and sat lengthwise. The library door swung slowly closed. After it clunked shut the department became silent again. On the bench she moved her arm and did something with her hair.

There were some monocular microscopes sitting on a demonstration bench showing glass slides of various tissue samples. He grabbed one and slipped the glass slide out of place. He upended the microscope, adjusted the eyepiece and concave mirror and pointed it down into the quad. It was one of the guys in Embryology who had showed him this trick – how to make a telescope out of a microscope. He had to rest the instrument on a shelf in front of the windowsill because the shake of holding it made it impossible to see anything. Then there she was – up close – filling the circular lens. She looked great. She moved her hand up and clawed her hair over her head, against the nap, while looking away off at something. It was good when women did that, concentrated on something. In music shops flicking through a pile of LPs, looking briefly at each one; in a library staring down, reading, the eyes moving slightly across the page line after line. A hand under the chin. Staring down into a glass case at an exhibition of books, moving a silver cross backwards and forwards on a neck chain. A face of such attractiveness. Intent. Looking at her. The feeling of swoon when she looked at him. He had nearly died. Touching the lobe of her ear without knowing she was doing it. He thought about a girl coming down the aisle with communion in her mouth. It wasn't the same thing, at all. It was the opposite of the first two things he'd imagined. Girls coming from communion were self-conscious and shy. They knew they were being watched – most of them were throwing their heads up like racehorses. It was the total lack of absorption of self which made women so attractive. They were at their most completely attractive when they were most completely themselves. It helped if they had nice breasts. This is what was happening now. This Australian was sitting by herself, in the evening sun, absorbed by her Victorian surroundings. She had nice breasts.

Even better was to see a woman by herself laughing – provided she wasn't completely doolally. The girl in the library reading her book suddenly smiles. What was funny on the page lives in her eyes momentarily. A woman walking down the street completely by herself remembers something said, something done and can't hold back laughing and puts her hand up to cover her lower face. She knows she is giving too much away in front of strangers. Maybe she's had a drink too many; maybe she's just left a good conversation in a pub or a coffee place. Whichever way it was, she gave her loveliness away to Martin as he waited for his bus one evening. It was like seeing a photo of her mind, the face, a kind of monitor to the inner workings.

Then suddenly the Australian was out of the eyepiece. He rose from the microscope and looked out the window. She was slinging her rucksack over her right shoulder and combing her hair the wrong way with her fingers. She headed for the front gate. Martin watched her until she disappeared into the cloisters.

The day after his A level results he spent an hour with a youth employment officer discussing everything from Art to Forestry and beyond to Customs & Excise.

'Do you fancy a science job? In the University?' The man pulled out a piece of paper from his top pocket.

'I'll do anything. In the meantime.'

'Get yourself up there, right away.'

He walked to the University and was directed to the Anatomy Department. It was the darkest, most Dickensian building he had ever seen. Climbing the stairs to the office he was aware of everything being brown. An indefinable smell, which stung the eyes, hung in the air. He knocked the office door and an oldish woman answered.

'I'm here about a job as a technician.'

'Yes, we've been expecting you.'

The woman had an accent like the Queen. She ushered him into an empty lecture theatre and gave him a form to fill in.

'I hope you don't mind waiting here.'

Martin sat on the bottom bench facing the blackboard. There was nothing written on it but he could see the grey rectangular tracks of a duster. On the wall was a picture of a transparent man to show his circulation – like a blue tree and a red tree which had become entangled. In here everything continued to be a mahogany colour: benches, rostrum, panelled walls. A blackout blind on an open window had come adrift and bellied into the room in the breeze. Each time it fell back the wooden spar at the bottom clanked. In the distance someone was whistling. He laid the form on the seat of the bench and filled it in. No matter what they asked him he would say as often as he could, 'I don't know but I'm keen to learn.'

After a while the oldish woman secretary came and showed him into the Professor's room. It was also brown. The Professor sat behind his desk in a huge ornate throne of a chair, carved wood and red velvet plush. He was a big, big man with round chins, white hair and a warm smile. Even his earlobes were chubby. Beside him stood a much smaller man in a white coat. To his right

263

a full skeleton hung from a stand. The Professor introduced himself and Mr Knox, his head technician. The head technician had a sort of permanent smile on his face as if he was always in very bright sunlight. It seemed a welcoming smile and, not sure whether it was the right thing to do in the circumstances, Martin shook hands with everyone. The Professor's hands were so big it was like shaking boxing gloves. The Professor indicated a chair and Martin sat down. To try and relax he drooped his shoulders.

'No need to be nervous with us,' said the Professor. 'The first question is – why did you apply for this job?'

'I was in seeing the youth employment guy – officer. He said there was a job going here. Now.'

'Those are circumstances, not reasons. Why this job?'

'Because it was the one on the piece of paper he gave me.'

'If it had said traffic management and supervision would you have applied for that too?'

'I don't know.' Martin hesitated. 'I'm not sure.' He smiled nervously.

'These are not trick questions. I'm just trying to find out a little about you. Do you like science, is what I'm really asking?'

'Yes.'

The Professor's accent was strange – thin sort of vowels. He leaned forward and looked at the form Martin had filled in.

'Have you any idea what the job would entail?'

'Sorry. I don't know but I'm keen to learn.'

'We certainly need an extra pair of hands at the moment.' Mr Knox nodded. 'We would allocate you to help with some research programme or other, a bit of section cutting – you would lend a hand looking after the animal house, help with the students – show slides at lectures. You'd have to attend night classes, get yourself some qualifications.'

'Of course.' He seemed to be nodding too much. Over-nodding. 'I'm keen to learn.'

'There might be some involvement with the mortuary side of things. Would this worry you? Are you squeamish about such matters?'

'No more than anybody else.'

'We are extremely indebted to people who leave their bodies to science. At all times they must be treated with respect and dignity.

A previous professor here was such a gentleman that he raised his hat every time he passed the Dissecting Room. But I shouldn't have to say this to another human being.' The Professor looked up at his head technician, then indicated Martin.

Mr Knox cleared his throat and said, 'Have you worked with animals before?'

'Not really. We have a cat at home.'

'I suppose it's a start. Can you wire a plug?'

Martin stared at the skeleton hanging by its skull. He hadn't a clue how to wire a plug.

'They don't teach that kind of thing at school.'

'Who wires the plugs at home?' said the Professor.

'The cat.' Martin gave a stupid kind of a laugh. There was a silence. Mr Knox continued to wrinkle his face, and the Professor raised one eyebrow. 'No, no – there's a man lives next door. He fixes hoovers and stuff for my mother. The cat is actually his.'

'I see here one of your interests is in photography. Are you any good?'

The Professor smiled. His question seemed to be outside the interview.

'I think so. I mean, I hope so.'

'We do a lot of that here. We are well equipped with darkrooms and the like. So you'll be in the right place.' Martin wondered if he had heard correctly. He had never done an interview before – yet this man seemed to be telling him he had got the job.

He began to dismantle the microscope-as-telescope. The quad was empty. The only movement was the slight ripple coming from the laburnum tree as the air moved through it. He hawed on the eyepiece and wiped it with a tissue and slotted it back. When it had all been reassembled he slid a demonstration slide of pancreas beneath the lens for the next student to find. He turned away from the window to the small historical section in the corner. It had a reproduction of Rembrandt's *The Anatomy Lesson of Dr Tulp*. Dr Tulp's left hand was in graceful mid-gesture above the left arm of a cadaver which he had just dissected as if wiring a very complex plug. Beside it was a modern silkscreen print based on the Dr Tulp subject matter, but with distorted figures. There were some

Vesalius drawings, a picture of Galen, also several plaster heads demonstrating the outdated notion of phrenology. One of the heads was that of a nineteenth-century murderer who had been hanged for his crimes. Martin thought that the features bore a great resemblance to Blaise.

Next to the historical section there was an alcove and a leather medical couch. This is where he had damply perched last year. One day the Prof had asked him if he'd like to make a few extra quid. Martin had nodded.

'You're thin enough for it. In fact you're ideal. How would you fancy being a model – in the surface anatomy exam?'

Martin hesitated.

'Nothing really embarrassing. It would mean – on the day – the occasional bit of pointing out on you. A bit of poking, maybe. Biceps rather than gluteus maximus.'

On the day of the exam he'd sat covered in a grey army blanket in the alcove of the Anatomy Library wearing only a pair of navy bathing trunks. He tried to read his book but it was difficult with all the distractions. The blanket smelled very faintly of oil of wintergreen and suntan oil, and there were bits of dried grass attached to the fibres. His thighs kept sticking to the plastic chair. Beside him, the leather couch took up most of the space in the alcove. He'd been listening to the drone of voices – examiners and students – from the other end of the room. Not every student was asked questions about the model. Up until now he'd only been examined by blokes.

Now there were footsteps and the Prof came round the corner of the alcove with a Chinese girl. Both were dressed in white coats.

'On the table, please, if you don't mind.' The Prof spoke to Martin in an unusual voice, kindly – as if the model was aloof from the whole business. Martin slipped the blanket off his shoulders and stood up. What if he got an erection? He slid his hip on to the old leather couch. As he lay down it was cold against his bare back and he gasped.

'Make a fist,' said the Prof. Martin clenched and the girl answered questions about the white strings in his wrist. He was being examined. She was being examined. Her voice was shaking with nerves and her English was not good. Her fingertip, the only

266

time she touched him, was ice cold. The Prof indicated similar strings in Martin's right foot. The girl seemed perplexed. Martin wanted badly to help her but he hadn't a clue what they were talking about. Somehow, just because they were talking about bits of *him*, he felt he should be able to help.

The Prof and the girl were now silent, the girl waiting for inspiration. Martin raised his head, chin on chest, and looked down at his bare feet lying at an angle of ten to two. He had no notion of getting a hard-on but thought it might have been better than the tiny accidental peak at present showing on his navy trunks. The material had gathered into this sharp point – like he was concealing a cocktail stick in his groin. He didn't want to smooth it down, or draw attention to it in any way. A shaking girl, in the middle of an oral exam – especially one who was doing badly – would not be the slightest bit interested in whether it was a small crease or a small penis. Martin coughed and made a half turn. The crease disappeared. He leaned back on his elbows. For some reason he began to sweat. It must have been something to do with nervousness, yet he didn't feel uptight. A trickle of sweat escaped from his armpit and dripped on to the leather of the couch. It was the girl. That's what was making him tense.

'Feet are extremely complicated items,' said the Prof. 'Twenty-six bones and as many joints and muscles. One minute they have to behave as a rigid lever and next as a pliable spring. Tell me what you know of the blood supply to the foot.' There was a long pause. The girl's answers were filled with stops and stammers. Martin wanted to say that her knowledge of surface anatomy was superficial. Unable to look at her distress any more, he looked away.

'What are you smiling at?' asked the Prof.

'Nothing – nothing at all, sir.'

'I thought I'd inadvertently made a joke of some kind.' The Prof waved his hand to indicate that they had finished with the model. 'Thank you for your co-operation.'

They both turned and left Martin alone. He slid off the couch and wiped away the drip of sweat with the blanket. It wasn't fair. These Chinese and foreign students had to cope with English as well as doing Medicine. He sat down to try to read again the first page of his book. He was interrupted almost immediately when he heard a new voice. It was Máire O'Malley, a girl he knew from St Dominic's. He'd been in her company many times in town when everyone had gone for coffee after the Central Library. Kavanagh had been in his element, surrounded by women. This Máire had lovely dark eyes and a nice smile. Fucking hell – what if she came over and started answering questions on his body. Him lying there with his pointy cock in the air and the sweat dripping from his armpits. He was too thin. His ribcage looked like a couple of xylophones.

They didn't bring her over to examine him – but when she was leaving she gave him a tiny wave from waist high just to let him know she had seen him.

He heard a distant ringing. The fucking alarm. He'd forgotten he had to kill another rat. There he was mooching around the Anatomy Library when he had work to do. He raced to his lab and banged the alarm clock into silence. Like many another one in the North of Ireland he had a night of killing ahead of him.

He heard the boom of the back door closing and went to the head of the stairs to see who it was. The metallic elevator gates closed. He bent over the banisters but could not make out who was inside. The lift motor hummed as it started to rise. The stairwell was gloomy and the light fanned out through the criss-crossed gates on to each floor as it passed. The hoist was large and slow for the transportation of cadavers. It stopped and the inner gates were pulled back, then the outer ones. Kavanagh stepped out carrying an Adidas bag.

'Ya bastard,' Martin said. His voice echoed in the stairwell. 'What are you doing here?'

'Checking up on you.' They both laughed.

'Yes, sir. All present and correct.' Martin pretended to salute. 'I thought you were supposed to be playing basketball in Dublin.'

'A group of hooded individuals decided otherwise. It seems their barricade was incomplete without our minibus.'

'What – you were hijacked?'

'That's what they call it.'

'Fuck – was that scary?'

'Too right it was. Lovely lad – with his balaclava and machine gun. Thought he was bloody John Wayne.' He dropped his bag and took both hands to slam the inner lift gate, then the outer one. 'Bastard. So we all had to take our kit and vamoose. Ireland's fight for freedom ruins basketball tournament.'

'Was there no other way . . . ?' Kavanagh shook his head.

'Northern basketball team fails to show. What sort of a bloody country is this?'

Kavanagh picked up his bag and they walked through to the lab.

'So how's it going?'

'I just killed one this minute. Seventeen to go.' Kavanagh reached out and patted him on the back of his white coat.

'Stout fellow. Keep it up.'

'What do you mean "keep it up". Are you not going to take over? Do it yourself?' He thought about his half date with the Australian girl. He could meet her at the jazz and they could maybe go on somewhere else.

'I've already phoned Pippa.' Kavanagh sat down astride the wooden chair, facing the back of it. 'Would you mind carrying on? As if nothing had happened?' Martin hesitated. 'It'd be a big favour.' Should he tell him about the Australian? There was a time when it would have been the first thing he'd have said but since Pippa had come on the scene things had gradually changed between them. All through the days when they studied down at the public library, she had kept Kavanagh at arm's length. Before the exams she would go out with him once a week and only at the weekend. There was work to be done, she said. He was completely mad about her. And Martin couldn't see why. Maybe it was because she was so unattainable. She was saved. A no-make-up Christian. But she didn't need any of it, she was so beautiful.

'And where are you going?'

'I don't know. To Pippa's?'

'I stay here and work my arse off for your fucking thesis, while you swan off with her?'

Kavanagh winced slightly at the swear word.

'Martin – it's a bad time for me.' He dropped his voice and shook his head. 'We had a row – last night. It's very serious and I need to fix it. As soon as possible.'

'About?'

'Everything – and nothing.'

269

'That's pretty clear.'

Martin didn't know what to say, or how to say you'd be far better off without her. She's a disaster area. It's women like her who will eventually drain you of any spark left in you. Her and her constant fuckin righteousness. Is *she* taking anything from *you*?

Kavanagh sat gazing in front of him, biting his lip. He went to scratch his head and Martin saw that his hand was trembling.

'Are you OK?'

'Yeah.'

Martin moved to put a hand on Kavanagh's shoulder. He half squeezed, half patted him.

'What about a coffee?' said Martin.

'Tea?'

'Yeah. I can take a break. From *your* work.'

'How's the bed?' Kavanagh stood and looked down at it.

'It's the most luxurious piece of canvas I've ever encountered.'

They walked the corridor to the tea room and Martin put the kettle on again.

'It's funny the way you can't stop the body reacting.'

'To what?'

'Flight or fight.'

'What are you talking about?' said Martin. 'Her or the hijack?'

'The sight of a gun − here.' Kavanagh held his index finger in front of his face. 'And it's not the gun. It's what the gun means. Talk is out. You do what you're told whether you like it or not. Result − anger.'

'Are you sure you're not talking about Pippa?' Martin laughed. But Kavanagh just smiled.

'Get stuffed,' he said and sat down.

The kettle boiled and Martin poured. He revolved a teabag with a spoon and when the water was brown enough he handed the cup to Kavanagh.

'No milk. Sorry.' They sat facing each other across the table. 'So − what's going on?'

Kavanagh cooled his tea with some water from the tap. He sipped it and set it down.

'She wants to break it off. She says that if we're to . . . continue − it's not enough for me just to behave myself. I must believe. She says she couldn't continue with somebody who has a totally different belief system to hers.'

'Well, get out then.'

'But I don't *want* out.' He couldn't look at Martin. 'Her Christianity is *so* important. It's not a superficial thing – like music or how you wear your hair. It's her whole life.'

'So what exactly can you do?'

'I have to promise I'll try to . . .' Kavanagh shrugged, '. . . believe more. It's no good just living a life of correctness. She says it has to come from here.' He touched his closed fist to his chest. 'I know she doesn't drink or do stuff before marriage – I accept all that. Always have done. But now she wants me to accept the Lord as my Saviour. I have to accept I'm a sinner.'

'Well, that's true.'

'This is serious.' Kavanagh's voice was turning snappy. 'She says it's just not good enough for me to go through the motions. I have to try and believe – or else there is no point in us going together. Our lives must be a threesome with Jesus at the centre.'

Martin went on fiddling with the teaspoon. He wanted to laugh. 'I dunno,' he said. 'But you *know* what I think of all this crap.'

'Pippa's faith doesn't believe in Lourdes-type miracles. But she says she's praying – a medical cure gives somebody a few more years on earth, she says, but the spiritual cure changes us for all eternity.'

'Hard cheese.'

'What's your problem with this?' Kavanagh lifted his cup and blew on the tea's surface. He sipped and looked up, then set the cup down. He seemed not to know what to do with his hands.

'It all sounds very *saved*,' said Martin, 'very Bible thumper.'

'You're stereotyping. You're just using labels.' Kavanagh nodded to the outside. 'All this sectarian nonsense isn't making things any easier. I thought the Protestant–Catholic thing was over, a thing of the past.'

Martin stopped smiling and said, 'If it matters at all then it must matter completely.'

'That kind of thing.'

'Blaise wouldn't approve.'

Kavanagh snorted.

'Blaise was a liability.' Kavanagh stood up and turned the chair beneath him so that he was sitting on it backwards, like he had been in the lab, his elbows resting on the back.

'Any word of him?'

'The grandfather was buried at the weekend. Remember him? With the white goatee. '*How dare you,*' Martin mimicked an old man shouting and shaking his fist. '*Bloody burglars.*'

'He was just deranged.' Martin could see that Kavanagh wanted to change the subject but Martin kept going.

'The bit in the paper said he was a W.B. Yeats scholar. Did you know that?' Kavanagh shook his head – no. 'I also hear that the father fixed things up when he was back for the funeral. He finally dropped the assault charges.'

'Did he?'

'The school is exceeding glad. Especially our friend, the Dean of Discipline.'

'I saw *him* the other day. Strutting up the Falls Road.'

'Condor,' Martin shook his head. 'Jesus.'

Kavanagh nodded in agreement.

'Bad vibes. Bad memories.' He took another drink of tea. 'Better left behind.'

'Why didn't you go straight to Pippa's place?' said Martin. 'Instead of coming here. I'd never have known a thing about it.'

'I want to be open . . . Anyway she won't be home until ten or so.'

'Where is she now?'

There was silence. Kavanagh changed his weight and leaned his elbows heavily on the back of the chair. Martin stopped what he was doing and turned and waited for an answer.

'She does dance worship.'

'I fucking don't believe . . .' Martin began to laugh. Kavanagh nodded.

'It's not really all that far fetched. It's using your body as a prayer. And, she says, it keeps her fit.'

'Dual purpose.' Martin was still laughing. 'That is *so* fucking Kumbaya, *so* tambourine . . .'

'In the past all the arts – painting, music, architecture – have been used for the glory of . . . have been used as a form of prayer.

I don't see what you're laughing at.' Kavanagh's face was heavy.
'Just wait till you reach your own Damascus road, Martin.'

'Christ, you're even beginning to sound like one of them.
Loosen up, man. Can I ask you a question?'

'Sure.'

'Why are you doing this?'

'I'm trying to find a way. To live my life as best I can.'

'So's you'll get to heaven.'

'Rewards don't come into it. What's wrong with Pippa
organising bread and cheese lunches in the basement for the Third
World? What's wrong with me being part of a community of
good? Beliefs are useless unless they're strongly held. As you said,
if it matters at all it must matter completely. The fact that Pippa
will not go to bed with me is not a restriction, it's self-imposed,
voluntary. It's Christ's law accepted with love – and if I don't
agree with that, she says, then I am free to leave. Her body will be
her gift to me when the time for marriage comes and not before.
When and where the Lord allows.'

Martin shook his head and stood staring at Kavanagh. He had
never heard him like this before. It was as if he was talking to a
stranger. He felt he had no right to punch him on the shoulder, or
ruffle his hair or say fuck in front of him. Kavanagh went on:

'There's nothing prissy or timid about being a Christian.
Christians are the strongest people on the planet. You have to be
strong to swim against the stream. We all admire the salmon, why
not the Christian?'

'That is straight out of a Sunday school teacher's mouth,' said
Martin 'Who said that to you?'

The cross-struts of Kavanagh's chair squeaked under his weight.
He pulled a face.

'The thought was Pippa's. The words were mine.' Kavanagh
looked defiantly at Martin. 'But this is for me and Pippa to sort
out. Nobody else.'

'I suppose so.'

Kavanagh threw what remained of his tea into the sink.

'I don't like it without milk.' He stood up. He was back to
smiling again. 'So. Will you do a night's business for me? As
planned?'

'Yeah – sure.'

'Any questions?'

'No.'

'The timing is crucial. But you know that.'

'Yes, Master.' Martin joined his hands and gave a little bow from the waist.

'I'll not forget this, Martin. You're a class act.' He put his arm on Martin's shoulder and they walked towards the stairs. 'And I'll see you, some time tomorrow?'

'Look – I mean now that you're back – maybe you could take over in the morning. You sort it out with Pippa tonight, and come in here in the morning and finish the rest. I'll be knackered no matter what.' Kavanagh paused and bit his nail. Martin said, 'I've got to get home and back at some stage. Maybe change the drawers.'

'OK. I suppose that's fair enough. I'll see you in the morning at the crack of dawn.' Kavanagh grinned. The lift was still at their floor. Kavanagh pulled back the gate. Martin stopped him with one hand.

'Did you hear the one about the test?'

'No.'

'The test for whether or not to wash your drawers?'

'No.'

'Throw them at the wall – and if they stick, you need clean ones. If they slide down they'll do you another day.' Kavanagh made a face of disgust.

'That's terrible,' he said.

Martin was laughing aloud at the joke. Kavanagh pulled the gates shut. They waved goodbye. Martin walked on back to the lab and followed the lift's descent in sound. The quiet fall. At the bottom of the shaft the clash of the gates opening and closing. The slamming of the outside door.

In the lab the knife sharpener was still shearing and grinding away. He felt depressed. How could this happen? They had been best mates at school and now Kavanagh was running after somebody who was saved. To the exclusion of all other relationships. He was allowing his brain to be deadened with this Christian crap. Blaise would have known what to say. Blaise would have wiped the floor with Kavanagh in any argument. Pippa was trying to trepan into the lad's brain. Bore a hole in his skull and fill it with a way of life – a way of death, more like. She was trying to twist his arm up his back until the bones cracked and he called a submission. Blaise was right – women were destroyers of men's friendships.

Kavanagh had been like this ever since he first met him. Obsessive. Never second best. Like when he'd taken up the pole vault. The Gym teacher had told him he was probably too big to be any good. It was an event dominated by average to small guys. It was about nimbleness and timing – being able to 'climb the pole'. But Kavanagh loved the event and practised every phase of it after school in the gym until it became second nature. Running at speed with the pole cocked, planting the pole in the box, climbing the pole, his weight making it curve, then the curve straightening and catapulting him higher. At the last second remembering to push the pole away, keeping his feet together and soaring over the bar, his stomach muscles tensed and arched, then the long fall to the cushions in the pit while at the same time looking to make sure the bar had stayed in place and was not going to come clanking down on top of him. By that time the pole itself would have slowly toppled on to the floor. Martin had seen all this because Kavanagh had asked him to help out on many occasions when the gym teacher couldn't be there. If Kavanagh wanted to practise climbing the pole – as opposed to running with and planting the pole – then it saved a lot of time and energy if there was someone to hold the pole anchored in the box. Martin had agreed. All he had to do was hold the pole at an angle, Kavanagh would run at it, jump, catch and climb and clear the bar.

He'd jump off the cushions, talking to himself, shaking his head, and walk back to come pounding down the floor at Martin and the pole again. This went on endlessly until Kavanagh was satisfied he had made some progress. Then they would walk up the road together.

It paid off for Kavanagh because he won the event and set a new school record by clearing a vault of 10 feet 5 inches on sports day. In front of a crowd, half of which were girls. Martin found that amazing – to see groups of girls in their summer clothes sauntering around the track of the Big Field which had been limed with lines for the day. To walk in their wake and smell their perfume. To hear them laugh and see their feet printing the ground where previously only boys had walked. To see a cardboard sign in the corridor painted with black paint which said **LADIES** →. To see guys blushing when they started to talk to the girls. To hear priests ho–ho–ho–ing, talking to boys' mothers and sisters. Clapping and rubbing their hands together. For some reason it caused an ache in him which he could not account for. There was something desperately sad about it.

And of course Martin was there to record the events on film. He got several really classy shots of Kavanagh in the act of pole vaulting but the picture he got of the actual record vault was not good. And whatever way Kavanagh was frozen in time you could see up the leg of his shorts. There was something up there – underpants or dick – it was insufficiently focused and Kavanagh was embarrassed enough to choose an earlier shot – with the bar at a slightly lower height – to use in the school magazine.

Then something had happened that almost took Martin's breath away. Through the crowds walking round the black ash of the track he saw the girl he had seen in the library – the one who had stared into the glass case and who had ended up giving him a wee smile. It gave him such a swoosh of panic when he saw her. She was walking along, oh so casually, talking to Eddie Downie. Martin stared at her, hardly believing they were occupying the same space. He kept her in his vision for most of the afternoon. At one point he ran and got Kavanagh. Talked almost gibberish to him – said he wanted to take a picture of him just standing by himself at the edge of the field. He positioned him and waited, did all the calculations in his head so that there would be no mistake. Eddie Downie and the girl approached and when they were level, but on the other side of the fence from Kavanagh, Martin started clicking. At any one time he knew exactly where she was: watching the long jump, walking between the colonnade of trees, buying an ice cream from a van the school had invited in to do the catering.

Blaise had been conspicuous by his absence at the sports. After it was all over Martin was on his way to the office to return the photographic gear to Cuntyballs when Blaise came strolling past the willow tree in the quad.

'Where have you been?' said Martin.

'Around. I went a walk.'

'Were you up at the Big Field?'

'No. Sports day is just one more way of humiliating the majority of the pupils in the school. All but the winners.' Martin shrugged. He didn't want an argument because his head was still full of the girl with Eddie Downie. 'It's another exam with a particularly low pass rate. I want no part of it.'

'Kavanagh broke the school record for the pole vault.'

'Did you get any good pictures?'

'Some.'

'How do you know?'

'I can see them in my mind's eye. You kinda freeze it.' Blaise looked at him intently. They both turned to walk in the same direction. Blaise smiled at him. Their elbows touched through their blazers.

'You don't want to heed the half the things I say,' said Blaise. 'Sometimes naive is good – for a photographer that's important. To see fresh. Don't lose that.'

When he had the gear handed in Martin couldn't wait to talk to Downie. If she was his girlfriend it would be so sickening.

'Who was she you were talking to, Downie?'

'Why is everybody asking me that?'

'Who was she?'

'My big sister – Patricia.'

And now he had a name for her. He could hardly believe his luck. Patricia Downie. A name with softness. Duck down. A feather falling.

The next day he developed the sports day pictures and the only ones he wanted to see were the ones of Eddie Downie's sister. He did an enlarged print of the picture of Kavanagh standing by the edge of the field, his arms folded. If anybody asked, it was a picture of his mate. But behind his mate was Patricia Downie, her lovely face turned to glimpse the athlete getting his photograph taken. Martin kept the picture among the books on the mantelpiece in his bedroom where he could look at it whenever he felt like it.

He had seen her only once again. In town on a Saturday afternoon, coming out of Robinson & Cleaver's and looking up distastefully at the rain. He was on the top deck of a bus and his first instinct was to knock the window furiously to draw her attention but then he realised how utterly fruitless such a gesture would be. An instant later she put up a white umbrella and then he could only see her feet. She walked round the corner into Donegall Place. She was wearing dark boots. He noticed that her feet were very big.

As he worked in silence he wondered if the Australian woman would turn up.

Just before nine o'clock he heard what sounded like music. Faint at first. Like a radio somewhere. It sounded like 'Blue Moon'. The jazz starting. It wasn't a tune, they were just warming up. Two floors away. Saxophone, piano, drums.

On the hour he killed another rat, then tidied up the bench. He washed his hands thoroughly – who wanted to go on a first date, however tentative, smelling of freshly eviscerated rat? He took off his white coat. He was wearing jeans and a denim shirt. He should shave. Just in case. He turned on the geyser and the gas plumped loudly and blue flames were visible. When he'd told his mother he had to work overnight she'd produced a drawstring bag for his 'kit', as she called it. Into it she put a toothbrush, shaving gear – although he really only shaved once every two or three days – and at the bottom a teaspoon. She recommended its use to scrape the tongue first thing in the morning.

He filled a beaker with hot water. To see himself he fetched the small mirror from the Ladies. When he finished, the beaker was full of grey blue soapiness with hairs like grains of sand rotating in it. A quick scrub of the teeth, a tongue strigil and he was ready for action. He put the mirror back where he found it.

The corridors were darkening and seemed very strange with this distant jazz sound in them. Usually after lectures they were full of students' talk and the banging of metal locker doors. He stopped at the top of the stairs and listened. The saxophone had a smooth Paul Desmond feel to it as it drifted up the stairwell. There was light down below and voices, as well.

Outside the door of the basement lecture theatre someone had set up a table and was taking money. He was talking to a bearded guy in leathers with a motorcycle helmet in his hand. The guy asked how much it was and made a face when he heard.

'Fuck, who's playing? Miles Davis?' The doorman sort of laughed and waved the biker into the hall. Then looked up at Martin. The only money Martin had was the change from his Kit-Kat.

'I work in here,' said Martin.

'Sorry?'

'I'm a technician in this building.'

'So?'

'I thought maybe I'd get a concession.' The doorman looked at him.

'We get the venue free,' he said. 'The money is for the band.'

'I've gotta hang around all night to close this place up,' said Martin. The guy held up a bunch of keys.

'We always do it ourselves.' Why was this fucker so stroppy?

'I just want to look in — see if somebody's there.'

The doorman seemed very reluctant to let him have a look around but eventually he waved his eyebrows in the direction of the lecture theatre.

'I suppose we need whatever audience we can get on a night like this.'

Martin nodded a sort of thanks and stepped inside. It smelled of joss sticks — probably lit to disguise the formalin and chalk dust smells. Or marijuana — jazz bands had that reputation. Martin knew the place in daylight, knew that the space was circular and raked only slightly. It was filled with curved benches around a raised dais. The curved walls were lined with glass cupboards. The place was dark except for a couple of spotlights beaming down on to the band, picking out the shining bits of the drum kit, reflecting the metallic yellow of the saxophone, whitening the tops of the musicians' heads. It took some time for his eyes to adjust to the low level of light. The saxophonist wore a cloth cap back to front. The pianist had sunglasses on and when he put his head back the reflected spotlight flashed from the lenses. It was so dark it was difficult to make out if there was an audience, never mind who was in it. The music finished and there was a spatter of applause and a few whoops.

The lights came up. The place became quiet enough to hear the biker unzipping his leathers. There was no sign of the Australian girl. The pianist leaned down to his mike and said, 'Thank you —

279

you're all very kind.' His voice sounded as if it was in a microphone cave. You could hear his breathing. 'All of you. All seven of you who braved riot and mayhem to get here.' He lit a cigarette and the smoke drifted up among the lights. He had an accent which was a mixture of Derry and New York. 'Until the crowd arrives – listen to this.' He began playing 'Blue Monk', with his head down, splashing the opening chords. People in the audience recognised it and clapped a bit, cheered a bit. Martin edged his hip on to a bench and listened. The music involved him. With jazz, he found he always had to let himself go with it – if he resisted, it didn't sound good. In some ways it was show-off listening – foot tapping or knee jigging, nod the old head, sway the body a bit and then he found he was really enjoying it. It was like religion: any scepticism or holding it at arm's length and it lost its power.

This was the lecture theatre where Pippa organised her bread and cheese lunches. People paid their money and could eat as much as they wanted. At lunch time the blinds were thrown up and midday light streamed in from the high windows. On the benches were industrial-sized tubs of margarine and piled columns of white pan bread, beside matching square slices of cheese – two types, orange and yellow. There was a basket of crispy French batons and smaller more select cheeses for the gourmets who strayed in. Soft drinks were sold by Pippa and her fellow workers, the profits all going to Christian Aid. Martin had suggested a bread and cheese and wine party would go with more of a swing but he was ignored. When he could, Kavanagh attended and sat talking to Martin, always staring over his shoulder at Pippa going about her chores – sympathising, exuding niceness, convinced she was saving lives.

Martin was surprised at how good the band was. There was something about live performance: the guys were making the music right here in front of him. They were plucking it out of thin air and shaping it and letting themselves go with it. It wasn't like listening to records. Martin saw the doorman come in and stand looking around. Even though it was pitch dark Martin bent and tied his shoelace. He didn't pretend to do it – he actually did it. Untied it, then tied it with a double bow. When he next looked up the doorman was away.

More people were coming in through the slice of light at the doorway. The place was filling up. 'Blue Monk' came to a long-drawn-out end. The close of the piece was signalled. Everybody knew it was finishing and they began clapping and whooping and drumming on the benches, mixing their applause with the music.

'Hi,' a voice said behind him. He turned. It was the Australian girl.

'It's yourself.'

'What?'

'It's yourself.'

'Who else would I be?'

'No – it's just a saying – a greeting we have here.'

'Gidday then.'

She slipped out of her shoulder strap and set her rucksack on the floor.

'Did you meet up with your boyfriend?'

'Not yet. It'll be bloody hard to find him in here.' She shaded her eyes from the glare of the spotlights and moved nearer the front to look at the faces in the audience. When she didn't see anyone she recognised she came back to Martin.

'No luck?'

'No.'

He liked that – the way she came back to him. She could have sat down on her own near the front, but she didn't. She slid on to a bench beside him.

'What is this place?'

'They use it for lots of stuff,' said Martin. 'Lectures, jazz – they have bread and cheese lunches in here for the starving of Africa.'

'It's a long way for them to come,' she said. He laughed for her. 'Did you get that thing killed?'

'Yeah,' he nodded. 'Stone dead.'

'I'm not sure I like that.'

The piano player leaned over to one of the microphones.

'You're all welcome,' he said. 'My name is Peetie Red Wallace. And this is the band.' He introduced them one by one as they played into the next number, 'Baby please don't go.' The audience applauded each one in turn. The area below the spotlights now looked like cones of blue smoke.

'You work in here?' said the Australian girl.

'Not exactly *in here* but — yeah.'

'The Anatomy Department?'

'Yeah, upstairs.'

'Strewth.'

Between numbers the house lights came up so that people could find their way to a seat. More people were coming in the door. Everybody was talking. The girl looked up, turning around.

'What's in all these cupboards?'

'Things,' he shrugged. 'Stuff.'

'Thanks for being so open and honest with me.'

'They've been painted with black paint on the insides of the glass, to stop people seeing in. They're pretty gruesome — some of them. You don't want to see the half of them.'

'What kind of *things* — what kind of *stuff*?'

Martin paused and looked at her.

'Things that go wrong — in bottles. Monster babies — hydrocephalics — Siamese twins joined at the chest.'

'And they're all in there listening to the music?'

'I think the worst thing is the skin of a baby's head, taken off the skull and flattened out — like Cinemascope. It's bloody awful looking.' The girl pulled a face. She leaned forward towards the cupboard door. Towards him. She smelled of talc. Or something like it.

'Some of the paint is peeling. Can you see in?'

'Only if you look hard enough. You'll see nothing with the lights out.' She cupped her hand round her eyes and put her face close to the glass. A number started and the house lights went down. They both sat there together. The drummer was playing wire brushes. Martin leaned over.

'It sounds like spilling sugar,' he said into her ear. A wisp of her springy hair touched his mouth. She nodded. The tenor sax man unhooked his instrument from around his neck and set it on a stand. He produced two pieces of a silver flute and slotted them together. As he played the light moved to and fro on it, up and down, again and again as its angle changed. The girl beside Martin began to fidget. After the number she said, 'What am I gonna to do? This guy hasn't showed and it's getting late.'

'Your boyfriend?'

'He's not my boyfriend. He was a drongo from Melbourne

282

who was going to get me a place to kip free of charge. If he doesn't show I'll have to find a youth hostel or a B&B. And they're so bloody expensive.' She looked at her watch by holding her wrist up so that she could see by the light from the stage. 'Bloody hell.'

'What?'

'Is there a telephone? I told the doorman I'd no money and I was just meeting somebody. He said join the club, and like an asshole I said how much is it. He said almost *everybody* in there says he's looking for somebody. I told him I hated this kind of crappy music and he let me in.'

'I thought you liked jazz?'

'Naow — I never said any such thing.'

'Do you want to phone from upstairs?'

'Yeah.'

Martin led the way out. She picked up her rucksack and followed.

As they climbed the stairs he looked at her moving in front of him, her head keeping her balance. In the main corridor he heard their own footsteps against a faint background of jazz. It was gloomy except for the light coming from the doorway of his lab into the corridor.

'This is such a spooky place,' she said. 'Is this where you do the killing?'

'Yeah.'

'Oh my Gawd — and this is an . . . an . . . anam an Anatomy Department?' She had stopped walking and was looking all around her.

'Yeah.'

She put out her hand and touched his elbow, stopping him in the middle of the corridor. Her voice reduced to a whisper.

'Where's the zombies?'

'What?'

'The dead bodies?'

'In there.' He nodded just to her left at the Dissecting Room.

'Jesus, how many?'

'Fifteen, maybe.'

She gave a low whistle.

'Is it locked?'

'Yeah – but I can get a key.'

'Ohhh,' she shuddered. 'Can I see in?'

'Naw – it's not just for nosying.'

'It's not that I'm nosy – but I'd really like to see. I've never seen a dead person.'

'Never?'

She shook her head.

'No dead relatives?'

'Not that I ever saw. I was a baby when all my grandparents passed away. I just love the way you talk.'

'Same back.'

'I could listen to your accent all night. You could make the telephone directory sound good.' Her smile disappeared and she wrinkled her nose. 'Oh my Gawd it stinks here . . . What's that smell?'

'Formaldehyde.'

'It's honkin. You'd think somebody was cutting bloody onions.'

'Aye, it goes for your eyes a bit. It's coming from in there.' He nodded to the Dissecting Room, then urged her on towards the light from the lab. Once inside, he pointed to the phone. She slid out of her rucksack and stood by his office chair.

'Feel free,' he said, then backed towards the door. 'Nine for an outside line.'

'Hey – where you going? I don't want to be here on my own-ey-o.'

'I just thought you wanted to . . . be on the phone. A bit of privacy.'

'Don't you dare leave me on my own.' She took out a notebook from a side pocket of the rucksack and opened it on the desk. 'In a place full of zombies.'

On the other side of the lab Martin looked at his watch, lifted another rat by the tail and popped it into the ether chamber. She was saying the number out loud to herself. The rat was dead even before she had finished dialling. He looked over his shoulder at her. She wrinkled her face in distaste.

'What's that hospital smell?' she said.

'Ether.'

284

'What's that noise?'

Martin shrugged. For a moment he couldn't think.

'The knife sharpener.'

'It makes my skin crawl.' He leaned over and switched it off. He'd caught it in mid-turnover and the blade was held aloft with a little black powder and oil dripping from it.

She stood with the phone to her ear looking around at all the equipment, at the bottles and jars labelled with Dymotape. The dialling tone purred for ages. He stood with his back to her, shielding from her what he was doing. He removed the rat's leg and put it in the jar of fixative. He labelled it with the time. She combed her hair through her fingers, the wrong way over the crown of her head. She looked at him and smiled. He smiled back at her. Finally someone answered the phone. She asked for the guy she'd met earlier. It was a wrong number. Martin rolled the bloodied rat carcass in several sheets of newspaper and put it in the waste bin. A picture of Nixon stared up at him. She checked that the number was the number she had dialled. It was. She replaced the phone.

'Bastard,' she said. 'I *knew* he was taking the piss with that number.'

'Approximate phone numbers are no good,' he said. She bit on her lower lip. 'So?'

'So what?' She thrust her notebook into the rucksack and sat down. She revolved in the chair, staring ahead. 'What's the name for this?' she pointed.

'A binocular microscope.'

'I think that's really crap – giving me a wrong number.'

'Are you sure you wrote it down properly?'

'Sure I'm sure.' She continued to swing in the chair. 'Do you look into it?'

'Yeah.'

'Can I?'

'Yeah sure.' He leaned over and switched the microscope on. He got a glass slide.

'Give me one of your hairs.' She pulled a blonde wisp down over her face, going almost cross-eyed looking at it.

'Wait,' he said and very carefully he selected a single strand and plucked it out by the root.

'Aiow – that hurt.' She wrinkled her nose. 'I didn't trust him. Don't ever trust anybody from Melbourne.' He wet his finger and stuck the hair to the moist print he made on the glass. He adjusted the focus and invited her to look. Parting her hair with her hands on either side, she faced up to the microscope.

'You don't need to close your eye – it's not a telescope.' She was at the wrong height so she stood. She let her hair go and leaned her two hands on the bench on either side of the microscope and stared into it.

'It's like a bloody iron bar,' she said. She didn't touch any of the controls. There was a tiny light in each of her eyes coming up through the eyepieces. Then she straightened up and raised her eyebrows. 'Some machine. Have you got a Yellow Pages?'

'There's one in the tea room.' He made as if to go and fetch it.

'Don't you leave me here.' She was joking but not joking. 'Speaking of which – is there a dunny? I'm dying.'

'A toilet?' She nodded. 'Yeah.' He walked towards the door and she followed him. He began to point into the darkness of the small staircase 'There's lights.'

'Oh no ya don't. You gotta come with me and show me.'

'OK, OK.' He was laughing – in a kind of embarrassed way. He led her up the flight of steps and put his head in through the door. He felt around for the switch and flicked it on. The fluorescent tubes blinked on, and off, and on.

'There you go,' he said.

'Leave that door open – and *don't you move.*' Martin sat down on the threshold and she went into one of the cubicles. Still the cisterns sang and dribbled. He looked beneath the cubicle door at her boots set square on each side of the white delf pedestal, her jeans accordioned at her ankles. He heard her piss then tug at the toilet roll. Then the flush was roaring and she was out slamming the door behind her.

'Double quick time,' she said. Martin turned off the lights and they went downstairs. In the lab she sat down on the office chair again.

'So what are you going to do?' said Martin.

'I dunno. It's a real bummer. I'm going back tomorrow. What time is it?'

'Almost ten.' She sat there, screwing up her face, thinking.

Martin said, 'I mean – don't take it the wrong way, or anything like that – but you can stay here – if you like.'

'In this place?' Her voice almost screeched in disbelief. 'By myself? In the house of the dead?'

'I'm going to be here,' he said. 'All night. I've things to do. It's the first time in my life I've been on night shift. We can take turns on the camp bed.' She pursed her mouth. 'I'm only joking – kidding on.'

'This is such a truly weird place. The Abos would be outa here like . . .'

'Abos?'

'The Aborigines. Black boys. They're very superstitious. A lot of spooky stuff to do with the dead.'

'I think you're making too much of this. The dead people thing. You just get used to it.'

'To being dead?'

'No – to being around dead people.' She put her feet up on the bench and swung the chair back and forth. She reached into her pocket and produced a tiny round jar.

'What's that?'

'Vaseline. Stops my lips being like dry paper.' She dipped her middle finger into the jar and applied the moistness to her mouth. Her finger moving over her lips pulled them sideways. Then she wiped the shining finger on a tissue and pursed her lips in and out to distribute the softness more evenly.

'Do you want a coffee?' Martin asked.

'Yeah.'

'The coffee stuff is in the tea room.'

'That's very Irish,' she laughed loudly. 'The *coffee* is in the *tea* room.'

Before he left the lab he switched on the knife sharpener again. To have it sharpening when they were elsewhere. On the way along the corridor he asked her, 'If you don't like jazz what kind of music do you like?'

'All kinds – I don't know. I suppose – everything.'

'For instance?'

'The Monkees, Sonny and Cher. Elvis, I don't know.'

In the tea room he filled the kettle and lit the Bunsen. She unslung

287

her rucksack and sat down. The chair creaked as it had done under Kavanagh. She gave an involuntary shiver.

'Are you cold?'

'I am not warm,' she said.

'I suppose the heating has gone off. That never occurred to me.'

She began to rub her bare arm vigorously.

'Look. Look at the goose-bumps.' She held her arm up for him to see. Her nipples were obvious beneath her T-shirt.

'Maybe it's just me. Heat's something we take for granted back home.' As they waited for the kettle to come to the boil he felt the beginnings of an erection, brought on by seeing her nipples standing out like that.

'We call it goose flesh here. You know what it is?'

'It's when you get cold.'

'Yeah, but also when you get hot − it's a sign of change of temperature.'

'I never get it in the heat.'

'When you get into a hot bath, do you not go all goose-bumps?'

'Yeah,' her eyes lit up. 'You're right. Hey, you're a genius. How do you know this stuff?'

He crossed his legs, tried to smother the hard-on.

'There's a muscle in the skin beneath a hair follicle − the arrector pili muscle. It contracts with cold or fear and the hair stands up.'

'Ooooh . . . a hair raising experience.'

'Sometimes it's not quick enough to know hot from cold.' He began to imitate a machine voice. 'Beep-beep temperature-change temperature-change.' Then back to his own voice again. 'So the hairs stand up when you get into hot water.'

'Clever boy.'

They sat facing each other. Each had an elbow on the table. She was closely examining the surface of her skin. The talk of erectile tissue was making Martin worse. *We could try hitting it with a cold spoon.* There was a blue and steel stapler sitting on the table beside the kettle. He smiled.

'What?' she said.

'Nothing.' He could bang a few staples into it along its length, along its *changing* length and that would soon shorten it. Dip it in Holy Water. Like the paschal candle on Easter night. Three times. Anoint it with ice cubes made from Holy Water.

'What's so funny?'

'Nothing,' he said. 'It's just that I'm not often asked to ride shotgun while a girl takes a leak.'

She smiled. There was a delicate crease at each side of her mouth like her smile was inside brackets.

'I wasn't going to be left on my own in this place.' There were several freshly laundered white coats sitting on a metal filing cabinet.

'Here,' said Martin. 'Why don't you put on one of these? It'll keep you warm.' He began to unfold the coat. It crackled with starch. He broke the sleeves open and stood and held the coat in front of him, hiding his condition behind it.

'Here.' He held it open for her to get into. She inserted her arms in the sleeves and pulled the crisp coat around her, still shivering.

'I'm a doctor now,' she said. She smiled nicely at him and sat down again. He was conscious of the silence and a bit embarrassed by it.

'So what's your name?' he asked.

'Dr Atkins.'

'First name, please?'

'Cindy.'

'Martin Brennan.' He leaned forward and shook hands with her.

'You're very formal, Martin – very polite.'

'That's the way I was brought up. Shake hands, ride shotgun whenever required and in whatever circumstances.'

'Back home that wouldn't raise an eyebrow.'

'Even two escaped eyebrows?'

'Yes – remember – the Grandmothers . . . What was the name?'

'Granny Greybers.'

'I really liked them, Martin. They were cute.'

'The Fleeing Eyebrow Show.'

'They were so businesslike. "We need to get somewhere very important – very soon."' She made bustling motions with her arms but was restricted by the starch in the sleeves. Martin spooned coffee into two mugs and filled them with boiling water.

'I'm sorry. No milk.' He offered her Coffee-Mate but she turned up her nose. She took hers black with two sugars. She gave a little *shiver* and wrapped her hands around the hot mug.

'It would be good if you had something a bit stronger.'

'Central heating,' said Martin.

'My mother's people were Irish, way back – McGimpseys.'

'What do you drink?'

'Wine. Australia makes a lotta good wine now. We used to have the image of beer-swilling rugby players. But that's all changing . . .'

'Now they're wine-swilling rugby players.'

'Do you play?'

'No – I'm a Catholic.' His hard had subsided. He felt relieved.

'What the hell has that got to do with it?'

'Catholics here play soccer or Gaelic football.'

'I'm Protestant.' She jutted her chin out at him and smiled in mock aggression.

'You travel light,' he said, 'for a Protestant.'

'That's my lesser backpack. My other one's in Scotland.'

'What's it doing there?'

'It's where I work. I'm in a hotel in Ballachulish, up the west coast.'

'What's that like?'

'It's a real bummer.'

'So what are you doing over here?'

'I had a couple of days off. I wanted to see Northern Ireland for myself. Everybody said "Don't go. You're mad." That always makes me want to do the thing. My dad always said don't do this and don't do that – so I knew what to try. I've never been to a war zone before.'

'What do you think?'

'Gimme a chance . . .'

'Are you scared?'

'In here – yes.'

'You've more reason to be scared out there. This country's full of mad bastards.' He sighed and looked at her. 'But the Troubles aren't all doom and gloom. It's had its lighter moments.'

'Like what, for instance?'

'That's called sarcasm.'

She blew on the surface of her coffee and took a wary sip.

'Where did you go?'

'All over.'

'And what did you think?'

'Irish guys are the nicest guys I've ever met.'

'Really?'

'It's called sarcasm.'

'OK, fair enough. Sounds like a bad experience. Where?'

'Somewhere called Limavady.'

'That figures.' He smiled at her. 'What kind of things did your dad tell you not to do?'

'That would be telling.' She bit her bottom lip and smiled back at him. 'My dad's a minister. Of religion.' Martin shrugged. 'He keeps bees. Do you know anything about bees?'

'They sting. I hate them.'

'That's a bit hard.'

'I got stung once and that was enough. No good reason for them to exist.'

'Honey.' He pretended to half turn and answer her.

'Yeah? Are you addressing me?'

She laughed at his joke. 'That is *so* brilliant – like something out of "Laughter – the Best Medicine" or "Life's like that". I might even write that in to *Reader's Digest* – they pay about five hundred smackers if they publish it.'

'For a joke?'

'No – for real.'

'Is that coffee OK?' She nodded.

'In a hive there's three kinds of bee – one queen, a coupla hundred drones and fifty thousand workers. The drones are males. They don't sting. Their big job is to mate with the queen . . .'

'Nice work if you . . .'

'Do you know about this?' Martin shook his head. 'Well, wait till y'hear. When she's ready the queen flies off on her nuptial flight and these poor bastards have to chase her. The fastest and strongest catch her up and have to do the job in mid-air . . .'

'Oh my God . . .'

'When they've finished the business and they try to pull out, their thingies are ripped off and they die and fall to earth.'

'Is that true?'

'Yeah.'

'What a crap ending,' said Martin. He pulled a face. So the dying fall did happen. The fantasy they'd had at school was possible – even though it only happened to a bee. You'd just got your hole for the first time when suddenly there was this enormous pain and your whole fucking apparatus is flying on without you. It's going horizontal and you're going down – with a hole torn beneath your belly. A hole that used to be your cock. And the wind is howling up past you, so strongly it's keeping the blood in. And you think 'Was that it? Was that what I droned all my life for?' The reward for being the biggest and best and fastest and sexiest was that he only got his hole once. But once was better than never.

'What's so funny?' she said.

'Nothing.'

'Do you have a girlfriend?'

'Naw.' The way he said it made it sound like there was no possibility.

'A good-looking boy like you?'

'Is that more sarcasm?'

'No, you are – you give off something. I dunno what.' He looked puzzled – sniffed the air as if she was making fun of him.

'B.O.?'

'No. Tell me this. What's an Orangeman?'

'The Lost Tribe . . .' Martin laughed. 'He's a sub-species of Protestant. They have this club – the Orange Order – and their only purpose in life is to pray to the Lord and march the Queen's Highway. To join you have to pass an unintelligence test.' He paused to see if she was taking it in. 'Or would you have to fail it?'

'How the hell would I know?'

'He has a bowler hat and an orange sash around his neck. There's Orangemen born who can march before they can walk. And there must be an element of causing annoyance in it. They wouldn't thank you for letting them march around a public park – it has to be on the Queen's Highway as it passes through Catholic areas. Up you, they're saying, we can do whatever we like. Of course, just to complicate the issue he could be a Blackman and wear a black sash and that'd make him from the Royal Black Preceptory or whatever it's called. And he could be both at once. Orange and black.'

'Like a bee,' she said and laughed.

'True enough. I've often heard it said, "Ya Orange B." Oh as if it wasn't complicated enough there's another crowd called the Apprentice Boys.' He picked up the Yellow Pages. 'Is this what you were looking for?'

'Thanks.'

He flicked it open and said, 'Eagle Tool and Equipment. Hire and Buy with Confidence. Saintfield Road. Hire – sales – service – repairs. Water pumps – Kango hammers – Rammers – contraction plates – dehumidifiers – strippers – rotovators . . . Next. ELITE Plant Hire. Daily Rates available. Chainsaws. Welders. Grinders. Transformers . . .'

'What do you think you're doing?'

'Just giving you pleasure.'

Still she shook her head in confusion.

'My accent.' Then she remembered what she'd said about his voice and laughed.

'Oh yeah. I thought you'd gone bananas. You make it sound like the dog's bollicks.'

On their way back to the lab she stopped and said, 'What's in there?'

'The library. But there's no books in it.'

'What's in it then?'

'Stuff. Specimens.'

'Can I see?'

'There's nothing *to* see.'

'Is it locked?'

'No.' She ran up the couple of steps and tried the handle of the door. It screeched open. Martin said, 'If you fancy seeing some old bones this is the place for you.' He followed her up the steps and found the light switch. A whole battery of fluorescent lights raggedly blinked on. She looked all around at the dark library furniture – at the glass cupboards which lined the walls.

'Spooky place number two. No, number three. Spooky place

293

number three,' she said. She wandered into the big room touching table tops on either side of her with her fingertips. He followed her in.

'Look at this,' he said. He took down a jar with a foetus in it. It had been treated so that all its tissues were clear, except the bones which had been stained scarlet with alizarin.

'What is it?'

Martin switched on one of several X-ray viewing boxes on the wall and held the jar up to the opalescent light.

'Jee-sus,' she said. 'Isn't that cute.' She kept staring at it and touching the glass with her fingers. It was as if she was trying to touch the embryo but the glass was getting in the way. 'Some mother's son.' She moved on, looking about her, touching.

'What's this?' She bent over and stared at a specimen in a flat jar.

'A lung.' She made a face. 'A smoker's lung. See all that black stuff.'

'Do you smoke?'

'I did at school. But then they told me what it did to you – in here.'

'There's so much bloody starch in this coat I can't even get my hands into the pockets.' Martin leaned towards her and tore the pockets open with a dry ripping sound.

'There you go.'

'Thanks, Martin.' She put both hands in both her pockets and leaned forward from the waist to look at the display around *The Anatomy Lesson of Dr Tulp*. Now when her hair fell in her eyes she blew it away, creating an up-draught by a twist of her bottom lip. She became interested in the modern print. She wrinkled her nose in distaste.

'Not very good at all,' she said. 'That's the kind of mark I'd have got at kindy.'

'Kindy?'

'Primary school. I was useless at art. Six outa twenty mighta been too good for me.'

'I don't understand.'

She pointed to the bottom of the print. On it was scrawled in pencil – 6/20.

He laughed and explained that this was a numbered print run

and not a mark given by a teacher. She made an embarrassed face by turning her mouth down at the corners and rolling her eyes at the same time. Then she laughed out loud with him at her mistake.

'I thought it was a mark.'

'That's great,' he said. 'Imagine the first print of a run of 100 and everybody saying *it's no good but you wanna see 99/100. It's brilliant.*' When she stopped laughing she put her hand out and touched the model head.

'I like the cut of *his* jib?' They sidled round the shelves laughing. Suddenly she stopped.

'Oooooooohh,' she said. It was like a noise made to frighten a child. She was staring into the corner at a complete skeleton which hung from a hook through the top of its skull.

'What?' said Martin. She pointed. For a moment Martin couldn't work out what was going on. He was so used to looking at skeletons he'd forgotten that they were supposed to be scary. She moved closer and put her hand on his upper arm and held on and peeked around him.

'You're only taking the piss,' Martin said.

'No, I'm not. I don't like seeing things like that.'

He laughed and put his arm around her starchy shoulder. He gave her a squeeze. She moved away from him towards the door.

'The beginning and the end,' she said.

'What?'

'De baby bones and de dead bones.'

When they reached the junction of the corridors the sound of the jazz became more obvious. It was a version of the 'St Louis Blues.' Cindy began to wiggle and walk funny inside the coat. She strutted and sassed along the central runner of the lino in the half-light. Then turned to face him and launched into a kind of twist or jive step. The white coat was open and she was moving inside it, like a clapper inside a bell.

'Come on. This'll warm us up,' she said raising her arms above her head. Just for a laugh he started to dance opposite her, mimicking her movements.

'OK. You're going well.'

But the music was so distant they could hear their own movements, the dry movement of their own clothes, the squeaking and shuffling of their feet. She reached out and they touched hands and she did a slow spin, used him as a lever to turn to the distant rhythm. Martin strayed off the lino and drummed the locker doors with his hands.

'Yeah, go for it,' she shouted. It was a bit embarrassing the way she said it – like a Girl Guide or a *Blue Peter* presenter snapping her fingers. Trying hard but not succeeding. The music stopped.

'There you go,' said Martin. 'Just my luck.'

'Wait,' she said. 'There's gotta be more.'

They moved down the corridor nearer to the stair head, listening to where the music had risen from. They were just outside the Dissecting Room when it began again. A slow blues sound very different to the number they had just danced to.

'That's "St James Infirmary",' he said. 'Just right for where we are.' He half sang, half spoke the words in an American drawl 'Saw ma baby there – laid out on a long white table, so white, so cold, so bare.'

'Oh don't. Why can't I see in?' she nodded to the Dissecting Room.

'It's not a zoo,' Martin said. 'It's sort of disrespect. We had a Prof here who used to raise his hat every time he went past.' She saw that the doors had an old-fashioned turnkey lock and knelt down to try and to peep through the keyhole.

'Why did he do that?'

'Honouring the dead.'

'Bunches of flowers – yeah. Lifting your hat? No thanks. I can't see a bloody thing.'

'Get up.' She got up off her knee and moved closed to him.

'Come on, Martin – just a look. Just once. I promise.'

'It's nearly dark. If I turn on the light at this time Security will be over like a shot.'

'A torch?'

'That would bring them over even quicker – the thought of catching a burglar.'

He began to move back towards the lab.

'Come on, pussycat,' she said. She held her arms out to him as if she was joking. He took her hand in his, slipped his other hand around her waist inside the coat. She felt firm and hard even beneath the material of her T-shirt. They were stepping slowly to the slow music.

'My dad taught me how to stroke bees,' she said: 'stroke their fur so's they go into a trance. Sends them into a kinda ecstasy.'

'What?'

'It's a way of hypnotising them. They love it – like putting a hen's beak to a white line.'

'What are you talking about?'

'Thingies.'

'If you talk I can't hear the music. Then I lose the beat.'

'To hell with the beat.' She put both her hands on his shoulders, then around his neck. He felt her join her hands at the nape hair of his neck – the way he had seen old women join their hands in prayer with fingers interlocked. They danced as if she was instructing him in the steps, his body still some distance from hers. He put his hands on her arms. He was aware of the way the hair on her forearms tingled. Electric – almost like static just above her skin. She was dee-dah-ing the words of the music, rocking her head this way and that. She shortened her arms and pulled his head close. The tops of their heads touched. He kicked against her shoe.

'Sorry.'

'No worries.' She began to laugh. 'Never look down at your feet when you're dancing.'

'I'm not, I'm looking at yours.'

He wondered if he should attempt to kiss her. Was it too early? Would she just burst out laughing? Or worse? A slap in the face, which happened in the movies. In Belfast it was a dig in the bake. Nora Rice was a local, good-looking psychopath who was supposed to deal out this kind of retaliation. Plenty of guys had screwed her and boasted openly of it. But if the wrong guy tried he got a thump in the mouth, a dig in the bake. So the rumour had it. That was the price. That was the prize. That would be what was in store for him if his face did not fit. But this Australian girl had said earlier he was a good looking boy. And she wasn't exactly backing away from him at this very moment. There was a sweet and beautiful aroma coming off her. He would compromise. Lay his head on her shoulder and see how she reacted.

'Are you tired?' she said. Grinning, he raised his head up and

297

his face was on a level with hers. He kissed her, his lips touching hers so lightly that he could still pull back, claiming it was a mistake. I'm sorry – I overstepped the mark. I thought that perhaps, that you . . . But her mouth moved against his, accepting what was happening. Not only did she lean into his kiss but she moved her own lips on his with a pleasant writhing sensation. Jesus, this is getting very interesting. She made a noise as if to say something but it was just a voice in her throat which never made it to a word. The next thing he knew was that her tongue was flickering into his mouth. Like a little lightning. In and out. Almost before he knew what it was. And again – quick like a viper. He nudged into her mouth with *his* tongue. She tasted like soft copper, in there. Rough, like suede. Then before he knew what was happening she had turned her face to the side and was dancing with her head up smiling at him. She said, 'Would you look at us? Dancing in a dead house.'

'Do you want to go somewhere else?'

'What age are you, Martin?'

'Why do you want to know?'

She shrugged.

'Maybe you look younger than you are?' Before he could say anything she added, 'That's meant as a compliment.'

The music stopped. Cindy began to walk towards the light of the lab. Martin followed her. Inside she hoisted herself up on to the bench.

'Is this OK?'

'Yeah.'

'I'll not get a disease in my backside or anything.'

'No.'

She swung her legs to and fro. Martin walked to her side of the island bench and switched on a blow heater beside his desk to MAX. The stream of air was warm around his ankles almost immediately. It also made a lot of noise, which masked the sound of the knife sharpener. He walked back to where the cage of rats was and dispatched another one.

'What are you doing?' she asked.

'Working.' When he had finished he washed his hands and dried them on the roller towel. He came round to her side of the lab. 'So what's your plan?'

'I dunno – it's a bit late to go out looking for a place now. Can I crash here?'

'Sure.'

'Doss on the old sleeping bag.'

'Good.'

'This coat makes me feel like one of your nuns or something.' She slipped down from the bench and took off the white coat, then opened her rucksack. She pulled out a white wool sweater and slipped it on. She handed the coat back to him and he hung it on the hook on the back of the lab door.

'Oh wait, I got something in my backpack. You must see this.' She reached into the rucksack and pulled out some sort of a doll. 'Isn't he just fabulous? My very own little leppercorn – one of the Little People. He was just *so* cute I just couldn't pass him. His green hat and his little stick. Look at that face. The woman in the shop called him a little rascal. She also had a name for that stick.'

'A shillelagh.'

'And another fabulous thing is, you get forms to fill in to say that you will love him for the rest of his natural. Look.' She produced the forms. 'A kind of contract.' Martin looked at them for a while then gave them back to her.

'I married a leprechaun,' he said.

'Leppercorn? How do you say it?'

'Lep-ra-hon.'

'Lep-ra-haun?'

'Correct.' Martin laughed, then looked at his watch. 'Do you want to see the animal house?'

'I'm easy. What's in it?'

'Guess.'

'Animals.'

'Spot on. I've gotta get another batch downstairs. Or maybe you wanna stay here?'

'It pongs a bit,' Cindy said. The animal house was full of twittering and scuffling noises. From floor to ceiling was shelved with zinc metal cages, each with its plastic water bottle. He showed her around. She crept from one small room to another looking down into the cages, at the same time holding her hair to each side of her head. She took one of the water bottles in her hand and tried to feed a rat some water. One sniffed and began licking.

'Hey look – he's taking it.' Martin told her that that was one of the jobs he hated. Filling those water bottles. The cold tap on full – holding each bottle underneath until it overflowed. Then replacing the dropper. His hands would throb with the cold. The only feeling he had was pure pain. It reminded him of the cold pain when he gave out the Holy Water in the church at Easter. When the hundreds of cages had had their water changed he would dry his hands and try and warm them at the fire.

'They are *so* cute with their little pink eyes and their whiskers. Are they all rats?'

'Some mice.'

Martin checked the label and selected the cage he wanted.

'Hey Martin! C'mere. Would you take a dekko at this.' In the corner of a cage a rat had had its litter. They looked awful – five or six pink things. They weren't shiny or slippery, but dry and pink, covered with a powdery bloom – like on raspberries. Their heads and faces were blunt, no sign of ears, their eyes still closed. Blind – hairless – yet, all the time, moving.

'They're like five little baby fingers,' she said in a baby voice.

'That's your mothering instinct coming out.'

Martin put coal on the fire and roared it up a bit. And they sat on a couple of stools getting warm, holding out their hands. She said it was like a place you would tell scary stories, and then covered her ears when Martin started to tell her one. He told her about the room next door where bodies were prepared by the mortician – veins and arteries were differentiated by having blue or red dye injected into them. He told her about the animal house attendant, mean Frank, who at one time kept quail for some experiments. He collected their eggs every day and fried them – about fifteen of them, tiny yellow and white fried eggs the size of ten pence pieces. And then he shovelled them between two slices of bread. Fried quails' egg sandwiches. Her favourite sandwich had been condensed milk – white jam, she called it – on bread. The coals burned away quickly and collapsed in grey ash. The back of the chimney was sooty and dotted lines of yellow lights threaded their way up and down.

'They call those soldiers marching,' he said.

'Hey, my face is getting red,' she said, feeling it. Martin kept his eye on the time.

As they climbed the stairs back to the lab they heard voices and laughing, car doors slamming and cars driving off. It must be coming up to midnight. The jazz was over. Martin was carrying a cage and he leaned it on the banister as he stopped at the top of the stairs to listen. The main front door closed loudly and it echoed up the stairwell.

'That'll be that prickly bastard leaving.'

'Who?'

'The stroppy guy on the door.'

Apart from the scrabbling noises in the cage there was silence. Martin looked at Cindy. She winked at him. At that moment the thought occurred to him that she might be an animal activist type. All the signs were there: the unmistakable hippieness – the way she sentimentalised dolls and creatures – the fact that she'd never mentioned anything to do with the animal cause, which meant that she must be hiding it. Maybe she was a journalist in disguise who would write a damning article which would mention him by name and give his address. Or she was here to release all the animals and burn the place to the ground.

In the lab Martin said, 'I have to do this.'

'Is this the killing?'

Martin nodded.

'Yeah.'

'How sweet. What are you going to kill?'

'One of these.'

'What did it ever do to you?'

'It's an experiment.'

'I'm on the rat's side,' she said and sat down on his office chair and spun around. She switched on a small radio and began immediately to change the station. It hissed and beeped and roared as she searched. She settled on some music – an old thing of the Beatles – and turned up the volume.

He went back to his work. Cindy nosyed around in the desk and found a cardboard box of glossy, black and white photographs.

'Can I?'

'Sure.' She leafed through them.

'Did you take these?'

'Yeah.'

'Hey, you're really good.'

'Thanks. I want to get the best of them and make a book.'

'A book? You're going to have a book of pictures published?'

'No. I mean I'm going to make up my own album.'

'Got ya. What are all these boys doing?' She held up the photo. Martin looked over his shoulder.

'Standing about. It was a religious weekend. A retreat.'

'Are you religious?'

'Not any more.'

She looked at him and he shrugged. Then she turned to the photographs again.

'There's you. Who are these two guys? This one's cute.' Martin stopped what he was doing and went over to her at his desk.

'That's Kavanagh. He's the guy I'm doing this experiment for. We were at school together.'

'He's really good looking. And him?'

'That's Blaise. Another guy at school. Mad bastard.'

'He looks it.'

'He got a bad kicking in school. We thought he was dead.' Her eyes widened.

'Who did it?'

'Some guys – in football boots – it's not important. They took him to hospital but he regained consciousness after a day. They had to get somebody to write his exams for him – they discovered he'd broken some bones in his hand. An amanuensis.'

'What's that?'

'The one who writes out your paper. You sit there with your arm in a plaster and tell him what to write.'

'I'd hate that. If I had to do that I'd fail everything.' She laughed a bit. 'I failed everything anyway. Where's this guy now?'

'Blaise got the highest marks *ever* in A levels in Northern Ireland. He went to Cambridge. To do Law.'

'A bit of a genius.'

'He was a great schemer. People said the amanuensis was open to bribes.'

'Is that true?'

'I don't know. I haven't talked to him since the day of the kicking.'

'So this one's doing Medicine,' she stabbed with her finger at the photo, 'and this one's doing Law ... Are you going to be doing this all your life?' she asked.

'I dunno.'

'What d'you reckon?'

'It's like a man rowing a boat. We've our backs to the way we're going. We can't see the future.'

'That's really neat – the way you said that. Ah! but what about astrology – do you read your stars?'

'Rubbish.'

'It's a *bit* scientific. I read my stars every day.'

'Stars, hide your fires, let light not see my black and deep desires.' She looked at him and raised her eyebrows.

'What's that all about?'

'It's from *Macbeth*. Did you do it?'

'No.'

'What was school like for you?'

'Crap.' They talked about the awful teachers they had. Hers were always 'yabbering their heads off', his were always 'droning on'. But he didn't tell her about the stealing of the exam papers. She'd be sure to ask him what marks he got and he'd have to admit that he only just passed even though he knew what the questions were. It made him look completely thick. When she'd finished with the box of photographs Cindy put the lid back on. Martin walked to the other side of the lab. She raised her voice and talked over to him.

'What's your experiment?' He wondered if this was the animal activist interrogation beginning.

'It's not *my* experiment. It's Kavanagh's. For his BSc. thesis.' The German excuse – we were only following orders. 'I'm the bottle-washer and Kavanagh's the scientist. Servant and fucking master. Naw – it's not as bad as that ... It's hard to explain.'

Because she was there he put a fresh wad of cotton wool on the bottom of the pot, then he splashed some fresh ether in.

'There's that smell again' she said loudly.

'I *love* the smell of it,' said Martin. She picked up the Dymotape machine off the desk and began fiddling with it. It was like a mobster's machine gun in chrome with a circular dial, which, when you turned it showed each of the letters of the alphabet. She pressed the handles together like a nutcracker. With each click the tape moved forward to allow another letter to be imprinted.

'I thought you were going to do some work.'

'The time is important.' At midnight Martin popped another rat into the stone jar. After he had removed the leg and disposed of the carcass he crossed the lab to where Cindy sat.

'Right,' he said. 'I deserve a break.'

'Look. I've done my name.' She pulled out the printed tape and snipped it from the machine with the little guillotine. She held it up for him to see – white letters printed on black. CINDY ATKNS. She grinned up at him.

'That was very nice,' she said.

'What?'

'The kiss in the corridor.' The office chair swivelled back and forth as she moved, pivoting it with her feet. He put his hands on her shoulders and began to massage her muscles lightly. Like a masseur – pressing with his thumbs, pulling with his fingers. But he was at the wrong height to kiss her again. She didn't stop him working with her shoulders, but put her head back. She straightened up again and stared at her piece of Dymotape.

'Shit – I left out the "I".'

'How very unselfish of you,' Martin said. She spun to face him. The toecaps of her boots touched his shins. 'Is it possible to perform an unselfish action? We used to argue about that kind of stuff all the time. You know, you lead a completely unselfish life in order to get to heaven. You do something for a stranger because you want to be liked. That mate – the one in the photo who got the kicking – he was very keen on philosophy.'

'Or you do things to people just because they're nice?'

'Nice people or nice things?'

'Both.' She turned the chair through 180 degrees and pointed to her shoulders. She lifted her hair in a two-handed bunch at the back. He began thumbing her muscles inwards towards her spine.

'That's your trapezius.'

'I don't care what you call it,' she said and leaned her head forward. Her eyes were closed. He wondered if he dare try. He hated the uncertainty – hated not knowing whether to proceed or not. He didn't know if touching her breasts would bring the whole episode – excessively pleasant to this point – to an end. Would she jump to her feet in a temper saying 'How dare you! Who the fuck do you think you are anyway? Who told you you could do a thing like that? Jesus – men! Men!' And she would be away with her rucksack over her shoulder stomping down the stairs to sleep the night on a park bench. Even worse was the thought of her mockery. 'And you thought I'd want to do that with a skinny bastard like *you*? I've refused real men twice your size. Have you ever seen the guys on Bondi Beach? You just don't know about sex, do you? You haven't a clue, have you? All you want it for is so's you can tell your mates.'

'Your trapezius is tight because of you carrying a rucksack,' he said. At least that is what he wanted to say. But it came out wrong. There was a catch in his voice. And he coughed a bit to try and cover up.

'Backpack,' she said. His voice was shaking because of what was happening. But he was trying to keep what was happening – still happening. Didn't want to draw attention to the fact that his voice was shaking because he was touching her.

'What?' She still had her eyes closed. Her head was revolving slowly and in response to the pressure from his thumbs. The sweater she'd put on was thickly knit, full of cable stitching and blackberry patterns, and he couldn't sense too much of her shoulders beneath it. But he could smell the smell of her coming up to him – a milky, sweet soapy niceness, shampoo from her hair maybe. The heat from the blower now filled the place, stirred the strands of hair at the side of her head. His hand sheltered her from the moving air. To get closer to her he inched his hands beneath the material of the sweater at the back of her neck. Her T-shirt material. Cotton. The DJ on the radio prattled on. Martin hoped he wouldn't say anything or play anything which would change the mood – a triumphal march or something. Or worse – a ceilidh band. And yet it would be too pointed if he turned the radio off. The DJ put on a slow bluesy track Martin didn't know. Cindy made the sound in her throat she'd made in the corridor. Then she put her hands on his hands to stop them. Held them firmly. This was it – this is where she drew the line. She will now turn to me and say something like: no this is not a good idea at all. Or there is no point in getting all worked up if it leads to nothing. I really think I should go now. But her hands remained on his only for a moment or two while she took off her sweater. Without him having to say a word she seemed to know what Martin wanted her to do. And she took off her sweater in such a way that he was astonished by it – not tugged off over her head because it would pull up her T-shirt with it and bare her midriff, but by extracting her arms downwards from the sleeves, modestly so that nothing rode up. Then enlarging the neck hole sufficiently to have it come off over her head without destroying her hair – like a priest getting out of his chasuble. Her white T-shirt was warm and the cotton barely distinguishable from what was beneath. She lolled back and, as she did so, let her legs relax and fall open. All the time he was waiting for her to stop him, to say something snappy like: that's enough, why don't we go for a walk. Or – I only agreed to stay because I trusted you. What amazed him was that she did things without being asked to do things. It was as if she wanted to do this and to have this done to her. That was what was so extraordinary. He touched her breasts through her T-shirt and they moved. She turned her head slowly and looked towards the uncurtained windows and asked if anyone could see in. He told her that the building which overlooked them was Theology and that there would be nobody there at this time of night. There wasn't a single light to be seen anywhere. He was going to say, even God's away home – but decided not to, for fear of breaking the spell. What if she were to laugh at his joke – slap her thigh and demand another cup of coffee. So he kept quiet. Not talking was good – it meant he was allowing her to concentrate on what was happening. Outside the window it was now completely dark, the only thing they could see was their own reflections. A girl swirling in a chair, a boy behind her massaging her neck and shoulders. He bent over and began kissing her. With their mouths together she still swung the chair to and fro. In the same way as she'd taken off her sweater, without being asked, she drew off her T-shirt. She was very brown – the colour of caramel – and her breasts were bare. There was no white bikini bar across her back. He knelt before her, between her knees. His face tilted up to her, she bent over, kissing down on him so that he felt a rush of her saliva into his mouth. When the kiss was finished he looked at her upper body. He said, may I? and she smiled and he touched her breasts as if they were an idea. The hematoxylin dye was still on his fingertips – like schoolboy ink. She paused and stopped his hands to have a closer look.

'Dye,' he said.

'No.' She placed his hands back on her breasts and he continued touching them because he only *sort of* knew what to do next. On the radio the music stopped and a DJ began to talk.

'Do you want the radio on or off?'

'I want everything off,' she said, pulling up his shirt. 'Including that fucking knife sharpener.' He laughed and got to his feet and switched the machine off. She switched off the radio. The silence was wonderful.

He knew what the aim was. But quite what that involved he was not too sure. Yes, he knew it involved his penis and her vagina. But that was a bit like saying chess involved a squared board and two sets of differently coloured pieces. There was more to it than that. More information was required to play a game with someone. How did you know about *the moving*? And he was *not* thinking of the chess pieces. Kavanagh had said *just think of the woman as your hand.* Fingernails? Knuckles? Did *she* do it or did you? Did it coincide with *the groaning* – what speed was *the moving* to be at? Was there any speed to *the groaning*? There was a joke about an alien watching humans doing it and when he heard that it took a further nine months to produce offspring he said *what was all the rush at the end for?* Jokes were unreliable for information. And knowing the names for things didn't help much. Kavanagh called it *thrusting.* But Martin stuck to calling it *the moving.* Was it possible to do it and not move? What if you put it in the wrong hole? It was full of holes down there. Would she tell you? *That's my urethra you're in.* Or – God, he would die – *That's my ass.*

When he hurried back to her she asked him again what age he was and he replied that *women* didn't like being asked that question. She laughed and rumpled his hair and told him that he was wet behind the ears. She said it was not where it was happening to her. And he asked her where – where was it happening to her and she stood up from the swivelling chair and pulled at the laces of her boots and looked sideways at him as she did so, smiling. And when the boots were off she stepped out of her jeans and stood in front of him in just her socks and a pair of white pants. She undid the buckle of his trousers and let them fall to the floor. Then with her thumbs in the waistband of his underpants she unhooked them from his cock and let him step out of them. He touched her and quick as a pen scrape, he came.

And he was profoundly embarrassed.

The little clots of his sperm fell to the lino with a strange repetitive sound – a pattering. He felt ashamed and repeated over and over again that he was sorry. She drew him to her and hugged him, her arms beneath his shirt and around his waist. She told him not to worry – such urgency was quite endearing. It was sweet when it happened. She said that they had all night to get it right. She tugged a tissue from a box on the bench and wiped the floor. She was still smiling. He made a joke that she was wiping up the lives of millions. This particular tribe was well and truly lost. He was still apologising to her, his body half crouched in shame. She asked him to take off his shirt and curl up with her on the camp bed. He said that he was too thin, too much of a skinny bastard to take his shirt off in front of anybody. She said how much better it was than being a fat bastard. She asked to see his muscles. He pulled up his sleeve, bent his arm and flexed his biceps. The muscle became a faint hillock. And he grinned. He said that it was funny how his elbows didn't come through his skin, they were so sharp. She kissed him and led him to the camp bed while they were still in the kiss. Shuffling, like inadequate dancers.

They lay together and talked, Martin half sitting up, her head against his shirt. She pointed to a small raised mole on his waist and made a face.

'That's my sultana,' he said. 'I'm saving it for an extreme situation. About to die of starvation halfway up Everest. Then I'll eat it.'

'You're utterly disgusting.'

They talked some more about the kind of music they liked. Then movies. Martin told her about one of his favourites, Stanley Kubrick's first feature, *The Killing*. About how it chopped up time and reassembled it in a more interesting way. The way Sterling Hayden chewed his matchstick. Then she remembered *In the Heat of the Night* and Rod Steiger chewing *his* matchstick. 'Mista

Tibbs,' she kept saying over and over with her chin up and her mouth turned down at the sides in a good imitation of Rod Steiger. He reminded her that the character's first name was Virgil. Virgil Tibbs. And her all time best ever movie *Love Story* with Ryan O'Neal and Ali McGraw. But he hadn't seen it. So she told it to him. It took a long time. As she talked he stroked her skin wherever it was near to him – her shoulder, breasts, neck, arm.

'That's nice,' she said. She had a great tan and her incredibly fine body hair was blonde. It reminded him of patterns iron filings took up in magnetic fields. He held his hand above her skin, hovered it there – felt something was touching but nothing was touching.

'I like your hair,' he said.

'Thanks.' She tilted her head and pulled a few strands down in front of her face.

'No, I mean the hair on your skin.'

'I'm not hairy.' Her voice was sharp.

'Then why do you get goose-bumps, as you call them? For every goose-bump there must be a hair.'

'Some on my forearms maybe.' She looked, rubbed a forefinger across her wrist. 'Sometimes beneath my watch. In the dark, like mushrooms. Euucch!'

'Did you ever hear of Mary Magdalene?'

'Is that a polite way of saying I'm a whore?'

'No. I saw these drawings in an art book at school and she was being lifted up into heaven by angels but she was hairy, like a gorilla.'

'I don't like the drift of this conversation.'

'She'd given up the bad life, thrown away her classy clothes and wandered off naked into the desert. But the problem was, if she received communion from a priest she would be an occasion of sin to him. So she prayed and her prayers were answered and her body was miraculously covered with hair.'

'That'll teach her. Who told you that?'

'A priest – he said it was a holy legend and not to be believed. I'd seen the drawings and asked him. That's what he came up with.' She started to undo his buttons. 'Take off that shirt and let me see how hairy *you* are.'

He stopped her unbuttoning and drew the shirt off over his head. Her eyes travelled around over his whiteness.

'Not a single one. Hey, what happened there?'

'I dunno.' There were some scratches and dried blood on the back of his shoulder. 'Oh yeah – I cycled through a bit of a riot earlier. I got hit with something. I was trying to cycle over the bridge.' She touched the vicinity of the wound with her fingers.

'What was it?'

'I dunno – a half-brick. I didn't hang around to find out.'

'It'll be bruised tomorrow.' She kissed around it. 'Maybe you better put something on it. Stop it getting infected.'

'And here, look at this,' he said, pointing to where he had cut his shin with the bicycle pedal. 'You were to blame for that – coming in the door.' She stood up from the camp bed and it tilted over with Martin's weight. He almost rolled off on to the floor and they both laughed. Cindy walked in her sock feet to her rucksack and pulled out a wash bag. She set the wash bag on the floor and squatted beside it. The ripple and curve of the bones of her spine. Again she tossed her hair with her hand.

'Why do you keep doing that?'

'What?' He mimicked her gesture. 'Oh that. It gives my hair more body.'

'As long as it doesn't give your body more hair.'

'Fuck you.'

'No – no, I'm only joking. You look great.' She found what she was scrabbling for and came back to him, grinning.

'You don't look so bad yourself.' She sat down behind him and he felt something cold on his shoulder.

'What's that?'

'Ointment.'

'But what?'

'It's a mixture of crocodile shit and Vegemite.'

'No – what is it?'

'It's an antiseptic cream. It can do you no harm.' She had a little left over on her fingers and she stooped in front of him to anoint the wound on his shin. She turned her face up to be kissed for all her good work. They continued to touch and caress. He could smell the faintly perfumed antiseptic cream from her hands. He found a softness between the clavicle bones at her throat, a hardness on the high dome of her foot. At some stage she had painted her toenails a dark maroon but she hadn't maintained them. He pointed this out to her. They kissed. He asked her what she did. She told him she'd gone straight from school into a hairdressing course and worked in a hairdresser's shop in Sydney – in King's Cross. Eventually, when she settled down after her travels, when she'd done roamin', she planned to set up a place of her own, maybe call it Scissors Palace – like in Las Vegas. Did he get it? Yes, yes he did. She hadn't thought up that name herself but she'd seen a hairdresser's called that somewhere on her travels and thought it clever. She was convinced that travel broadened the mind and her one really, really true ambition was to visit Disney World in Florida. He had found the heat of the inside of her thighs strange. They kissed. Gradually she stopped talking and removed her pants and said he could kiss her if he wanted. He was unsure and looked at her face, then down at what Gray called her 'organs of generation'.

'Your hair – it's not the same.'

'Yes – my downstairs hair and my upstairs hair are different colours because I'm a skilled hairdresser.' She pointed between her legs and he hesitantly bent down and kissed her – not quite a peck on the cheek, but more of a brief goodnight kiss and she said, Gee thanks. Whatever was expected of him he knew he wasn't doing it right. It was like an exam – like being asked to compare Milton and Keats and he hadn't done any Keats and only one poem of Milton's. He was definitely missing a large part of what was required for a pass mark. But this was so much worse. This was embarrassing stuff. Nobody was embarrassed when they knew fuck all about Milton. He remembered Kavanagh's advice about paying attention to the face. He found it difficult, if not impossible, to pay attention to her face *and* her perineum at the same time. He bent to her again and did the same thing.

'What are you afraid of?'

'Nothing.'

'Then why all the enthusiasm?' He looked at her. He was sure she was making fun of him.

'We just started bacteriology.' She looked at him, unsure of the word. 'Hygiene.'

'You think I don't wash?'

'No – no, of course not.'

He had been in this kind of trouble before. He recognised the danger signals. The first time he had come into contact with the female 'organs of generation' it had been dark, at a barbecue. He had been snogging this girl – she must have been one of the organisers because she smelled of paraffin and wood-smoke. Then they went for a walk, and later a lie down where various mutual fumblings occurred. She made him come in the sand and when it was over they walked to the sea's edge and he said, 'Do you mind if I wash my hands?'

'Feel free,' she said. He squatted down and waited for the wave to come up to him. When it did he paddled his hand in the salt water. He looked around and she was away, half walking, half running back to the barbecue.

Again Cindy pointed down to herself. He half expected to see the little straight lines labelling her parts. He knew the diagram in Gray, like the map of Ireland – yet what he was looking at now was like Ireland upside down. Was that Galway or Cork? Belfast had become Dublin. The real lines were the tracks of elastic on her waist and inner thighs.

If he was to say any of the anatomical words out loud how would they be pronounced? How would he begin to have a stab at saying urethra? Or the glans of Bartholin? Knowing the medical name wasn't a help. And school names for things weren't any improvement. Her rug. Her bush. Her tush. Her cunt. Her asshole. She would slap his face if he used words like that to her.

'I like your undergrowth,' he said. She smiled at his word. Pudenda, when he looked it up in the dictionary, said: the external sexual organs, especially those of a woman. From the Latin, literally 'things to be ashamed of'. He straightened up and said this to her.

He continued to stroke her with his fingers. She changed position, shrugged and said, 'I know some Latin.'

'What?'

'*Terra nullius* – an empty land – Australia.'

'*Terra incognita*,' he said. 'An unexplored region.'

'Ohh, that's nice. Yes.'

'Our Latin teacher was called Ned Kelly.'

'I don't believe you.'

'Wasn't he an Australian gunman?'

'Bloody good bloke. Down a bit.'

'I know he was hanged.'

In response she reached down and touched him. 'Lazarus is back from the dead.'

'Did you know he was a brother of Mary Magdalene's?'

'Are you nervous?'

'No.'

'Martin?' She turned and looked at him. It was as if something had just dawned on her. 'Is this your first time?'

'No,' he said. But it didn't sound convincing enough so he added, 'It's always been dark before.'

'I want you inside me,' she said. Jesus. What did she mean by that? Could she swallow him? Or part of him? Was it like communion or what? It was just such a confusing request. Sounded like it was worth forty marks – one of the big questions, like the essay.

'Eh . . .' he said.

'Yes. It's safe,' she said. 'I'm on the pill.' Somehow he knew she was close to taking over. Questions about where to put your tackle and how to move it were on the verge of being answered. 'Let me show you.' As she moved, the bed again tipped. 'Fuck this for a lark.' She unzipped the sleeping bag all around so that it became a quilted blanket which she spread on the floor. She invited Martin on to it. Then she sat astride him and eased him up into her. Then he heard a shot. It was definitely a shot. Not a car backfiring. It was followed by another burst of firing. He lay there watching her move, gliding up and down on him with little lifting movements of her hips. He looked at her face to see if she'd heard the shot. If she did she said nothing, she just kept moving. He wondered if he should tell her he loved her, to make her feel better. He certainly felt extremely grateful to her. Generosity like hers was something he had never encountered before.

'I love you,' he said.

'Don't be so stupid,' she panted out the words. 'Don't be such a drongo.'

As she gyrated she held her hair with both hands, as if it was going to fly off like a wig. Then she began to touch herself. At first slowly. Martin felt as if he didn't need to participate any more. He was in danger of becoming a spectator at his own initiation. She groaned and made those throat noises again. Louder and louder. Martin wondered would any of the security staff be patrolling the place. Would they have heard the shots? Would they, indeed, have been the ones who fired the shots? All that was needed now was for some bigoted Orangeman in a uniform to come in and find them at it. Get the Catholic boy the sack, for having sex on the premises. But there was something wrong with Cindy. There was definitely something wrong with her. She had her eyes closed and was shouting, threshing her hair from side to side. Jesus – she was having a fit of some sort. At a time like this, for fuck sake. Martin might as well have been in the animal house for all the attention she was paying him. He wondered if he had done something to her, triggered some bad reaction. A heart attack? Her breathing was all over the place. He hardly noticed himself coming, so concerned was he for this woman pounding on top of him. It scared the living daylights out of him. Or maybe she had been shot. A stray bullet had got her in the back. He went through the sequence of phoning the porter's lodge and reporting a dead body. In the Anatomy Department? Is this a hoax call? Is it in connection with the recent shooting? Or, if not the porter's lodge, then Kavanagh. I lost my virginity but the woman is in hospital in a serious condition. In intensive care. With a half yell she stiffened and stopped breathing. Jesus. Fuck me one. Fuck me two. Fuck me three. Your honour, she just stopped breathing. Then after what seemed like an infinity she slumped forward shuddering on to Martin's chest. Waves moved through her and she kissed into the side of his neck. Oh Martin, Martin, Martin, Martin she was saying. She was panting close to his ear.

'Did you come again?' she asked.

'Come again?'

'Yes.'

'Yes.'

He put his arms around her. What was he supposed to do now? She kept saying Hmmmmm and snuggling into him.

'*Consummatum est,*' he whispered in her ear.

'What?'

'Just some more Latin.'

'What does it mean?'

'A consummation devoutly to be wished.'

'You talk the greatest load of shit I've ever heard.'

It was a long time before her breathing returned to normal. It sounded magnified because her nose was right beside his ear.

'You remember you said you stroked bees?' he asked her.

'Yeah.'

'Their fur. Is it real fur?'

'I dunno. Feels like it.'

'D'you think would it be possible to make a coat – fifty-eight thousand bee pelts stitched together? A bee coat?'

'Yeah sure,' she said. Then nothing was said for a long time. 'When did *you* first . . .'

'I dunno. I was late where we come from. Just turned fifteen.' She raised herself up and looked at his face. 'This *was* your first time.'

'How do you know?'

'I can tell. It's nothing to be ashamed of. Was it?' He nodded yes and grinned. She tousled his hair and hugged him. 'How sweet. It's really sweet to know. And I'm absolutely delighted to have been the bad apple.'

He wondered if he should walk down the corridor and phone Kavanagh from the tea room. But he didn't have the number for Pippa's house. That would be a little triumph. Getting Tambourine Woman on the phone and telling her to give Kavanagh a message – that he, Martin had just got it for the first time. But then Kavanagh would come on the phone and want to know about the experiment. Jesus – he'd missed killing a rat. Maybe two. Time flies when you're . . . Martin had well and truly fucked up. What should he do next?

Cindy turned and lay on her stomach. Maybe she was married and hadn't told him. The Muybridge book lay on the desk. When somebody screwed Muybridge's wife he'd come after them with a gun. Maybe it was Cindy's husband who'd been shooting outside.

'Come here,' said Cindy. She patted the sleeping bag beside her. It was wet. 'Yuk, you're like a snail – you leave slime.' When Martin sat down he turned to her and grinned.

'You're a bit of a slippery customer yourself, if I may say so.' She slapped his bare back.

'You're like one of those animals that go round marking out your territory.'

'It's *you* that left it. I gave it to you. You leaked it.' He got up again and reached for a cloth beside the sink. He was just about to wipe the mark when he stopped.

'Wait a minute – wait,' he said. He got a glass slide from a box on the bench and touched it against the wet on the sleeping bag.

'What are you doing?'

'Wait till you see.' He picked up a pipette and put a droplet on to the glass. 'Saline. Harvested from the Dead Sea.' He covered it with a wisp-thin glass coverslip. 'Come here.' He put the slide on the stage of the microscope. And focused. And adjusted the light to a low oblique level, 'Look at that.'

She got up from the floor and draped the sleeping bag over her shoulders. She bent to look into the binoculars.

'Worms.' She looked up at him. 'You've opened a can of worms, Martin.'

The sleeping bag blanket covered her unevenly. Her backside was bare. Martin snuggled in behind her and they made standing spoons.

'Let me have a look,' he said. She moved her head. Her hair fell all to one side. He stared down at the moving image. His own microscopic seed thrashing and weaving. At the edges were outriders, their tails propellering. There was a terrible blind urgency about them, like creatures fleeing. Climbing over each other, like snakes. A nest of vipers. 'There's life in the Dead Sea.'

'They're very impressive. Your spunkies.'

'Are you sure you've . . .'

'Yeah – of course . . .'

'It was a Dutch guy – Leeuwenhoek – who discovered sperm, in the seventeenth century.'

'I'm sure there were guys who'd discovered it before that.'

'And Paracelsus believed if you cooked human sperm and horse dung for forty days you could make a small man . . .'

'How long would a big one take?'

'Paracelsus reckoned he wouldn't have a soul. That'd be the only thing'd be missing. And he was supposed to be a scientist. How wrong can you be?'

'I've no idea.'

'This is the kind of crap you pick up at night classes.'

The sky paled, was becoming a slate colour. Cindy asked him, 'What time is it?'

'A quarter past four.'

'It's getting brighter. Another day another dollar.' Martin didn't answer her. She came up to him and put her arms around his waist. 'When it gets bright, can we look in that place?'

'Where?'

'Where you keep the bodies.'

'What is this?'

'I just want to see. I'm naturally curious.' She pretended to be afraid. 'Will you stand beside me?' He looked at her. She simpered and pretended to beseech him.

'OK – if that's what you want.'

'Don't go away from me but . . .'

'No.'

She let a long low groan out of her. Martin thought it was something to do with the sex. Something else he didn't know about.

'Ooooaawww,' she said. 'I am starving. I could eat the decorations of a hearse. Sex gives me an appetite.'

'Greater love hath no man – than he share his last sandwich.'

'Are you serious?'

He nodded.

'Good on ya.'

'Are you a vegetarian?'

'An Aussie veggie?'

'Damn.'

'Why?'

'If you'd been a vegetarian I could have eaten them all myself.' He produced the pack of ham sandwiches and smiled as he unwrapped them. There they were, cut four ways with crusts removed. It was like having his mother beside him with this stark naked woman.

'Do you like mustard?' She nodded. They ate without saying much. She rearranged the sleeping bag on the camp bed and sat down, then rolled over on to her side, still chewing.

'I'm knackered.' She tried to stretch the sleeping bag out so that most of her was covered. She made a pillow of her folded arm and its soft inner elbow.

Martin started to get dressed. He hopped around trying to get into his trousers.

'I hate when that happens – when you get your crotch caught between your toes. Have you been to Italy?'

'Uh-huh.'

'For the Italians fingers and toes are all the same thing. Digits. The only way you can tell them apart is by the context.'

'Uh-huh?'

'If I say, don't pick your nose with your finger. You know it's not your toe.'

She didn't say anything. He tucked his shirt in and tightened his belt. When he moved his bare foot he left a momentary steamy outline on the lino. He pulled on his socks and shoes, tying his laces as he rested his foot on the stool. His white lab coat was where he left it. He considered whether or not to put it on.

'Fuck it,' he muttered. It was almost 4.30 in the morning – who needed a white coat?

When he looked round at Cindy she was asleep. He went over and crouched down. The back of her knee was exposed – somehow the sleeping bag hadn't covered it. He saw a pale letter H creased on her skin. It reminded him of Kavanagh and the day in the Waterworks when they had sworn to phone each other just as soon as they got it. He stood remembering and savouring. He sniffed his fingers and she was still there. Her aroma. He looked at her. She was breathing deeply and her face had gone slack. At the end of each intake of breath there was the slightest vibration of a snore. Then – it was barely audible – twice, quietly, she let two little farts. They sounded like slight hand claps. Maybe he should phone Kavanagh. Tell him the whole story. The hole story. Forget it. He'd just be mad – getting phoned at this hour. It was a daft notion.

He killed the right number of rats all at once to bring himself up to date, 'going about it as quietly as he could so as not to wake her – sliding the glass lid gently on and off the ether chamber. He looked at his watch but it didn't make any difference. He labelled the specimens as if they were killed on the hours of one, two and three o'clock. It would ruin Kavanagh's results and maybe even

318

screw up his thesis and he – Martin – would be to blame. Would Kavanagh believe him? He'd have to repeat the experiment and then he'd find out that Martin had cheated. Things were never as clear cut as that. It was rarely like the titration which went, with the addition of one drop of acid, from black to white. He could leave it – say nothing. If Kavanagh wanted to repeat the experiment because these results didn't tally, he would help him. But it was a hell of a lot of work. Martin could maybe tell him he forgot, slept in. Jesus, why was he telling lies? Why could he not tell his best mate the truth? I got sidetracked. A woman. Sex. Because Kavanagh was a changed man. Kavanagh had betrayed him. Blaise was right about the effect women had on friendship.

When he had all done he went to the tea room and brought back a wooden chair. There wasn't room beside the camp bed so he went to the other side of the island bench. He could not see her from there. He lined the chair up with two others. He knew he wouldn't sleep, but he felt tired and wanted to stretch out. He kicked off his shoes and lay down on his back across the three chairs – one for his legs, one for his bum, one for his head and shoulders. He joined his hands across his stomach and felt a bit like a corpse. But the middle chair from the tea room squeaked a bit and that reassured him he wasn't dead.

He must have slept a bit. The next thing he knew the lab was a lot brighter and he had an erection. The sky was changing colour. Birds were singing. A blackbird, by the sound of it, full of twirls and twiddles. Then he remembered the girl. For a second he wondered if he'd dreamed her. But he heard her little cat snore. The chair squeaked as he swung himself up and he sat stunned for a moment, his head in his hands, on the middle chair. He put on his shoes and padded round the island bench. It was almost the hour and time to kill another rat. He worked quietly so's not to wake her. The only part of her he could see now was her head and her bare arm and shoulder. As he stared down at her, her eyes opened and she wrinkled her nose and smiled.

'Hi,' she said.

'Good morning.'

'Whatcha doing?'

'My job. I'm a rat serial killer.'

'What are you killing them for?'

'For my mate, Kavanagh.'

'Ha bloody ha.' She yawned loudly and stretched.

'I'm not entirely sure. I'm only the bottle-washer round here.'

'Don't put yourself down. What's it all for?'

'It's something to do with the way this drug affects bone and bone marrow.'

'What drug?'

'I can hardly say it. Phyto – haemo – something or other. Glutinin. Anyway Kavanagh injected this stuff into all these rats at five o'clock yesterday and I've to assist one to pop its clogs on the hour, every hour. Then he'll look at what happened to the bone. And the marrow.'

'And it's not a cure for anything?'

'Nope. Not unless something goes drastically wrong. But who knows. Then he's going to inject it at different times of day to see if that makes any difference. Did you know we have circadian rhythms?'

'I certainly did not.'

'The day is twenty-four hours long – right? The body reacts differently to invasion at different times of the day. Most people die at three o'clock in the morning. People on night shift get irritable and stressed.'

He paused and looked at her, then began to tear at his hair and shout at the top of his voice. 'This is so fuckin awful. This is my first night ever on night shift and I am so fucking irritable . . .' Her eyes widened and he stopped shouting. 'Joke over.'

'I thought you were serious. Jesus you gave me a fright.' Martin finished what he was doing and washed his hands at the sink. Cindy clutched the sleeping bag tightly under her chin. 'I react badly to invasion at any time of the day or night. Hey – I've just realised. You missed a whole lot of rats.'

'I didn't notice at the time. I was doing something else.'

'You cheat.' He smiled at her and dried his hands on the roller towel. Then he crouched down.

'What about a pleasant invasion?' He kissed her. 'Is there a place in under there for me?'

'Only if I can get in to see the room.'

'Which?'

'The dead room.' Martin nodded. 'Promise?'

'Yeah.'

'Say it.'

'I promise.' With that she shuffled a little to the side and admitted him under the sleeping bag. Her mouth tasted slept in. He caressed and touched her and she luxuriated and made her little throat noises. When he touched between her legs he said, 'You *are* a slippery customer.'

'It takes one to know one,' she said. They had sex again and this time Martin thought it was better – probably because he remembered Kavanagh's advice and paid considerable attention to her face. Jesus – what if Kavanagh decided to come in early? And wandered into the lab and found the two of them at it? Martin almost looked over his bare shoulder at the door. What could he do? Just say, 'This is *thee* most important day of my life. Could you give us a couple more minutes.'

Afterwards Martin asked her if she'd like a cup of tea. He dressed and carried the chair back. He knew where to get the key for the Dissecting Room.

'Breakfast,' he said. He pushed the door open with his foot, a cup in each hand. Cindy was dressed and standing reading a book which lay flat on the bench. He set the cup down in front of her. There was one piece of Kit-Kat left and he halved it with her.

'Jesus,' she whispered.

'What?'

'Look at this.'

'What?' She was looking at *A Textbook of Histology*.

'This is awful. I can't believe anyone could do stuff like this.'

'What are you talking about?'

She pointed to a picture of a white mouse. She read in a kind of flat school voice: '*Photograph of a mouse that received a fertilized mouse ovum in the anterior chamber of the right eye 12 days earlier.*'

'So?'

'That is *so* awful. Look at the poor thing.' The eye bulged and shone, almost extruding from its socket.

'That's not nice.'

'You got it. Somebody thought that up. That is pure torture.'

'I'm not defending it but it's just an experiment. It's a fact of life. If you go into hospital with blood poisoning, some guinea pig is going to die.' He leaned over and flipped the book closed. 'Don't upset yourself. I told you there's lots of things about here which are not for the general public.'

She lifted her cup and wrapped her hands around it.

'Jesus,' she said quietly.

'Let's cheer you up. Let's go look at the dead.' She smiled ruefully.

'Can I bring my tea?'

'It'll not help.'

Martin unlocked the Dissecting Room door. He pushed one half of it open and stepped in. He held the door open for her. Outside she cocked her head to one side and hesitated. He couldn't make up his mind whether she was genuinely frightened or play-acting. She covered her mouth with her free hand and stepped inside the door.

'Jees Zus.' She looked around the fifteen tables in the milky light. There was still a dawn feel to the air. The windows overlooking the quad, even though they were on the first floor, had been painted white to prevent anyone seeing in. Students had scratched their names and dates in the white paint with scalpels. She was pretending to be a baby, pulling her mouth into a straight line behind her hands and standing as close as she could to Martin. Then the smell of the formaldehyde got to her more than the sight and she pinched her nostrils shut with her finger and thumb. She set her mug of tea on the draining board of a sink and reached out to hold Martin's hand.

'The spell is terrible. How does eddy boddy breathe?'

'You just get used to it. Like looking at dead people.'

'How bizarre,' she whispered. 'Dote − dote go away frob me. Dote let go by had.' She peeped over his shoulder. She let go of her nose. 'Why have some of them got their legs in the air?'

'They are dissecting the . . . that bit − underneath.'

'The asshole?'

'Yeah − all around there.'

It was like she was going in for a bathe at the seaside. Taking it slowly. Feet, ankles, adjusting to the new icy temperature. Then, in over the knees. Looking and looking away quickly. Looking back again. She moved him, as if she was dancing with him, nearer the closest table and rested her forehead on his shoulder, looking down at the floor. Then her face came up and she looked over his shoulder. She shivered the way people shiver when they immerse themselves totally – when cold water closes around the heat of their back.

'It is *so* strange to look at somebody dead.' She moved away from him and let her hand trail away from his. She stood looking directly down at a cadaver's face. 'Even somebody you never knew. The light's gone out. The shop's shut. This is as low as we get.' Cindy turned her head to look at the face properly – the way someone turns their head to read the title of a book on a shelf. 'Auntie Dinkie.'

'That's what the medics do. Give their body a name. To make fun of it. Mildred or Tarquin – that kinda thing.'

'She's the image of my Auntie Dinkie.'

She eye-rolled a bit then started to pay attention to the body on the next table. It was that of a thin old man with his legs in the air. His skin was leathery grey, a rhinoceros colour. The points at which the body had been in contact with the aluminium table had gone yellow and had remained flat – the way a chicken goes if left on a plate overnight. Now the yellow parts were exposed because the body was raised to dissect the perineum. His little grey cock had been folded over to one side and kept out of the way, speared with a cocktail stick. His mousy pubic hair lay flat, like grass by the bank of a flooded river.

'This is truly, truly awful,' she said.

'I thought you'd think it was the dog's bollocks.'

Although she'd let go of her nose she still held her hands up half covering her lower face. Sort of looking over her fingers. She moved across to another table.

'So many,' she said.

'You've never seen one – all of a sudden you see fourteen.'

'Is this a man or a woman?' The head hair had been closely shaved to a grey stubble. The chest pouches could have belonged to either sex. The sex organs were in process of dissection. 'They all look like they've been half chewed. I want to cry but I can't.'

Martin had his hands joined behind his back. The white tiled walls were covered with plastic diagrams: of the nervous system, the muscle system, the skeleton. He walked up to the blackboard and back again. Cindy was looking down at another dead woman's face. She turned and made a horrified face, pointing beneath the table.

'What's that?'

'What?'

'That stuff dripping out.'

Martin shrugged.

'It's just fixative.'

'It's the first table I've ever seen with a penis.'

There was an overflow pipe pointing into a bucket beneath each of the stainless steel tables. 'You see that bucket – that's where they put the bits.'

'What bits?'

'The leftover bits of each body. The chicken bones, the skin. When they dissect it.'

'Yeuchhh.'

'Each of them will get a Christian burial – correction – a burial of their choice. All their bits get gathered together in a coffin. Whether you're a Jew or a Muslim or an atheist we can cater for you. Burnt or buried, sir? And you don't want to go mixing them up. You don't want Auntie Dinkie's knee bone turning up in some old rabbi's coffin, do you? So everything has to go into the right bucket. And from the bucket into the coffin with the right name on it. I've seen them, in the basement. At the Last Judgment the trumpet shall sound. And it'll cause no end of bother if people have been mixed up.'

'You shouldn't make fun,' she said. 'Don't forget I'm a minister's daughter. And I still believe in God.'

'God is the great lie and we are the generation who found it out.'

'This is very heavy for so early in the morning.'

'I used to think there was some sort of justice. The fat capitalist when he died would get his comeuppance in hell, and his thin victim would get to heaven. But we all end up like this. This is the only way things even out. The scales balance. Everybody dies, everybody disappears.' Martin looked around the Dissecting Room. 'Maybe comedownance would be better.'

There was a number of high stools for the students, like bar stools at each table, and Cindy slid on to one. Martin came and stood in front of her. Her legs were ajar.

'I wish I hadn't come in here,' she said. 'I thought it'd be horrible. But it's just sad. So so so sad.' He began to touch the insides of her thighs lightly.

'Don't,' she said.

'Sorry.' She was on the verge of tears. She slid off the stool and stood staring down at a woman. From behind, Martin chastely put his arms around her and put his face to the side of her face. They both looked at the body. 'She probably had about six nippers,' said Cindy. 'Tied their hair in bunches. Ginger Belfast kids with freckles. Good stone throwers.'

'She's probably not from here.'

'What?'

'They ship them in. We ship ours out – to Leeds, or London.'

'Why?'

'If they're not local then there's less chance of a student getting his granny to cut up.'

'Christ Almighty. Not only is she dead, but she's away from home.' She closed her eyes and fought hard against crying. Martin joined his hands across her stomach.

'Let's go then,' he said. 'I knew this was a bad idea.' He put gentle pressure on her to move towards the door. She allowed him to push her. In the corridor he kissed her but she did not respond. He began to touch her but she stopped him and stepped away.

'I'm raw,' she said. She moved back along the corridor to the lab. Martin locked up and followed her. 'I forgot my tea,' she said. Martin went back and unlocked the Dissecting Room and brought her tea. When he came into the lab she had the histology book open again. She was staring down at the photo doing her lips with the Vaseline. She nodded at the page.

'This is worse than in there,' she said. 'They're dead. They don't feel anything.'

He went over and closed the book.

'Why do you look at it, if it annoys you?'

'Because I can hardly believe it. A pregnant eye. Can you imagine the pain of that? And somebody causes you to have it?'

325

He tried to put his arms around her but she turned away and began to pack her toothbrush and things into her rucksack.

'I'm going to try and catch the early boat. I think there's one at seven.'

'It wasn't *me* did that experiment.'

'I know. But I associate it with here, with you, with this place.'

'Hey – don't go all serious on me.'

She shook her head with all its hair as if to get rid of the thought.

'Hey – I associate . . . this was something good. I associate you with something really good. Cindy.' She allowed him to lean his face against her shoulder, then to put his arms around her.

'I still want to get that early boat,' she said. 'Your sannies were good but I badly need some breakfast. My belly thinks my throat's cut.'

'Do they say that in Australia too?'

'No. But they do in bonny Scotland.'

He put the Dissecting Room key back exactly as he had found it then walked down the stairs with her. Again the echo and scrape of their feet on the stone.

'It was great to meet you,' said Martin.

'Liar.' Cindy still looked sombre.

'No, no really, it was,' said Martin. 'Hey, come on – we had a really good time. Well, I had. I really like you.' She looked at him and raised an eyebrow.

'Gee thanks,' she said.

'Why for the sarcasm?' Cindy continued down the steps. She hitched her rucksack higher up on her shoulder. 'Cindy?'

'I think what you do is really sad.'

'What?'

'Being cruel to animals. Killing them, cutting them up.'

'I'm not cruel to animals.'

'You could have fooled me.'

'It's part of my job, for God's sake. How could I be a technician in here if I refused?'

'You could get another job. Be a hairdresser. Work in a hotel.'

'A hairdresser.' His voice went high pitched and echoed in the stairwell.

'You see – you *do* think I'm a piece of shit.'

'I do not.' They stopped on the stairs.

'All night you've been examining me and letting me know I'm a piece of shit.'

'Cindy.' He tried to put his arm around her but the rucksack made it awkward. 'That's not true. Not true at all. You're great.' He pulled her head with its bush of hair into his shoulder. Then she allowed him to kiss her on the mouth. After the kiss she tightened her lips as if she was about to cry again. 'You can't say that.'

'OK – maybe I'm paranoidal.'

'You are, you are.' He opened the door and swung it wide. 'Tonight was great. What about an address?'

'I'm thinking of moving on from that hotel,' she said. 'I'll give you my father's address in Australia if you like. You could contact me there. If you ever came over. See Bondi Beach.'

'OK.' She had a tiny notebook with a spiral spine and he handed her his ballpoint pen. She wrote the address and tugged the page from the book with a tiny ripping sound. Martin glanced at it – saw *c/o Rev. Jake Atkins* in big fat backhand. 'Thanks. It was great,' he said. 'Take care.'

As she walked away she raised her hand and waggled her fingers instead of waving goodbye.

Back in the lab he turned on the knife sharpener again and listened to its rhythmic scringeing. He just stood there watching it, in a hypnotic state – watching the sliver blade turning over – the glass plate slowly revolving. Like the hypnotist swinging a gold watch. A pendulum. Simple harmonic motion. If there was no gravity there could be no pendulums. Or should it be pendula? Would Baldy Ned Kelly know an answer to a thing like that? Time was a part of it too. How long each swing took. It also depended on the length of the pendulum. Why was he thinking in this dumbfuck kind of way? He had to force himself to move. To snap out of the little trance he had allowed himself to fall into. He moved his arm. And scratched his upper lip. His fingers smelled of sex. Of Cindy. He smiled and slipped on clear plastic gloves. That way he wouldn't have to wash his hands when he'd finished what he was doing. He felt totally knackered. He needed to get his head down for a few hours at least. The only thing that would help was sleep. He remembered one of his mother's supper evenings when they had addressed themselves to the subject and examined it in some detail.

'And how's Mary?'

'I can't complain, Father.' She lowered herself into the armchair, with a sound of deflation. When she got settled she said, 'What am I talking about? I'm among friends. I'm bate to the ropes. Awful. I haven't slept well one night this week.'

'It must be something in the air,' said Nurse Gilliland. 'I haven't slept a wink since Tuesday.'

'What about a wee cup of hot milk?' said Mrs Brennan.

'Och, no thanks dear. I'll just wait for the tea.'

'No – I mean for the sleeping. At night.'

'Sorry, love,' said Mary Lawless. 'I thought you were offering me hot milk now. At this minute. Says I, what's come over Mrs Brennan running around offering people hot milk in the middle of the evening.'

'I was wondering,' said Nurse Gilliland. Father Farquharson smiled and then began to chuckle to himself.

'What's tickling your fancy, Father?' said Mrs Brennan.

'Nothing, Mrs Brennan. Nothing at all.' But he went on smiling. Mrs Brennan asked him a second time. He straightened his face.

'I'm very easily amused. My funny bone is very near the surface tonight,' he said. 'Have any of you ever heard tell of the great churchman Monsignor Ronald Arbuthnott Knox?'

'Was he not a Scottish Protestant?'

'You're right there,' said Mary Lawless.

'No,' said Father Farquharson. 'He was an entirely different kettle of fish. You're talking about John Knox – a bad pill, if ever there was one. The man I'm talking about was a scholar and a gentleman. Ronnie Knox engaged himself in the piffling task of translating the whole of the Bible. The New Testament first. Then the Old Testament.'

'Would he not have been better to go at it the other way round?'

'Start at the beginning.'

'That is not the issue here,' said Father Farquharson. 'What I'm saying is that he was a man of high intellectual gifts. And for relaxation he wrote detective stories.'

'Did he write them under the pen-name of Father Brown?'

'No . . .'

'Agatha Christie?'

'Jeff Chandler?'

'As far as I know he wrote them under his own name.'

'That was brave of him.'

'Why have a dog when you can bark yourself,' said Mrs Brennan.

'The point is,' said Father Farquharson, 'that he was not a great sleeper.'

'He didn't know about the hot milk, did he? Eh, Mrs Brennan?'

'Divil the bit.'

'And I remember reading somewhere – or did someone tell me about it? No, I think I read it – even as a four-year-old child he suffered badly from insomnia, and he was asked how did he cope with it – as a child – and he said "I just lay there and thought about the past." At four years of age.' Father Farquharson chuckled and patted his thigh lightly. Mrs Brennan looked all around.

'Most children can talk by the age of four,' she said.

'Wasn't he the right wee tinker, too,' said Nurse Gilliland. 'I'd have given him a bit of a smack and let him cry himself to sleep. Bible or no bible.'

'At four years of age,' said Mary Lawless, 'he couldn't have had much of a past to worry about.'

'That's my point,' said Father Farquharson. 'That's what's amusing about it.'

'Oh I'm with you now, Father.'

'All days even to the consummation of the world.'

'I remember the old ones talking about taking valerian. To get over to sleep.'

'I've heard of valerian, but what is it?'

'A sedative,' said Nurse Gilliland. 'Something to make you sleep. A drug.'

'I always keep a book on the bedside table,' said Mary Lawless.

'A thriller. Most times, one page and I'm asleep. But not this week. No sir.'

'Did you ever wake up with the book on your chest and the light still on?'

'Many's the time.'

'Are you worried about anything?'

'I'm worried about *everything*.'

'It's not getting over that's my problem,' said Nurse Gilliland. 'It's when you wake up in the dark at half four or five. And you're as bright as a button. And you find yourself up, wandering the kitchen, making herb tea and whistling like Ronnie Ronald.'

'Lemon balm is supposed to be very good.'

'And maybe a few hops.'

'Hopping would put me off my notion of sleeping,' said Mrs Brennan.

'Hops – the plant – like leaves. They make beer out of it.' They all began to laugh. They laughed so much they had difficulty speaking. Mary Lawless rolled around in her chair and her bosom shook. Nurse Gilliland stuck her legs out straight and threw her head back. Father Farquharson covered his eyes in embarrassment for Mrs Brennan and her mistake and clumped his false teeth. Mrs Brennan herself tried several times to speak but lost what she was going to say in the next bout of laughter. Eventually she got it out.

'And there was me thinking of hopping around the kitchen at four in the morning trying not to spill my cup of hot milk.' And they laughed all over again. Gradually the laughter disappeared, but it came back in little ripples – eyes were wiped with handkerchiefs, smiles were left on faces. There was a lot of nodding.

'If the crack was any better you couldn't stick it,' said Mary Lawless.

'As I've said before – the hot milk is hard to beat. With maybe a spoonful of honey in it,' said Mrs Brennan.

'And no hops.'

'No – divil the hops.'

They were back on even keel. No one said anything for a moment or two.

'Och, there's no doubt about it, we're all becoming a bit dotery.'

'Every last one of us.'

'The march of old age. It'll trample on us all.'

'We're becoming a dotery coterie,' said Mary Lawless and that was them all away laughing again.

'And what was laudanum when you're writing home?' said Mary Lawless. 'My granny used to talk about that too.'

'I think it was opium – pure and simple,' said Nurse Gilliland. 'More drugs.'

'Every day ends with the mystery of how we sleep,' said Father Farquharson, 'and each morning begins with the miracle of how we wake.'

'Well said, Father.'

'Oh I nearly forgot,' said Mary Lawless. 'Martin, hand me over that handbag. I've some photos.'

'I love photies,' said Nurse Gilliland and rubbed her hands vigorously together making a dry skin sound. Mary Lawless fed the photographs to her left to Mrs Brennan who handed them on to Nurse Gilliland who handed them on to Father Farquharson who returned them to Mary Lawless. Mrs Brennan scrutinised the first picture.

'She's arms on her like thighs,' said Mrs Brennan. 'Whoever she is.'

'It's my sister.'

'Oh is *that* your sister? She has such a sweet smile.' There was silence for a moment or two. Murmurs only as each picture was looked at and passed on.

'I'm always cutting the heads off people,' said Mary Lawless.

'With me it's the feet,' said Nurse Gilliland. 'I'm always cutting them off at the ankles. I can't seem to get the camera angled down.'

'Would you look at the age of you in that one. Mary Lawless, you'd swear you were twenty-five.'

'You're far too young looking for your age.'

'Very photogenic. As they say – the camera loves you.'

'Isn't it a great invention altogether? The camera.'

'It's like everything else,' said Father Farquharson. 'It can be used for good or ill.'

'What could you do wrong with a camera, Father?' Mrs Brennan knitted her brows. Father Farquharson looked at the ceiling, then down to Martin where he was sitting on the floor. Mrs Brennan twigged.

'I suppose you're right, Father.'

'Never spoke a truer word.'

'I would enlarge that one,' said Nurse Gilliland.

'I'm big enough, says you.'

'The photos bring back memories.'

'They certainly do. It's a long time since we had a look in the Black Magic box.'

'If you're going to do that, I'm off,' said Martin.

'Aww, he's shy.'

Later the Black Magic box was produced and the Brennans' family past was gone over again. School photographs, small black and white photos – some sepia.

'I don't know what you're all talking about – we couldn't *afford* a camera,' said Mrs Brennan.

'But who took all these?' said Mary Lawless.

'Neighbours, friends. Lots of them are school photos – you paid for each one as it came along. And people would give you ones they took.'

'Street photographers, d'you mind them? They'd snap you on the street or the promenade at Bangor – but they were only kidding on. They'd crouch in front of you pretending to click. Nearly always a guy with a girl, wanting to show off. If you said you wanted to buy, they took another one. The only one. Cute eh?'

'Aw, you couldn't be up to them.'

'There's some slippery customers, right enough.'

'There but for the grace of God . . .'

'It wouldn't happen nowadays – giving your name and address and handing over the money with nothing to show for it.'

'No siree,' said Father Farquharson. 'Trust is a thing of the past. The St Vincent de Paul men have to watch the collection plate like a hawk when it's passing round.'

'In case people help themselves?'

'You said it, Nurse Gilliland. You said it.'

Mary Lawless was leafing through the pictures.

'You're always squinting into the sun, Martin,' she said.

There was an enlarged studio photograph of Martin as a boy of five.

'A wee cherub,' said Nurse Gilliland.

'Aww – I could ate him up,' said Mary Lawless. Every time it was produced his mother told the same story.

'I had the quare job getting your hair to lie down flat that day. At the finish up I had to use egg white to make it stick the way I wanted it.'

'I'm going,' said Martin.

'Sit where you are,' shouted Mary Lawless, 'and take your praise like a man.'

It took him about half an hour to catch up with the rest of the night's work – going down to the animal house for another batch of rats, killing and dissecting out, labelling the specimens with the false times. He moved sluggishly, felt very tired. Everything seemed at a distance, as if there was a pane of glass between him and what he was looking at. He heard the door at the bottom of the stairs closing and the clash of the lift gates. That would be Kavanagh. Martin walked out to meet him. There was the sound of talking as the lift ascended. Kavanagh had somebody with him. The lift jolted to a halt.

'Martin,' said Kavanagh. 'Look who's here.' The gates were pulled back.

'Pished to the eyeballs, but good to see you, Martin, nevertheless.' It was Blaise wearing a Frank Sinatra hat. He wore denim dungarees without a shirt: the shoulder straps and buckles were on his bare shoulders.

'For fuck's sake . . .' Martin stammered and shook hands.

'Pished *and* stoned.' Blaise hugged him with his free hand and whooped a few times. Martin was conscious of hair against his cheek. Blaise had grown a goatee beard. In fact he looked like a negative of his grandfather. 'Where did you pick up this beardy bastard?'

'We ended up at the same party,' said Kavanagh. 'And nothing would do him but he would come along and see you.'

'And there was no drink left. And no people left. And nowhere open. And it was my birthday. Not today – yesterday. And so on and so on.'

'We were just talking about you earlier,' said Martin. The three of them walked along the corridor. Kavanagh was in the middle.

'Remember this,' Kavanagh said and bounced into the air levering himself up on both the others' shoulders, straightening his arms. Martin and Blaise staggered a bit but kept him up there for five or six paces, until the strength in Kavanagh's arms went and he collapsed back on to the floor between them. 'Stout lads, both of you. It was the touch of your naked flesh, Foley that finally did for me.'

'We were trying to carry you as far as that low doorway,' said Blaise. Then he whooped a couple more whoops and they echoed around the department. They walked into the lab.

'Fuck, I do not believe this,' said Martin. There was something glittering on Blaise's cheekbones.

'Pippa and I were at this party in University Street and everybody was yacking on, and I said *I know that voice*. And it was your man – giving out in the corner.'

'You mean to tell me,' said Martin, 'I was in here working for your thesis and you were at a party?'

'It's just the way it happened last night. I needed to talk to her – to sort things out. A friend of a friend had a party – you know how it is.'

'I'd a bit of a party myself in here.'

'Really?' Kavanagh waited for an explanation.

'Naw,' Martin said, 'I was getting your work done.'

Blaise flopped down on the camp bed and tilted his hat forward over his face.

'I'm still fractionally pished,' he said. 'Make me a black coffee, Martin. Because it's my birthday.'

'So you told me,' said Martin. 'What's with the gear?'

'It's party time.'

'You look like an American farm boy.'

'I had the straw hat earlier but some bastard went off with it and left me this fucking thing.'

'Which birthday is it?'

'The big two oh.' Blaise spoke into the crown of the Frank Sinatra. 'Naw, I'm a liar – I'm more than that.' Martin took Blaise by the hand and pulled him to his feet. Blaise put his arm around him.

334

'The coffee makings are in a different location.' Martin turned to Kavanagh and pointed to the cage. 'Maybe you should take over. It's almost the hour.'

'Yeah, yeah. I think I need a coffee too,' said Kavanagh. 'Or else I'll cut my own fucking finger off.'

'You're muttering,' said Martin looking at him. Kavanagh grinned. 'You *are* pretty pissed. So how did it go – with Pippa?'

'Total disaster. She walked out. It's over.' Martin made a sympathetic face for Kavanagh but very quickly turned to Blaise. 'Let's go. In search of beverages.' With their arms around each other, they unsteadily walked the corridor towards the tea room. Kavanagh followed them. Martin was aware of the bareness of Blaise's shoulder beneath his hand. Blaise lurched a bit to one side.

'Keep to the lino,' said Martin. 'So what are you doing these days?'

'Huh!'

'I heard you were doing Law in Cambridge.'

'You are ill informed and behind the times.'

'So?'

'Remember that day in the Waterworks.'

'Yeah, that was a good day.'

They all smiled.

'The backs of the girls' legs. The big H . . .' Kavanagh grinned.

'Naw – it was the sun and the smell and the green of it.' Martin nodded.

'I remember the man rowing the boat,' said Blaise. 'That was good. A man rowing a boat. He couldn't see the future and neither could we.' In the tea room Martin aimed him at a chair and Blaise plumped down. Martin put the kettle on. Blaise leaned his head back and recited to the air above him,

'*Children of the future age, reading this indignant page, know that in a former time, Love, sweet love, was thought a crime.* Blake.' Martin set out three cups and spooned coffee into them. 'Martin is there no drink about this place?'

'Afraid not.'

'I remember you once saying that Oxford and Cambridge were fucking awful. And yet you went there. Why?'

'They are places of excellence. When I said that, I didn't have a clue about the nature of excellence.'

'So if you are not doing Law what *are* you doing?'

'Nothing. Sweet fuck all.'

'Stop talking in riddles.'

'Speaking of which – I need a piss.' He stood up. 'Where's the nearest one?' Martin led him from the tea room. The door of the Ladies was open and it was still too early for anyone to be about.

'Go in there. The Gents is on the next floor.' Blaise was quite unsteady on his feet going up the steps. He raised his leading leg but didn't put it down immediately, like the way a chicken sometimes does. Martin was sufficiently worried about him to wait outside. Just as he had done with Cindy. Different experience altogether.

The sound coming from Blaise's cubicle was loud. Blaise shouted out, 'Like a man on fuckin stilts.'

When he came out he didn't bother washing his hands.

'Martin Brennan,' he said. 'I really liked you at school.'

'It wasn't obvious.'

'Aw come on now. It was only a term . . .'

From the top of the steps Blaise put his arm around Martin and the two of them walked back to the tea room. Kavanagh was nearly asleep in his chair. Blaise sat down by the door.

'Well, Martin what have you been up to?'

'Fuck all, really. Learning to drink . . .'

'Where?'

'The school Old Boys.'

'With my old man,' Kavanagh was laughing, wakening up.

'Do *you* go?'

'But rarely – nights my old man is not there. I'm over this side of town mostly. But that's all going to change now.'

'And what do you do in the Old Boys?'

'Play snooker.'

'Who with?'

'Brian Sweeny – other guys. Sometimes we play poker,' said Martin. 'Isn't it amazing – everything they stopped you doing at school, they encourage you to do when you're an Old Boy.'

'And?'

'Night classes. For the lab.' Martin looked up, thinking. 'And I joined a camera club.'

'Seedy? Raincoat brigade?'

'Naw – fawn cardigans. They've some good people. Good darkrooms.'

'And he's still foraging for sex,' said Kavanagh.

Martin started pouring water into the coffee cups.

'You can have it black or black,' he said.

'What's that smell off you?' Kavanagh sniffed at Martin.

'Ether, maybe.' Blaise sprang upright in the chair.

'Ether! You've got ether in here?'

'Yeah.'

'Why don't we have a go at it?'

'What?'

'The ether – it's an old Northern Ireland tradition. Did you never hear of the ether drinkers of Ulster?'

'What?'

'One of the few nice traditions to come out of this hole.'

'You're mad in the skull.'

'No, really. Up around Tyrone – at the end of last century the boys were throwing it into them. You have to hold your nose. But then you're out of your tree for ten minutes.'

'It would kill you,' Martin was laughing.

'You would just vomit,' said Kavanagh.

'What do you mean "just"? Wouldn't that be enough? Where's the bottle?' said Blaise. 'The belching is supposed to be monumental.'

'I don't believe a word of this.'

'The *BMJ* reckoned there were fifty thousand ether drinkers in mid-Ulster in 1890. I want to try it. I feel left out.'

'Fuck off, Blaise,' said Martin. 'I've a job in here. And people are about to come into work. What would I say to the Prof? Oh I just let him drink the ether.'

'Lead me to it.' Blaise stood but Kavanagh tipped him on the chest with a finger and knocked him back down on to the seat.

'Martin's right. You're out of order, Mr Foley.'

'I want to try it – just once.'

'There must be safer ways to blow your mind.' Martin handed Blaise a coffee.

'That's fucking *it*. That's the Martin I know. Always looking for a *safe* way to do something dangerous.'

'Hold on,' said Kavanagh and disappeared.

Blaise was now slumped in the seat. He spread his arms to Martin and said, 'Would not play false and yet would wrongly win. Am I right Martin?'

'No. You're not. It's "Wouldst not play false and yet wouldst wrongly win." '

'Fuck you and your notions of correctness.'

Kavanagh came back with a gallon bottle of clear liquid.

'This is the boy to start the day,' he said.

'What is it?' Blaise took off his hat and squinted at Kavanagh.

'Absolute alcohol. Almost one hundred per cent.'

'Oh wondrous to relate.'

'It tastes of nothing, really – like the very best of vodka.' Kavanagh splashed some into Blaise's coffee cup.

'That'll put hair on your chest.'

'No, thank you.' Blaise sniffed at it. The vaporising alcohol went with his breath and made him cough.

'Take it easy.' Kavanagh poured a little into his own cup. Martin put his hand over the third cup.

'Naw – I'm on the bike.'

'Fuck off,' said Blaise. 'Join us. It's not often we get together. For old times' sake.'

Kavanagh waited for Martin to nod.

'Just a splash,' said Martin. Kavanagh poured him a lot more than a splash. 'That's enough.' Blaise's coughing fit had made him wary. Martin raised the cup to his mouth slowly and as he did so smelled Cindy off his fingers. The aroma was intense and wonderful.

'Here's to us,' said Blaise. 'The fucking Provincials.'
They clunked their cups together and drank.

'Why wouldn't we be provincial,' said Martin. 'We live in a province.'

'With provincial attitudes,' said Kavanagh. 'I mean, just look at us – sitting at seven in the morning in a dead house drinking hooch talking about old times.'

'I'm really sorry we didn't have a go at the ether. A missed opportunity if ever there was one. And who's talking about old times?' said Blaise. 'Certainly not me.' Kavanagh sat down at the bench. Martin leaned his chair back against the wall. The alcohol

338

in the coffee tasted good and gave it an after-burn. Kavanagh sighed heavily.

'Oh fuck,' he said.

'It's a long time since I heard you say that,' said Martin.

'What am I gonna do?'

'About Pippa?' Kavanagh nodded and put his head in his hands. 'That girl is everything to me.'

'Maybe she doesn't deserve you,' said Blaise. Kavanagh put his head back as if he'd just thought of something else.

'I'm going to be seeing her in here every day. Working beside her.'

'How was it left?' asked Martin.

'Over. Done with.'

'It might be on again.'

'No chance. That's why I got drunk with this one.'

'What is "this one" doing? He refuses to tell me.'

'This one,' said Blaise, 'was doing Law and then with great difficulty he transferred to Philosophy. To be metaphorically at the feet of Wittgenstein – a man of astounding genius. Have you heard of him?'

'Vit – who?'

Kavanagh shook his head: no, he hadn't.

'He was a great whistler. A virtuoso whistler. It's said he could whistle the Brahms *St Anthony Variations* from start to finish.' They all laughed. 'I am not making this up. This is the absolute fucking truth. But not only did he change the face of philosophy, he did it twice. He wrote two masterpieces which contradicted each other. He saw that philosophical problems come from the inadvertent misuse of words. Careless talk costs lives. There are still people in Cambridge who knew him.'

'How utterly riveting,' said Martin.

Blaise ignored him and went on, '*A cry of distress cannot be greater than that of one human being.* I thought this very hopeful at first – very uplifting – until I remembered the capacity of some human beings for suffering. I was getting on splendidly, not that I'd say it myself, until such times as the authorities thought it better that I carry on with my own particular Philosophical Investigations outside the academic establishment.'

'The bum's rush? I suppose you'll say you didn't deserve it,' said Kavanagh.

'For what?' said Martin.

'He won't tell me.' Kavanagh went round the cups again with the absolute alcohol. Martin refused, snatching his cup away and holding it close to his chest with his hand over the top. His stomach was empty and the first half of the coffee was making his head light. Blaise raised his right hand.

'Wittgenstein says that to improve the world you can only improve yourself.'

'And what about you?'

'I'm doing my best.'

'To what?'

'To improve myself,' said Blaise. 'All I will say on my behalf is *De maximus ni curat lex* and for those people whose Latin is a little rusty – or those people taught by fucking Baldy Ned Kelly, a translation is – the law does not apply to giants.'

'Aye but what law was it they applied?' said Martin.

'It's a question of supply and demand,' said Blaise. 'And at this very moment demand far outstrips supply. Maybe Martin here could supply us. Are you into the marijuana, Martin?'

'Nope.'

'You had enough to stone a regiment last night.'

'But at this moment I am bereft.'

'Was *that* what they sent you down for?' said Kavanagh.

'The police took a great interest in me. In my habits. In my *place* – once unfortunately when I was out. And I broke my own rule. I didn't cover my tracks. A hundred quid fine. The University couldn't or wouldn't look the other way.'

'Bit of bad luck there,' said Kavanagh.

'Yes, indeed. Hit me again.' Blaise held out his cup. 'I'm out of coffee.'

'Use some water or it'll burn the mouth off you.' Kavanagh stood shaking his head, looking down at Blaise. 'Martin, is there a camera?'

'Yeah.'

'We'll have to get a picture of this bastard – in this outfit – with that beard.'

'Photography is about surfaces,' said Blaise. 'That's why Martin is so interested.'

'Go on, get a camera,' said Kavanagh.

'Naw.' Martin didn't want to move. He turned to Blaise and said, 'Using a camera teaches people how to see. Without a camera. And to see things as they are is every bit as good as imagining stuff in novels. If not better. Cartier-Bresson talks about trying to seize the whole essence of something in a single photograph . . .'

'Well, he's a dumbfuck then.'

'Martin — go on,' said Kavanagh. 'Take one of the three of us. Like the last time in our house. Then we'll take one in another three or four years. We'll document our lives . . .'

'Only if I can have one taken with a skull,' said Blaise. 'Like Hamlet. We're in the right place for a skull.'

'Even the right room,' said Martin. He opened the filing cabinet beside him and produced a creamy white skull which he handed to Blaise.

'Yes, ya beauty. Is it real?'

'Of course.'

'It's not plastic or anything?'

'No.' There was a cut around the forehead and the top of the skull could be lifted like a lid. But now it was held in place by little brass hooks and eyes. Blaise opened it and looked in. He spoke in a sepulchral voice into the cavity:

'Where is your soul?'

Martin went out and came back with a sheet, a tripod and a camera. He rigged up the sheet over one of the bookcases as a background and positioned Blaise in front of it. He didn't bother with the tripod. Blaise held the skull up and he stared into its empty orbits, profile to profile. The bib of his dungarees creased in such a way as to bare his chest from the side.

'Put that fucking thing back in,' said Martin.

'What?'

'Your nipple.' Blaise adjusted the bib and shoulder strap.

'I know who this is,' he said. 'I knew there was something familiar about the face.'

'Who is it?' Kavanagh was grinning in anticipation.

'Mary Anne McCracken. Henry Joy's sister.'

341

'That only works once,' said Kavanagh. Martin told them both to shut up and took some readings with a light meter. There was quite a bit of daylight coming from the window. He adjusted the aperture and depth of field.

'He's trying to blind us with science,' Blaise said to the skull. 'Stop grinning – it's not funny.' Martin began to snap away. Quickly advancing the lever with his thumb after each shot. Clicking the shutter, hearing the camera mechanism make the satisfying noise. Taking some landscape, some portrait.

'How did you get the gold stuff on your cheeks?' he asked.

'I put it there before I went out last night.'

'Pardon me for asking,' Martin said. 'Did you hear about Sharkey?'

'No.'

'You remember who Sharkey was?'

'Yeah,' said Blaise still staring at the skull, 'he was in our so-called religious class. The Republican bastard. Gifted with stupidity.'

'He was also the one who led the charge to give you the kicking,' said Kavanagh.

'That's all a total blank to me. Days that disappeared.'

'Well, he's no longer with us,' said Martin.

'Shame!'

'He was shot dead about a year ago by an army marksman.'

'What was he doing?'

'It was at night. How would you know? He was probably trying to kill the army marksman.'

'Men who shoot straight in the cause of crooked thinking.'

'That's good.'

'So it should be. It's Louis MacNeice.'

'Oh.' Martin imitated Blaise's sepulchral voice of earlier as he circled round him clicking away. 'Where is your soul, Mr Foley?'

'I don't have one.'

'Leave Yorick out of it now.' Martin took the skull and put it on the table. He continued to snap Blaise. Looking this way and that. His hat tilted. His hat off.

'You've learned a thing or two in here, Martin?'

'I know how to empty a big bottle.'

'Aye, drink it.'

'Naw – there's more to emptying a bottle than you'd think. If you just upend it, it takes ages. It goes ker-plunk, ker-plunk, ker-plunk into the sink.' He was crouching, still taking pictures. 'But if you swirl the liquid it creates a vortex then it just gushes out. Speeds the whole process up.'

'That's really useful to know,' said Kavanagh.

'That's why I told you.'

'Why don't you write a book about it?' said Blaise. He took another sip from his cup. ' "Bottle Emptying for Beginners." It's nothing to be ashamed of. Wittgenstein was a laboratory assistant in Guy's during the war.'

Kavanagh elbowed his way into several of the pictures beside Blaise and tried to look mad.

'Now all three of us,' he said, beckoning to Martin, 'with a bottle of abs alc.'

He was getting really drunk now. Saying stupid things. Slurring his words. Martin mounted the camera on the tripod and switched it to self-timer. He used what remained of the film to take pictures of the three of them with their arms round each other. Pulling faces in much the same way as they did the last time. Squinting and eye rolling. Kavanagh pretending to pull Blaise's goatee beard. And Blaise letting him. He was getting every bit as drunk as Kavanagh.

'To pluck the beard of a Russian is the supreme insult. It's worse than spitting in his face.'

Martin rewound the film.

'We'll have to wait for prints until the boss takes a day off. He doesn't like us doing homers.'

Blaise moved and slumped on to a different chair. He pointed to the skull on the table. 'I know. I know what would be nice. We could have a drink from this skull.'

'Don't be daft,' said Martin. 'It would only run out the holes.'

'Not if you're clever,' said Blaise.

'Why on earth would you want to?' said Kavanagh. 'When we've got cups.'

Blaise flicked back the tiny brass hooks and lifted the lid of the skull. Kavanagh pointed down inside, spoke in a pretend dumbfuck voice, 'The foramen magnum. Big hole for spine. Alcohol dribble out.'

343

Blaise flipped over the top of the skull he held in his hands so that it became a small dish. He held it out like an inverted skullcap.

'Hit me,' he said. Kavanagh didn't move.

'Oliver fuckin Twisted, right enough,' said Kavanagh.

'Just a splash.'

'Hey that's going a bit far,' said Martin. 'That *was* somebody.' Blaise laughed and mimicked Martin.

'*That was somebody*. It's no big deal.'

'Why would you want to?'

'For the sheer fucking hell of it.'

'You'll have to do it yourself,' said Kavanagh. But Blaise couldn't be bothered to get up off his seat. He replaced the top of the skull and fastened the brass hooks.

'This would look great on my mantelpiece,' he said. 'Would it be missed?'

'Too fuckin right it would. It's Dr Cowie's demonstration model.' Martin lifted the skull and replaced it in the filing cabinet drawer. 'And if they found out I'd get the fucking heave-ho.' He was about to turn away, then he thought better of it and locked the drawer. He pocketed his keys and sat down and yawned. His act of yawning made him want to yawn again. He leaned back on his chair. He angled the chair so that it was propped against the wall at a steep angle. That meant his head could lean against the wall.

'I'm bate to the ropes,' he said. His eyelids, the top and the bottom, came slowly together. It happened simultaneously in the left eye and the right eye or at least he was not conscious of it happening therefore he assumed that it happened simultaneously. The voice of Blaise seemed to fill the room, then to fill Martin's head. Occasionally Kavanagh spoke. He had a deeper voice. They sounded like music together. And at the same time Martin knew that he should not be falling asleep when the two people he liked best were in the same room as himself and they were drinking and talking. His chair was balanced on its back legs like a fulcrum. Show me a fulcrum and I will move the earth. Who said that? Martin made out what the two others were saying but could not respond to it.

'Look at your man.' Kavanagh's voice.

'Sound asleep.' Blaise's voice.

'He's been up all night.'

'But, sure, so have we.'

'No staying power.'

'Drink is fuel for getting you through.'

Martin felt as if he was hypnotised. Aware but unable to act.

'We got away with it, didn't we? The exam papers.'

'Yeah.'

'No one *ever knew*.' Blaise smiled. 'Who left them back?'

'Me. Martin got rid of your pictures. Says he burned them. Condor never knew.'

'Oh yes he did. That fucker stood the Thomas à Becket thing on its head: it was the priest saying, "will no one rid me of this troublesome pupil"?'

'How do you know?'

'He said it to me – not in so many words. The day of the inquisition. Martin should have sold the photos. Shouldn't you?' Blaise shouted. 'Eh Mr Brennan? Wittgenstein says about conversation that it's like a custom where you throw someone a ball and he is supposed to throw it back to you. But certain people don't understand and put the ball in their pocket. End of conversation. ISN'T THAT RIGHT, MARTIN?' Why was he always falling asleep? Was he suffering from sleeping sickness? Why were there other times when he couldn't sleep at all? He heard Blaise get up and heard his voice getting nearer. He was paralysed with exhaustion. Kavanagh's voice said:

'Naw – naw, that isn't fair.' Blaise kicked the chair leg outwards and Martin fell. He woke with a start and a roar. And was conscious that both Kavanagh and Blaise had caught him before he reached the ground. The wooden chair clattered loudly away from beneath him. They laughed and their hands cushioned his fall.

'For fuck sake, lads, what *are* you doing?'

'Saving your life.'

They lowered him on to the lino and he lay there stunned. After a minute or so he got to his feet.

'I'm off,' he said. 'I have been away from home too long.'

Blaise hugged him. Martin was again conscious of the touch of his beard. He felt uncoordinated with tiredness. Blundering. He could hardly speak.

'Where's home for you these days?'

'A flat in Cambridge.'

'It's a squat,' said Kavanagh.

'See you some time,' said Martin. 'Sorry, I'm fucked. But that's another story.'

'See you.' Kavanagh patted Martin on the shoulder on his way out the door. 'Maybe tomorrow.'

'The future is only the past waiting to happen,' said Blaise.

'A Blaise phrase, if ever I heard one.'

Blaise waggled his fingers to say goodbye in much the same fashion as Cindy had done. Kavanagh slumped back heavily on to his chair and put his head in his hands.

The big door slammed behind him and he walked away from the department out into the day, pushing his bike. The cold helped waken him. In the quad the early morning sun was bright and hard. There wasn't much warmth in it yet. The light made dark shadows of every university building. Birds were singing, going at it hell for leather. The cherry tree bark shone like dark brass. The yellow of the laburnum hung utterly still. Two pigeons were flying in and out of the quad, making a noise with the flapping of their wings. They flew above the roofs and toppled out of the blue sky and, just in time, saved themselves from falling by spreading wings – gliding with a flash of blue-grey and white feathers. When they settled they cooed and cuk-cooed. There were several sets of steps to negotiate so he didn't immediately get on his bike. He liked pushing it by the saddle. A fractional lean to the left or to the right and the handlebars tilted and the bike went in the direction he wanted it to go. Leading from behind. It was a fine balancing act totally within his control. Coming to the steps he bounced it and helped the bike rear up like a horse.

Cycling on the road was a strange feeling, seeing people who had spent the night sleeping, coming hunched and puffy eyed from their houses, lighting up their first cigarettes. He saw himself, all those years ago, white faced from sleep, waiting around outside the paper shop for Kavanagh so's they could walk to school. The big fella laughing, throwing his head back. For a while a thing of the past but now there was hope it could go back to that – with Pius Pippa giving him the bum's rush. Martin would have to work hard if he wanted the situation to stay that way. It was for Kavanagh's own good. For him to become 'saved' for the sake of a woman was the height of nonsense. He hoped he wouldn't get too depressed or be hurt too badly. He would hate that to happen. To anybody.

He pedalled slowly, taking it easy, his hands at the centre of the handlebars. Meeting Blaise again was amazing. He was definitely homo – or gay, as they were now calling it. But, for some reason, it didn't worry Martin – it was just so typical of Blaise to go a different way. It was the way he was. He remembered the weird poem by St John of the Cross – of the man pursuing Christ and kissing him, getting a love bite. 'My neck he wounded'. He accepted the poem and what happened in it, the way he now accepted what Blaise was. Martin had not the slightest desire to be like him, but he had no desire to stop him either. Just as he didn't want to be gay he didn't want to be wild either. Blaise was an intelligent, thrawn, mad bastard. Martin was not. He felt that once Blaise was on the scene there was an air of danger, of unpredictability in everything – as dangerous as a sharpened blade, not in its box. In a way he loved that, and in another way he didn't. He, Martin, was a 'Do I dare to eat a peach?' guy, whereas Blaise would eat them stones and all. Watching Blaise was like watching a movie: you enjoyed it but you were glad you were not in it. This morning, Martin was glad he was able to cycle away from Blaise, leaving Kavanagh to tidy up.

There were lots of policemen about, looking uneasy. He wondered if there had been an explosion and he hadn't heard it. If anybody had been killed. Sometimes, if the wind was in the wrong direction, you didn't hear a thing. These fucking Troubles had gone on for years now. Hundreds had been killed. How long was it going to go on? How many more would die? Recently in the parlour they had talked endlessly of the situation.

'Tell me this and tell me no more,' said Mrs Brennan, 'what is it all about?'

'Ask the Other Crowd,' said Nurse Gilliland. 'Wasn't it them started the whole thing?'

'You might be right.'

'Wasn't it your man up the Ravenhill Road who started the riots in '64 goading the police into it – all for the sake of a tricolour in a shop window.'

'Don't tell me it was Catholics jumped out of a car and stabbed that poor man on the Falls Road.'

'And wasn't it the Other Side who murdered that barman – shot him stone dead – for nothing other than his Catholic religion. And wasn't it the Prods who let off the first bombs, blowing up water mains . . .'

'Wasn't it them that killed the first policeman.'

'It wasn't the Legion of Mary who burned out Bombay Street.'

'What were they thinking of?'

'They were retaliating before the event.'

'And they were in the driver's seat, too. They had no grievances. It was *us* didn't have the jobs or the houses.'

'You never spoke a truer word.'

Martin was no longer obliged to carry in the trays for the supper evenings but if he was in the house he would always contrive to be in the room when the food was handed out. Nothing much had changed – except that Father Farquharson had been given a different parish at the other side of town. It meant he came less frequently, it being dangerous some nights even to 'venture out'.

'You'll have done *Macbeth*, Martin,' he said.

'Yes, Father.'

'*I think our country sinks beneath the yoke; it weeps, it bleeds and each new day a gash is added to her wounds.* How's that for memory? Forty-two years since I looked at it.'

'They could teach in those days. Father,' said Mrs Brennan. 'Not the faffing about they go on with nowadays. Leaving it up to the pupils.'

'They say we're the world's experts here at putting the body back together again,' said Nurse Gilliland.

'Humpty Dumpty land,' said Mary Lawless.

'The land where nobody is safe.' Mrs Brennan was almost in an anxiety state about what was happening.

'Steel pins for joints,' said Nurse Gilliland, 'titanium plates for bone that's disappeared.'

'What can a body do nowadays?'

'If they run out of materials, Mrs Brennan, they could use your tart plates,' said Father Farquharson. 'The best of tin.'

'And welcome. If my oul tin plates could save a life . . .'

'Beaten into shape of course.'

'The boy from Belfast with the titanium cranium . . .' said Nurse Gilliland.

'Rhubarb or apple, sir? Which would suit you best?' said Mary Lawless. 'Protestant or Catholic?'

There was a slight decline towards Shaftesbury Square, which meant he could almost freewheel. He imagined himself as Billy Graham – hiring football grounds for pagan rallies – preaching to the converted. 'There is no God. We're in this by ourselves. Nobody else. Sinn Fein – ourselves alone. If you don't believe – stand up – go out the nearest exit. And if you still want to believe listen to the testimony of my friend Mr Foley. And if you don't believe him lend an ear to my other – recently reformed – mate, Mr Kavanagh.'

The night was over. Fuck, and what a night. The night of the bad apples. Cindy letting him. Blaise walking back into their lives. His thing still felt raw red. From usage. But it was now pleasant – an after-glow. Like the absolute alcohol. He had been bursting to tell Kavanagh and Blaise about Cindy. However, Kavanagh would have twigged that precious little attention would have been paid to accuracy in his experiment. But Kavanagh had been fairly drunk. Martin might be able to blame *him* for the mistakes. He mightn't remember too much about it. Maybe some day he could tell him. Whether it was before or after the BSc thesis, he had still to decide.

The best thing about the sex was that it was all over. He wouldn't have to worry about it any more. He could raise a superior eyebrow like Kavanagh and say, '*Thee* most important day in the life of a young man is the day he first gets it.' But it wasn't as simple as that. The actual event, the getting of it, had been awful. What he had liked was the lead up to it. But maybe he would improve. Who plays basketball well his first time on court?

He began to feel more alert, was beginning to get a second wind. But he couldn't stop himself smiling. He must look daft –

cycling and smiling. The girl smiling to herself as she came out of the pub, at something said, or someone seen, and he remembered liking her for it. He imagined a person on the pavement seeing him, Martin, smiling at this very moment and liking him for it.

At the other side of the road he saw a girl coming down the hill of a side street on to the main road. From a distance he felt she was someone familiar. Or he even thought he knew her. Or wanted to know her. She was wearing a yellow outfit, very summery. Her back was straight and she carried herself well. He had to keep glancing for fear he would run into something, like the back of a bus. He stared at her for as long as he dared. Jesus. It was Patricia Downie – the one at the glass case in the library. The ghost, the reflection. Her hair was different, but it was definitely her.

Again he was immediately taken with her, as he had been at the school sports. If anything, she was even more attractive. A greater proportion of her hair was now blonde. Sunshine sometimes did that. And it was longer. Martin swerved and jinked between cars. He applied his brakes and nipped up on to the pavement beside some railings. Keeping his eye on her on the far side of the road he locked the bike to some church railings. He was afraid she would disappear. Into a shop, on to a bus. He wanted her in his sights for as long as possible. She was carrying a bag slung over her shoulder. Martin looked this way and that and threaded his way through the traffic to her side of the road. She turned on to the main road totally oblivious of him. He tried to take in everything about her with his eyes.

But she stopped at the bus shelter and made a face, even though she was by herself. Because there was no one else queuing she'd obviously just missed one. She'd be late for work. He stopped. Should he approach her? He felt he still had some bravado from the early morning alcohol. It had not worn off completely. And it had the advantage, because it was pure alcohol, that it couldn't be smelled off his breath – like vodka. Maybe he was so tired it didn't matter. Maybe he had changed in some way.

'Hi.' He greeted her with such conviction that she was slightly taken aback. She smiled, thinking it her fault that she didn't recognise him. There was sleep still in her eyes. She waited for him to speak, still smiling. 'I was at school with your wee brother, Eddie. How is he?'

'He's fine.'

'What's he doing?'

'Teacher training. In London – Strawberry Hill.'

'You used to go down to the Central – the library. To study.'

'Once or twice.'

'I remember you. How are you?'

'I'm fine.'

'I didn't know you lived around here.'

'Just up there. Magdala Street.'

'So what are you doing? How did *you* get on?'

She was tall and looked directly into his eyes. He wanted to die. Wanted to swoon. But this was rush hour. Swooning would get him nowhere. There would be a bus along any second. She gazed at him, trying to recall who he was. A man joined the queue behind them and lit a cigarette.

'Not so hot,' she said. 'I didn't get enough to get *me* into teacher training. That's what I wanted to do as well.'

'There's this book I read – *Wisdom from the East* – it says if you have a desire to teach, wait till it passes. Teach, only if you have no compulsion to do so.' She stared at him and raised an eyebrow. But smiled at the same time. She doesn't know me from Adam. There was the danger of a silence developing. Then he noticed that she was wearing the same small silver cross at her throat as she had worn that day in the library. Two more women stopped in the bus queue. 'I'm sorry – that's not a criticism of you. It's just wisdom.'

'Thank you for it.' She was laughing.

'So what did you end up doing?'

'The Civil Service.'

'My mother is a great one for civility.' She looked at her watch. Then took a step forward to look up the road for her bus.

'And you?' she said. 'Where did *you* end up?' She'd asked him a question. A whole new line of conversation was beginning. Patricia Downie was showing an interest in him. To a certain extent. She'd asked the question over her shoulder while she was looking up the road for her bus, but it was still a question. She had initiated something. He was getting on famously. The bus queue now extended out of the back end of the shelter. Her eyes were detaching certain connections in his brain. He could no longer

351

think. He was tired, he wanted to fall asleep on her breast there and then. The link between thought and tongue was almost completely gone. Her look had scissored vital pathways. She was showing an interest in him only because she didn't know him very well. So far. Just wait. He was falling. Skydiving in her presence. Plummeting. Without protection because the loose flesh of his cheeks was rattling and his hair felt as if it was straight up. Behind her lovely head the Perspex of the shelter was covered in felt-tipped graffiti. Obscenities. Cocks and balls. Perineums.

'The Uni. I'm working up at the Uni.'

'Very good.'

The bus stop was across the road from *the* Bonne Bouche. A woman was going into the premises, unlocking the double glass doors, opening the place up. Once inside she stopped to pick up the mail lying on the mat. He was aware of the listening queue behind him and dropped his voice.

'Have you time for a coffee?' The words just came out of him. A coffee would waken him up. A caffeine injection. Restore coherence to his gibbering. She leaned slightly forward.

'Sorry?'

'Have you time for a coffee?'

She laughed. Her mouth was wonderful.

'I'm on my way to work.'

'I'm sorry. I'm all disorientated. I've been on the night shift.'

'At the University?' It was his turn to laugh.

'Yeah – emergency philosophy. A callout.' She smiled and turned her head quickly to look up the road again. Her hair momentarily remained behind, then followed, like the swish of a skirt.

'Oh come on, come on.' She kept moving her feet. He noticed again they were very big. 'D'you think there's been a bomb scare?' she asked.

'No, the buses are obviously running.'

'They're just not going where I want to go.'

'Tomorrow maybe?' he said.

'What?'

'A coffee. What day's this?'

'Friday.'

'A coffee tomorrow. The weekend. Here.' He nodded across the road to the Bonne Bouche. 'Are you working?'

'No.'

'Eleven o'clock?' She didn't say anything for a moment.

'But . . .'

'For old times' sake . . .'

'Two o'clock would suit me better.' Again she looked at her watch, then looked up the road. She kept fidgeting. The tops of her feet were tanned. A bus turned the corner and she relaxed visibly. He couldn't believe what she had said. She had accepted his invitation. He had a date. With Patricia Downie.

'If it's for old times' sake I'd better know your name.'

'Martin Brennan.'

She put her hand out. Martin raised his hand automatically. For a moment he was confused. He thought she was trying to shake hands but her hand was gesturing out and away from him – impossible for him to reach. He half attempted to . . . then he realised she was putting her hand out to stop the bus. Oh fuck – had she noticed that he had moved his hand? There he was, going to shake on a deal like a horse trader and all she was doing was flagging down the fucking driver. The bus stopped and the queue shuffled forward.

'I'm Patricia Downie,' she said. And she was away. He stood rooted to the spot and saw her take her seat downstairs on his side of the bus. As it pulled away from the pavement, in the act of sitting down, she smiled at him and gave him a small wave. No dumbfuck he.

He walked back to his bike and unlocked it. He could hardly believe what he had just accomplished. With Patricia Downie. The bike moved off as if it had a life of its own and he mounted it at the run. It felt part of him – he had never been on a horse or mount of any other sort but he imagined that this is what it would have felt like. The control he had over it – the leaning, the weight, the nuances of nudging and steering – threading the eye between bus and pavement. Pegasus was a horse with wings and as he cycled around the complexity of the Square it felt he was on such a creature, gliding. It was about gravity and defying gravity at the same time. The morning air parted as he moved through it and closed again behind him. The rush hour traffic was beginning.

It was coming at him from all angles but it seemed of no consequence. He was above it all. He feinted between vehicles, shouted warnings to pedestrians. His upward glance took in Frink's two huge verdigris figures high up on the white side of the Ulster Bank. The top body was horizontal, the lower one at 45 degrees to it appeared to be winged. He should really stop some day and take pictures – it was such a strong image. Two strong images. He had taken the laboratory job 'in the meantime' and the meantime had lasted too long. Maybe Cindy was right: he should look at something else. He should think about something in photography. In his bones he felt it was becoming more and more important to him. It was what he would like to do. But how could he get into it? How could his life be shaped by darkness and light? Like Macbeth. By space and time? By silver salts on paper. What is a photograph, after all, but an image which invites contemplation. Like the one hovering above him on the wall of the Ulster Bank. Before the fall, the stall. Martin had always guessed they were in the act of falling – like angels chucked out of heaven. Sent down – like Blaise. Falling apart and falling together. Horizontal, stretched – like the pair on the motorbike who were killed beneath the bus in his street. Or he thought of them as 1920s American stockbrokers hurtling to the pavement in a death plunge. Victims of both gravity and capitalism. His falling dreams were like adolescence. You never knew where you were. You didn't know what you knew – at least you couldn't trust it. People could burst out laughing. Or they could nod and agree. The same as in a dream or real life. You had no way of knowing. You could be catching on to something solid and permanent which was anchored or something solid and permanent which was falling at the same speed as yourself. That was in fact what was happening. People believed themselves to be on solid ground when in fact they were falling through space on the earth itself. Newton's Unknown Law of Motion. A bad apple falls at the same speed as a good apple. He had another notion that the Frink statues were bodies rising – two of them, lofted, buoyed up on thermals of hope. About to come into bodily contact with one another. With a loud metallic clanking. A dying fall – that was a term in music – for a trumpet. Had that woman just shot him down? Tomorrow at two o'clock would she be laughing in her bedroom remembering the boy at the bus stop – or even worse – not remembering a thing about him. Or would she be sitting across from him, her mouth red after a strawberry tart, playing with the spoon in the sugar bowl, occasionally looking up at him with those eyes and saying yes, I do want to make my life with you – even before you've asked me.